BUTTERFLIES IN THE STORM

NICOLE RENEÉ WYATT

DREAM PUBLISHING
Lawrenceville, GA

BOOKS BY NICOLE RENEÉ WYATT

Butterflies Are Free?

Butterflies in the Storm

Visit www.nicolewyatt.com for updates about upcoming books.

ACKNOWLEDGMENTS

I would like to take a moment to thank a multitude of people for their inspiration, encouragement, and honesty. Thank you to my friends and family who provided me with excellent feedback. Their opinions and advice were invaluable!

Thank you Emily Mullins, Cathie Brailey, Lorrie Mullins, Tammie Smith, Lori Wyatt, and Susan Blackmon who were such avid supporters (and pushers) that I'm not sure I could've made this journey without them. Thank you for never letting me quit or settle for less than my best.

Thank you Sanford Tullis. You truly have an incredible eye!

But mostly, thank you to Brittany and Caity, my children. Thank you for allowing your mother to play with her imaginary friends – all the time. Even when you thought I wasn't. Even when I was supposed to be paying attention. In a multitude of different, sometimes little and sometimes big ways you have been the wind beneath my wings. Without your steadfast support, honesty, and sacrifice, this novel and subsequent novels never would've been completed. Thank you!
I love you with every breath I take.

NICOLE RENEÉ WYATT

How does one become a butterfly?
They have to want to learn to fly so much that they are willing
to give up being a caterpillar.
–Trina Paulus

CHAPTER 1

Angela and Ted stood at the entrance of Angela's beloved flower garden. A sea of meticulously maintained yellow tulips greeted them. A pollen-coated, cobble-stoned path wound its way through the aureate flower blanket. With Angela's arm gently tucked into Ted's, he escorted her as the warm spring day in southern Georgia began drawing to a close. Energetic bugs buzzed and flitted to and fro under the umbrella of a clear sky and slowly setting sun.

After they were deep into the garden, Ted removed all semblance of peaceful energy with earthshattering news: "I don't know how to tell you this, Ang, but I suspect your little cash cow hasn't been totally faithful to you."

"What do you mean?" she asked in a calm, distracted tone. The delightful fragrance of the nearby fruit orchard perfumed the air around the couple.

"Alan? Your husband?"

"Yeah. What about him?" she inquired as her eyes scanned the gently swaying yellow blossoms.

Ted was surprised at the ease in which she was responding to his news. "Well, you know that little stable hand, Mary, right?"

Angela didn't immediately respond. Instead she stopped dead on the path and threw her hands on her hips. "What the hell is that?" she said through clinched teeth. She stomped to the edge of the flower bed.

"What?"

"That!" she exclaimed and pointed at two red tulips in the midst of all the sunny blooms. Her flawless face was masked with burning red anger, which was a harsh contrast against her soft wavy blonde hair.

"It's a little patch of red ones," Ted said with a laugh; his auburn beard nodding to the rhythm of his laughter.

"I said I wanted *yellow* tulips! Not red!" She immediately trampled through various yellow tulips, squashing many to the ground, until she arrived at the innocent red flowers. After ripping both from their bulbs, she threw one to the ground and stomped it. She then held the other in the air and shouted, "Someone's head will roll for this!"

"Ang. It's a couple of red tulips," he said in a tone that was obvious he thought she was overreacting. "I think it's kind of neat seeing a little patch of red amidst all these yellow ones," his hazel eyes scanned the expansive area of yellow in search of another anomaly.

"No one asked what you think! This isn't what I wanted! I said I wanted an entire ocean of yellow as bright as the sun! This? This looks like someone *bled* in my beautiful garden!"

"Oh come on, it's not that bad!"

"You wait until I get my hands on that good-for-nothing gardener!"

"Really? Don't you think that's being a bit extreme?" he asked as he ran his fingers through his tousled red hair. "It's not like he could see what color they were before he planted the bulbs."

"I said I wanted yellow tulips," she explained as she crushed more yellow blooms with her exit of the flower bed. "How does this red tulip translate into yellow tulips?" she demanded as she waved the sad flower in his face.

Ted rolled his eyes. "You're being a diva."

"Am I? Am I?!" she said with increasing irritation. "I'm Mrs. Alan Brooks! Why the hell can't I have everything I want? If I have to live on this God-forsaken farm, the least I can do is have what I want!"

He scoffed a little. "Of course, my dear."

"This is my garden! Alan gave it to me! And I want *yellow* tulips!" she said as she smacked the red tulip against Ted's chest with

To Brittany and Caity, the greatest loves of my life.
You're my reasons for living, breathing, and loving.

To my sister, Lori. Her journey, courage, and undying love
have been the inspiration for much.
I love you.

each sentence.

"Ok. Ok. Yellow tulips. I've got it," he said as he backed away from her tulip abuse.

"Damn right. I *deserve* yellow tulips! Not this ridiculous red shit!"

"Ok. Yellow tulips," he repeated. "Now can you settle back down and listen to what I was saying?"

With a pronounced pout, Angela cut her eyes toward him. "Fine. What did you say again?"

"I said I think Alan has a thing for that stable hand, Mary."

Angela coolly sniffed the despised red tulip. "Really? Interesting. Isn't she the one you think can help you train horses?" She was trying to appear indifferent.

"Yes. That's the one," Ted replied, shocked at how composed she was being. "You seem oddly calm."

"Well, we are separated you know."

Ted stopped and turned her to look at him; his face was filled with hope. In his eyes, Angela was everything he could've ever hoped to have in a fourth wife – rich, powerful, no-nonsense, stunningly beautiful, and the greatest lover he'd ever had. He looked at her tall frame, nearly as tall as he was. Her insatiable curves tempted him every time he simply thought of her. Her flawless oval face never gave away her true age. Was she finally giving up on Alan? "So you don't care? Does this mean you're actually going to leave him and be with me?" he asked optimistic for a positive answer.

Despite her best efforts, Angela's eyes squinted and her pretty face contorted as if she'd just tasted something sour.

Ted was confused. He put his hands on her shoulders and asked, "You ok?"

She clinched her eyes until they were almost closed. "That bastard! How dare he undermine me like that?!" She yanked away from Ted while gripping the delicate flower's stem in her fist. "First he takes my money away, and then *this*!"

"Yeah," Ted said with devilish delight. The sooner he could convince her that Alan was as evil as he thought Alan was, the sooner he could keep her for himself.

"How do you know??" she demanded.

"Well, just this afternoon I saw them coming out of the top

pasture together on his four-wheeler. She was on the back with her arms around his waist and her face buried in his back."

Angela scoffed. "Have you ever ridden a four-wheeler?"

"No."

"Well that's how you ride it when you're on the back," she said as she spun the stem of the dying bloom between her fingers. Her initial anger cooling somewhat as she continued strolling down the path. *How stupid of him to draw such a conclusion*, she thought.

"Maybe. But when they stopped and got off, I saw him cradle her face in his hands and lean down to kiss her."

Angela stopped walking. "Did he kiss her?" she asked without turning to look at Ted.

"I couldn't tell for sure. It seemed that way, but if he did, it was a quick kiss. The kicker was when they parted ways; they held hands for as long as they could with their arms extended out to each other as if they didn't want to leave."

"Hmm," Angela said as she thought.

"There's no telling what's going on behind closed doors."

"You don't think they're lovers; do you?" she asked, aghast at such an idea.

Ted looked at her suggestively. "What would *you* do behind closed doors, away from prying eyes, just the two of you?"

"With *him*?" she asked with a sneer. "Probably not what you're thinking."

"But what if you were nothing more than a simple-minded stable hand?"

"Hmmm," Angela commented as her thoughts continued.

"Maybe a simple-minded, *gold-digging* stable hand!"

"Yesss...," she said quietly, lost in devious thought.

Ted felt uneasy. What was Angela thinking about? Was she considering leaving Alan and being with him? He sat down on a white iron bench, crossing his strong, slightly bowed legs. His mind entirely wrapped around hope.

Angela, deep in thought, quietly paced and spun the delicate bloom back and forth by its stem.

Ted urged her, unsuccessfully, to join him on the two-seater garden bench.

Finally, after considerable silence, Angela returned from her eerie calmness and spoke with a sad, pitiful voice. "I can't believe he would have the audacity to do something like this right here in front of everyone. What if this separation turns into divorce, Teddy? How will I survive?" Getting Ted on her side was her most important mission.

"You can marry me," he suggested.

"We've been through this; you can't afford me." Angela's face was manipulatively sullen.

"You don't know. Maybe I can."

Completely ignoring him, Angela continued, "If Alan divorces me, I'll have to sell the horses and get a real job." Slowly, she lowered herself onto the bench next to him.

"I'll take care of you," he promised her while he put his arm around her narrow shoulders. "Just give me time. I'll have enough money to take care of anything you need."

"I won't have time for you anymore," she said with a pitiful pout.

"We'll always have time for each other, Baby." Ted caressed her face and leaned in to kiss her, but before he could, Angela turned from him and rested her back against him.

"I'm going to have to step it up," she thought aloud. "There's no other option."

"What are you talking about?" Ted asked.

"Alan. I can't let him go so easily. I have to have a fool-proof plan to keep him right where he belongs."

Ted stroked his red beard and sighed. Had she not heard a word he'd said? "And where's that?" he asked, even though he already knew the answer.

"With me, of course!"

While expelling a deep sigh, he said, "Ok." He closed his eyes and shook his head. "So what's your plan?" he asked dully, realizing Angela was still no closer to leaving Alan and being with him than she was prior to hearing his juicy news.

"I've got to get him to sleep with me."

"What?! No!!" Ted was immediately on his feet, causing Angela to have to catch herself from falling back against the bench. "I won't share you!" he shouted at her.

"That's just tough, isn't it? It's the only way, Teddy. I've got to get pregnant to make Alan stay. He's wanted a baby for as long as I can remember. If he knew I was pregnant, he'd move heaven and earth to stay with me and the baby."

Ted felt as if his world were suddenly crashing around him. *Pregnant?* he thought. "I'll kill that bastard first!"

Angela was stunned by his comment. Her carefully made-up face became blank as it stared at him. *Ted kill Alan? Hmm, now there's a thought,* she pondered. "Now, if there were some way I could keep Alan's money *and* marry you."

Ted's face displayed his scandalous contemplations. "Well, we *could* kill him, you know? Then you'd inherit all his money."

Angela gasped as if the thought had never entered her mind. "I don't think *I* could kill anyone."

"I didn't mean that *you'd* do it; I meant we could hire someone. Once he's taken care of, our worries will be over." Ted returned to the bench next to her. Getting rid of Alan, permanently, was the best idea he'd had in years! Having Alan's money would far outweigh anything Ted had planned.

"But...," she sighed, "oh, don't tease me, Teddy."

"I'm not teasing you. I've got a friend; he's a former jockey. He'd do it."

"How? I don't want anything bloody and nasty."

"You leave the details to me."

Angela smiled a shy smile at Ted that turned quickly to a school girl's pout. "I don't know, Teddy. He's got a new CD coming out. If you kill him now, we'd be giving up any future money."

"Not really. Think about how much more his stuff would be worth after he's dead? Think of Elvis. Michael Jackson. You could make millions just off of royalties and residual fame."

"Hmm...." Angela ran her manicured fingers through Ted's auburn hair. "Still, I don't know about just killing him outright. That's a little extreme, don't you think?"

"Well, to me, the sooner you're all mine, the better."

"I'm all yours now, Teddy," she said while she cupped her hands around his bearded cheeks. "All I'm saying is maybe killing him right now when he's got a new CD coming out isn't quite the right time. Besides, my plan seems much less difficult. All I've got to do is get pregnant long enough for Alan to come crawling back to me. It will get rid of that Mary, too. Two birds with one stone. He'll focus entirely on me and the baby. Then everything will go back to the way it's supposed to be."

"I don't like it, Ang."

"I don't care if you like it! This isn't your future we're talking about, it's mine. The only way I can be assured Alan won't leave is if I'm pregnant."

"And if it doesn't work?"

"It will."

Ted sighed. "But what if he leaves you anyway? I wish you'd just let him go," he whispered.

"I can promise you, if my plan doesn't work, we'll put yours in place," she said sweetly. "And then we'll be together forever."

"But then you'll have a baby in tow," he said with a disgusted frown.

"You don't get it do you? I have no intention upon actually *having* any baby." She shuddered at the thought. "Eww! All I have to do is get pregnant and stay pregnant long enough to bring Alan around and run that little tramp off. Then I can just have an abortion again."

Ted seemed surprised by her callous, matter-of-fact statement. "And that doesn't bother you?"

"It doesn't seem to bother you killing Alan!"

"True. But still…"

"Oh come on, Ted! I've had to do this before, only it was an accident I got pregnant before. I'll just tell Alan I had a miscarriage. He bought it last time."

Ted only sighed his surrender to her plan. Killing Alan seemed like such a much better plan. His heart pounded in hatred against his enemy. He wanted to be the one to destroy Alan!

"We've got to act pretty soon, though. Once his CD is released, he'll be gone most of the time on tours promoting it, and then getting pregnant will be impossible."

With a noticeable scowl, Ted nodded.

"But if I find out that Mary's fucking him, we'll destroy them both!" she exclaimed as she crushed the tulip blossom in her hand.

CHAPTER 2

Alan sat in the leather office chair behind Johe's desk. "Ok. What the hell were you talking about on the phone? The only thing I got was 'serious problem' and 'poisoned.' Who was poisoned?" he said into the barn's landline. With Johe still in Athens tending to Biscuit and Old Gem, Alan was free to use her office as he liked. He leaned back in the chair, which made a loud creaking noise. The clapboard walls of her comfortable office surrounded him; the air lacked the routine rich aroma of coffee.

"Biscuit!" her raspy voice nearly shouted. "He's dead. Poisoned. I-I don't know what to do. I-I-I can barely breathe! How could something like this happen?!"

"I don't know," Alan said, almost not believing his ears. In his mind, Babbling Brooks was as secure a sanctuary as he'd ever had. The idea that it had been infiltrated made him feel anxious. He wondered who could have gotten onto his private farm. He'd had crazed stalkers in the past and had spent millions fortifying the property. Was it possible someone had breached all his security measures? "How do they know for sure?"

"Dr. Berg, the vet here at UGA, said the toxicology screening showed Biscuit was poisoned," Johe said. "I'm so pissed I can hardly stand it! Who the hell would've done such a thing?"

Alan's cerulean eyes aimlessly scanned the chaotic desk, confused on what to say. "I honestly don't know," he slowly said.

"I faxed you a copy of the toxicology report. Check the fax

machine."

"Hold on." Alan laid the phone down and retrieved the piece of paper from the nearby fax machine. He paused trying to make heads or tails out of the report. Sitting back down in the noisy chair, he picked up the phone and said, "I don't understand any of what this is saying."

"Dr. Berg said she was surprised to see such a toxicological report. Most animals and humans who are poisoned with ethylene glycol react considerably differently. She said it's likely an elevated level of copper caused the anomaly," Johe added.

"Or just his sheer determination to live," Alan said as he furrowed his brow in an angry yet worried look. "How'd he get into antifreeze?"

"I'm not sure. That's where the mystery comes in. I guess it could've been…" Johe's comment trailed off incomplete. *Just how had Biscuit been exposed to it?* she wondered. "I suppose maybe someone was changing their engine coolant and didn't dispose of it properly, and Biscuit somehow drank it."

"Yeah. Maybe. But I thought Frankie had everyone change over to environmentally friendly coolant that didn't contain ethylene glycol," Alan said about his chauffeur.

"I don't know. I don't keep up with that kind of stuff. I just know I'm caught between wanting to cry my eyes out and wanting to claw someone else's eyes out. The thing that scares me the most is there are really only three possibilities for how this happened: accidental; intentional from a stranger; or intentional from someone who already has access to the barn."

"Yeah," Alan said as his thoughts returned to the safety of the farm in general. It had been just over two years since he'd had a stalker try to penetrate Babbling Brooks. She'd made his life so difficult that he'd had to use disguises and aliases in order just to move around. "You don't think it was Danielle, do you?" he asked about his last stalker. *She would be getting out of jail right about now,* he thought.

"I don't know. I suppose it could be. Maybe she saw you and Mary riding, and she thought Biscuit was the horse Mary was riding," Johe said with a palpable twinge of irritation.

"Wait. What?"

9

"You know what. You and I both know you and Mary go riding a lot. Her horse looks like Biscuit on steroids."

"So. What's that got to do with anything?"

"I'm just saying…"

"I know what you're saying, and I don't like the implication," he said with a defensive posture.

"Then why don't you explain just what the hell you and Mary are always doing together."

Alan chuckled lightly. "I don't have to explain anything. It's my farm, and I can do what I want on it."

"Touché. Still. I've noticed. I'm sure others have too."

"It's no different than if I were to ride with you – oh but of course, you don't ride," Alan said with a note of teasing derision.

Johe briefly chuckled. *He knows damn good and well why I don't ride,* she thought. *He visited me in the hospital after the accident at the Atlanta Olympics.* "Yeah, maybe so, but she's my employee. And while you're gallivanting all over the place with her, the work around there isn't being done."

"Then hire someone else to take up her slack."

"What and pay her to play with you all the time?"

"I believe I still pay the bills around here, don't I?"

"Yes, but it's my job to maintain a balanced budget."

"And when has Angela ever once let you maintain a *balanced* budget?"

"That's beside the point. I'm not so keen on introducing another unknown to the farm. We got lucky with the staff we have. Don't you think we've been disrupted enough?" she asked referring to Biscuit's poisoning. "You don't think someone put it in his food do you? Or what if they injected him with it?"

"Ok. Ok," Alan said in an attempt to quell her growing anxiety. "Stop worrying. I'll call Felix and have him start investigating what happened," Alan said about his head of security. "Felix will get whoever he needs to help. Will that make you feel better?"

"Yes. Thank you." Johe's pleased smile showed through her words of gratitude. "But don't you think we should call the police?"

"Police? No. I'd rather not. I don't need the bad publicity of it all. Lord knows I've had enough bad publicity in the past few months from Angela. I'd rather investigate this in-house first. Felix can handle it, and he'll take care of it as quietly and delicately as possible. If he thinks someone from the outside did it, then we'll get the police involved. Ok?"

Johe sighed. "Ok – I guess."

He pulled out his dead cell phone to call Felix. "Hmm. I completely forgot, my phone is toast."

"What happened to it?"

"It got wet."

"How?"

"Mary and I went fishing; she fell in the lake, and I jumped in to save her. My phone was in my pocket," he explained while trying to shake more water out of the phone.

"Uh-huh," Johe suspiciously said. "And when was this?"

"Just a little bit ago. We sat out on the lake for a while trying to warm up and dry off before we came back. Why?" he asked without looking up from his phone.

"No reason. Just wondering." After a momentary pause, she continued, "Do y'all do this often?"

"Do what?"

"Go 'fishing.'"

Even though Alan couldn't see her, the inflection in her voice made it clear she didn't believe they were fishing for actual fish. "Wait. You don't believe we went fishing?"

"Oh I believe you went out on a boat, but I'm betting there was far more going on than feeding some fish."

Alan laughed his melodic laughter that showed his sincere amusement. "You think so little of me!"

"No, I know men. And providing you and Angela are separated, and probably not sexually active, I'm guessing you've got some of the bluest balls ever at this point."

Alan only laughed harder, louder. "No. Nothing like that. In fact, it was her first time ever fishing. She was adorable learning how to fish."

"Really?" Johe asked, a little surprised by his response. "What possessed you to take her?"

"It was my choice. She said I could spend an entire day with her any way I wanted, so I picked fishing."

"Did she now?" Johe asked, interested in hearing more. "So,

just what *is* going between you two?" Johe asked again, more suspiciously this time.

Alan realized he'd inadvertently said too much. "Nothing. Why?"

"Because even when we were dating, you never took me fishing. And what's this mess about how she said you could spend an entire day with her? Sounds to me like she's playing you. I just want you to be careful."

Alan smiled his appealing dimpled smile that stretched up to his eyes. "You'll just have to trust me. She's not playing me. Not at all."

"Then what's going on?"

"Johe," he said as he leaned toward the desk, "it's none of your business."

Johe could hear the chair creaking, which, in her mind, meant she was getting to him. "I think it is. If one of my employees is acting inappropriately, I would like to nip it in the bud."

"There's nothing you need to worry about, and no bud nipping required. We're f-friends. That's all."

"Are you sure? You kind of stumbled there over your words."

Alan looked left and then right. He listened intently for sounds of anyone else nearby before he spoke again. "Ok. But you have to swear to Almighty God you won't repeat this, ever!"

"I swear."

"The truth is, she intrigues me. I can't get enough of her."

"Have you slept with her?" Johe asked as she braced herself for the blow she anticipated was coming.

"No. No. Nothing like that."

Whew! she thought. "Ok. So what have you done with her?"

"Just kissed a few times."

"Alan! You're a married man!" Her judgment came harshly and quickly.

"Thank you, *Mom*, I'm aware of that," he said sarcastically. "But I also know Angela and I are separated and well on our way to divorce."

"It's progressed that far, huh?"

"Yeah. I'm just tired of her shit. And the more I think about it, the more I'm aware there's something special about Mary that fits me perfectly. We mesh."

"You mesh," Johe mocked him.

"Yeah."

"I'm surprised you haven't fucked her yet," her words were biting.

Alan immediately felt their sting. "I never 'fucked' you when we were dating, as you so eloquently put it," he sarcastically said.

"Yeah, but that's because you were too young to know what to do with a woman like me."

"Well that's what you get for dating someone so much younger. You should've told me no."

"Uh-huh. There's no way any woman could resist those eyes of yours!"

"Ha! Wanna bet?"

"Have you even tried to sleep with her?" Johe asked, changing the subject back to Mary.

"No. She's not ready for something like that. It's obvious she's gone through a really rough marriage and divorce. I don't want to push her into something she's not ready for." Even though he said the words, the truth was, he hadn't made any sort of sexually charged moves on Mary, so he couldn't say for sure what she would do if he did. All the moves he'd tried were pretty benign in comparison. Maybe since they'd kissed he could step up his game. He was hopeful.

"Good. Because if Angela finds out about any of this, there's no telling what would happen to the both of you. And heaven help you if she found out you were actually screwing around on her. You'd wish for just a divorce."

"Humph," Alan said. He wanted to talk to Johe about his suspicions that Angela and Ted were already involved in an adulterous affair, but he kept that information under his hat. Besides, he didn't want to be with Mary as some sort of revenge, and he definitely didn't want anyone to think that way about her. "Look, just remember to keep your mouth shut!"

"I will. But you've got to learn to hide it better. People watch your movements more than you realize."

"What the hell?!" Alan growled as he stood up and began pacing as far as the phone cord would allow. "This is my farm! I should be able to do whatever I want without judgment!"

"Yeah, but that doesn't mean you can fornicate with the help on your whim!" Johe blasted back at him.

He stopped and looked directly at the leather couch on the opposite wall of the office. "Is that what you think all this is? Some ploy for me to get my rocks off?"

"Isn't it?"

"No. Mary and I are similar souls. I l-love her," he said, realizing how true it really was.

"You what?"

"I love her," he said with a smile. *Wow that felt good,* he thought.

"Oh boy," she said dully.

"Oh boy what?" he repeated.

"Oh boy, are you in for trouble."

"How do you figure?"

"Angela. You don't think she's going to walk away from you quietly, do you? Even if she is completely stuffed up Ted's ass, she's still not going to be willing to give you up without a fight."

"Why not?"

"You're her meal ticket."

"You don't really think I would leave her destitute, do you?"

"Well, no, I know you better than that. But what I'm saying is she's likely to try and take you for everything you've got! Why take some milk when she can have the whole damned cow?"

He thought for a moment before he spoke. "That'll be for Earl to work out. Besides, I'm in no rush. I just kissed Mary for the first time today; let's not get the cart before the horse," Alan said with a laugh.

"Ok. But don't say I didn't warn you."

"Consider myself warned. When are you coming back?"

"I'll be back in about a week."

"All right. Be safe. I'll talk to you later." Alan and Johe said their goodbyes, and he hung up the phone.

Has anything changed since we kissed, he wondered. "I guess there's only one way to find out." He picked up the phone and dialed Marcus' number.

"Marcus, I want you to call the Olde Pink House in Savannah and reserve a private dining room for me and a guest."

14

"What day? What time?" Marcus asked.

"Tonight. And let's say 8:00."

"Will do."

"Get Frankie to get the stretch limo ready. I want this to be completely first class all the way."

"Yes, sir. So you'll be needing your tuxedo as well?"

Alan sighed, frustrated that Marcus needed such detailed instructions. "Yes. And bring in a personal shopper with evening gowns and jewelry." Yet, Alan hoped Mary would want to wear the pearls he'd given her.

"For Angela?"

"No."

"For who then?"

"Just do what I told you."

"They'll want to know what sizes to bring."

"I'd say small. For a woman who weighs maybe 100 pounds."

"So, very small?"

"Yes! Sheesh! I might as well do it myself if I have to answer all of these questions!"

"I'll get on it. Is there any particular color dresses you want?"

Alan hung up the phone without answering Marcus' question and stood up from Johe's desk. Mary had promised him a whole day; he had every intention of extending it into the night as well.

CHAPTER 3

Mary shut the door to her cabin; her entrance evoked a diaphanous puff of yellow pollen that hung in the setting sunbeams shining through her windows. With eyes half-closed and an ethereal smile on her face, she placed her fingertips to her lips and relived the feeling of Alan's lips on hers. Her heart pounded wildly at the thought – the memory. The incomparable country music star Alan Brooks had kissed her. How could it be possible?

The snugness of her quarters didn't seem to matter. Her heart was flying on tiny wings. Hope. She hadn't felt that kind of hope since she sat at her dinette table in her apartment on West Roger Road in Tucson and read her formal acceptance letter into the doctoral program at the University of Arizona. It was also the last time she'd tried to leave Roger. To her surprise, there were no overpowering flashbacks accompanying that thought. All that remained was the lighter than air feeling of hope.

Her fingers gently, weakly dropped from her puckered lips; a deep, soulful smile pushed her eyes the rest of the way closed. In her mind, she could see Alan's imposing presence moving into her space, his face erotic and demure. As if pushed by the gentle lift of angels, her lips met his. The sheer heat from them was enough to make her want more. Her knees felt wobbly as a warm tingly sensation washed through her body.

Moving to the couch, she thought of the pearl necklace Alan had given her months ago. She'd never worn it, yet she wondered why exactly. Opening the coffee table drawer, inside were the pearls, right next to the gun Tunda had demanded Mary take with her when she left Arizona. For a moment, Mary only looked at the two items. They were both such extremes – one possessing the potential for violence, the other for love. One a constant reminder of how precarious her situation was, the other a reminder of hope for a future that didn't revolve around perpetual fear.

Her slender fingers reached for the necklace. The pearls – cool, iridescent with a natural pink overtone – were perfectly round and gradually got smaller the closer to each side of the diamond clasp they got. Mary slid individual beads slowly through her fishy-smelling hands.

Her once cold, frightened heart warmed.

"Alan," she said to no one. *Who would've ever thought he'd mean so much?* she wondered. The freedom to feel something – anything other than terror – was a welcomed relief. Still, the gun remained in the coffee table drawer reminding her that she wasn't completely free to feel anything other than anxiety that her cover might be blown.

Would he have kissed you if he knew you were Mary Franklin? her mind asked.

You can't think about that right now, her heart replied. *Don't ruin this!*

He believes a lie. All you've done is lie to him. He doesn't even know who you really are, her mind said again.

"But I can't tell him," Mary said aloud. "I can't. If I did, how could I guarantee my safety? And if he knew, would he leave? Would I ever feel this way again?"

It would be nice to know he loves you for who you really are, her mind added.

"Yeah...," Mary said with a sigh. Somehow she always had a way of thinking her way out of anything happy.

Before her thoughts were entirely finished, there was a knock on her door. Her heart skipped a beat in anticipation – Alan. Would he kiss her again? Could she kiss him freely now? She flitted to the door as if her feet had wings.

"What do *you* want?" she coolly greeted her guest.

"I saw ya comin' in, so I figured I'd stop by. How're ya?" Cliff asked.

"Fine," she replied with her arms crossed. With quick thinking, she'd narrowly escaped Cliff's demands just the night before. What did he want this time? "Did you come over here to twist my other arm off?" Her arm was still sore from how he'd man-handled her less than 24 hours earlier. The jury was still out on sharing such information with Alan.

"Maybe," he said as he tucked his chin and glared his hard eyes on her. "Ya mine if I come in?"

"Yeah. I was just about to get into the shower," she said.

"Trus' me, this cain't wait,"

Mary scoffed. "Whatever you have to say, you can say right here on the porch."

"Really? 'Cause this is about you and Mistuh Brooks."

She quietly gasped. "Fine, but be quick," she reluctantly agreed. If she denied him, would he force his way in anyway?

Cliff sat down on her couch as if he owned the place. His dark sapphire eyes lighted on the strand of pearls sitting on the table. "He give ya those?" he asked.

"Who?"

"You knowed who."

"No, I'm sorry, I don't," she fibbed.

"Your precious Mistuh Brooks."

"I-I bought them at a thrift store," she told him the same lie she'd told Ginger. Quickly she pushed the pearls into the coffee table drawer and shut it.

Cliff grabbed her around the waist and pulled her onto his lap on the couch.

As if Mary had sat on a tack, she tried to jump back up, but his hold on her was too great.

"Knock it off!" he snapped.

Mary did as she was told, but her skin crawled being so near him. His breath made her sick to her stomach. It reeked of the bittersweet smokeless tobacco that frequently was stuck between his teeth.

"Now, I knowed you 'member what I toll you yesterday, right?"

She nervously remained stoic.

"I done toll you ta stay away from that Mistuh Brooks, right?"

She nodded. "B-but we're friends."

"Yeah, well see, here's the sit'chee-asion. I was out fishin', mindin' muh own business when I sees this boat pullin' into the cove I was fishin' in. Now, I knowed that there lake ain't open ta jus'

18

anybody's use, so I knowed it was Mistuh Brooks. I sits fer a while and watch, an lo an' behold if you ain't there with him…"

"I can explain…"

"Oh I ain't done, Shuga. Jus' after you cast out yer pole, Mistuh Brooks turns ya to look at him. I'm thinkin' what in the hell is goin' on here?"

Mary stroked her opposing arms with her hands. A cold chill traveled down her spine; she wanted desperately to get off of Cliff's boney lap. *If only Alan were here,* she thought.

"Da nex' thing I knowed, there's Mistuh Brooks plantin' a sloppy one on ya! So I grabbed muh cellula phone and snapped a few pics."

Mary's blood ran cold. *He took pictures of us kissing?!* she thought in a panic.

"Then there you go overboard. I dropped muh phone, bout ready to jump in after ya, when Mistuh Brooks done the same." Cliff rubbed his chin. "So from what I's seen, I's figurin' there's somethin' more goin' on wid you two than you was lettin' on. An' I'm bettin' that somethin' is somethin' y'all ain't wantin' folks to know 'bout, right?"

Cliff relented his grip on her enough to where she could climb out of his lap. She deftly moved across the room, and hid her anxiety behind empty eyes.

"And from where I sees it, you ain't nothin' but a no-count liar! Ya lied ta me last night."

"No…"

"Shut up!" Cliff shouted at her as he jumped up from the couch.

Mary's gaze dropped to the floor. Terrorized thoughts conjured up from the depths of her psyche like zombies rising from graves.

"I don't need ta hear anymore of yer lies! I could sell these here pictures to jus' about anybody."

Her primary focus was hiding the panicky dread such an idea was bringing.

"But here's the way I figure it. If yer wantin' to keep what I seen a secret, I'm-a need a little somethin' to keep muh mouth quiet." Cliff slowly stalked her.

She knew exactly what he meant, and raised her head to stare at him. Burning the image of his leathery face with its dark, relentless eyes into her mind overtook any anxiety about her secret relationship with Alan. If he was going to rape her, she was going to give a complete description of him and know for sure that it was Cliff. It wouldn't be like before when she didn't think to pay close attention to details about her rapist. "And that something is me, huh?" She backed up one step for every step Cliff took toward her.

"Bingo! Yer gettin' it jus' fine. Now come-on over here and gimme a kiss."

"No!" she shouted with her lips curled in disgust.

"You ain't in any position to be refusin' my offer. All I'm a-wantin' is a kiss – for now," he said with a devious grin that showed his missing tooth.

"I don't know what you think you're doing, but you're not getting anything from me!"

"Oh yeah? Well, how 'bouts I make muh way up to the main house there and talk to Missus Brooks? Huh? I'm sure she'd like ta know what's going on wid you an' her hubby."

"Go ahead. There's nothing to tell. I've already told you; we're just friends."

"See, I may look stupid, but I ain't. When Mistuh Brooks kissed ya, it didn't look like no friends. I don't kiss muh friends like that. Something's up. An' if you don't want folks knowin' 'bout what I seen, you best get over yerself 'n' kiss me. 'Cause I gots photographic evidence provin' differen'. Ya ain't gonna lie yer way outta this one. Now pucker up, 'cause I'm claimin' what's rightfully mine."

"I don't care what you think you saw. Alan... Alan...," she stuttered as she tried to come up with another lie. The truth was, there was no denying it. Alan had kissed her, and she'd kissed him. If Cliff had photos of it, such evidence could ruin both of them. Roger would be on her faster than the speed of light!

"I-I-I'm, uh, I-I-I'm not kissing you."

"I took muh dip out 'n' everythin'," he said as he pulled his bottom lip out, providing proof.

Mary moved backward; the raw sexual power he exuded made her mind continually flash between reality and images of her attacker. She struggled to keep herself focused.

She cringed as Cliff's puckered lips invaded her space.

Cliff's ominous words bounced around inside her mind: "All I'm wantin' is a kiss – for now!"

The wall stopped her backward escape. Before she could find another outlet, Cliff had his large, strong hand gripping the back of her neck at the base of her skull. His body pinned her against the wall.

"You didn't have any trouble kissin' Mistuh Brooks."

Cliff's cat-that-swallowed-the-canary grin unnerved her. His sultry, aggressive eyes seemed to undress her.

"And what do you think Alan's going to do to you when I tell him you're trying to blackmail me?" she said with her head pulled back by his steely grip.

"I can make up jus' 'bout anythin' I want 'bout what I seen, so he ain't gonna have nothin' to say!" Firmly, Cliff encapsulated her; any attempts of escape were futile. "'Sides, he ain't gonna know, 'cause you ain't gonna tell him."

"Get away from me!" She tried unsuccessfully to push him away.

In an instant, Cliff was through taking her nos for an answer. The intensity of his hold on the back of her head increased; Mary winced in pain. He shoved her face to his, engulfing her mouth and lips with his mouth.

Mary could smell the vileness of his spit as Cliff invaded her senses and space. She fought as hard as she could against him, but his control was unrelenting.

The terrorizing feeling of being trapped was overwhelming as Cliff's body throbbed against hers. Her head pounded. The flashing images of her rapist immediately became her prevailing thoughts. Her eyes clinched tightly shut.

Fear's icy cackle created clouds inside her mind.

She tried to scream, but it only allowed Cliff's slimy tongue to slip inside her mouth.

Mary's breaths were quick and shallow. Beads of sweat appeared upon her forehead as her thoughts grew into full-blown panic. Her heart was pounding so loudly that her mind could no longer think.

Fear laughed loudly as he pulled her puppet strings.

Cliff crassly rubbed his free hand down her arm from her shoulder across her chest and between her breasts. He stopped to massage firmly her left breast as if it were a piece of meat.

Mary's body began to tremble as thunder crashed inside her mind and thoughts morphed into her reality. Before she even knew what happened, her mind snapped. To her, Cliff was her assailant; his slight moaning was nothing more than the guttural growls of a mad man. She felt helpless again – cornered and under attack. With strength she must've gained from so much manual labor, she finally pushed Cliff off of her. In an instant, she shrieked and smacked his face as hard as she could.

Immediately, Cliff backhanded her across the cheek, which knocked her off her feet.

"Sos you like it rough, eh?" he shouted at her.

Mary's face instantly throbbed as the memories of Roger's attacks came back to her.

Cliff grabbed both of her arms in his work-worn hands in an attempt to regain control of her. "Knock it off!" he yelled at her.

With her arms held firmly by her sides, she screamed violently and turned into a tiger flailing her legs at him.

He put his hand firmly over her mouth and nose. "Ya better shut yer stupid mouth 'fore I shut it fer ya! Permanently!"

With determination to survive, Mary ferociously bit at his fingers.

"Ow!! You bitch!" He swung back to hit her again, but with one swift kick that nearly landed on his aroused genitals, he jumped back from her.

"*Nooo!!*" she cried out as she slapped at the air, and then ran down the hall to her bedroom.

Cliff strode quickly behind her. No woman was going to get the upper hand on him. "Get yer ass out here!" he growled.

Before Cliff could reach her, Mary's slight body slid under the bed and just out of reach.

He tried to pull her from under the footboard, but the bed itself protected her.

To her surprise, the quilt and mattress were tossed off the box springs. In desperation, she crawled out the other side of the bed.

Just as she'd made it past Cliff and back into the hallway, he grabbed her and spun her around to face him. Something inside her snapped. As if in one quick motion, she reached back as far as she could and punched Cliff square in the jaw with every ounce of strength she had. Her fist could feel his teeth rattle against each other with her punch.

"Don't you *ever* hit me!" she shrieked.

Like lightning, Cliff threw her against the wall again, trapping her. This time he drew back his fist to hit her square in the face.

Before he could throw his punch, Mary's knee came smashing against his crotch.

Cliff's punch landed just next to Mary's head and went through the warm-colored drywall as his knees buckled. His tall, lanky body landed with a thud on the thinly-carpeted floor, gasping for breath.

"Don't fuck with me!" Mary yelled at him before she quickly bolted out of the tiny cabin. Her adrenaline was pumping so hard she couldn't even feel her cheek. Getting as far away from Cliff as possible was her immediate concern. Was he following her? What would he do to her if he caught her again?

Without ever once looking back, her trembling legs carried her hastily out the front door of her cabin and straight to the barn. *There's no way he'll follow me into public*, she thought.

Aja was the first person she ran into.

"You ok?" Aja asked.

"Yeah," she breathlessly answered, "I'm ok. I-I just saw, uh, a-a-a snake." Her face throbbed; could Aja see a red mark? Mary kept that side of her face turned from Aja.

"Oh sugar, honey, iced-tea! I'd be freaking out too! You want some water? I just put some bottled water in the fridge. You're welcomed to some."

Mary shook her head for a moment. "What did you just say?"

"Sugar, honey, iced-tea," Aja repeated with a smile. "No self-respecting Southern lady would be caught saying the s-word."

Mary thought for a moment. "Huh?"

Aja rolled her eyes. "Sugar, honey, iced-tea, now take the first letters of each word."

"S. H. I. T. Oh my gosh!" Mary said as her face turned flush. "That's one way of saying it."

"Yeah. My mama would've worn my tail out for saying such things, so I learned how to say them without being vulgar."

"I see. Anyway, don't go out the back of the barn. There's a big, nasty snake. Wait for it to go away."

Aja smiled sweetly. "Will do. Thanks."

Getting as far away from Cliff as fast as she could was her immediate need. She didn't bother with a bridle; she just hopped on Sun's back and bolted out of the barn. The two immediately hit the woods in the opposite direction of the trails. Getting lost in the dense forest wasn't such a bad thing.

Mary clung to Sun's neck as she tried to keep herself from catching all of the spider webs between the trees. The idea of having a spider crawling on her was as disgusting as Cliff's lips!

"Cliff," she whispered into Sun's mane. "What am I going to do with him, boy? Everything has gotten way out of control. He thinks he can use violence to overpower me, and the sad thing is maybe he's right. I've got to stand up to him. He's not..." The words were difficult to say. "He's not Roger, but he's pretty damn close."

Her cheek throbbed.

CHAPTER 4

It was unmistakably dark by the time Mary stood inside the thick woods near her cabin. The distinct fetor of Cliff's tobacco-laden saliva clung to her swollen face; it was an overwhelming and nausea-inducing smell that reminded her of Cliff's behavior. The stench from Cliff's nasty wet kiss made her breathe from her mouth. She could still taste it; the last thing she wanted to do was smell it also.

Her ears strained to hear anything.

Nothing.

Her eyes throbbed from the uncontrollable crying she'd done in the relative safety of Sun's presence. It made it hard to see. Was Cliff still there?

There were no lights on in her cabin. Was he waiting in the dark for her to return?

Her mind flashed to the times Roger would sit quietly in the living room without a single light on. She'd sneak inside, thinking he had to work late and wouldn't mind her staying late at the lab. Only to have his voice stop her dead in her tracks: "It's nice you finally decided to return home, Mrs. Franklin." Nothing good ever started with that sentence. It still resonated in her ears and made the hair on her arms stand up.

Could she handle this whole Cliff thing on her own? Or should she involve Alan?

She thought of angry Cliff pulling the mattress off of the bed. No one had touched the bed since Alan had sat on it with his feet poking out the footboard. Beds were still as evil as they ever were.

Should she do like she always did and clean it up, hiding what happened? What about her face? Would she end up with a black eye?

Nervously, she tapped Sun's sides with her heels. "Eeeeasy," she whispered. Creeping out of the thickets as slowly as possible was best. The golden horse responded exactly as he'd been trained to do; each step he took was measured and deliberate.

"Whoa."

Sun completely stopped.

The back door to Mary's cabin was no more than 25 feet from where Sun stood. The idea that Cliff was there lying in wait made her tremble. Her eyes scanned the peaceful courtyard of tiny cabins. In an instant, her head snapped to the cabin next to hers – Cliff's cabin. A light had turned on in the kitchen. Inside was Cliff, dressed in only a towel. He had his hands behind his head as he thrust his hips to a song Mary couldn't hear. His thin, muscular physique was amplified as he danced.

The thought that her bedroom window could be seen from Cliff's kitchen window made her rethink the mess he'd left behind. Perhaps it was best to shut the door on it. "Shit head," she said to the night air. "He doesn't even give a damn about what he did to me."

She felt raw, angry, and hateful.

"I can't believe you're allowing him to steal your joy," she quietly, venomously told herself. Gently, her fingers ran across her cheekbone. How many times had she felt the same pain from the back of Roger's hand? She clucked and directed Sun to turn to the left, away from the cabins. Carefully, they maneuvered through the edge of the brush.

"It's like I'm a prisoner all over again! Dammit!"

Once she'd made it to the end of the forest where the trail to the other pastures began, she stopped and looked back at the cabins, which were now a fair distance away. The light in Cliff's kitchen window still burned in addition to every other light imaginable inside. Flickering light came from his bedroom window.

"No doubt from that damned 55-inch TV he has," she told Sun. Mary felt moderately assured he was in his cabin for the night. All she had to do now was put Sun away and sneak her way back into her cabin, where she suspected she'd spend the night in the pitch darkness and in constant terror that he'd return. Her face genuinely hurt. There was a bag of frozen peas in her freezer just begging to be on her cheek.

"Come on, let's get you in bed," she said softly to Sun while she tapped his sides with her heels. Her eyes stayed glued on Cliff's illuminated quarters. If there was any movement there, she'd be the first to know. Her burning eyes made it difficult for them to focus.

Just yards from the barn's entrance, she heard "Hey, you!"

The words' intrusion startled her so much, she clung to Sun's mane in a failed attempt to maintain her balance.

"Oh. My. God. Alan! You scared the shit out of me!" she exclaimed as she hopped off Sun's back.

"I didn't mean to. I've been looking all over for you! Where were you?"

"I, uh, I went out for a little ride." Her eyes remained continually locked on Cliff's residence.

"By yourself?"

"Yeah. Why?"

"Well, I had planned a nice, romantic evening for us in Savannah…"

Mary flashed a sweet smile to Alan, but returned her eyes to Cliff's cabin. "Really? I'm so sorry." Strategically, she kept Sun as a barrier between herself and Alan. She didn't want Alan to see she'd been crying, and she definitely didn't want him to see her swollen face. If he noticed, there would be no option about hiding Cliff's behavior anymore.

"Nah, it's ok." He pulled out his new cell phone. "It's too late now anyway."

"I'm really sorry."

"Well, the whole thing made something abundantly clear to me."

"Oh yeah?" Mary asked nervously.

"Yeah. I don't like not being able to reach you."

She released a pensive sigh. "Oh, well, you don't like that my world doesn't revolve around you, is that what you're saying?"

"Um, no, Honey, I'm over here," Alan said as he reached over Sun's neck and waved his hand in front of her face. "You ok?"

"Uh-huh," she said while she moved to lead Sun into the barn.

"You seem distracted."

"I've got to take care of Sun."

"Can I have a little kiss first?" he asked as he reached for her hand and held it under Sun's head.

"N-n-not right now," she answered and turned her head away from him. *Oh I hope he can't smell that disgusting smell of Cliff's spit!* she thought.

Alan suspiciously looked at her. "This isn't another one of your one-step-forward-two-steps-back, playing-hard-to-get moves is it?"

She closed her eyes and shook her head. "I don't have a clue what you're talking about."

"Then kiss me to prove me wrong."

"Let me get Sun taken care of first. I don't want anyone to accidentally see."

"So. Let them see. I'm not ashamed. Are you?"

"No. I'm not ashamed; I'm just private."

He chuckled with a scoff mixed in. "Private, huh? You're holding my hand, you know?"

"Yeah. I'll kiss you all you want when we get in my cabin." The words left her lips, but made her question just what she was thinking when saying them.

A pleased smile planted itself between Alan's ears. "I'm going to hold you to that, you know?"

"I'm sure you are." They entered the barn and made their way down the aisle.

"You need any help?"

"Nah. I've got this. Sun and I are pretty simpatico; he doesn't always like anyone else taking care of him."

"Ok. Well, I'm going to head on up to your cabin. I'll see you when you get done."

"Ok." Mary slid open Sun's stall and led the obedient horse inside.

I've got to get rid of this nasty smell! she thought as she immediately went to Sun's automatic waterer. She filled it with fresh water and splashed it on her face, scrubbing it as best as she could with just her hands. The coolness felt good on her sore face and reduced the swelling.

"If I never encounter that stench again, it'll be too soon." Sticking out her tongue, she scrubbed her tongue, too. *I wish I had some soap, but is simple soap going to be strong enough to get rid of this?* she wondered. She contemplated using some wood shavings mixed with water to scrub her face, but decided against it merely because her face would definitely be red and cause Alan to inquire into why. There was a chance her cheek wasn't red at all anymore. After all, he hadn't mentioned it. "I hate that Cliff slobbered away Alan's kiss," she muttered.

"You'll just have to kiss Alan again," she told herself, smiling at the thought.

As she swished water around in her mouth, she thought of the two men. Alan's lips were so different than Cliff's. Cliff was like kissing a dirty, wet toilet plunger. "Eww," she said when she spit the water into the basin. Her wet lips curled in disgust. Alan's kiss, while eager, was tender, enticing, and... *experienced?* her mind asked.

"Don't be a prude, Mary. You have to know he's kissed a lot of women in his time. One he's older than you. Two he's... he's Alan Brooks!" She wiped her face off with her shirttail.

Sun sneezed behind her as he nibbled from his hay rack.

"Oh no!" Terror suddenly seized her. If Alan was in her cabin unattended, would he find the mess Cliff had made in her bedroom? The hole he'd punched into her wall? With nervous, determined, and oddly familiar steps, she closed the stall door and worked to think of a lie to tell Alan.

Breathlessly, she busted into the dimly lit cabin. Alan sat quietly in his usual seat on the end of the sofa.

"Hey," he greeted her with his eyes half-closed.

"Hi," she said overly cheerfully as she tried to smooth things over and not draw attention to what had happened.

"Have a seat."

With wobbling knees, Mary sat in the faded pink chair across the room from Alan. Roger's exact threating words rumbled inside her mind.

He sat forward, resting his elbows on his knees. "What happened?"

"With what?"

"You know," he said as he dropped his chin.

Mary nervously fidgeted. He knew. There was no point in trying to hide it.

"I-I-I l-l-lost an earring," she could hardly believe she was lying for Cliff. She sounded just like she did when she'd lie for Roger.

"Don't give me that. What happened?"

Her head immediately hung to her chest. The tears she'd cried deep in the quiet, secluded forest pooled in her eyes. The look on her face was worried, scared.

"Hey. This isn't an interrogation or anything," he sweetly said as he moved over to her. "You didn't do anything wrong."

"Didn't I?"

"Come on. There's nothing so bad we can't fix it." He took her hand and led her down the hallway to her bedroom. There among the other yellow-coated bedroom furnishings was the mattress with its bedding still attached. In addition, it appeared Cliff had enjoyed destroying her room by throwing various items onto the floor.

"I had to use the restroom and noticed that something was grossly wrong here as I walked past."

Mary only sniffled.

"I'm not going to force you to explain. I wish you would, but I'm not going to force you to. Just don't lie to me."

"I…"

"And I know what you said before is a bald-face lie."

She nodded without looking at him.

"Now, come on. We'll set this all straight." With his massive reach, he grabbed each side of the full-sized mattress and placed it over the footboard and back onto the box springs.

Nervously, she tugged on the quilt with the circular pattern. Just the idea of touching it made her afraid. She only used two fingers to slide the quilt back in place.

Alan busied himself picking up other things that had been knocked onto the floor.

Standing back and looking at the almost-made bed made her stomach churn. *Smooth the blanket all the way out,* she could hear her mother's voice tell her.

Delicately, she touched the stitching on the quilt covering it. Thoughtfully, she analyzed some of the stitches; as well as it was made, it still was clearly handmade. That knowledge encouraged her to make the bed appropriately, it was the least she could do for whoever made the quilt.

She took special care with the quilt. When she went to tuck the sheet under the mattress, she flipped up the corner of the quilt and noticed some stitching on the backside of the blanket.

The stitching read "Made, with all my love forever, and ever, and two weeks. To: Alan Foster Brooks, Sr. 'Wedding Rings' by: Fiona Marzena Nielsen Brooks. May our circle always go unbroken. Christmas, 1985."

To the very depths of Mary's soul something inside her was moved. She looked more carefully at the quilt with the intertwined circles; how had she not noticed the pattern before? It was wedding rings; rings that were hooked together, never to be parted. Alan's mother, a woman she'd never met, had made that quilt with love in every stitch.

Mary gently touched the needlework with her fingertips. In the midst of her terror, she was surrounded by pure love, and she didn't even know it. She rubbed her outstretched hand across the quilt quickly, almost as though she expected something dreadful to happen – nothing happened.

She exhaled sharply. *What did you expect?* she thought.

Perhaps Mary's avoidance of beds had been foolish; perhaps her fear had been misplaced. It was Roger who had made things so bad, not the bed. After all, in the midst of Cliff's pursuit of her, she was unknowingly in the presence of a grand display of true love that had protected her and helped her escape. The idea that it actually exists, and it exists there in the Brooks family, made her stop and think. All this time, she had been too afraid to see it or even notice it, yet there it laid waiting patiently for her.

She smoothed the bedding out, effectively removing the remnants of her terror, and returning the bed to its unassuming look. Every time she looked at it, she would think of Fiona Brooks, instead of her rape.

You're safe now. Cliff's gone, and the house is as it should be – with Alan, she thought.

Mary moved over to Alan and placed her hand on his shoulder. "Alan?"

"Mary?" he asked as he turned to her.

"I did lie to you," she confessed while looking directly into his calming blue eyes.

"I know you did. You're not a very convincing liar."

If you only knew, she thought.

"Are you going to tell me what happened?" Alan skeptically asked. "Because I know you've been crying. And there's a hole in the wall that's too high for you to make."

She hung her head and then looked up at him. "You're right. And I'm really sorry I lied to you."

"It's ok. Just don't do it again." He stroked down her cheek with the backs of his fingers.

Mary tried hard not to wince, but couldn't resist the temptation to flinch. She covered her recoil by rapidly bobbing her head in agreement.

He leaned down and gently kissed her, which brought immediate warmth radiating throughout her guilty body.

His arms enveloped her; she wanted to climb inside his skin and hide in his protection. The room that had just moments ago been host to such terror was now host to Alan's protection, tenderness, and forgiveness.

"I'll have maintenance come out and fix the hole in the wall."

"Ok," she meekly said.

"You're not going to tell me what happened, are you?" he asked as they walked down the short hallway back to the living room.

"You told me you weren't going to force me to tell you."

"That's true, but I had hoped you'd volunteer the information."

"I-I'm not ready," she whispered as they sat on the sofa together.

Without another word, he leaned down and pressed his lips against hers. Slowly, thoughtfully, his lips moved to kiss her top lip before moving to caressing her bottom lip.

Sooooo much better than Cliff, Mary thought as her entire body prickled in arousal. *I hope he doesn't smell Cliff,* she instantly thought. What if she hadn't scrubbed away every bit of Cliff's residue?

Concerned that he might discover Cliff, she pulled back from Alan's lips. "You're going to make me melt into a trembling pile of mush if you keep that up!" she said in an attempt to remove the concern she felt.

"So? I'll be here to scoop you up into my arms," he said as he brushed a wayward lock of hair from her face and tucked it under her red bandana.

Mary eagerly kissed him this time. If nothing else, she wanted to completely rid her memory of Cliff's invasion. Gently, she sucked on his tongue as their passion increased.

Alan ran his hands down her back and laid her down on the couch. In a flash, his body was between her legs. His goatee tickled her chin.

She moved her lips to kiss down his chin to his neck and placed delicate kisses all the way along his thick neck and back up to just in front of his ear.

His hand slid its way down her body, stopping briefly at her hip before making its way back up again. He massaged the same breast Cliff had roughly groped.

As much as she wanted to let go and let whatever happened, happen; she couldn't.

"Stop. Alan. Please stop."

"Good. God. You're sexy," he hotly murmured.

With considerably more force, she wiggled and pushed against him. "Please. Stop!"

Alan pulled back. "What?"

Immediately, she slipped onto the floor. "I said stop." She buried her face into her knees that were tucked against her chest. "Please," she weakly added.

"I-I-I'm sorry. I-I just got caught up in the moment." Alan tenderly lifted her chin to look at him; her fearful eyes shot right through him to his heart. "I'm still a man, with very manly desires."

"I know," she softly whispered. After Cliff's near assault, there was no way she could have sex with Alan. Not yet. "I'm so sorry." Her words barely made a sound. Her very being wanted him, but something inside her stopped her cold. "I just can't. Not yet."

"Don't be. It's my fault. I know you're not ready." He quietly chuckled with a blast of air through his nose. "But *damn!* That was just such a turn on…." He ran his fingers through his tousled blonde hair.

"I don't *want* to be this way," she said as she clinched her puffy eyes. If anything, she wanted to just get over the whole situation, but she seemed to run smack into a stone wall when she tried to let go.

"I know."

"Besides, there's still Angela. And I wouldn't want to do anything that would compromise that," she explained.

"I know you wouldn't." *Angela,* he thought. *Yeah. I definitely need to do something about her.*

The room quickly filled with silence and the gentle hum of the refrigerator.

Mary leaned her back on the couch and struggled to fight off tears. Her thoughts swirled around telling Alan about Cliff and playing out various scenarios of what would happen should she tell him.

Alan sat on the couch and sipped his flask. *Damn*, he thought. *I don't know what her ex-husband did to her, but I'd like to punch him in the throat right about now!*

CHAPTER 5

"I'm really sorry," she meekly broke the reticence.

"There's no reason for you to be sorry. I'm the one who is sorry," he said and gently stroked her shoulder.

Mary's immediate response was to jerk away from him.

He sighed and sat back up. The delightful warm embrace of bourbon poured from his flask down his throat.

Mary turned to him. "I guess I'm just..."

Before Mary could finish apologizing, he interrupted her with, "I know you won't believe me when I tell you this, but I didn't come over here to make out with you."

"Oh really?"

"Nevertheless, consider it quite a benefit," he said with one of his smiles that made Mary's toes curl. "I had planned a wonderful evening for us, but when I couldn't find you, I decided to get you a little present." He tugged at his pocket.

She silently chuckled to herself. The hard thing in his pocket wasn't his arousal after all; it was her gift.

Alan presented her with a small white box.

"Um, thanks, but no thanks," she handed it back to him.

"What?" He looked at her and then the box, confused.

"I don't want you buying me gifts," she said flatly.

"O—K, consider it a business necessity."

"Bullshit. It has nothing to do with business and you know it."

"All right, maybe then I'd like for you to have it for your own safety," he said, hoping the excuse would work. He opened the box and placed the white iPhone in her hand.

"I told you, I don't want you buying me gifts. If I want a phone, I'll go out and buy myself one."

"But I *want* you to have it. I programmed my phone number in there for you and everything." He smiled trying to encourage her to take it.

Mary only glared at him. *He never takes no for an answer. The pearls in your coffee table drawer are proof of that,* she thought.

"Look, I bought myself a new one too." He produced a new ridiculously large phone.

"What the hell is that?"

"It's a 'phablet' – half phone, half tablet."

"It's huge!"

"Yeah, I know, but I rather like it, so far."

"Glad you didn't get one of *those* for me!"

"Yeah, well, with your tiny hands, I thought something so big would be too much." He chuckled to himself about how close he came to getting her the same phone. "Look, we can text each other any time we want."

"What are you driving at with all of this? Are you trying to keep tabs on me now?"

"No. Well, maybe. I want you to be able to reach me always."

"And you reach me, huh?"

"Exactly. I didn't like it today when I didn't know where you went or how to find you. I had quite an evening planned, and you were nowhere in sight."

"Sorry about that."

"So, I figured since my phone died today when I baptized it in the lake…"

Mary put her hand up to her mouth and turned toward him. "Oh my gosh. I didn't even think of that."

"Yup. It's gone. Anyway, after waiting impatiently for you to not show back up, I decided you needed a phone, too."

"Don't you think Angela is going to be pretty pissed about this?" she asked as she began tinkering with the phone.

"Angela?" he repeated with a scoff. *Not her again,* he thought. "Please. Angela doesn't have a clue, nor will she. This is just a way for us to talk any time, any place, with no one interfering."

"What?" She looked up from her phone, having missed pretty

much everything he'd just said.

"Ok, ignore the phone for a minute and listen to me." He smiled in amusement at what he assumed was her change of heart with the phone idea. "I said I miss you when we're apart. The phone will make it easier for me to reach you. Keep it with you all the time. Fuck Angela."

She blushed at his crassness. "Why don't you tell me what you really think?"

Alan chuckled lightly. "I have news to tell you, too. I talked to Johe a little bit ago."

"Yeah? When is she coming back?"

"In about a week. She said Biscuit was poisoned."

"What?!" Mary immediately looked up from the phone and nervously stared at Alan. "Who would do such a thing?!"

"I don't know. I've got Felix looking into it."

"Felix? Who's he?"

"Head of my security. I don't know what to think about all of this. Johe has some wild speculations, but I'm not going to make any suggestions until the facts get sorted out."

"Is he dead?"

"Felix? No, of course not!"

"I meant Biscuit."

"Yeah. Yeah he is."

Mary gasped and covered her mouth with her hand. "How's Johe taking it?"

"In typical Johe fashion."

"Not very well, I'm guessing."

"Bingo. I just wanted to keep you informed in case you see a bunch of unfamiliar people prowling around the barn and asking a bunch of questions."

"Ok. Thanks. What about the police?"

"No cops, for now. God knows I don't need any more bad publicity."

"Good thinking," she said with a silent sigh of relief. A police presence would mean she'd have to leave. Police are trained in a way normal people aren't. They'd figure out that she's actually Mary Franklin, the missing wife of Roger Franklin, in no time. "I would just die if something like that were to happen to Sun."

"I know you would."

"Do you think he's safe here?"

"Yes, of course. Why wouldn't he be?"

Why wouldn't he be? reverberated inside her mind. She couldn't tell him that if Roger were to find her, he'd likely go after Sun just to hurt her. "I-i-t's just that Sun and Biscuit look so similar."

"You know," he said as he scratched his head, "Johe said the same damn thing! I never thought they looked *that* much alike."

"But they do – or I guess they did," Mary said uneasily. "Alan," she started as her grossly concerned face looked directly at him, "what if Sun *was* the intended target?"

"Don't be ridiculous! No one would want something like that to happen to Sun."

Or would they? she asked herself. *Oh God, what if Roger is closer to me than I thought?* Her face turned noticeably pale.

"Stop worrying your pretty little self! Would you feel better if I hired a team of security guards and posted them outside of his stall?"

Security guards, Mary thought. *Would they help? Could they help?* "No. I-it's just a waste of money."

"It's not a waste if it gives you some peace of mind," he said as he reached his hand out to her, encouraging her to sit next to him on the couch. "I'll hire some security guards for Sun. I don't need your permission."

She nervously chuckled. "True. But still. Won't that look funny? Security guards guarding just my horse but none of the others?"

Alan drew his mouth into a straight line. "Good point. How about this: I'll hire a team of security guards to simply guard the entire barn? That way no one will enter without permission."

"But what happens when we put the horses out to pasture? A wayward hunter's shot could put one of the horses down in a second." It was clear her worry was getting out of hand.

He cupped her face in his hands and forced her to look directly at him. "There are over a thousand acres here. No one is allowed to hunt on Babbling Brooks; that's why I have separate hunting land. Breathe, ok?"

Mary did as he instructed.

"All we can do is our best. I can't coat him in a bullet-proof blanket, but I can assure you there's no hunting allowed here."

She timidly grinned. "I know. Still. It just freaks me out to think about such a horrible thing." The desire to be next to Sun was bubbling below the surface. "He means more to me than my own life!"

"No one means more to me than your life," he said as he gently kissed her forehead. "I'll do my best to protect him and you, ok? The idea that someone may have infiltrated the farm means that no matter what, security will have to be beefed-up."

Mary exhaled sharply as if she were releasing the fretful air she was holding back.

"You ok now?"

No, she thought. "I think so," she said. "Thank you."

"I'm proud to do it," he said just before he delicately touched his lips to hers. "You know, so often I'd like to just walk away from all this mess and be a normal person again," he said thoughtfully.

"Really?" Mary asked, looking quizzically at him, surprised by his statement.

"Yeah." It almost felt liberating to him to say those words; it felt like he was confessing some secret sin.

"I would've thought stardom was your ultimate dream."

"At one point, I guess it was. But now it just seems to be more of a problem than anything."

"I can understand that. Still, it would be a shame not to share your talent with the world."

"What if my true calling isn't to promote myself, but instead to help others along the way?"

"That would be a noble thing."

Noble, he thought. *Like the Brookses before me?* "Hmm, maybe."

CHAPTER 6

Cliff's perpetual bad attitude toward Mary grew increasingly worrisome. With one glance, he could make her jump out of her skin. To her relief, her eye didn't blacken and Alan didn't know about Cliff's backhanding her. Nevertheless, she felt like one of the feral cats walking along the rafters of the barn – one wrong move and everything would come crashing down.

The stress alone made it difficult for her to make herself eat regularly. Yet, Alan always made it a point to make sure he was there at meal times, even if those times were later in the night. The disapproving look on his face when she would push the plate away persuaded her to eat, even if it was only a few bites.

Alan had been surprisingly patient and hadn't again mentioned the incident with the mattress or the wall. Maintenance men came, patched the hole, and painted over it. Mary wondered if he'd forgotten, but she knew him well enough to know such a thing wasn't probable. He was simply waiting for her to be ready. The trouble was, as the days passed, Mary got less and less ready to talk about it.

It was over a week after Alan and Mary's fishing trip when Johe finally returned from Athens. Mary was relieved to have her back. If anyone other than Alan could keep Cliff in place, it was Johe, and Mary had grown quite weary of constantly looking over her shoulder for Cliff *and* Roger.

The only disappointment in Johe's return was that she didn't bring Biscuit's body back with her.

As Mary unloaded Old Gem from the trailer, she inquired after Biscuit. "So why didn't you bring him home to be buried here?"

"I talked with Alan, and he agreed to donate Biscuit's body to UGA for research. I came back as soon as I could. According to Ted, things have been falling apart around here."

Mary scoffed. "Ted probably didn't get to do everything he wanted to do, is all."

"Well, you and I both know the world doesn't turn unless he twirls it," Johe said with a laugh.

"No kidding." Mary pulled on Old Gem's lead line; the horse was eagerly grazing on grass. "He just didn't get to train as much as he wanted since the increased security around the barn was put in place. Ted has been very vocal about the fact that he's not happy. He also has been most displeased about our training sessions. They haven't gone so well," Mary explained while she led Old Gem toward the barn.

"What happened?"

"He moved me to over three-foot fences, and, well, I seem to fall off more than I stay in the saddle."

"Ouch. You haven't been hurt, have you?" *The last thing I need is Alan crawling my ass*, Johe thought.

"No. Just my pride. I haven't jumped hardly at all since Monday, though."

"Oh! Now I see. It's important to get back at it or you'll lose your nerve," Johe told her.

"Not me…"

"Just remember my story," Johe said as they entered the barn. "Don't be like me. Don't give up."

"I won't."

"So, Angela and Ted worked a lot, and when Ted wasn't working with Angela, he was arguing with Cliff?" Johe asked.

"Yeah, pretty much. Cliff has been another issue altogether."

Johe inhaled through her pursed lips. "Oh yeah?"

"Yeah. I don't know what's gotten into him, but he's been a complete jerk lately," Mary reported. *Surely you can read that Cliff's been making my life a living hell!* she hoped.

"Hmm, that's a volatile situation there. I don't know what's going to happen with the two of them. There needs to be some attitude adjustments and soon."

"I don't know. I just know Ted yells at Cliff, and Cliff yells at me. It's a vicious cycle."

"Hmm…," Johe mumbled contemplative. *Does Alan know about this?* she wondered. *If he did, he'd fire Cliff on the spot.* The changes Alan's infatuation with Mary would make on the barn's dynamics would be difficult to navigate. *I'll have to be careful when it comes to Mary,* she thought. *And so will everyone else. But how to communicate that without violating my promise to Alan?*

"Well, Ted yells at me, too, so I sort of understand how Cliff feels," Mary said.

"Yeah, well, you at least take his criticism with a stiff upper lip and work to improve yourself," Johe replied.

Mary put Old Gem in his stall. "I sure did miss you around here, though. It's surprisingly dull without you!"

"What's so surprising about it?"

"I don't know. I guess you don't realize how much of a difference one person makes in a place until that person is gone. I found myself standing in your office looking at your empty desk feeling very sad."

"You're pathetic!" Johe said with a hearty laugh.

"I know," Mary said, returning Johe's laugher. "But now that you're back, everything can go back to normal. Whew!"

Johe smiled at her. *Normal? Ha! As long as you're with Alan, things won't ever be normal again,* Johe thought. "It was hard being there in Athens. Facing the harsh realities of Biscuit's death was harder than I care to admit. I couldn't stop crying for days. It was just awful! I came to bring Old Gem back, but in reality, I wanted to drown my sorrows in anything other than coming back and seeing Biscuit's empty stall." She shook her head.

"I understand fully. I-I'd be a mess without Sun." Mary followed Johe into her office.

"Good God, what happened in here?!" she exclaimed at the sight of her disorganized desk.

"Um, well, you can thank Alan for that one. He was looking for stuff – he claims your checkbook, address book, and some other little things – and well, that's the end result." Mary wondered just how different her desk looked compared to how it was when she left. It always seemed to be a jumbled mess; what was so different now?

Johe sighed deeply. "I'm almost sorry I left. It's going to take me forever to clean up this mess."

"I'd stay and help, but I've got stuff I need to work on."

"No, no, there's a method to my madness. You go and do what you need to do."

"It sure is good to have you home." Mary looked over her shoulder and smiled at Johe.

"It's good to be home."

It was almost quitting time by the time anyone else noticed Johe's return.

Aja pounced on her, excitedly hugging her neck. "Oh my gosh! I can't believe you're finally back!"

"I'm beginning to wonder if I shouldn't leave more often," Johe said with an astonished chuckle.

"No!" Mary and Ginger responded in unison.

"How's Biscuit doing?" Aja asked, changing her tone to a more serious one.

No one had had the guts to tell Aja the truth about Biscuit's death. She was so softhearted and sweet that such news would be devastating to her. There was a particular time when she accidentally ran over a squirrel on her way into work. One would've thought she'd run over a child or something! She cried and cried – totally incapable of being consoled. She ended up spending the entire day on the couch in Johe's office crying.

"Not well, I'm afraid. His condition was very serious, and quite unique. Dr. Berg there at the hospital said she'd be interested in keeping him for research and for use for her students, but that any hopes for him as a stud were unlikely. They'd like to learn as much as they can from him. Mr. and Mrs. Brooks have agreed to donate him to the university," Johe explained without disclosing he was dead.

"Oh!" Aja's hand shot over her mouth. "I'm so sorry." Her eyes were instantly sad and glistening as tears automatically appeared.

Everyone braced themselves for Aja's broken heart.

"What caused it?" Aja barely spoke.

"They're pretty sure he was poisoned," Johe explained quickly trying to stave off any overemotional sadness Aja may be heading toward. "That's why we have all the new security. We're not sure how he could've been poisoned."

"Oh! I asked about the new security, but no one seemed to

know why," Aja said.

Ginger nodded toward Johe. Everyone knew why Aja didn't know the reasoning behind the increased security – they all made a pact not to tell her, and let Johe handle it.

"How have things been around here? Ted and Alan are the only ones I've heard from." Johe patted Aja's back.

"Fine. You know how Ted is," Ginger chimed in, trying to defuse any potential emotional bomb that may be about to explode.

"I know, Mr. Grumbletones," Johe said.

"The other day I really thought he and Cliff were going to fight," Aja innocently mentioned as she dried the edges of her eyes with her shirttail.

"Shh!" Ginger immediately interjected, giving Aja a harsh look.

"What? He didn't mention this," Johe said with obvious interest. She looked to Mary.

"What?" Mary uncomfortably asked.

"What happened?" Johe demanded.

"I don't know what they're talking about. I didn't see anything." Mary had heard about the whole fight between Cliff and Ted secondhand from Ginger and Aja, but wasn't comfortable repeating it.

"How did you miss such a thing?" Johe inquired.

"I wasn't there. I don't always listen to everything that happens around here," Mary said, but it was evident she was nervous. Her ardent attempts to avoid Cliff at all costs had to remain hidden from Johe and the others. "I've gotten quite adept at blocking things out," she said, implying toward the many arguments between Alan and Angela.

"You know something," Johe said with a skeptical squint at Mary.

"No, I really don't. If you want to know, go talk to Cliff," Mary suggested.

"Maybe I will."

"Tell her the latest with Sean," Aja said as she elbowed Ginger.

"Oh! Yeah! Now *there's* a story!"

"Ok. Fill me in on the latest," Johe asked as she went into the kitchen to refill her coffee cup. "You've got to be kidding me! No coffee?! I'm gone a short time and the whole place goes to hell in a hand-basket!"

"I'll get some coffee going," Mary volunteered.

"Well, let's just say that Sean is the quintessential asshole fish that I should've done like you said and flushed," Ginger reported.

"I told you!" Johe said while carrying her empty mug.

"Yeah, I should've listened. He's such a lying prick!" Ginger exclaimed with palpable irritation.

"Tell her what happened," Aja encouraged Ginger.

"All right. So you know I spent a few days with him and had some of the most amazing mind-blowing, headboard-crawling sex of my life, right?"

"Yeah," Johe said.

"But I said I'm through with him because he likes to play Dutch oven, right?"

"Yeah! Get on with the story," Johe said as she sat down on the black leather couch in her office, impatient for the delightful aroma of fresh coffee.

Ginger sat on the other end. "Well, I found out he's *married!*" she said with a shrillness that could break glass.

"He's what?!" Mary asked. It was the first time she'd heard the story.

"Married. I know. There was none of the tell-tale white line on his finger. Nothing that would give it away. Even his house wasn't neat or reeking with that feminine touch."

"How did you find out?" Johe asked.

"Accidentally. I was down at the Piggly Wiggly in Metter, and there he was with his wife."

"How do you know it's his wife?" Mary asked.

"Because, I stopped to talk to him, and she introduced herself as his wife. No doubt in a jealous attempt to exert her claim on her man. I wanted to say 'Bitch please! He's obviously not in love with you anymore,' and then it hit me. He's just another loser man looking to get his love spuds off anyway he can."

"Now, come on, they're not all losers," Aja said.

"I never said *all* men are losers. Some definitely aren't. It just seems that lately all the ones I've come in contact with are demented flushers," Ginger said.

Johe crossed her legs, and stated, "Did you really think he was any different than the rest? I mean, outside of the farting under the covers bit."

"Actually, yeah. A part of me was hoping so," Ginger said. "I mean, the sex – day-mn! – the sex was out of this world! I don't blame his wife for staking her claim. Hell, I would too with sex like that. I just don't understand men these days. What happened to the sanctity of marriage? Does it mean nothing anymore?"

Mary quietly stood thinking of Alan. Was she wrong to think he was different than any other man? He still wore his wedding ring, and he hadn't mentioned anything about divorcing Angela. But then again, did she really want him to divorce her? *You can't very well marry him or be with him forever,* her mind told her. Still, her heart hovered in some make-believe world on tiny wings of hope.

"I guess it doesn't matter so much. I mean, I certainly got my fill of screaming orgasms, so I guess I used him as much as he used me," Ginger added. "But I had hoped to at least go back in for another shot of that kind of satisfaction."

"How did you pull off those screaming orgasms with the wife around?" Johe inquired.

"She must've been out of town or something. She never once came into the house," Ginger replied.

"Maybe she knew what he was up to," Aja added.

"Yeah. Maybe she's a freak who likes watching him have sex with strange women," Johe suggested.

Ginger's face became uncertain.

"It could happen, you know?" Johe said.

"Surely not. Ew. Just. Ew," Ginger cringed when she spoke.

"Makes you rethink all that headboard-climbing sex, huh?" Johe said with a laugh.

"Makes me want to hook the hose up to my vagina and wash it!" Ginger exclaimed.

"That's just nasty!" Aja said in disgust.

"No, what's nasty is the idea that his wife may have been there watching! Ewww!!" Ginger shuddered and stood up from the couch. "I think I need to go shower."

"Yeah, I need to take care of Sun," Mary told them all. "It sure is good to have things back to normal."

"I agree," Aja said. "We need to all get together soon and go celebrate."

"After my showerssss. And for the love of God, ladies, don't let me pick up anymore weirdo fish!" Ginger added.

"All right, all right, girls. Let's all agree to put a chastity belt on Miss Ginger before we go," Johe commented.

"Agreed," the girls said in unison.

"Good. Now, let me rest my tired old bones some, and get caught up around here, then we'll go out, ok?" Johe told them. Johe left her office to retrieve some freshly-brewed coffee.

Mary quietly clocked out and left the office. As glad as she was to have Johe back, she still preferred Alan's company over anyone else's.

In short order, she found herself at Sun's stall. "It's not right. I shouldn't allow myself to feel like this, you know boy? It's just not right." She picked up a curry comb and began to groom Sun's coat.

"I don't know what exactly happened on that stupid boat." Her mind wandered back to the feeling of Alan's incredible kiss; a warm sensation enveloped her. *Oh my God, it shouldn't feel that good!*

She could hardly believe her thoughts actually continued further to later that same night when they were on the couch. His gentle embrace on her breast was so different than Cliff's coarseness. Her entire being wanted him.

She actually wondered what sex with Alan would be like. *No. No I can't even allow myself to think like that,* she told herself. Yet as she groomed Sun thoroughly, that's exactly where her mind wandered off to.

While noticeably distracted, she finished up the last few things she had left and headed up the slight hill to her cabin.

She needed to find something – anything – to take her mind off such thoughts. *You're not ready for something like that!* she thought. Sex again? It simply wasn't possible, nevertheless, at the same time, if it was ever going to be possible, it was a thought she needed to at least start entertaining. *Right?* she asked herself.

Walking in the front door, she picked up a book on the mechanics of jumping. Ted had given it to her after she'd bit the dust so many times during their training. *Yes, this is just the distraction you need to take your mind off of Alan,* she thought. Her mind instantly added: *And sex.* Although it hadn't worked previously, it simply *had* to work this time.

Just as she opened the cover, there was Alan's signature knock on her door. *Damn.*

CHAPTER 7

Warm morning sunbeams shone through the original, hand-made window glass of the Babbling Brooks main house. Heavy taupe and black striped curtains flanked both sides of the windows; large plantation shutters were neatly folded and tucked away inside the thick walls. Angela lounged on a plush pink velvet window seat. The warm late-spring breeze shook the fully-green tree branches to and fro, but Angela's eyes were locked on the splashing water of her favorite fountain located in the circular part of the driveway. Impatiently, she waited for Felix to meet with her – he was late.

The chasm between me and Alan just seems to grow. Damn that Mary! If it weren't for her, he'd be content, she thought. With a deep sigh, her thoughts continued. *But I can't kill her. If I do, Alan will never be where I want him. He'll ache for her and leave me anyway. But then again, maybe that'll inspire him to write more music.*

Angela watched the water splash down the fountain she'd designed and placed in the center of the drive. She thought of her days at the Savannah College of Art and Design – where people believed in her art, unlike her father. *Daddy*, she thought. "Jackass," she whispered.

There was no one on the planet that Angela hated as much as she did her father. He'd abandoned their family when she was only four years old. The ten times in her childhood that she'd seen him were moments she once thought were precious, but they fell to the wayside as time passed. Once she'd started college, she tried to use her art to reach out to him. His only response to her work was a very cold statement: "You won't amount to shit!" Her heart ached as she replayed his words in her mind. In her memory, she saw the shattered remains of her sculpture after she'd smashed it against the tile floor of her apartment. The tears she'd cried were bitter, hate-filled.

"I guess I showed him," she whispered. Alan may have his faults, but he'd at least given her prestige. When his career pursuits made him neglect her, just like her dad had done, she swore she'd never let a man have such power over her again. She would have the power. No matter what it took.

Gus interrupted her thoughts by walking into the parlor and announcing Angela's guest, "Mr. Felix."

"Send him in." Angela turned from the window and adjusted her whimsical silk charmeuse blouse's billowing sleeves. The yellow and blue flowers set against the nearly sheer white background created the allure of innocence and sweetness, images that Angela always wished to display to anyone closely associated with Alan. The sunbeams shining through the windows made her blonde hair glisten.

"Thank you for agreeing to meet with me, Mrs. Brooks," Felix said upon entering.

"It's my pleasure." Angela said in her sweetest voice. "Won't you have some coffee?" she asked as she moved from the window seat to a conversation area that the maid, Lynn, had set up with a coffee service. Angela picked up the sterling silver teapot that had been in the Brooks family since before the Civil War. She routinely used it for coffee, and never for tea, as it was intended.

Lacking the grace of a well-bred, well-trained hostess, she poured out while the cups remained on the tray. Alan's mother always found her mannerisms unsophisticated, and complained loudly every time she used the teapot for coffee. Angela continued to use it simply because she knew it bothered Fiona.

"Why thank you," Felix replied.

"I'm afraid you were rather cryptic when you requested this meeting," she said as she poured two cups of black coffee. "Cream? Sugar?"

"No, black is fine." Felix took the cup and saucer from Angela's willowy, graceful hand.

She placed the coffee pot onto the matching tray and retrieved her own cup. "What's it concerning?"

"This has to do with Biscuit. Mr. Brooks has charged me with the task of determining what happened to the horse," Felix explained.

"I thought it was clear – he died of a heart attack."

"Not really. There's been evidence uncovered that indicates there could be foul play at hand here."

Sitting on the edge of a noticeably worn baroque chair that Alan refused to allow her to repair, Angela inquired further, "Foul play? In what way?"

"In short, the toxicology report came back indicating that Biscuit was poisoned. An autopsy is underway to determine how the poison was administered. In the meantime, I'm investigating the situation to make sure that the utmost security at Babbling Brooks is maintained. We're checking into the possibility of security breaches."

Angela's eyes glistened with melodramatic tears. "Poisoned?! How is that even possible??" She pulled out a white linen handkerchief with matching yellow and blue flowers embroidered on it. Daintily she dabbed the corners of her eyes.

"Yes." Felix sipped his coffee as his keen eyes watched Angela's performance. He placed the cup and saucer back on the coffee table, next to the matching silver tray. "We're checking into how it happened."

"You'll have to forgive me. I'm a little out of sorts this morning."

"Oh yes, ma'am. I understand. Is there anything I can do to help?"

"No, no. I'll be fine. It's just such unsettling news has me feeling quite vulnerable."

"I wouldn't worry too much, Mrs. Brooks. Mr. Brooks has insisted I hire the best security guards available. Babbling Brooks is as secure as I can make it."

"But what if someone is after Alan? Would they try to get to me first? Given that Alan and I are separated, does that security extend to me? Or has he cut me off from that as well?" she asked acting as best as she could like she was trying to quell the hysteria hidden behind her pseudo-refined façade.

"I can't imagine Mr. Brooks would do that to you, Mrs. Brooks. He's a good man…"

"Good man?" she hastily interrupted. "Do you have any idea

what he's doing to me??"

"No, ma'am, I don't."

"He's restricted me to a paltry amount of money and expects me to survive…"

"Mrs. Brooks. That has nothing to do with my investigation."

"I see. What can I do to assist you then?"

Felix pulled out a pad of paper from his jacket pocket. "Are you aware of anyone who would want to cause harm to the horse?"

"What do you mean?"

"Is there anyone who was angry with the horse or had even flippantly stated a desire to harm him?"

"No," she immediately answered.

"Ok. You don't want to think about it?"

"I don't need to. If someone wanted to harm him, I wouldn't know about it. I don't consort with the help."

"Have you seen anyone present around the barn who doesn't belong?"

Yes, that damn Mary, she thought. "No. I've seen nothing out of the ordinary."

"We're concerned about Mr. Brooks' stalker, Danielle. It's possible she may have played a part in this. Have you seen her?"

"No."

"Have you heard from her or had any forms of contact with her?"

"No."

Felix's acute eyes evaluated Angela's behavior and mannerisms. She seemed nervous and trying too hard to be elegant. He felt there was more there than meets the eye, but he wasn't certain what that something was. "Are you dedicated to solving this situation, Mrs. Brooks?"

"Of course I am! The lack of security at Babbling Brooks affects me just as much as it does Alan! What kind of question is that?"

"It's just that you're not offering any assistance."

"I can't assist with what I don't know. Have you interviewed the help? They'd know more than I would. What about that Mary? She's still relatively new here. Perhaps she had something to do with it," she implied while struggling to maintain her ladylike appearance. "I simply ride, and that's all."

"My team is interviewing the stable hands as we speak."

"Good. Mary is one I'd be worried about if I were you. God only knows where she's from or who she's associated with. For all I know, her plan is to destroy Alan and everything connected with him." She took the corner of her handkerchief and lightly dabbed the mascaraed edges of her eyes. "Even me. My marriage has been in shambles since she showed up. No doubt she's got Alan fooled into thinking she's someone she isn't."

"And who might that be?" Felix asked, knowing full well Alan had already disclosed his involvement with Mary.

"She's a home-wrecking tramp to me!"

Felix wrote on his pad. "Do you have evidence of such infidelity with Mr. Brooks and Mary?"

Angela breathed in deeply before she spoke again. "No. But I know he likes to go riding with her."

"And that makes her a home-wrecker?"

Angela sighed with a noticeable amount of irritation. "No. I guess not. But Ted…" she started, and then stopped. She didn't want to involve Ted in any of this. With Felix snooping around, she didn't need Alan finding out about her relationship with Ted. "Alan was perfectly content with me before this Mary came along. Now? Now we're separated," she said with a melodramatic, tearless sob.

Felix patiently waited for her over-the-top display to quiet down before he continued, "And you think this Mary woman has something to do with that?"

"I don't know. But doesn't it seem rather odd that one minute we're happily married and the next minute we're separated and Biscuit drops dead? The only thing that's different at the farm is this Mary creature. Surely it makes sense to you that she's the likely culprit."

Felix wrote more notes. "Did you run a thorough background check on her prior to her employment?"

Angela sipped some of her coffee. "What? A background check? I thought your people took care of things like that."

"Typically we do…"

"Then you should be asking yourself that question. Not me. I don't keep up with things like that. Why do you think we pay you?"

"As it turns out, Mrs. Brooks, we indeed run background checks on all Babbling Brooks and Brooks Industries employees."

"And…?"

"And she wouldn't be working here if she had anything questionable on her record."

"Then you have nothing to report?"

"On Miss Stephenson, no. Mary Stephenson is from Tucson, Arizona and she has no criminal record to speak of."

Frustrated, Angela asked, "Are we finished here?" Her genteel façade was fading, and she didn't want Felix to see her unraveling.

"Not quite. Have you seen anyone using antifreeze around the barn?"

"No."

"Have you seen anyone working on their vehicle anywhere on the grounds?"

"Just Frankie, the chauffeur."

"What about Cliff?"

"What about him?"

"Have you seen him working on any vehicles or having antifreeze in his possession?"

"No! I've already stated I haven't seen anyone. Are you finished?"

"Yes, ma'am." Felix stood up. "Thank you for your time, Mrs. Brooks. If I have any additional questions, would it be ok to come talk to you again?"

"Y-yes, of course."

"Good. There's just one more thing. We're checking into any insurance policies held on the horse. Is there anything you might want to disclose?"

Angela's eyes blinked rapidly. "No. Why would there be?"

"I don't know. That's why I'm asking you first."

"Well, I have nothing to say about any of that. I told you, I just ride. I don't keep up with the business side of things. I suggest you talk to Johe about that sort of thing. I'm sure she keeps those kinds of records."

Felix nodded. "Of course. Thank you for your time."

"Gus will show you out." Her trembling fingers reached for the bell to call for Gus.

"Yes, ma'am?" the dutiful butler entered the room.

"Please show Mr. Felix out."

"Yes, ma'am," Gus replied.

"Thank you again for your time," Felix said with a polite nod.

As soon as the door was closed, Angela pulled out her cell phone. "Alan!" she loudly stated into the phone. "I don't appreciate one of your thugs coming into my home and interrogating me like I'm some kind of criminal!"

"What are you talking about?" Alan asked.

"Felix! He just left! He's accusing me of poisoning Biscuit! What the hell are you doing??"

"He's just doing his job, Ang. Calm yourself."

"I don't appreciate it! I felt so humiliated that he even came here and spoke to me about this! As if I had something to do with it!"

"Grow up! He's not saying that. He's just leaving no stone unturned."

"So you don't care that he verbally assaulted me?"

"Oh come on! You don't really think I believe that, do you? He's the best at what he does. If you felt assaulted, then maybe he's on to something."

In anger she pressed end on her phone and tossed it across the room to the chair Felix was sitting in. "Damn him!" she grumbled.

Insurance policies repeated in her mind. What would he find if he dug around?

CHAPTER 8

On the fourth day since Johe's return, the morning's light crept into Mary's small living room bit by bit. She'd spent the night like most nights before – reading and re-reading the same chapter, listening to Alan's CDs or Alan in person, and trying hard not to think about what sex with him would be like. It wasn't working.

Feeling his rippling muscles through his button-down shirt, or T-shirt, or jacket; and his delicious, enticing kisses certainly didn't help matters. The feeling of his hands on her body lured and thrilled her. The feeling of his clothed body against hers made her want more. Fear kept her from partaking in more.

Save for that one attempt to coax her into sex, he hadn't tried again at all. Mary was both relieved and disappointed. Part of her couldn't wait for him to rip her clothes off; the other part of her was fearful.

"It's hell living inside my head," she whispered to the morning. The entire night had been filled with conflicting thoughts. Her prevailing thought had been wrapped up in the "if-only" world: if only she'd killed Roger; if only Alan wasn't such a public figure; if only she had met Alan instead of Roger while in college; if only her rapist hadn't stolen her desire to feel sexy. "If only," she whispered. "He deserves someone so much better than you anyway, so just drop it," she mumbled to herself.

Mary turned off her alarm clock. She was awake long before the alarm was due to sound. She wondered why she even bothered to set it.

Shoving her hat down firmly on her head, she walked through the morning's thick fog down to the barn to start the day's work.

She was determined to keep her head down and her nose to the grindstone. It seemed like the perfect plan. Working harder than ever would exhaust her enough to where she wouldn't be awake all night thinking. Dreaming. Hoping. Desiring. Fearing.

Immediately, she went to work feeding the horses.

"Well, good mornin', Sunshine," Cliff said sarcastically at the sight of her. His favorite past time was annoying her.

Mary said nothing.

"What's wrong? Alan got yer tongue?"

Mary glared at him, but said nothing in her defense.

"Oh? Is there trouble in paradise?" he asked with a haughty laugh.

Mary remained silent and kept walking.

"So he loved ya then left ya, huh? I knowed you can't possibly be surprised. He's married, or did ya forget that? And to think, you could have me all to yerself."

Mary poured grain into the first horse's feed dish.

Cliff leaned against the sliding stall door. "'Course, the offer still stands. All ya gotta do is gimme some of that no-strings-attached nookie, and nobody will find out 'bout you and Mistuh Brooks."

She walked stoically past him to move to the next stall.

He slid the door shut before she could enter. "It's ok, you ain't gotta answer right now."

"Open the door, Cliff," Mary demanded.

"Say you'll do it."

"I already told you, I'm not interested."

"A'ight. I sees what you're sayin'. So I'll be by t'night for a little piece of dat ass," he said with a cackle as he squeezed her butt cheek. He spit snuff juice onto the concrete floor.

"Get your damn hands off of me before I break them off!"

"'N I've done tole ya that ya better make me happy – or else. All it'd take is jus' a little an' the world would know 'bout you and Mistuh Brooks. Is that what you're wanting?"

She wanted to say, *How about I tell him about how you practically twisted my arm off? Or chased me under my bed and then tore it apart trying to get at me? Or backhanded me across the face? Or groped my breast like it was a cow's udder? Or grab my ass every chance you get?* Instead, she only said far more feebly than she'd planned in her head, "If I tell Mr. Brooks about your constant feeling me up and blackmailing attempts, you'll regret it."

"Ooooh. You act like I'm scared of him! I'll post them pictures all over Facebook and the innernet. Then what? Huh? What's been seen, cain't be unseen."

Frustrated, Mary slung the stall door open and went back to work. "Just go away, Cliff," she muttered.

The other stable hands' voices mingled with the distinct smell of the horses.

"I ain't through with ya," he threateningly growled under his breath.

Mary kept working, never acknowledging he'd left, yet worried about how to handle him. If she involved Alan, what would that say? Would it only be proving Cliff's suspicions were correct? Would word spread throughout the barn about her fraternizing with Alan? Would that make Alan leave her? Would Angela make things more difficult for Alan?

"Ah, there you are. We're going to put you back over fences. You've had plenty of time to read that book. Now I want to see how well you can apply it," Ted informed Mary as he ran into her in the aisle.

Internally, she groaned. She'd read the first chapter multiple times without any of it sinking in, but reading any further hadn't even occurred to her. Instead, most of her thoughts were encapsulated around her flurry of contradictory thoughts about Alan.

Moments later, Mary was aboard Rascal, circling him around the arena; the three-foot jumps were looming in her future. *You can do this*, she told herself.

Ted seemed unusually demanding and irritable. "How's he feeling?" he asked Mary while they were training.

"Fine," she replied succinctly.

"Fine," Ted sarcastically mocked her answer and threw his hands up in frustration. "How about giving me more details than that?!" he angrily shouted at her.

She didn't speak another word; she simply continued around the arena passing by one jump at a time, dreading when she'd actually have to jump them. *How many times will I fall off today?* she wondered.

Ted stood in the center of the arena watching with a sour look on his face and his hand on his hip, clipboard in the other hand. "Hello?! Are you alive up there?! What the hell is going on in the saddle?"

Mary remained quietly indifferent.

In a fit of rage, he threw the clipboard to the ground. "Forget it; just forget it! When you're ready to talk to me, we'll pick up where we left off!" Ted marched out of the arena like the diva he was. "I'm not wasting my precious talent on a damned mute!" he growled.

Mary pulled Rascal to a stop. It irritated her that the fear of falling off was interfering with her training. Adding into it the lack of sleep and all the confusion with Alan and Cliff, and she was a mental wreck. Yet, she didn't feel compelled to do much about it. What she truly wanted to do was be with Sun in the middle of the pasture – away from the world. She wanted to feel like a stone – no feelings, no confusion. The desire to escape the world of her making was becoming a distracting situation.

Leading Rascal down the aisle, she ran into Johe, Ginger and Aja who were all bent-set on ganging up on her.

"Ok, ho, what gives? You've been skulking around here like your best friend's kicked the bucket or something. What's wrong?" Ginger asked.

Mary was taken aback. "Nothing's wrong, why?"

"Because you've hardly said boo to anyone this past week. You were acting like you were on top of the world, and then suddenly someone let the air outta your bubble. Hell, Ted just chewed your ass out and you didn't even blink. Come on, normally you would've at least tried or said something back. What gives?" Johe added.

"Nothing." Mary attempted to push past them.

"Nuh-uh. No. Don't think you're going to get away with this kind of stuff, Honey. We know something's up. Hell, even drama-queen Ted knows something's not right. Otherwise, he'd still be out there with you. Are you going to tell us, or are we going to have to drag it outta you?" Ginger asked again while shaking her index finger at her.

"I answered him; Rascal *was* fine," Mary told them.

"Yeah, I know he was, but you know that's not enough. Come on. Why are you so blue?" Aja asked in her sweetest voice. Her precious, child-like face shined with a tender smile. "You haven't been this sullen since you first got here."

"I'm not," Mary said. Out of the corner of her eye, she spied nasty Rob walking down the hallway toward them. "Ugh. Here comes Rob," she warned them.

The women scattered like roaches to avoid him.

Mary led Rascal down the aisle toward the tack room, quickly hooking him to the cross ties. Even facing Rob didn't seem to bother her as much as usual. He was far better than facing Cliff! She simply continued as if Rob weren't around.

Jumping practice had been a colossal failure. Ted would be expecting her at the dressage arena soon. *At least, I think,* Mary thought. *Maybe he's through with me altogether today.*

She removed Rascal's forward-seat saddle and swapped it for the high-backed dressage saddle. Just as she'd begun to tighten the buckles on the girth, Rob started talking to her. "I saw you out there riding," Rob said behind her.

"Oh?"

"You looked good."

"Thanks." She touched her knee to Rascal's belly.

"You didn't even jump one jump. Why'd you quit?"

"Ted told me to." She pulled the next buckle tight and wandered into the tack room

"Oh," Rob commented as he followed her. "I haven't seen you around in a while; where've you been?"

"Right here...the same place I've always been." She retrieved Rascal's dressage bridle.

"So, you're riding for Ted now?" he asked in an almost apprehensive voice.

Mary wondered what was going on with him. She'd been riding for Ted for months; what was he getting at? Rob, who never said anything to her except nasty comments, almost seemed nice. What did he want? Had Cliff put him up to something sinister? "Yeah. I have been for a while now."

"Oh. I guess I haven't been paying attention, huh?" he said.

"I guess so." She traded out Rascal's bridle. "What do you want, Rob?" she asked, trying the direct approach.

"Nothing." He shuffled his feet.

"Ok," she said and went back to work.

"Actually," Rob started again, "Cliff sent me over here."

Mary rolled her eyes. *I knew it!* she thought. "Good grief," she said under her breath.

"You really dating Mr. Brooks?" Rob asked.

"No!" she replied, aghast that Cliff was now spreading rumors. Maybe she *should* just sleep with him, but then that would be letting Cliff win.

"Then why won't you go out with my boy, Cliff?"

"Because I don't like him that way."

"So, you can get to know him better. It's just one little date."

"And if I said yes, he would beg me again for a second, and then a third. I don't feel like opening a can of worms," she said as she patted Rascal's powerful neck.

"You're assuming he'd ask."

Mary blankly stared at him. Cliff obviously hadn't told him the whole story, especially the parts about Cliff's manhandling her.

"Come on, just one date."

A brilliant answer came to her: "I don't date people I work with."

"How're you ever gonna meet anyone then?"

"Who says I *want* to meet anyone?"

"Why are you being like this? You act like he wants to fuck you or something!"

Inside, Mary smiled. There was the typical, asshole Rob coming out. "Maybe he does, maybe he doesn't; either way, I'm not giving him the chance."

"Yeah. It's 'cause you're already fucking Mr. Brooks, isn't it?" Rob said quite loudly.

"Absolutely not!" Mary angrily shouted at him. "Get out of here, Rob! I have work to do!"

She grabbed Rascal's reins, which caused Rascal to jerk his head up in surprise.

"Eeeasy, boy," she said as calmly as she could fake.

She and the horse walked toward the dressage arena. Maybe Ted had cooled down enough to resume her training.

Ted was there impatiently waiting for her. Timidly, Mary approached him at the dressage arena. "I'm very sorry, Ted," she meekly said. Her mind swirled with thoughts of what Rob had said. Was Cliff making good on his threat to tell everyone about her and Alan?

Ted puffed his chest out. "Good. Don't let it happen again!

Now get out there and show me how much better you are."

Mary mounted Rascal and began warming up.

Her dressage training with Ted went better than the over fences; Mary made a concentrated effort to be more focused and more communicative. Every movement was calculated and strategic. Perhaps it was Rob and his knowledge about Alan that pushed her into putting on a better face in front of others. Whatever the reason, she put on the familiar everything-is-great mask and pushed herself harder than she ever had.

Ted made sure he worked her extra to make up for her lack of focus over fences.

By the end of the day, her body felt like she'd been beat with sticks. Even lifting up her arm to clock out felt as though she were lifting a sack of boulders.

"Ok, Miss Thang," Ginger's voice said behind her, "you may have escaped once, but not now. It's just me and you. So, who killed your dog?"

"No one. I don't even have a dog." She looked at her confused.

Ginger rolled her eyes. "It's just an expression. Sheesh! Don't take everything so literally. Why you so sad?"

"I'm not. I'm just beat. Ted worked the crap out of me today."

"Uh-huh, I don't believe you! You looked like this before Ted ever laid even a finger on you. So, you know the only solution for such blues, right?"

"No?"

"Get your ass in gear, we're going out."

"What? No. I don't feel like going out, really."

"Errrr," she made a sound like a buzzer, "wrong answer, Honey! Whatever his name is, or whoever ran over your dog, we're going to set it all straight. A few pitchers of beer, a few dances with a few good fish, and you'll forget all about whoever-he-is."

"And my dog?" Mary added with a gentle, yet forced smile.

"There ya go! Come on, go get ready," Ginger said.

"We're not going back to that awful club again, are we? I don't want to run the risk of running into Mike. You know what happened last time."

"That's true. And I definitely don't want to run into Sean again. Get a few drinks in me, and I'm not so sure I could resist the temptation of earthshattering sex. Married or not!"

Mary shook her head at Ginger. "You're crazy!"

"Maybe. Maybe," she said contemplatively as she tapped her finger to her chin.

"Anyway, I'll go as long as we go somewhere else," Mary said, remembering her previous agreement with Ginger. She definitely wasn't willing to tell Ginger her dissertation was a complete waste of her time.

"There's nowhere else to go, unless," she said as she slid her fingers to cup her chin thoughtfully, "yes, we could go clubbing in Savannah and make a whole go of it! Oh yes, Savannah is where you'll find some *fine* fish to take your mind off of this Prince Harming that's dragging you sooooo way down," Ginger's voice mimicked how down she assumed Mary's spirits were.

"There's no Prince Harming, and I don't need any fish to take my mind off anything. I just need a nice, hot shower and a good night's sleep." The gross lack of sleep since even before Alan kissed her the first time hung heavy on her shoulders like sacks of wet cement.

"Hogwash! Get your ass in gear!" she exclaimed and slapped Mary's behind. "You know, I'm sick and tired of having to force you to do shit with us! How quickly you forget our deal! March your ass right up there to that cabin! You've got an hour before we'll be there to haul your sorry self out. So you decide. You can either get ready and go, or we're gonna take your smelly, sweaty ass the way you are!" Ginger commanded.

"Yes, ma'am!" Mary jokingly said.

In the shower, Mary thought of Cliff. She wondered if he'd come to her cabin tonight expecting sex from her. "It's probably best that we're going out," she said as the hot water washed away her sweat. The shower felt amazing! Her sore muscles appreciated the warmth.

Once she had all of her hair hidden neatly under her hat, she picked up her cell phone and texted Alan: *The girls and I are going out to Savannah tonight. Don't wait up.*

Alan's response came quicker than she'd anticipated: *Have fun. Don't go home with any guys!*

Mary checked her look one last time in the mirror. Her hair was carefully pulled into a bun and successfully hidden under her hat. It had been months, and she'd never once let anyone see her long crowning glory. *And no one will,* she thought. Slipping her cell phone into her pocket, she left to meet the girls and go to Savannah.

Most of the night and into the early hours of the morning were spent in Savannah – dancing, drinking, and club hopping.

Mary was determined to drink all thoughts out of her mind, but every time she thought she'd accomplished it, there Alan was in her thoughts kissing her lips – making her heart skip a beat. And then there was Cliff groping her and threatening to expose her. She had to curb her drinking just in case she got weak and said something about either issue.

Ginger enjoyed dancing with several "fish;" only this time, she went home with the same people she came with, which was quite a change.

As the four women drove back to the farm early in the morning, Johe drove in utter silence.

"What's wrong, Johe? You've hardly said a word since we left Churchill's," Aja inquired.

"Oh she's just pissed that we made her the designated driver *again,*" Ginger drunkenly said.

"No, there's more to it. Maybe she's caught whatever's got Mary." Aja cocked her head and tried to get Johe's attention. "Is that it? Did your dog die too?" Aja poked her bottom lip out; her big brown eyes reflected the dash-panel lights.

"You look like a muppet when you do that! It's disturbingly gross!" Johe snapped at her and shoved her away.

Aja laughed obnoxiously. "I just wanna know what's bothering you." Aja was drunk, but not as much as she'd been on many other nights. She giggled at Johe's reaction.

"If you don't leave me alone, I'm going to put you out on the side of the road and you can walk home," Johe growled.

"Oh! You better watch it, Aja! She sounds like she meant that one!" Ginger said with a giggle.

"Of course she didn't mean it. She's just messing with me," Aja said.

Immediately, Johe slammed on the brakes.

"Ok, ok! I'm sorry! I'll shut up and leave you alone!" Aja said and looked hard at Ginger. "What's up with her?" Aja mouthed.

Ginger mouthed back, "I don't know."

Mary did nothing but stare out the window. Their attempts at taking her mind off of everything had been futile. It was as though her mind and her heart were torn entirely in half: one part wanted nothing more than to love Alan and let him love her; the other part was keenly aware of how increasingly hazardous those kinds of thoughts were. In the depths of her soul, a terror began to stir. *What happens now?* she quietly wondered. *Don't be stupid. This is all nothing but a cheap dalliance. And you're making it into more than it is,* she thought.

CHAPTER 9

By mid-morning of the next day, Mary was well rested and ready for practice.

Johe was still in the same frame of mind she was in the night prior. At every turn, she was barking out orders and growling at anyone who talked to her, but her frustration seemed to be focused on Mary.

After snapping at Mary for leaving her spoon on the counter, Mary pulled Johe aside and inquired after her attitude. "Johe, what have I done that has made you so pissed at me?"

"Nothing. Just forget it," Johe said as she tossed the forgotten spoon into the sink. The spoon loudly ricocheted against the sink walls until it settled on the bottom.

"No, I can't forget it. You've done nothing but yell at me since last night. What did I do?" Mary asked again.

"Don't tell me you don't know," Johe's voice seethed with bitterness; her fiery, dark eyes made Mary's skin crawl.

"Apparently I don't. Why don't you let me in on it?"

"You didn't see it? At Churchill's last night?" Johe asked with her hands on her hips.

"No, I'm sorry. I don't know what you're talking about."

"The picture of Alan with his arm wrapped around you. How could you not see it? It was right there on the wall!"

A wave of dread washed over her, soaking every inch of her in panicked feelings. She had to get to Savannah and get that photo off the wall! Where did someone get a picture like that? Her mind raced around trying to recall when something like that could have been produced. How many more of them were out there?

"N-n-no... I-I-I don't recall any such thing. I-I-I don't know where anything like that came from!" Then it hit her – Cracker Barrel. Valentine's Day. *Damn Alan making me be in all your pictures!* Mary thought. *Damn Valentine's Day always screwing up my life!*

"You don't? How could you not? You're practically shoved up his butt all the time! And then Cliff said he went over to your cabin the other night, and Alan was there." Johe frowned and breathed in deeply. It was her way of saying she knew something was going on between Mary and Alan without violating her promise to Alan. "Are you sleeping with him?" she asked with her eyes closed and face clinched.

"Cliff?! God no!"

"Alan!" Johe snarled.

"*No!*" was Mary's immediate and emphatic response.

"You think I don't know? I don't ask questions I don't already know the answers to."

"There's nothing to know," Mary tried to defend herself, even if her defenses seemed as weak as a wilted flower.

"Look, I've been around here a long time, and I know Alan better than he knows himself. I've seen the way he looks at you. I've seen y'all together. There's more going on than you're letting on."

"You're just imagining it."

Johe's face was grave, stern. She'd never been one to out-right lie, but then again, she'd never been in a situation like this before. "Understand that I'm talking to you as the daughter of my dear friend, Tunda. It-it pains me to see you falling for his m-mess." She paused for a moment, took in a noticeable breath, and then burned a line directly to Mary's green/gray eyes and said, "Do you really think you're the first girl he's been fixated on like this?"

A wave of doubt covered the original panic that had washed Mary from the top of her head all the way to her toes.

"Trust me, you're not. Don't depend on him like that. He'll abandon you in a second for the next pretty young thing that looks his way. That's just the way men like him are."

Mary's knees felt weedy. She could taste the sharp, acrid taste of the reality she'd barely allowed herself to consider. Could this be true? *Of course it could! He's Alan Brooks!* she told herself.

Immediately, she worked to cover up the shock she was afraid was written on her face.

Johe continued unabated. "And then where will you be? You won't want to stay here, that's for sure. And from what Tunda told me, you need this job pretty badly. So if my behavior was gruff or alarming to you, there's a reason for it. I don't want you to end up like the countless others before you."

"T-thank you, Johe. But I promise you, t-t-there's nothing going on. I mean, we've hung out together a few times, but I swear to you I am not sleeping with him."

"Are you sure?"

"Yes. You have to believe me," Mary said while her eyes were locked on Johe's. "It's like you said. I-I-I don't want to jeopardize my job like that." But just what was she doing with Alan? Dating him? Kissing him? Dreaming of sex with him? Clinging to him as her only bright spot in the midst of her tumultuous secret life?

"Isn't dating the rich, good-looking boss what all young girls aspire for? And then marrying him so that she can live the life of luxury?"

If you only knew, Mary thought. "Maybe for some, but not me. My marrying days are o-ver! I've had enough of such foolishness. I like hanging out with Alan. He makes me laugh. We have a good time together. But that's it. If you or anyone else thinks anything differently, you're wrong."

Johe was actually impressed at Mary's ability to be convincing. She acquiesced. "Ok. I can see that. Still, watch your step with Alan. You're not the first of his arm-candy flings, and you won't be the last."

"Ok. Thanks for the advice."

"Tell me about the picture," Johe commanded.

"The only thing I can think of was when Alan and I went to buy tack for some of the horses, some people stopped us to take his picture. I tried hard not to be in the picture, but he wouldn't let me beg out. He made me stand next to him with his arm around me."

Johe nodded. "Yeah, that sounds like something he'd do." She decided to let it go – for now, even though she knew Alan felt far more for her than she seemed to feel for him. The seeds were planted. "All right," she said with a deep sigh. "I can't tell you how much it bothered me thinking about having to fire you!" Johe hugged her. "How would I explain that to your mother?" All the while, Johe inadvertently communicated the very real tenuous nature of her job's future.

"I don't know! And trust me, firing me would bother me a lot too!" Mary laughed and hugged her back.

"Just cool it with him, ok? I know how he is; he likes to hang out with us, but getting the wrong idea about his flirtatiousness will only spell trouble for you, ok? What people perceive and what it actually is can be two different things, and rumors are easily started. With all these new security people around, well, we have even more sets of eyes, and these eyes are trained to watch our every move. Make sure you don't give anyone room to doubt what you say or do, ok?"

Mary felt like Johe's intent was to warn and advise her, yet there seemed to be a hint of asperity in her voice – enough that Mary felt on edge. "Ok." Her main mission had to be to destroy that picture! There's no telling who else had seen it.

Ted broke up their make-up session by announcing he was changing Mary's training routine. "From now on, you and Angela will be training together," he sternly informed Mary.

Trying hard to hide the second wave of panic, Mary only blinked her eyes in astonishment.

"Let's get going!" Ted commanded.

Mary dutifully left Johe and Ted to saddle Rascal.

"What do you know about her, Ted?" Johe asked.

"Nothing, except she's got a more natural seat than Angela, the horses respond better to her, and Angela can't stand her," Ted replied, omitting the kiss he'd seen occur between Mary and Alan. "Why?"

Johe shrugged. "No reason, I guess. I'm just wondering."

"Well, whatever she is, I'm planning to use her to make Angela at least work during training."

"You like living dangerously, don't you?"

"I have to. Angela has this crazy notion that she'll be ready to show this season, and if she doesn't at least make an effort, she's not going to make it."

"Hmm, yeah. Good luck with that." Johe turned to her computer; Ted left.

Moments later, Mary joined Angela and Ted in the dressage

arena. "It'll be nice to have someone so skilled teaching me," she said as professionally and politely as she could to Angela.

Angela only scowled at Mary.

"Exactly," Ted reinforced. "Angela, Darling, please begin; Mary you follow behind her and do everything she does at each letter."

Mary did as she was instructed.

Angela, though, seemed determined to show Mary up at every single letter. Whenever Ted called out a command, Angela worked harder than ever.

Mary immediately sensed what was going on, and would not be outdone. She too performed each maneuver as well or better than Angela.

"Very good, very good," Ted said, halfway praising himself at his ingenious plan. The two women fed off each other's competitive natures. *Why didn't I think of this sooner?* he wondered.

After they had trained diligently for several hours, Ted finally released them from dressage. "Take my horse and get him ready for jumping," Angela arrogantly commanded Mary.

"Yes, ma'am," Mary submissively said.

"And when you are done, you're fired!"

"What?!" Mary exclaimed nearly simultaneously with Ted.

"You no longer work here! You're a poisonous viper, and I don't want you here anymore!"

"No. Angela! She's done nothing wrong!" Ted said trying to defend Mary.

"She tried to make me look bad!" Angela rebutted.

"I wasn't doing anything!" Mary begged.

"Angela, please, she just did what I told her to!" Ted exclaimed.

Mary began hyperventilating. How could Angela be so cruel?

"Don't start crying! Just get out!"

"Angela!" Ted authoritatively shouted at her. "She didn't do anything!"

Angela crossed her arms with a scowl on her face. "I don't like people with negative energy to work here."

"How do you get she has negative energy?" Ted asked.

"She's determined to make me look bad!" Angela demanded.

"That was not my intent! I was trying to replicate you! I think you're an amazing rider, and I just wanted to be as good as you are," Mary desperately lied. *If Angela fired me, could Alan overturn such a hasty decision? Would he try?* she wondered.

"Angela, don't be ridiculous! No one rides better than you, my dear! Be reasonable."

Mary's eyes eagerly searched for Alan, but he'd texted her early that morning saying he'd be rehearsing all day and he'd see her that night. Searching for his assistance was futile.

Angela glared at Mary's pleading, defeated face. With a deep cleansing sigh, she said, "Fine. But you better hurry up and get my horse ready!"

Mary scurried away with Centurion and Rascal in tow.

Once Mary was in the barn and away from sight and earshot, Angela opened the flood gates of criticism against Ted. "Just what in the *hell* do you think you're doing?!" she complained.

"What?" Ted innocently asked.

"I don't ride so I can be abused by my own trainer, on my own horse, in my own arena!"

"I didn't abuse you."

"My god! How can you not see that?!"

"You're being overly dramatic, don't you think?"

"No!!" she shouted. "If you *ever* have me riding with that-that piece of *filth* again, I will fire *your* ass right here on the spot!" Angela shouted at him.

"But you rode beautifully, Darling," he sweetly responded.

"That ugly tramp is trying to ruin me! And you..." Her eyes became small slits that allowed her heavily-lined azure eyes to still show through. "You have the audacity to shove Alan's fuck-toy down my throat! She's stealing my husband, and now you're letting her steal my horses, too! I am *not* riding with that filthy whore ever again!" Her smoothed back golden hair practically steamed with anger.

"Now, Angela, you know none of that is true. You are the best rider on the planet! But I'm not making any progress with her, so I was hoping I could use you to train her better," Ted lied. The truth was quite the opposite.

"You keep that piece of trash away from me!"

"Ok, Sugar. I'm sorry."

"She's evil! She's trying to destroy me! And it's blatantly obvious that you're encouraging her!"

"How could she possibly succeed? Have you looked at yourself?

You're stunning! You're a goddess! And I would never encourage anyone to hurt you. You know that." Ted gently stroked her cheek.

"You make everyone hate me! You make me look like the bad guy all the time!"

"Everyone loves you. They can't get enough of you. I know I can't."

"I'm going home!" Angela turned away from him.

"No, come on, don't be like this," Ted said as he pulled on her arm.

"All you care about is her!"

"All I care about is *you!*"

"I hate her!" Angela's face displayed her clear repudiation of Mary. "I want her gone!"

"You can't do that, and you know it."

"Why not?!" she shrieked. "This is *my* farm!"

"Because if you try to get rid of her, you'll probably end up getting rid of Alan too, and that could have the opposite effect you want."

Angela frustratingly growled and stomped her feet.

"*I* wanna be the star!"

"And you are, Precious. Shh," he said as he pulled her head against his shoulder. "You are the *only* star. I promise."

"These are *my* horses, not hers," she said with a faux sob.

"I know, Sugar. And you are amazing with them! No one is better than you."

Angela lifted her head from his shoulder and weakly smiled.

"Oh, now, you can do better than that, can't you?" Ted caressed her chin.

"I just hate her so much!"

"I know. But revenge takes time, patience, and planning. You'll never win if you act impulsively."

"Felix said he ran a background report on her before she was hired, and it showed nothing. How is that even possible? No one can be as conniving as she is without a record!"

"Not having a record only means you're smart enough not to be caught. She's no dummy, that's for sure."

"Oh! So now you're her number one fan, huh?"

"No, not at all. I'm just saying. Anyone here could have a criminal record; they've just been clever enough to not get caught."

"What about you, Teddy?" her tone turned to a manipulatively sultry tone. "Are you some secret criminal mind?"

"Maybe," he matched her aroused tone with a low, guttural answer.

"Then you're going to make this up to me, right? I want her destroyed!"

"When you let me eliminate Alan, I'll get rid of her, too."

"Patience, Teddy." Angela smiled a saved-from-the-brink-of-tears smile.

Ted gently kissed her.

Angela wrapped her left leg around his waist, expecting Ted to grab her and hold her up. "Don't make me beg; you know I hate that shit."

"But I like making you beg," he growled from deep in his chest and pulled her opposing leg up to join her other one.

"You're a naughty boy, Teddy!"

He held her against him and nuzzled his lips to her ear. "I know."

"Stop it!" she said with a playful giggle.

"Then don't make *me* beg."

"Right here? Right now? You know I can't," she said with silly, high-pitched titters. "I'm not done training today."

"Ok. Afterwards."

"Mmmaybe," she purred in her most sexy voice as she put her legs down on either side of him. "Maybe," she winked and then walked away. Knowing she possessed such power over him delighted her.

"Day-mn," he whispered as he watched her sashay toward what he assumed was the house to change into her jumping attire.

Once Angela was out of sight, Ted patted himself on the back for coming up with such a plan to make Angela perform better and to appease her perpetual diva ego. He entered the barn all while continuing to praise his cleverness. He wondered just how far he could push Angela. Would having her frequently around Mary increase Angela's desire for angry sex? Would it increase her desire to completely rid them of Alan *and* Mary? Or was he toying with disaster with such a plan?

Just outside the tack room, he found Mary getting Hurricane ready for Angela's jumping lessons. Ted leaned against the wall and watched her work for a moment. She really was a beautiful woman. She certainly was not the curvaceous beauty Angela was, but in her unique way, Mary was appealing. He could understand why Alan was attracted to her. Her petite wiry frame, understated curves, and lithe arms and legs were perfect. He watched her adjusting the saddle to Hurricane's back. Still, there was something weird about her. He'd never really pinpointed what it was, yet it remained as he quietly stared.

Mary took her riding helmet off and wiped the sweat from her brow.

Seeing her bandana-covered head made Ted realize: *I've never seen her hair. Why is that?* He was intrigued. Could she be hiding something other than her hair? He stood up and walked over to her. "Hi," he said, his hand followed the contour of Hurricane's neck. "We're planning to attend a special horse show event at the end of July in Kentucky; I need you to get Centurion ready for jumping. Angela is insisting we take him and not Hurricane."

"Oh! Ok." Mary immediately began unsaddling Hurricane.

"I'd like for you to go," Ted added. He hadn't really thought much about the words until they had already been said.

"Wait. What? No. I'm not ready for that."

"Well, you wouldn't be riding just yet."

"What would I be doing?" Mary asked as she loosened the last buckle of Hurricane's forward-seat saddle.

"You'd be watching, being exposed to other techniques."

Mary thought about his offer. "What kind of event is it?"

"Well, it's sort of like three-day eventing, only this time, there's indoor cross-country jumping instead of the true cross-country course, like Angela wants to do. It's something that seems popular in the UK, but is still new here in the US."

Mary's mind scrolled through a litany of reasons why she couldn't go. The most important one was Roger. Like a Rolodex, her mind flipped through every person she could think of who Roger knew or was associated with him in a way that involved her. "I don't know Ted. I-I just don't know."

"Besides, Angela needs a stable hand to go with her."

"Who would normally go?"

"Well, Cliff, but I'm not taking his good-for-nothing self this time!"

"Why not take Ginger or Aja?"

"They have college still."

"But…"

"No buts! You can learn a lot by watching others."

Mary loosened the buckled chin strap of Hurricane's bridle. "I just…"

"Stop arguing. It's an order. You're going and that's that. We'll be leaving a few days before the show and will be gone just over a week, when you count in travel time. So you'll need to find someone to cover for you."

"Is Centurion even ready?"

"Well, we've got a lot of training to do, but I'm sure we'll make it," he said, pleased by his current plan to get more work out of Angela, which would equate to more training for Centurion.

"Are you going to ride too?" Mary asked him as she unfastened Hurricane from the cross ties and led him toward his stall.

"Yeah. I'm going to take Quantum with me to ride," Ted replied as he walked with her.

"Oow! I bet Cliff's going to be pissed!"

"Why? He's training Quantum to be shown; why would he be angry?" Ted asked with his haughty voice.

Mary realized she'd said too much. Cliff had mentioned to her that he was planning to take Quantum to a show in Brunswick during the show in Kentucky, but since it was obvious Ted didn't know, she wasn't going to divulge any further information to him. "No reason. I guess I misunderstood. I guess I thought he was training Quantum for him to ride."

"Well, maybe so, but that would be wrong. Quantum's at the level now where he can be a serious competitor, despite Cliff and everything he's done to undo my work. I think this year may just be Quantum's year." Ted grinned at her. "But don't you worry about all of that. I'll deal with Cliff."

Mary put Hurricane in his stall and went seeking Aja, who was walking Centurion around to cool him.

Ted left Mary to take care of swapping horses; moments later, he ran right into a red-faced Angela.

"You think I didn't hear you, but I assure you I did. You're *not* taking her to the Kentucky show with us!"

"She's going to help."

"We can take Johe or Cliff! But *not* her!"

"They're busy."

"Why are you bent-set on stuffing her down my throat!?"

"I'm not! Come on, Sweetie, don't be this way," Ted said in an attempt to sweet talk her. He massaged her shoulders gently.

"Get your damned hands off of me!" Angela snapped.

"Are you going to ride for me?" he asked in a coaxing voice.

"I don't see why I have to be around her all the time. I'd rather puke than look at her!" Angela complained. "I can't even stand to hear her breathe!"

"I know, but just think, at least you'll be able to keep an eye on her."

Angela angrily shook her head. She wanted her way, and she was willing to do anything required to get it.

"If she's with us, then she's not with Alan," Ted pointed out.

"But why does she have to go with us? You're trying to torture me!" she said with an angry child-like whiny voice.

"What better way to remind her of where she belongs than to take her as your groom?" Ted said with a deceptive smile. "You can boss her around and treat her like shit all you want."

"Yesss, I see your point." She smiled devilishly. "So, this might be a good thing?"

"Exactly," Ted said.

Even though Angela's thoughts were devious, his were primarily to keep Angela heading in the right direction. To him, Mary was a lot like Old Gem, and he wanted to make sure Angela stayed focus on the competition. Besides, it would be the perfect time for him to have Alan killed without Mary or Angela getting in the way.

CHAPTER 10

Mary had barely touched her supper before she gave up trying. Her mind was a muddy mix of things. Churchill's flat refusal to return the picture; Cliff's continual tormenting and come-ons; Johe's revelation about Alan and his philandering; the close call with Angela's threats – it all meshed together as a congealed mess of worry that blocked any sort of alternative thought. She moved from the dinette table and sat in her chair.

Worrying made her tuck her knees against the faded pink fabric; attempting to take her mind off of the worry made her open the book Ted assumed she'd already read.

If Cliff has told Rob about me and Alan, who else has he told? she wondered. *What if he shows Angela or Johe those pictures he took? Then they'll know about my relationship* – she stopped.

"Relationship?" she audibly questioned. "Is that what this is?" Her eyebrows rose at the thought. It felt that way, somewhat. Yet, how would she label it? Or should she? *Alan's married, so it can't be a relationship.* Perhaps Johe was right – he's just looking for a conquest.

On the other hand, he didn't seem that way at all. "You need to talk to him," she told herself. Every creak and groan in the house made even her hair on edge. Was it Cliff coming to assault her again?

"I wish Alan were here." She picked up her phone and texted him: *Are you coming over tonight?*

Moments later, he texted back: *Sorry, not 2nite. Mega busy w/ the band.*

A frown immediately pulled her face downward. *Still?*

Yeah. Sorry.
Oh. Ok, she texted back.
U ok?
Yeah.
U sure?
She shook her head at how he knew so easily she wasn't. *No. But it's ok.*
What's wrong?
Don't worry about it. Get back to work. We'll talk later.
They can wait. What's wrong?? he insisted.
It can wait.
I'm on my way.
NO! It's not urgent. Sheesh! Stay there. We'll talk later, I promise.
I'll come by later then.
Ok.

Should she tell him about Angela? About Johe? About the picture? About Cliff? What would he do if he knew? "Nothing. What can he do? You're just overreacting," she told herself. "Oh who are you fooling? You want him here simply because he makes you feel better than at any other time."

She nodded. It was definitely true. Still, the quietness in her cabin made her ears listen intently to any little sound. Hearing some of Alan's music just might be the comforting she needed.

Closing the book, she rose from her chair and sat in front of the espresso-colored coffee table. Her laptop was tucked next to the couch. The Windows music played as her computer booted. The sound still made her skin crawl. Each time she heard it, she anticipated that her door would be abruptly kicked in again, like it was when Roger busted into her apartment on West Roger Road in Tucson. "Stop being such a baby," she told herself. "It's been months, and no Roger whatsoever. Just relax."

Once she had Alan's baritone voice filling the lonely room, she realized that with everything going on, she hadn't checked her email or the news since just after her fishing trip with Alan. The last email she'd sent to Tunda was information about Alan. How had she forgotten about that? Eagerly, Mary logged into her email – even skipping glancing over the news. Inside, were two emails from Tunda. One was a response to her message entitled "He kissed me!", which was sent shortly after Alan had kissed Mary the first time on the boat. *It's got to be about Alan,* she thought. *I wonder what she'll tell me. Will she tell me to stay away from him?* The thought hadn't entered her mind until that moment. Did she really want to click to read her message? "Yes, of course you want to! Even if she says to stay away from Alan, that doesn't mean you have to!"

Mary positioned the mouse cursor over the first email message:

> *Honey,*
>
> *Loving someone means giving him the ability to hurt you, but trusting him enough to know that he won't. If you love him, you know what you've got to do – tell him about Roger. Tell him the truth. Give him the chance to understand and love you anyway. Alan will protect you. I just know it.*
>
> *Love,*
>
> *Mother*

Mary could hardly believe Tunda's advice! She'd even used Roger's name so plainly – something they'd both avoided in the past.

How could she ever tell Alan everything about Roger? She read Tunda's email once again, and leaned back against the couch. No, Alan could no more know the whole truth than Tunda could. He knew too much as it was, and if he knew it all…. She shuddered at the thought. *He could single-handedly destroy – everything!*

Mary shook her head. No matter how she felt about Alan or how hopeful her heart was, telling him everything could mean certain destruction. Roger was probably foaming at the mouth now in his pursuit of her. She knew she was playing with fire, and as difficult as it was, she had to stick to her guns and keep her mouth shut.

Alan knew she'd been abused, and that was enough. If she actually let Alan into the deep, hidden fortress of her trust, it would make it impossible to leave him, should the need arise. He would be the only person on the planet who knew everything, with the exception of her and Roger. *Besides,* she thought, *Tunda said "if you love him." I'm not certain it's love, yet.*

But then again, maybe his knowing wouldn't be such a bad thing, her heart told her. *Give him the chance to know and still love you.*

You're crazy too! her head came back.

Her heart cringed as she wrote to Tunda:

Mother,

Thanks for the advice, but I'm afraid I disagree. Roger is like a demon who torments me every step I take! Perhaps if there wasn't the ambiguity of my husband lingering over my head with every thought and every move, then things would be different. Strike that, I'm absolutely certain that if it wasn't for him, I would let myself be free to be with Alan.

But that's not the case. Yes, the realization of that is <u>absolutely killing me</u>! You and I both know, though, that the minute I let my guard down, my husband will be on me and destroy everything I have – including my life, and maybe even Alan's.

No, Mother, I'm sorry. I simply can't risk it.

Love,
Mary

Mary clicked send and then went back to her inbox to read Tunda's second email, which had been sent only the day prior.

Mary,

You won't believe what has happened!! I don't have the words to even express my shock! So I'm pasting the news story below:

<u>Prominent Tucson Attorney Charged with Wife's Murder, Authorities Say</u>

TUCSON, AZ — Roger Donovan Franklin, the husband of missing Tucson native, Mary Elizabeth Franklin, has been charged with first-degree murder in the case.

Friends and colleagues of Mary Franklin, 25, have been on an exhaustive campaign to seek justice for Mary. "Mary was unlike any woman, and yet like every woman," says friend Tammie Holmes. "It's only a matter of time before we find her body."

Franklin was last seen almost a year ago on September

15, just before the November elections where Roger Donovan Franklin was running for Arizona State Representative.

The following Monday, she was due to teach freshman physics at the University of Arizona. Professor Freddie Fleming told police, "I thought she'd canceled classes on Friday, but when she didn't show on Monday, I knew something was wrong." Authorities found Mrs. Franklin's car on the university campus with her keys, empty purse and cell phone inside.

Citing the ongoing investigation, Tucson Detective Joseluis Rodriguez declined to comment further on the case or a possible motive. "I hope this arrest will bring some peace and closure to Mary's friends," he said.

Attorneys in the Pima County District Attorney's Office declined to discuss the case but did say that Franklin had seemed out of sorts since the disappearance of his wife.

Despite the fact that no body has ever been found, Chief District Court Judge Raul Rivadeñeyra on Wednesday signed an order stating that Mary Franklin was likely the victim of a homicide and that Roger Donovan Franklin was likely involved in her death.

Franklin, who has maintained his innocence, turned himself into authorities on Thursday morning. His representative, former law school classmate, Earl L. Forsyth, stated that Franklin has no comment to make. A sizeable reward for information leading to the discovery of Mrs. Franklin's remains has been offered; no one has come forward to claim the reward.

Mary limply fell back after she read the news article. Part of her felt relieved! *Roger. In jail. Amazing!*

Then her paranoid, yet logical, thoughts took over. *You've got to know this is going to make Roger insane!! He knows he didn't kill you. He's going to be doing everything in his power to find you,* her mind told her. *Damn Roger! I should've followed Tunda's advice and killed him before I left. But that's neither here nor there. I can't change that now. Maybe they won't let Roger out on bail. That would keep me protected at least for a while. But if he makes bail, any kind of future with Alan will be far too risky of a thought to even entertain!* Her heart ached as she thought of those words. Mary clenched her chest.

Johe's information about Alan and his womanizing came back to her thoughts.

"You've made the biggest mess imaginable!"

She felt fearful. Both Cliff and Roger had successfully resurrected Fear's unmistakable grip on her. Fear's chilling cackle filled her ears. The comfort of Alan's arms around her seemed to be the only thing she wanted. *No. You've got to be strong,* she thought.

Alan's twangy country voice continued to bounce off the walls.

Quickly, she whipped up a short email to Tunda:

> *Thanks, Mother. Please stay vigilant and let me know if you hear anything new – like bail information.*
>
> *Love,*
> *Mary*

She clicked send, and immediately hung her head in disgust at herself. *You've got to pull yourself together and not forget the mess you're in. You can't escape Roger. Jail or no jail.*

Fear pulled his puppet strings and forced her to get up and start pacing the living room. His hauntingly eerie laughter continued. *You've totally forgotten yourself, haven't you?* she thought. *He's Alan Brooks, for crying out loud! You can no more have him than you can have anyone, but especially him. He's a public figure, and heaven help you if Cliff found out who you* really *are! Word would get back to Roger and blamo! You'd be dead meat!*

On the other hand, Alan was huge in stature and had plenty of security, but could all of that protect her from someone like Roger? Roger was the type person who would keep coming back and back until one of them ended up dead! Was being with Alan worth the risk?

And what if Alan did abandon you like Johe said he has in the past? Then what? Would you face Roger alone?

"Maybe you should just sleep with Cliff," she said aloud.

As she paced, her mind argued with her heart. *Absolutely not! There has to be a way you can be together,* her heart pleaded. Her heart disputed her head's logic with what seemed like justifiable reasons of why it could work between Mary and Alan.

Mary pulled out her cleaning supplies and gloves. Cleaning her kitchen was the only peace she could find. Her mind ran as rapidly as her hands scrubbed already clean surfaces. But none of her thoughts formed into actual words.

Fear's frightening taunting immediately dissipated the second she heard a knock on the backdoor. *Alan!* her heart shouted with joy.

In practically two leaping steps, Mary was at the backdoor. When she swung it open, she instantaneously clung to his neck.

"Whoa! That's one helluva welcome!" he said as he embraced her. He smiled as he heard his familiar music playing in the background.

"Please. Hold me."

He smiled as he walked inside with her in his arms. "No problem."

Mary could smell the distinct smell of bourbon on him, but she didn't care. Having him there was everything she needed to defeat Fear.

"I couldn't stay away," he said as he kissed her bandana-covered head. "It's nice to know you feel the same way."

"I didn't want to bother you while you're working, but I'm so glad you're here!" Her ear was filled with the sound of his heart beating. It quieted Fear's ethereal, tormenting voice. It didn't even bother her how weak she thought she must've appeared to Alan. Simply being near him and feeling his embrace was enough to make her feel strong again. "What made you come over?"

"You," he said with his lips just inches from her head. His hands comforted her like a frightened child. "You sounded like you needed me, so here I am."

Mary lifted her head from his chest and smiled up at him. "I'm so glad!"

"Besides, all I could do was stand there on the stage and wish I was here with you."

"Yeah?" Such news made her heart tell her mind and Fear off.

"Yeah. What's up, Honey? What's got you all shook up?"

"Just demons," she said as she took her gloves off.

"Demons, huh? The problem with demons is their surprising ability to wiggle their way into the insecure and frightened souls living inside us. Then they relentlessly torture your defenseless soul."

"Yeah," she whispered.

"It's all smoke and mirrors, you know?"

"Yeah."

"Hey," he said as he pulled her face up to look at him. "You want to get out of here?"

"And go where?"

"I don't care, really. I just need a change of scenery. We could go to Savannah."

At the mention of Savannah, Mary remembered the picture of them in Churchill's. "By the way, Johe informed me there's a picture of us hanging in Churchill's."

"She did, did she? Well what's wrong with that?"

"She was quite accusatory! She claimed I am sleeping with you."

"I wish!" Alan filled the kitchen with his melodic laughter. It mixed beautifully with his recorded voice singing in the next room.

"It's not funny!"

"I know. At least I know where your demons are coming from now."

"Yeah, I guess. I didn't know what to say to her."

"What *did* you say?"

"I told her we most definitely weren't sleeping together."

"Which is true," he affirmed.

"Exactly. But she, uh, well, she said some other stuff too, but, she was mostly displeased about the picture."

He reached behind him inside his jacket and pulled out a picture frame. "You mean this picture?" he asked as he handed it to her.

"Yeah! How'd you know?"

"Because she chewed me out, too. I personally went down to Churchill's and took care of it."

"How'd you get it from them?" Mary asked as she looked at it. It was the one pictures taken at Cracker Barrel when Mary didn't hide her face. "I tried, and they wouldn't even entertain the idea."

"Aw, there's not much I can't talk people into."

"You paid them for it, didn't you?"

"You say that like I did something nasty. Everyone has a price, Sugar. Theirs just happened to be a new picture with me, a promised autographed copy of my next CD, and a promise to come there and perform."

"I hate that you had to do all that," Mary sheepishly looked at him. "All because of me."

"Don't you worry your pretty little head about it. It's my job to protect you from prying eyes and questions. Now does your hero deserve a kiss?"

"Mmm, you bet!" she said as she stood on her tip-toes and kissed him.

"Good God, I can't get enough of your lips!" he hotly whispered.

"Thank you," she whispered back.

"For what?"

"For the picture. For coming here. For finding me attractive." *For saving me from myself,* she thought, but didn't say.

"What else did Johe say?"

"Huh?"

"You said she was concerned we're sleeping together, pissed off about the picture, and then you said she said other stuff."

Mary chuckled lightly. *He was listening.* "She said some stuff about you and other girls."

Alan stiffened up. "What other girls?"

"She said you tend to chase after the latest pretty girl and then you end up abandoning them for another woman. She implied it would happen to me too."

"You've had a tough day, haven't you?"

"Yeah," she said as she looked up at him. Her face displayed her concern. "A tough couple of days, really."

He placed a hand on each side of her face, cupping her ears with his fingers. "Listen to me. Like I told you back when we were in my granddad's cabin, there's been no one else since Angela, until you. Whatever Johe might possibly be talking about was back when I was a young buck chasing anything in a skirt and cowboy boots! I'm not leaving you. If anyone is going to get left, it'll be Angela. Ok?"

She nodded.

"Ok??" he demanded.

"Ok," she said with a half-smile.

"You can do better than that," he said as he tilted his head and looked at her with his eyes half-closed.

Mary smiled full-on – amused by his reaction.

"Now, come on. Let's go in the living room. I want to hold you properly."

"Yes, sir," she playfully said.

Once he was settled on the couch, Mary planted herself in his lap. His arms were immediately around her. "God, you don't know how much I missed you," he whispered with his face near hers. The spicy aroma of bourbon filled the tiny space between them.

"We haven't been apart that long, you know?"

"I know. But even five seconds is too long. You don't understand. I haven't felt this way in ages. I'm so afraid it's going to go away, and then I see you, and like magic, the feeling is back!"

She blushed and hid her face against his chest. "Nu-huh."

"Uh-huh. So, I've been thinking…"

"About what?" she interrupted him.

"Let me breathe a second, and I'll tell you. I've been thinking, maybe it's time to divorce Angela."

Mary thought about Roger being in jail and about all the trouble she'd been dealing with lately. Would divorcing Angela help things? "Do you really think that's wise?"

"W-what?" Alan asked, completely shocked that she wasn't jumping up and down with joy.

"It's just that a lot of things have been going on lately." She moved out of his lap and onto the couch, but turned so she was facing him.

"Like what?"

What do I say? Dare I tell him about Cliff? she wondered. "Well, with Johe's accusations, and well…," the words about Cliff hung on the edge of her lips.

"Annnnnd…"

"Cliff."

"What about him?"

"Nothing."

"Oh no you don't! Don't give me that stupid shit! What about Cliff?"

Silence fell as she tried to think about what she should say.

"Say!" he demanded.

She closed her eyes and blurted it out: "Cliff took pictures of us kissing on the boat, and he's been trying to use them against me." The words rambled out of her mouth faster than she intended them to.

"He what!?" Alan's brow crinkled.

"Just yesterday, Rob asked me if I was dating you now."

"What did you say?"

"I told him he was crazy! But I knew it came from Cliff. He thinks he can get what he wants with those pictures."

Alan sat upright from the couch. "How long has this been going on?!"

"The first time was a while ago, when you found the mattress on the floor. But it happens nearly every day."

"And you're just now telling me," he gruffly said as he stood up and angrily looked at her.

Mary felt afraid of him. "I-I-I didn't, uh, I didn't mean to hide it from you. It's j-j-just that he keeps threatening me with it."

"Threatening you?!"

"Yes. He said he's going to post them on Facebook and the Internet. That's why I said maybe divorcing Angela right now isn't such a good idea. Everything could blow up even worse then."

Alan gritted his teeth; his muscles flexed as he tensed up. "So he's trying to blackmail you, huh? What does he want? Money?"

"I-I-I don't know."

"Yes you do."

"Sex. He wants me to have sex with him," she said with her eyes closed and hid her face. She knew Alan would know there was more to it just by looking at her, so she tried to hide.

Alan's face was immediately deep crimson with rage. "Look at me!" he demanded.

Mary followed his orders.

"What else has he done?" he asked with his fists clenched. "Tell me what happened."

Mary timidly held the stare of the agitated man; his soothing recorded voice continued to sing on the computer. If she told him Cliff hit her, he was liable to go over and annihilate him.

"Tell me!" he demanded. "Your silence is as telling as anything, but I want to hear you say it."

Slowly she nodded. "He-he grabs me – sexually."

Alan's enraged breaths quickened.

Mary kept talking, hoping to keep him in the cabin, "He keeps saying if I don't have sex with him, he'll expose those pictures."

"Have you done it?!" he asked not certain he wanted to know the answer.

Mary earnestly defended herself. "No! I slapped him the first time he grabbed me, but he hit me." And the words tumbled out of her mouth.

"He did *what*?!" Alan shrieked with his eyes bulging out.

"He hit me," Mary quietly repeated.

The incensed Alan wasn't listening to her anymore. He didn't say another word before he practically tore her front door off the hinges and charged through it.

"Alan, please don't!" Mary begged. "Please!!" She ran after him. "I'll handle it. Please stop!"

Alan pounded on Cliff's door with his fist. The entire structure shook.

"Please, Alan, you're making this so much worse." The plain violence that oozed from his entire body frightened her. Would he turn on her?

His austere fiery face snapped to glare at her just before he kicked Cliff's door in. "Get your stupid ass out here!" he shouted.

Mary was close on his heels.

Cliff emerged from his bedroom, and Alan instantaneously tackled him into the wall, breaking through the thin drywall.

"Alan, no!" Mary shouted.

Before she could let out another scream, Alan was on top of Cliff landing a series of blows that quickly splattered bits of blood on the broken wall. "Just who the hell do you think you are?!" Alan shouted at him as he punched him.

"Stop it! You're going to kill him!" Mary shrieked. When blood splattered onto Mary's face, absolute panic made her run back to her cabin and hide in the closet.

"Don't you ever even *look* at her again!"

"I didn't do nothin'!" Cliff lied.

Alan punched him squarely in the jaw. "You know what you did!"

"She's a lyin' whore!" Cliff tried to defend himself with his arms over his face, but Alan's blows continued to rain upon him through the holes in his defenses.

"Shut your damn mouth!" Alan shouted with a final blow to Cliff's mouth.

"You broke muh tooth!" Cliff groaned.

Alan pulled him up by his shirt collar. "You're going to hand over those pictures, get your shit, and get out of here! Now!" he growled and dropped him back to the floor. Even as Alan stood up, he didn't notice the blood pouring from his right hand. "And if you ever come near her again, you won't live to regret it!"

"You'll be hearing from muh atturnee!" Cliff shouted as he touched his bleeding mouth.

"Good! I *want* to hear from your attorney! Get your ass off my property!" Alan pulled out his cell phone. "Felix! Get over here to Cabin A. I want this fucker off my property before I kill his ass!"

"Uh-huh. Get yer boys ta handle the dirty work, huh?" Cliff taunted him. "Pussy!"

Alan hung up the phone. "What?! You didn't get your ass kicked enough?" Before Cliff could get back on his feet, Alan began kicking him in his ribs and punching him again.

Felix and his guys burst into the cabin. "Mr. Brooks!" Felix exclaimed and pulled Alan off of Cliff.

The two body guards positioned themselves between the irate Alan and injured Cliff.

"What's going on?" Felix asked.

"He broke muh ribs and…" Cliff started.

Two large bodyguards moved on either side of Cliff; their body language made it clear they didn't want to hear anything he had to say.

"Mr. Brooks, you need to have your hand looked at. Would you like for me to call Dr. Sabia?" Felix asked. He produced a white handkerchief for Alan to wrap around his hand.

"I'm fine. That fucker's been harassing and trying to blackmail Mary with pictures he claims he took of us. When Mary wouldn't give him what he wanted, he hit her!" Alan informed Felix.

The two bodyguards turned to Cliff, picked him up by his armpits, and pinned him against the wall.

Felix turned to Cliff. "I want those pictures."

"I don't know whut yer talkin' 'bout," Cliff defiantly said.

"So, are you saying there are no pictures?" Felix calmly asked.

"Of Mary and Alan? Yeah, I's got 'em."

"Hand them over," Felix demanded.

"No," Cliff firmly stated.

The two bodyguards growled low in their chests and hoisted him higher up the wall.

"I don't think you understand fully who you're dealing with here. When you were hired, you signed a waiver indicating that anything you witnessed you could not disclose to the outside world. This waiver precludes you from any of the threats you've made."

"Whut's seen cain't be unseen."

"Yes, but if you expose those pictures, you can face serious lawsuits and jail time. Is that really what you want? Wouldn't it be far smarter to just delete those pictures and go on about your business?" Felix's words were firm, commanding.

Cliff didn't respond.

"Where are the pictures?"

"On muh cell phone."

"Which is where exactly?"

"In there in the bedroom."

Felix entered the bedroom, retrieved the cell phone, and returned to the scene. "So these grainy, indistinct pictures are the ones you were using to blackmail Miss Mary?"

"They's not indistant!"

Felix showed the pictures to Alan.

"Good grief. You can't even tell that there are people on the boat! Just delete them," Alan commanded.

"Indeed." Felix deleted the pictures.

"Mary. She was right here; where'd she go?" Alan asked.

"She wasn't here when we got here," Felix informed him.

Alan's face went white. *Oh hell*, he thought and tossed the handkerchief back to Felix. "Mary?" he called out for her, but there was no answer.

Images of her terrified face worried him. "Mary?!" he called as he ran out of Cliff's door. Blood left red tracks as it ran down his fingers and dripped to the floor.

Alan entered her cabin and called for her again.

Mary heard him, but was too afraid to reply. Part of her compelled her to go to him, but another part of her was simply too petrified to leave the dark safety of her closet.

"Mary??" Alan called again; noticeable worry resided in his voice.

This time, Mary meekly replied. "Yeah?"

A scarlet trail followed him to her sanctuary. "Are you ok?"

"Why did you do that?!" her voice asked with all the indication of how afraid she was.

"I-I-I was defending you."

"Why? I told you I'll handle it."

"But you're still afraid of him."

"I'm afraid of a lot of things. Are you just going to beat the shit out of all of them?"

"I would if I had to."

"You didn't have to do that."

"Yes I did. Trust me. If I didn't, it would never stop with him."

"Do you really think it's over??"

"Yeah. Felix is evicting him now."

"You don't get it do you?!" she cried as she pushed against his chest.

"Apparently, I don't. Why are you defending him?"

"I'm not! I'm defending you…"

"I don't need you to defend me!" he tersely interrupted her.

"You didn't let me finish. I'm defending you and me and what we have together. I don't want to lose that."

"How do you get that kicking his ass would do that?"

"Because everyone here already looks at me weird. Now that you've made a scene, everyone is going to be talking about what you did. I'm not prepared to handle that!"

"Who looks at you weird?" he threateningly asked.

"Every…no one," she said, changing her mind. What would he do to the others if she said anything else? "Please just stop!"

"I won't tolerate anyone treating you badly."

"Just let it go." She tucked herself against him and wrapped her arms around him. "Come on," Mary begged as she tugged on his arm. "Let's get your hand bandaged up."

"I'd kill that fucker if it wasn't for you!"

"I don't want to have to visit you in jail, so let's not, ok?"

Alan relented and let her lead him into the bathroom.

"Let me run some cool water over these cuts."

He didn't flinch at all as the bloody water ran down his fingers. Her hands shook as she took care of his cut and bruised knuckles. Her breaths were shallow and tremulous.

"I'm sorry," he whispered as he dropped his head. His intent was to protect her, not frighten her.

"I know," she quietly murmured.

CHAPTER 11

The Georgia pre-summer sun seemed determined to show off its prowess. Red clay dried and cracked from its unrelenting demonstration, and the grass faded and bowed to its might. There was no breeze to speak of, and even the shade from the tall oaks was sweltering.

Mary never realized Georgia could get so hot or that 90 degrees would seem so miserably smothering. Arizona's 90 degree weather was nothing like this, and could even be considered a glorious day. She could at least breathe in Arizona even when it was well over 100 degrees. But this? This was stifling! Her lungs struggled to pull in the thick, humid air.

The heat seemed to suck the energy out of everything. The feral barn cats lazed around trying to stay cool instead of pouncing on random flies or unfortunate mice. Even the stable hands seemed quieter with Cliff gone.

Angela too was unusually silent. Her normal outbursts in the barn hadn't been heard at all. Ted had continued to train Mary and Angela together, yet the normally highly vocal, rarely pleased, boisterous Angela had been quiet as a tomb.

Perhaps it was all because of the heat, but Mary felt it was too quiet. Collectively, it unnerved her. Were people afraid to talk because of the Cliff incident? Everyone knew Cliff had been fired, but it wasn't clear why. Rumors flew to and fro during the following weeks. Mary played dumb and didn't provide any clarification. From what she could tell, Alan did nothing to set the record straight either.

Casually, Mary mentioned the tense feeling at the barn to Alan. On a 95-degree day without a drop of rain in sight, Johe stepped up and put a stop to the speculation by stating she'd fired Cliff because of his fights with Ted. When Mary heard that, she could only shake her head. It was clear to her that it was Alan's way of dealing with it – letting his staff cover up the situation. Mary wondered if Johe knew the truth.

On another stiflingly warm evening, Mary sat in her chair across the room from Alan. Her book on the mechanics of jumping sat in her lap as she tried to read it yet again. Sweat dripped down a path from her neck between her shoulder blades until it soaked into her bra strap. The bandana covering her head had noticeably moist edges. An oscillating fan stirred the hot air in the tiny room.

At the end of the couch, Alan sat in a sweat-marked button-down shirt, nursing his flask. He also hadn't said a word since she welcomed him inside, said hello, and kissed her. It was almost as if speaking a single word only added to the smothering heat.

The crisp turning of her pages seemed to echo like a shout left at the Grand Canyon. Her eyes occasionally glanced over at the muted object of her affection. Knowing that Alan was capable of the violence she saw against Cliff made her feel edgy; nevertheless she did her best to hide it from Alan.

His hat sat on the table in front of him; his hair was windswept, mixed with sweat. His face was stoic. The normal dimples she enjoyed seeing were only faint parentheses on the edges of his closed mouth. His typically vibrant and impish eyes were fixed and steely grey while his slightly furrowed brow hung heavily above them. His square jaw was set and rigid. Strong shoulders that often held the entire weight of his world appeared weary.

He seems distant, she thought. *I wonder what's going on.* The fan only blew hot silence around the room. *Angela. It's probably all about Angela,* her thoughts continued. *There has to be a reason she's been so weird lately. I wonder if they're fighting again.*

"You're awfully quiet tonight," Mary said without looking up.

"Am I?"

"Yeah." She closed the book and looked at him. "What gives? You usually talk my ear off while I'm trying to read." Mary squinted at him. "What's going on?"

"Nothing much, just thinking."

"Thinking? About what?"

"A million different things," he said hoping his words placated her. The truth was his mind was engaged otherwise. His thoughts swirled around in a semi-congealed mixture of uncertainty and unfamiliar desire. It seemed like Mary had been different since Cliff had left, or was she? The pressure Alan had been feeling from his record company to finish his latest CD had become insurmountable, so maybe it wasn't Mary. Maybe it was just his stress. He wasn't sure. The one thing he knew for certain was that the album his recording company wanted to release wasn't right. It was missing something. What that something was, he wasn't sure.

He spent most of his time arguing and less of his time writing or searching for an answer. He needed something – a jolt – to stoke the fires of creativity. But his attempts at writing or finding just the right song had been futile. The very presence of Mary had promised to provide that jolt, but instead it only increased his disillusion with his career and the sincere desire to run away from it all. The whole situation frustrated him.

He looked up at Mary. A smile immediately graced his lips, showing off his previously shy dimples.

She gently grinned back, an automatic reaction to him. It amazed her how just one smile could quiet the demons inside and make her feel happier than she'd felt in months, years—ever. Roger was securely in jail, Cliff was gone, and she simply felt free to love Alan. Yet there was still that shred of fear that kept her from giving him her entire heart. "Care to tell me about one of those million things?"

"You," he said rather decisively and quickly. "I'm always thinking about you." He patted the seat next to him.

Mary took the hint, placed her book on her chair, and moved from her seat to the couch, snuggling her head against the nook in his shoulder. His shirt was damp with sweat.

Alan immediately wrapped his arm around her. He took a drink from his flask. "I don't know how I lived before you," he told her as he placed his other hand, still gripping the flask, on the couch's arm.

"The feeling is mutual. But I know there's more on your mind than just that."

He quietly chuckled; his smile increased. Kissing her covered head softly, he whispered, "How do you know me so well?"

"It's not that hard. You're pretty much an open book."

"Then how is it that Angela doesn't have a clue about me after ten years?"

"Easy. She never bothered," Mary lightheartedly said as she patted his chest. "Her loss is my gain. Now what else are you thinking about?"

"Just business. Nothing else."

The silence between them returned more quickly than either of them expected.

"So you're just going to sit there all quiet like?"

He took another drink from his flask and sighed. Across the room, sitting on her chair, was her book. If he didn't say something soon, she would surely start reading and ignoring him again, but what to say?

His heart felt a million things that he seemed incapable of communicating through words, lyrics or music. He'd tried repeatedly to write what he felt about her, but everything he'd produced seemed to fall short. How could he put into words what he couldn't describe for himself? Words just seemed to lack the power he wanted. Lyrics seemed to be limp. Music notes were noise in comparison. Maybe if he could find them, he could also finish his album. Maybe he could figure out a definitive future for them. Yet, there always seemed to be something holding her back.

He scratched his head and took another sip from his flask.

"If you're going to sit here and drink, then I'm going to go back to my book." Mary stated nearly the exact sentence Alan predicted she would.

"How about we just make out for a while?" he asked with a twinge of hopefulness.

Mary twisted her mouth to the side as she thought. "It's too hot for that. Why don't you play me some music?"

"Nope."

"Why not?"

"'Cause that's too much like work. That's all I've done all day. I want to do something I *like* to do."

"Something you like to do, huh? But I thought you liked music."

"Yeah, I do. But I've been running on empty for so long that I'm too frustrated with it. I'd rather do something more stimulating."

"Stimulating?" she said with surprise and anxiety. "I'm not sleeping with you," she said quickly.

"Funny, but that thought didn't enter my mind," he lied. His mind often ran rampant with imaginary sex with her. It was the first thing he thought of in the morning, and the last thing he thought of before bed. It often kept him awake at night and interfered with any thoughts throughout the day. But considering how long it took for him to touch her without her flinching and then to kiss her, he suspected sex wasn't something he'd get to enjoy anytime soon. Still, in his mind, he enjoyed it quite often.

"Of course, I wouldn't resist if you just started tearing my clothes off right here, right now, but as funny as it may seem, that wasn't something I was considering." *At that second, but now that you mention it…*, he thought.

Mary's brow furrowed as she looked at him. "Are you sure you're not sick or something? That's usually the first thought in a man's mind."

"True, true. And it has been quite a while since I had any. But still, that wasn't even a consideration."

"Uh-huh," she said in disbelief. She snuggled against him; the silence returned. "Have you noticed it's been unusually quiet around here lately?"

Alan's life had been anything but quiet. "No. Why?"

"It just is. Hardly anyone has said more than 'Hi' to me. Even Angela has been acting weird."

"Weird? How?"

"She hasn't yelled at me or anyone in weeks! What did you do to her?"

"Nothing."

"Nothing? Hmm…," she put her hand to her chin.

"There's nothing to worry about. Maybe she's just focused."

"I doubt that," she said with a laugh.

"She does have that big show coming up soon. She takes competing very seriously."

"Hmm. Maybe." Mary shifted to where her back was to him; she leaned against him with her head lying in the crook of his shoulder.

Yet again, the only sound came from the fan.

"You still worried?" he asked.

"No. Not really."

"Not really means yes in girl code."

"I didn't realize you spoke girl code."

"I've been around the block a time or two and picked up some of the language along the way. What's going on?"

"I don't know. I can just envision Angela and everyone knowing all about me and you, everyone down at the barn afraid to even speak to me because of what you'll do to them, and Cliff being even angrier and plotting his revenge."

"Is that so? Well, then, consider him gone," he nonchalantly said as he pulled his cell phone out.

"No! That's not what I meant!"

"Did you think I was going to have him killed?"

"Yeah!"

"What?!"

"Yeah. And what were you going to say 'This guy has made my girlfriend's life hell, I need him rubbed out.'?"

Alan laughed his beautifully melodic laugh. "'Rubbed out'?"

"Yeah. Isn't that what the gangsters say?"

"You've been watching too much *Goodfellas*. No, Honey, I was just messing with you. I couldn't do something like that even if I tried." Alan looked at her from under his eyelashes. *Girlfriend,* played over and over in his mind.

"What?" Mary shifted uncomfortably in her seat. "Why are you looking at me like that?"

"Girlfriend?" he finally said.

She closed her eyes and dropped her head. *How impetuous of me!* she thought. "I'm sorry…"

"What?"

"I mean, I should've said mistress or something else. I mean, girlfriend is so serious sounding."

An immediate burst of laughter left his lips.

"It's not funny!"

"I'm not laughing."

"Yes you are!"

"It's a…a… breathing spasm! Yeah. I'm just having a breathing spasm," he said while unsuccessfully hiding his amusement.

"Really now?"

"Yup," he said with a broad smile at his cleverness.

"Oh just shut up," she said with a silly grin as she wiggled away from him.

He grabbed her by the waist and drew her back to him and onto his lap. "Come over here, Girlfriend."

She buried her face into his shoulder. "I'm so embarrassed!"

He struggled to stifle his giggles. "Come on. I love it! And one day, I'd like to call you my wife instead."

The words made Mary's ears ring like a sharp piercing sound. Yet she didn't flinch. Every part of her insides did, but her exterior was like a stone. *Alan wants to marry me?* she thought. Mixed emotions washed over her. She couldn't look up. *Change the subject,* her mind demanded.

"What do you think about that?" he said with a delighted smile.

"Umm," she struggled to come up with something to say.

"Don't worry. I know you're not ready yet. Neither am I. But one of these days, I'd like to call you Mrs. Alan Brooks."

"Uh, um, I-I-I don't know..."

He hugged her tightly with one arm and took a long drink from his flask. "I don't know how I lived before you, and I sure as hell don't want to go back to living without you anymore!"

"Um. Ok?" Her mind was a jumbled mess of panicky thoughts. *Change the subject!!* was all she could clearly think of.

He quietly chuckled; his smile increased. "This is nice."

"What's nice?"

"This. Holding you like this. You not pulling away from me all the time." He leaned down and gently kissed her head. "Having the freedom to do that sends thrills all the way down to my toes."

She sat up and looked at him. "How is that even possible?" she asked with an incredulous tone.

"Just kissing you is as thrilling as whitewater rafting down the Nantahala!"

"I don't have a clue what you're talking about."

He chuckled. "Just shut up and kiss me, future Mrs. Brooks," he commanded as he leaned into her for more.

Mary stopped her ascent toward his lips. "You never told me about the scar on your lip," she said noticing how bad it really was. *Yay! We changed the subject!* her mind told her.

· "I told you about that."

"Not really." She looked directly at him and gently ran her fingertip along the vertical pink line dividing his bottom lip.

Alan sighed deeply. "Ok, if I tell you the entire story will you make out with me the right way? And that means you let me get past first base."

"Maybe."

"Maybe," he repeated with a tone of dubious belief.

"Yeah, maybe."

"I guess that's better than no." Alan drew in a deep breath. "Angela bit me."

"Yes, I know. But *why* did she bite you?"

"I wish I knew. We were on the brink of make-up sex, and well," he paused, "see, we had been fighting, like usual, and I don't know. I got pissed off with her constant rejection…."

"Whoa! You tried to force her to have sex?" Mary interrupted him, drawing her own conclusions. Showing her disapproval of his alleged action, she sharply moved away from him.

Alan hesitated before he spoke again. "Well… no, not really. It wasn't what you're thinking. I just thought if she'd try to reconnect with me things would be better. She never tries! I wanted so badly to be near her again, and, things went a little too far."

"So she bit you in self-defense." Mary moved even further away from him.

"Not exactly. If she had said no, I would've stopped."

"So, you're saying she never said no? That doesn't seem likely," Mary said with a highly skeptical look.

"No, I mean, her body language didn't say no."

"What?! Are you some rapist or something?!" she asked him, fearful about what the answer was. "No means no." She narrowed her eyes to little slits as she looked at him disapprovingly.

Alan put his hands behind his head and ran them down his hair. "What?! Hell no!! She's my wife for crying out loud! How can I rape my own wife?!"

"Because if she doesn't want to and you force her, that's rape. Were you going to force her?"

"Uh-uh no," he said, stumbling over his own words.

"It sounds to me like you were forcing her."

"No, no, you're taking this all wrong. I wasn't forcing her. I carried her to the bed," he paused as he tried to remember the details. "And then we got started, and out of the blue she bit me."

"Ok, let me ask you this, if I were to tell you no, what would you do?" Mary asked him with her arms across her chest.

Alan turned to face her directly. "I haven't made a single move toward you! I think I've taken no quite well; don't you?"

"I'm just saying. Would you force me to have sex with you if I didn't want to?"

"Of course not! Don't be ridiculous!"

"Then what happened with Angela?"

"I don't know. I was a little tipsy at the time, and…"

"Oh!" Mary exclaimed as she tossed her head back and threw her hands in the air. "So you were drunk! That explains a lot."

"I wasn't drunk!"

"Alan, when you think you're tipsy, you're not, you're really close to falling-down drunk!" She shook her head at him and returned her arms across her chest.

"I don't drink that much!"

"Mm-hmm," she said with disbelieving, scrutinizing eyes. "You were drunk the night you beat the shit out of Cliff, and you were drunk the night you tried to rape Angela. What's going to happen to me?!" She could feel the anxiety rising inside her. Was she safe with him?

"Oh come off it, Mary! You're being ridiculous!"

"Am I? Am I?! I don't think so. You have no idea what you're like when you're drunk!"

"I don't get drunk!"

"Sure you don't."

Mary sat in silence; she wasn't exactly sure what to make of the story Alan had just told her. The idea that he was capable of beating Cliff up frightened her, but this? This was much worse. Deep inside, she knew every man was capable of that kind of behavior, but Alan? Her sweet, precious Alan. She rubbed her forehead with her fingers as she contemplated what he'd just said.

"I guess you're not going to kiss me now, huh?"

"How very astute of you!" she said as she stood up and returned to her chair.

In an attempt to hide her anxiety, she crossed her legs, tucking her feet under each leg. Still, she couldn't hide her bouncing leg. Her right knee twitched rhythmically to the beat of her pounding angst. Eagerly her fingers flipped through her book, but her mind remained focused completely on Alan. He seemed like such a gentleman. She could justify his attack on Cliff with his desire to protect her, but this? Could she still trust him? Could she even chance being around him? What if he were to stop taking no for an answer from her? Could she handle such a situation?

Alan came to her and knelt in front of her.

Mary couldn't look at him. How could she be secretly aroused and frightened at the same time? She certainly wasn't aroused at all by her rape; it was the single-most terrifying moment in her life! But Alan seemed to be different. Maybe it was the idea of controlled domination, where he would stop if she said so. Or would he? Would she have to bite him to make him stop? Was she safe being with him? There were no definitive answers.

She could hear Fear's familiar icy cackle in the background of her thoughts.

"What? So you're not talking to me anymore?" he asked. "It's not as sordid as you're making it out to be."

"No? I thought I knew you...," she said, but all the while wondering if she knew herself. In her mind's eye, she envisioned Alan – broad shouldered, thick neck, ripped biceps all overpowering her. The look of absolute ecstasy written all over his face as he entered her. Her heart thumped wildly in her chest.

"He's an animal!" Fear's gritty voice shouted from a distance.

"Oh come off it Mary! Of course you know me! Nothing's changed. I'm still the same person!"

Mary closed her eyes. "Are you?"

Gingerly, he pealed one of her jade eyes open. "Yes. I'm still the same man. Nothing has changed, or ever will change."

"How do I know you won't turn on me like you did Angela? Or Cliff?"

"What?! Oh hell, I'm sorry I even told you!" He released her eye and stood up, pacing the small room. "I'm the *victim* here! *I'm* the one who got bitten! She led me on! She made me think she was into the idea of sex, and then she attacked me! Hell, I can't even remember the last time I had sex with her! Imagine how excited I was at the prospect! Put yourself in *my* shoes," he implored her. "A man has needs, you know?"

He returned to kneeling in front of her. "Do you think I really and truly would have forced her to do anything she didn't want to do? Honestly. In your heart of hearts, do you think I would have? Don't you think she had to've at least led me on a little?"

Mary forced herself to look at him plainly. His eyes were no longer steely grey, instead they were startling blue. "Alan, you were drunk. How do you know what she did or didn't do? Or for that matter, what you did or didn't do?"

"I wasn't *that* drunk. I was well on my way, but at that moment, I wasn't drunk."

"Yeah, whatever."

"Don't do that. Don't put up a wall between us. You have to trust me. I didn't do anything to her that she didn't encourage me to do. I was just as shocked as anyone when she bit me. It-it was like she was a spider luring a fly into her web! Bringing me in for the kill."

"But why would she do that? Why? If Angela had any common sense whatsoever, she wouldn't do something like that. Think about it logically."

"I don't know. Angela and common sense don't belong in the same sentence!" he said with a smile that he hoped would charm her back into his arms.

"Still." She looked away from him, trying hard to ignore his attempts to wiggle past her defenses with his smiles that attracted her like a moth to a flame. "I find it hard to believe that she would bite you unprovoked. I think you were drunk, and you f-f-forced yourself on her."

Memories of the powerless, frightening, defenseless feelings she'd felt during her rape flooded her mind as Fear began to obtain control of her thoughts.

Alan sat back on his heels, profoundly thinking. Maybe she was right. His memory of that night was cloudy at best. "All right, you win."

Fear settled himself on the throne of her thoughts, fogging Mary's mind. He was now in control.

Her line of sight shifted toward the ceiling. Just the thoughts of the words she knew Fear would force from her lips were difficult.

She pugnaciously fought against Fear and his deadly words. The urge to go scrub the already clean kitchen was overwhelming.

"I-I-I don't want you to get drunk and-and something like what happened to Angela or Cliff happen to me," she said.

Fear wouldn't allow her intense green eyes to look directly at Alan.

"What?!" Alan hopped to his feet. "How…. Hell, give me a break! I was *defending* you with Cliff! Don't even bring that into this!"

"What about Angela? What's your excuse there?"

"I already explained that to you. She duped me. She made me believe we were on the cusp of make-up sex. You don't know her like I do. She's a manipulative bitch!"

Mary's leg fervently shook as she sat silently trying to resist the temptation to clean the kitchen.

Though Alan didn't know it, he was engaged in an all-out war with Fear. As much as Mary wanted Alan to win, Fear had ruled her for so long that he had the advantage. Where Alan's reaction to a difficult situation was to stay and fight it out, Mary's reaction was to run away – letting Fear take control of her.

"I-I promise you, I'll *never* speak to you or acknowledge your existence again if you do something like that to me! *Ever!!*"

Alan knelt before her and leaned into her lap, covering her book and thusly quieting her leg. "Understood. I'm so sorry. If I could, I'd go back and change the past. But, I can't. All I can do is assure you of how sorry I am. I shouldn't have fallen for Angela's trick. I shouldn't have punched Cliff. I was wrong," he said with a soothingly calm voice. "Will you please just look at me?"

"No," she said, her voice quivering.

Fear demanded her attention.

Mary's mind meekly curled into a ball in the corner of her thoughts. Her attempts at a valiant battle with Fear were quashed.

Fear had won.

"Please?" Alan asked.

"I-I-I can't," her voice trembled, "You're t-too dangerous," Fear made her say.

"Dangerous?? What on earth are you talking about?" he asked as he hopped back onto his feet.

"You're a…," she could hardly say the words, but Fear forced them past her lips, "…a rapist."

"A what?! Of course not! Don't be ridiculous! You're blowing this way out of proportion." The pitch of his voice displayed his shock and confusion.

"Am I?" she whispered.

"Yes! I'm the *victim!*"

Mixed emotions pulled at her like two conflicting currents. Her mind feebly reached for him, but Fear smacked her hand away.

Was Alan far more dangerous than she thought? And why did that danger excite and terrify her at the same time? Would she burst into flames if he so much as touched her – sexually?

Alan strategically moved so she had no choice but to look at him. He instantly furrowed his brow. "That far-away look there in your eyes is freaking me out. What is it?"

"It's nothing." Fear made her close her eyes, failing to truly see anything.

Fear screeched in her ear, "He's as much of an animal as Roger! You'll never be safe with him!"

"No, it's something. Talk to me; don't shut me out. I promise you, you're making way more out of this than it is," Alan gently implored her. "Don't you think if Angela would have thought it was something, she would have turned this into a huge ordeal? She's the biggest drama queen around!"

Mary's lip trembled; her eyes stayed closed as they began to burn from the tears forming. Yes, that made sense. If Angela had felt attacked, surely she would have used it against him in her campaign to discredit him. Yet, there was no word of such an ordeal.

Fear roared in her ear, "He must've paid her off! Don't believe that drivel! He's just like Roger!"

It angered her that she couldn't keep control of her conflicting thoughts better.

Comparing Roger and Alan when they were at Cracker Barrel was one thing, but in this situation, it was quite a bit different. Was Fear right? Was Alan indeed *just like* Roger? Her heart begged for it not to be true. Fear waved his boney hand and swirled her thoughts so much that she couldn't form words. She remained silent.

"I hate the silent treatment, please talk to me. You can trust me, I promise." Alan reached out to her and lightly touched her slender cheek.

Her immediate reaction was to react as if he had shocked her.

He sighed, dropping his hand to the arm of the chair. "So we're back here again, huh?" he whispered.

In the past several months, he'd learned that when she reacted in such a way, it was best for him to back away and wait for her to come to him. As he stood to return to the couch, he leaned down and whispered, "Please forgive me" into her ear. Without another word, he sat on the couch and returned his flask to his lips.

Her thoughts raced but were too muddy to make any definitive sense. What frightened her the most was the idea that Alan was capable of such violence. Seeing him lambaste Cliff was hard enough, but knowing that he'd tried to force himself onto Angela was a different story. Mary had given him a lot of her trust; did she need to rethink that trust?

"Yesssss," Fear hissed.

The urge to clean was too great to resist anymore. Mary rose from her chair and on wobbly knees made a bee-line to the kitchen where her ever faithful sponge and cleaning products were waiting for her.

Alan waited a few moments, finished off the bourbon in his flask, and followed behind her. He crouched down to her and whispered, "You know it's already clean, right?"

She didn't look up. Her glove-covered hands were busy scrubbing non-existent dirt. The overpowering aroma of alcohol on his breath sent chills through her body.

Fear immediately joined them in the kitchen.

After considerable, confusing silence, Mary coolly whispered, "I think you should go."

"I can't. Not with you like this."

As if someone were murdering her precious heart, Mary heard Fear make her coldly say the words she knew would make him leave: "I don't want to see you anymore."

"You what?!"

"I-I-I can't see you anymore."

Limply, Alan's head and hands dropped. He was a deflated balloon.

"You're too dangerous," she hardly whispered.

Fear triumphantly gripped her still-beating heart in his boney clutches and cackled in victory as he tore it apart.

"That's bull shit! I don't believe you!"

"I can't." Her words barely made a sound. "I want to, but I can't."

Fervently, he grabbed her by the shoulders, stood her up, spun her around, and made her look at him. "That's just bull shit! Of course you can! Tell me what's so dangerous about me!"

"Everything," she said as she looked back down.

"It's all that Angela shit, isn't it?"

Mary didn't reply.

He pulled her face up by her chin. "Please look at me."

Her grey-green eyes were rife with a storminess he'd never seen before. It startled him. It was almost as if his precious Mary wasn't there and someone else was.

"Please. Just. Go," she coldly said. The control she wished she had over her thoughts and emotions wasn't to be had. Fear was in complete control; Alan barely stood a chance.

Intently, Alan searched her hypnotic, spooky eyes for a glimmer of hope.

Nothing.

"You're the first chance I've had at true happiness in my entire life! I can't walk away from that. I *won't* walk away!"

He leaned down to gently kiss her, but Mary pushed him away. "Just leave," she said with a coolness that shot icy daggers through his heart.

Every bit of Alan's tall frame stood erect. His desperate grip on her released. He wouldn't win tonight.

Immediately, Fear pushed Mary back to her scrubbing duties.

Alan's sorrowful eyes looked longingly at Mary as she washed the bottom cabinet doors with her back to him. What was going on? Should he say something, or just leave? *Dangerous* reverberated in his mind.

"You ok?" he asked with his hand on the backdoor.

She only nodded.

"You sure?"

She nodded more animatedly.

How could she quell the uncompromising hold Fear had on her? Nearly everything about her psyche was too weak to fight against Fear. The only chance she had was the unbridled desire for Alan that was a lone, tiny ember below the surface. She was in no position to fan the ember, yet there was still the secret desire of her heart to find the safe hiding place in his arms, to easily taste his kisses, to run her hands over his rippling body, to feel his body pressed upon hers, and to feel him inside her. No matter how hard Fear tried, he couldn't completely quiet the still nearly insignificant voice that told her Alan could give her the safe, impenetrable place to fall apart and be who she really is – Mary Elizabeth Franklin. Yet at that moment, Fear's shrill voice was the only one she could hear.

Without another word, Alan sucked up the tattered remains of his pride and left Mary behind the closed door.

As soon as the door knob clicked closed, Mary wanted him to come back. Still, the torment pushed her to scrub already clean cabinets and made her take the sparkling clean stove apart to wash microscopic dirt.

While trying to choke back sobs, she scoured the sparkling clean drip pans. Why could she not let go? Why couldn't she see Alan for who he was – Alan and *not* Roger. Alan and *not* her rapist. Why should Alan pay for Roger's sins? For her rapist sins? Why did Alan have to drink?

CHAPTER 12

Alan felt like his head was going to explode. *What the hell just happened?* he thought as he stomped down the stairs of Mary's back stoop. His throat ached for a strong drink, but his empty flask betrayed him.

As soon as Alan's feet hit the gravel walkway leading to the barn, Johe spotted him. With a polite yet deprecatingly cool smile, Johe nodded toward Alan, who made no attempt to acknowledge her existence.

How could she think I'm dangerous? he thought. "Damn Angela!" he muttered. His footfalls should've left giant foot-shaped indentions in the ground. *Where does she get such a crazy idea? I'm the victim!*

His arms swung apoplectically as he strode straight to the main house. The strong desire for a drink pulled him as if he were on a string. Once inside, his hand quickly found a nearly full bottle. Gulping the brown liquid down, his insides felt as if he were swallowing liquid fire.

He didn't care.

His mania forced him to finish off the bottle and open a brand-new liter of another. Nothing seemed to pacify the frenzy raging inside.

Dangerous? he thought again. *How am I dangerous? Damn Angela!* He poured more bourbon down his throat. "I'll kill her," he said aloud.

He took his cell phone out of his pocket and dialed Earl.

"You've reached the law office of Earl L. Forsyth. We are

closed for the day. Our normal hours are 9:00 a.m. to 5:00 p.m. Please call back…" Alan hung up before the message could finish.

He dialed Earl's cell phone.

"Earl Forsyth," he answered after 3 rings.

"Earl. It's Alan. You know those divorce papers you keep on file?"

"Yeah."

"I need them – now!"

"I'm sorry, but I'm visiting an old college buddy. Can it wait? What's going on?"

"Nothing. I'm sick of her shit!"

"Go on…"

"She's messing with my personal life."

"She's your wife; I would think that's sort of what they do," Earl said with a wry chuckle. "I know my Natalie does."

Alan was not amused. "Truth is, I met someone."

The other end of the phone was quiet for a few moments.

"Earl? You still there?"

"Yeah, I'm still here."

"I thought I'd lost you."

"No. Who is this someone?"

"No one you know."

"Maybe I do, and you don't know it."

"Her name is Mary Stephenson. She works here at the barn."

"You're leaving Angela for some barn cat?" Earl said with an incredulous tone.

"If you were in front of me, I'd choke the life out of you!" Alan angrily growled.

"Ok, ok, I'm sorry."

"Look. I'm serious this time. I want Angela gone – out of my life for good!" He gulped from the bottle again.

"All right. So does Angela know about this Mary?"

"No."

Earl expelled an inordinate amount of air, expressing his concern. "If she does, that could be a problem."

"Why? She's screwing that Ted!" Alan exclaimed as he flung his hand, knocking a nearby beer bottle onto the floor. Glass shards and beer shot in random directions.

Alan's housekeeper, Julia, heard the bottle shatter and entered the room to clean it up before he hurt himself.

Without noticing, Alan walked through the mess and began pacing between his recording studio and bar area. The glass stuck to the bottom of his cowboy boots crunched against the hardwood floors.

"You don't know that for sure," Earl reminded him.

"Oh I'm sure!"

"But that's not enough to stand up in court. No judge will grant a divorce based on infidelity with no evidence."

Alan sighed in frustration. "Just hurry up and get me my damn papers!"

"What's the rush? Is this Mary pregnant?"

"No! I haven't laid a finger on her! I haven't cheated, so there's no cheating on my part. Just Angela's." He turned the bottle up again. *Dangerous?* he thought while he swallowed the burning liquid. *How's that even possible??*

"That's good," Earl said. "Still, this could cost you, my friend. All Angela needs is the idea of infidelity, and she could drag this divorce out for years! Heaven help you if she actually proved you had been unfaithful. She'd no doubt take you for a lot more than the 6 million your prenup guarantees her."

Alan gulped from the bottle the entire time Earl spoke. By the time he removed it from his mouth, nearly half of its contents had been consumed. Warm booze dribbled from his mouth to his goatee.

Julia presented Alan with a short, wide-bottomed drinking glass.

He brushed her off.

Nevertheless, she offered the glass to him again, this time with a stern, motherly look on her face.

Alan knew the look well and relented. The emptiness in the glass was half-replaced with bourbon.

Julia silently motioned for him to put the bottle on the bar, and take the glass.

With a loud sigh, he picked up the glass, and said into the phone, "Then give her 12, but not a dime more. I just want her *gone!*"

"All right. I'll have to re-write them to reflect the changed amount."

Exasperated, Alan said, "Fine." He sipped from the glass.

Julia victoriously smiled as she swept up the broken beer bottle mess. Making him drink from a glass seemed to at least slow down his drinking.

"What about the rest?" Earl asked.

"Yes, she can still have my hunting land. I'll even agree to build her another barn there and a house. She can take all the horses with her."

"Ok. I'll have to add that into the papers. What about alimony?"

"Alimony? Good grief! Isn't the 12 million enough?"

"I'm sure her attorney is going to fight for alimony."

"Well, let her. I'm not offering it."

"If you go ahead and offer it up front, she just might sign the papers easier," Earl suggested.

Alan sighed deeply. "Fine. She can get exactly what she's getting now."

"$250,000 a year?"

"Yes."

"For how long?"

"Two years."

"Five might encourage her to sign them faster."

"Whose attorney are you?!"

"I'm just saying, if you want her to sign the papers without an argument, you're going to have to pay. You see? Perhaps it would be best to start at the bottom and work your way up."

Alan finished the drink and headed toward the bar to refill it. "Good grief!"

"It's up to you. If you don't start at the bottom, it's probably going to cost you even more."

"Look, offer what I just said on the condition that she only gets it if she agrees without an argument. If she refuses to sign them, then we'll start back at the bottom."

"Sounds like a plan. I'll be back in town in a few weeks," Earl said.

"*A few weeks!?* I want them now!"

"Well, Peg's on a well-deserved vacation while I'm here in Arizona."

"Arizona? What are you doing there?" Alan thought of Mary and how much she loved her home state. His heart burned like the alcohol he'd poured into his stomach. Perhaps he should just go to

Arizona and get the papers from Earl. *Maybe Mary would go*, he wondered. *Of course not!* he countered. *She doesn't want to see me anymore! But if she knew how serious I am, maybe she'd think differently.*

"I told you. I'm visiting a college buddy of mine."

"Then cut it short and get your ass back here."

"I can't do that. He's got some serious legal issues that are far more important than yours."

"Earl. You're *my* attorney. Get your ass here!"

"I would. But once you cool down, you'll destroy those divorce papers like you do every time…"

"Not this time," he said with a grave tone. He placed the empty glass on the bar and poured it half-full again. "How about I come out there? I need this done right away."

"I see. Well, then, what's the rush? The judge won't even sign them for 30 days. And you'll both have to go through divorce counseling first. Besides, if I leave now, my friend will be sitting in jail for something he didn't do, and I don't want him spending even one second longer than he has to. Let me get him squared away, and then I'll come help you."

Alan sighed loudly. "Fine," he said with a definite note of exasperation at the idea. He sipped from the glass before he asked, "What did he do?"

"He didn't do it."

"Ok. What *didn't* he do?" Alan drank again.

"His wife disappeared, and now he's being blamed for her murder. But there's no body, so they can't prove she's even dead. The whole thing is just ridiculous."

"No body?"

"Yeah. From what I've found out so far, most of the evidence is circumstantial and barely even points to him. In my opinion, he should never have been arrested. It's all a witch hunt!"

"Man, that sucks." Alan took another nip and then asked, "Is there anything I can do to help?" What he really wanted to know was how he could speed the whole thing up. *Dangerous?* he questioned again.

"I'm sure he'd take a donation to help with legal fees."

"I thought that's why you're there."

"Yeah, but I don't work for free."

"He's your friend!" Alan refilled his glass, nearly to the top this time.

"So. You don't perform for free, do you?"

"Yeah! I have many times, especially for friends."

"Well, this case promises to be long and drawn-out for sure."

"Even without any evidence?"

"Oh, they have evidence. But it's just weak. I think they were simply trying to arrest somebody – anybody."

"Why doesn't he just get an Arizona attorney?" Alan flopped down on the plush Italian leather couch; the delightful aroma of the rich leather mixed with the distinct aura of bourbon, which accidentally spilled. Gently, he sucked the liquid from the top edge of the glass, and placed it on the adjacent leather-topped table.

"He will. But not just anyone will do, you know? He's an attorney, too, so he's not likely to trust just anyone. Besides, I owe him a favor."

"A favor, huh? What kind of favor?"

"He helped me fulfill a-a fantasy of sorts. Something I've always wanted to do."

"Well, then, that's all the more reason you should be doing it for free." Alan licked the bourbon off of his fingers.

"It's not like I'm going to charge him my normal rate. But I do have expenses. And then there will be the issue of bail, if he's granted bail. He has a bail hearing in a few weeks."

"Bail?"

"Yeah. The evidence they have is so flimsy, I can't imagine the judge not granting bail. The trouble is getting the bail together."

Alan took a generous swig from his glass. "If he's a friend of yours, I would think he would have no trouble making bail on his own. Don't you only associate with the fabulously wealthy?" he wryly asked.

"Not everyone has means like you. And normally he wouldn't have a problem making bail, even if it's a sizeable amount. But when you're involved in a case like this, you don't typically have access to everything you're used to having access to on the outside. Including money."

Alan reluctantly sighed.

"Look, if you help this guy out, he can hook you up with the most amazing hunting land ever! His wife is, well, I guess, *was* really close with the Indians on the Tohono O'odham reservation, and through her, he has permission to hunt out there."

"Yeah? They got good game?"

"Oh yeah! He has access to the areas protected from outsiders."

Alan nodded his head. "All right. I'll make a deal with you. I'll post the bail for this fella, if you'll get those papers to me quickly and plan a time when we can go hunting. Deal?"

"Deal. Maybe I can work on them at my hotel room and email them to Peg to get to you."

"Sounds good. Get with Greg. He'll cut you a check for whatever you need. Just keep it on the down low, ok? My image has already suffered enough from Angela's shit."

"Will do. Thanks, Alan."

"You can thank me with divorce papers and one bad-ass hunting trip!"

"Absolutely!"

Alan hung up the phone and gulped down more liquor.

He felt hot – sweaty and nasty. After assuring Julia had left, he threw off his shirt and boots, and retrieved the bottle of bourbon he'd started on. By the time he made it to the piano bench, he was down to just his boxers.

Pieces of blank sheet music lay higgledy-piggledy around the grand instrument; crumbled up balls of failures littered the far right corner of the room. He'd austerely instructed Julia not to touch them. Being surrounded by such failure forced him to continue to try.

Alan glared at the keys. His mind was filled with thoughts of Mary. It only took moments before he turned the bottle up again.

"I'll bet your daddy's real proud of you," he whispered into the empty room. He held the bottle's edge to his lips as he spoke.

You're our only hope for carrying on the Brooks name, replayed in his mind. The sound of his father's voice was as poignant and clear as if he were standing in the room with him.

"I can't, Daddy," Alan muttered.

"Can't never could, boy!" his father responded.

Alan hung his head.

"You're bringing shame on this family!" his father said.

"I don't mean to."

"The road to hell is paved with good intentions. Get off your backside and do something!"

Alan stood up from the piano bench. Like a robot, he retrieved his granddad's violin, tucked it under his chin, and closed his eyes. The delicate rhythm of the bow vibrated under his skillful fingers. The violin's melody was soulful, gentle – pure.

In his mind, he could see his granddad's weathered smile as he waltzed with his grandma while young Alan played. The love shining in their eyes made him want to play music forever. Their joy couldn't be matched. If he could only bring that kind of feeling to everyone he played for, he could never want for more. Yet, here he was, 35 years old, disillusioned with music, and wanting so much more than his empty soul contained. He never got to see the love in his fans' eyes – just the fanaticism. Mary was his only hope at something more, and now she was gone.

Without missing a beat, he delicately and with precision shifted straight into a melancholy song his granddad had written and taught Alan to play. Between the crisp notes, the violin cried the tears Alan kept locked inside. The tears he couldn't let himself cry without accepting defeat. The tears of his bitter failure as a Brooks man. The tears that the Brooks name would die with him.

The abundant amount of alcohol he'd guzzled was creeping up on him. Even his notes seemed slurred. He wanted to be better. To be everything Mary could ever want in a man. Instead she had called him dangerous and cast him out. What did that mean?

With a screech across the strings, he stopped.

"Dangerous," he repeated. "Puh. I'm no more dangerous than a butterfly!"

As he packed up the violin, his mind thought of Mary's hauntingly stormy eyes. Their image flashed before him. He was rarely if ever afraid of anything, but what he saw in her eyes made his heart hesitate to beat. What was it? What was it that was so disturbing?

He fervently wanted to be with her – just being in the same room as she gave him peace. Certainly he could give her the same kind of peace. "We need each other. We're both just butterflies caught in life's storm, but together, there's peace." He drank a long drink from his bourbon bottle, leaving only about a third of it left.

"Of course!" he shouted before he'd swallowed all of the whiskey in his mouth, causing it to dribble down his bare chest.

He could feel the effects of the alcohol seeping into his motor skills as he staggered back to the piano bench. Briefly, his bottom lip listlessly hung from his teeth. What was he there to do?

Limply his hands flopped onto the piano keys; the instrument responded with a disjointed sound. Warm liquor dribbled down his goatee.

His every thought fixated on Mary; there was an appeal about her that he could neither deny nor resist. He couldn't articulate exactly what it was – the fact that he couldn't have her, her aloofness, her sad and tempestuous eyes, her infectious laughter – none of those seemed strong enough to justify her appeal, and yet collectively, they all made him want her more. Many times he'd sit at his piano thinking of her and trying unsuccessfully to put into words just how she made him feel whenever she was near him, yet once he thought he had something written, he always realized how insignificant it was. This time, it was there, delightfully out stretched before him.

What was it again? he asked himself.

"Butterflies," he said aloud. "Butterflies in the storm of life. The storm of trouble. The dangerous storm. The delicate butterfly and the vicious storm. Two extremes," he said as he brainstormed.

His fingers danced lightly on the keys. The instrument responded exactly as he anticipated it would – gently, thoughtfully, mournfully.

"I see the storm raging
In those eyes of yours.
Tears you won't cry
Fear you ignore," he sang.

His heart longed to have Mary sitting on the leather sofa, just as she'd done the day it snowed. He closed his eyes and envisioned her there beside him – her slight frame sitting with her legs crossed; her happy green eyes scanning the pages of his childhood; her prominent cheek bones highlighted by her generous smile; her delightful laughter filling the room as she looked through his family's photo albums.

Alan tried to emulate the sound of her laughter through the music he played and the sounds of her delicate sighs hidden between the notes he gently stroked.

The melody came as naturally to him as if it were ordered by every feeling in his heart. His fingers automatically sensed exactly where they should go next. As if on cue, his mind filled in lyrics.

Lyrics about a butterfly trapped in the storms of a life, and everything keeping her from escaping.

As he played what he initially thought was the final note, he realized, "We're all just butterflies in the storm. Trying to hold on. Trying to fly to safety."

He added a final piece that included such a sentiment.

Alan played the last note of the song. "Wow," he whispered. "That's it."

Immediately he stood up from the piano to record what he'd just played and sang, but it was then that the profuse amounts of alcohol he'd consumed made the room spin wildly out of control. The acoustic paneling lining the walls of his studio became a jumbled blur before his eyes.

He staggered as he brushed back sheets of blank sheet music to reveal his microphone. He had to record the song as quickly as he could before he forgot it. "Butterflies in the Storm," he said into the microphone.

Wobbling unsteadily, he sat back down on the piano bench and began playing and singing, but he only recorded a few bars before his thoughts succumbed to the massive amount of alcohol he'd consumed. The numbness he'd so desperately wanted had arrived, yet much too soon.

CHAPTER 13

Two and a half weeks had passed since Mary had thrown Alan out of her cabin. Despite all of Alan's desperate attempts to get her attention, he remained rebuffed.

It didn't help that the song he thought he'd written for her, he couldn't remember but bits and pieces of. He'd spent a week in Nashville trying to recreate the song he was so passionate about, but was unsuccessful.

His producer, Josh, this time was adamant and demanded Alan let go of the song and release the album. Reluctantly, Alan acquiesced. He simply didn't care anymore. Nothing mattered more than Mary.

Between Mary's rejection and his music's rejection, he was low. Lower than low. On his first day back at home, he spent the entire day and night sitting completely despondent and slumped on the plush leather sofa in his studio.

Julia had tried unsuccessfully to get him to eat something, but Alan showed no interest in food. His self-loathing was evident by the nearly-empty bottle resting in his hand and the several completely empty bottles littering the floor around him. Every time Julia tried to clean them up, he vehemently demanded she leave them.

Angela took this opportunity to have her way with him. Slowly she crept into the studio, dressed in a skimpy red silk G-string teddy while wearing thigh-high patent leather boots. It was Alan's favorite look.

"Hi Sweetheart," she whispered in his ear from behind the

couch. "You down here all alone?"

"Yeah," Alan muttered.

"Want some company?" Angela breathlessly asked, but didn't wait for an answer.

Alan sat numbly.

Angela sparkled from head to toe. Her blonde hair was swept up to expose her elegant neck. Her hips swayed from side to side as she smoothly walked to the other side of the couch. She smelled lightly of Chanel No. 5 and moved in a sensual, seductive way. When she tried, she could be the most elegant, appealing woman Alan had ever seen.

Stopping in front of him, she straddled his leg and leaned toward him. Her blue eyes spoke volumes without saying a word.

Alan only stared past her. His mouth gapped listlessly open.

"Do you see anything you like?" she said with a sultry smile. Without waiting for a response, Angela squatted down on Alan's leg and planted a delicate, red-lipstick kiss on his bottom lip.

In an instant, he was rudely awakened. "What the…," he said with a start. "Get off me!"

"What?! Why??"

"What the hell are you doin'?" he said with a thick tongue. He was drunk, but not drunk enough to forget.

"I want my husband."

"Yeah, right." He stood up and staggered to the empty bar, finishing off the bottle in his hand as we went.

His butler, Gus, and the other servants had raided his bar while Alan wasn't looking. Gus took his job very seriously. As low as Alan was, Gus kept all of the staff on alert. The bottles that Gus allowed in the bar, he watered down significantly.

Alan rummaged fruitlessly through the empty shelves and cabinets for something more to drink.

Angela scowled. *I'm going to have to do something extreme,* she thought. *But what?* She strutted around the studio, hoping Alan would catch a glimpse of her.

Angela looked at all the bottles on the floor. *That much alcohol could kill a horse,* she thought. *But even that's not working. Hmmm,* she thought as she tapped a long bright red nail against her prominent chin. She spied him staring at her; a seductive smile graced her ruby lips. Her feet carried her directly to him. "Come on, baby, you know you want me."

"Angela. We're separated," he apathetically said. "There's a reason for that."

"And I'm saying I still want you."

"But I don't want you. I've had enough of you," he said while steadying himself on the granite bar. "Earl is working on divorce papers. I can't do this anymore."

"What?! Are you insane? Do you really think I'm going to sign them??"

"Yes. I'll be more than generous. We've just got to admit there's nothing left for us anymore."

"I would never break up our family!"

"We don't have any children, you know?"

"I cannot believe you'd say that! Our child just turned over in his grave!"

"I think he'd want us to be happy. And neither of us has been happy for years." He found a hidden fifth of bourbon, twisted the cap off, and turned it up.

"This isn't over, Alan! You're just drunk."

"I'm not drunk. But I can assure you, this," he motioned between him and her with the opened bottle, "isn't happening."

"I'll never agree to a divorce!"

"I don't really care," he said as he walked away from the bar and down the hallway to his bedroom.

Angrily, she growled and stomped up the stairs, fuming mad. By the time she got up to her room, she had Ted already on the phone.

"Look, I've already talked to Vince. He said he'll do it," Ted said of his jockey friend.

"At this point, I'm willing to let him!"

"He said it would cost $50,000, which I thought wouldn't be too hard for you to come by."

"Fine. I'll see about getting the money to you," she said and then threw her cell phone on the bed. "Damn Alan. Damn his stupid ass!"

The next morning, a sullen Alan sat alone at the breakfast table. His blood-shot eyes were glued on the barn outside the picture window. Occasionally, he nursed a cup of strong, black coffee. His brief moment of sleep was disturbed with a realistic dream that troubled him.

Over and over in his dream, he saw Mary screaming as she ran away; he wasn't exactly sure what the significance was, but the whole idea haunted him. Was it some kind of warning message to him that Mary was truly frightened by him?

Maybe it was showing him exactly how strong his feelings for her had morphed, or how difficult it was trying to come to the realization that she didn't feel the same. If he could only get her attention and talk to her, he felt certain they could work things out. It was simply killing him that she didn't want to see him anymore.

His head ached, but he didn't seem to care. He wished his coffee had some bourbon in it or something. He longed to feel the numbness of acceptance, yet his soul wouldn't let him give her up. It felt as if the other half of his very existence was gone. He loved her too much to walk away. The only numbness he could find was in the bottom of several bottles of liquor, and even that wasn't enough.

His mind tormented his soul by replaying Mary's words over and over again: "You're t-too dangerous. You're a rapist."

A rapist? How absurd! he thought. *I'd never do something like that! There must be something more to it. But what?* The only conclusion he ever could come to was that she was afraid he would hurt her, but hadn't he already proven the opposite was true? He'd protected her from Cliff; he'd do anything in the world for her. But how could he prove it to her? How would she know for sure that the pure and genuine feelings he had were unlike anything he'd ever experienced? *She won't have anything to do with me,* he thought. His repeated texts and phone calls went unanswered. The fear that he'd miss a possible text from her was the only thing keeping him from smashing his cell phone to bits.

"You never did tell me how your last trip to Nashville was," Angela interrupted his thoughts as she sat down to the table with her newspaper in hand.

What was she doing there? he thought. He hadn't noticed she was even nearby. "Too long," he didn't give much thought to his reply.

"Really? Why?"

"I get tired of having to deal with all the mess." He drank some of his coffee without moving his eyes from the picture window. The barn's activities played out as if the window were a large television. "I came closer than ever to telling them to take all this and shove it."

"You've got to be kidding!"

"But in the end, we reached a compromise," he said.

"Well I'm glad about that! You can't walk away." She could hardly believe he was contemplating such a thing; she wondered how much a thought like that was Mary's fault. If he walked away from recording and performing, the money would stop! *Stupid little hussy!* Angela thought of Mary. *Yes, killing him is the right thing to do after all.*

"Sometimes I sure would like to." He mindlessly looked down at his coffee cup. The hustle and bustle at the barn hadn't produced even a glimpse of Mary. "We finished the CD."

"That's good!" Angela replied with a faux sense of cheer. *Then again, maybe not.*

"Yeah. In the end, I'm the one who had to compromise, though."

"Well, compromise is good."

"I guess," he said as he drank from his mug.

"Well," Angela said with a seductive smile, "I, for one, am glad you're home. I missed you while you were gone."

Alan raised his eyebrows in disbelief. "What? That's twice in ten years you've said you missed me. Is it me that you miss or my money?"

"You, of course! Are you so surprised?"

"Actually, yeah," he said with a confused smile. He turned from the window and leaned back in his chair with his coffee mug in his hand. "There's nothing to miss, Angela. We're over. Earl will have the papers ready any day now. As soon as he does, he's sending them to Peg for me to sign. You might as well know," he said, repeating what he'd already told her the night prior. He had only a foggy recollection of what they'd talked about before.

Angela became an award-winning actress. "What?? You're divorcing me??" she practically shrieked with tears welling in her eyes.

"Yes. You had to know it was coming."

"No! What brought this on? I've been trying everything imaginable to make up with you, to make you happy, and you... you go and do... this??"

"Angela. Don't be so melodramatic. I'll generously provide for you. I'm just tired of it all. I want out. We both deserve the chance to be happy."

"But... but... I love you."

"Honestly, I wish that did it for me. And this time last year, it probably would have. But not anymore. I'm done. I can't do this anymore."

Angela's lip trembled as her eyes poured out her tears.

Alan abruptly interrupted any impending manipulative, tear-filled fit. "I'll talk to you about this later. I'm going to visit my mother." He stood up; turning back, he said, "Look, I'm being more than generous in the papers. Once I get them, you can have your lawyer check them out or whatever, but it's over." Without another word, he put his hat on his head as his cowboy boots shuffled across the mahogany floors and retreated back downstairs.

Her face instantly changed to one of complete anger. She could hardly believe his divorce talk wasn't just some drunken ramblings. He was actually divorcing her! "Damn Mary!" she growled. "It's all *her* fault! No trashy tramp of a stable hand is going to steal from me!"

Methodically, she drummed her fingers on the table, deep in thought. *So the new CD is coming out after all. That will equal millions! No. Killing him now won't be good at all. He's got to promote it, and how will he if he's dead?* she thought. *But, if I can seduce him....* Slowly she began to nod. "Yes, I'll just go back to the original plan. Mmm, this will be deliciously sweet!" she whispered. "No one messes with me – no one." She smiled devilishly.

Julia quietly appeared and removed Alan's half-empty coffee mug from the table.

In a moment of inspiration, Angela quickly trotted off to her purse and retrieved her cell phone. Desperate times called for desperate measures. She was going to make Alan stay with her even if it took nailing his feet to the floor!

"Ted, Darling. I need you to find me some of that date-rape drug you were talking about. It's time to take this whole thing up a notch!"

"But I thought you were hiring Vince..."

"Change of plans," she interrupted him.

CHAPTER 14

Alan's lips pursed as he walked downstairs. Breaking the news to Angela about their impending divorce felt right, but it wasn't enough. His mother, no doubt, would chastise him for not making his marriage work, and then there was Mary. Life without her was empty – pointless. He had to get her back, but how?

"God I want a beer!" he grumbled to himself as he cleaned himself up for a visit to his mother at the nursing home. If he showed up with beer on his breath, he knew all too well she'd smack him on the back of his head with whatever she had handy, like she'd done many times before, so he waited.

In short order, he climbed into his Viper, put the top down, and zipped out of the garage. Briefly, he stopped, put his Wayfarers on, and watched the goings on at the barn. His eyes quickly spied Mary leading a horse with Ted leading a horse also.

"What the hell...?" he said as he watched the two mount their horses and begin riding toward the trail leading to the other pastures. Enraged suspicion boiled beneath his skin. *What is she doing with him?* consumed his thoughts.

He reached into his jacket pocket to get his cell phone to have Johe or Marcus follow them, only to realize, with an aggravated growl, that in his drunken stupor he'd forgotten to charge it the night prior. He plugged it into his car charger. Every ounce of him wanted to command someone to follow them and find out what they were doing and saying.

His mind replayed the feeling of her kisses on his lips; he

couldn't recall a time when he wanted someone as badly as he wanted her. The idea that she could or would share her lips with Ted made him slam the car in park and get out. Was Ted moving on from Angela to Mary? He had to say something – but what? He paced outside of the trembling car, watching.

What was going on? Jealousy rattled his brain and kept him from thinking as clearly as he would've liked. His mind was totally enraptured with the feeling of Mary's tender lips upon his and wondering if she would kiss Ted the same way. Would Ted try something with her?

His muscles flexed as he tried to keep himself from moving farther than a few steps away from the car. If he started walking away from the car, he couldn't be responsible for what he'd do to Ted. The knowledge that Mary would be unequivocally angry at him for such a thing was the only thing keeping him at the anxious car.

"Just get in the damned car," he growled at himself. "She doesn't want you!"

His words were like daggers to his heart. Surely he was wrong. Surely she still wanted him.

He spun tires as he sped down the driveway.

Mary and Ted immediately turned to look toward the source of the sound.

She closed her eyes. *He saw,* she thought of her riding with Ted, *and he's pissed.*

Tires squalled when he pulled onto Brooks River Road; the car's engine roared as he tore down the street.

In no time, he pulled into the parking lot of the local florist. He hung his head for a moment before looking straight ahead. "You've got to pull your shit together," he told himself before he got out of the car.

Upon entering the store, he greeted Ruth, the owner, with a false sense of cheer, "Hiya Sweetheart."

"Good morning, Mr. Brooks. How are you this fine morning?"

"Doing fine. I'm heading off to see my mother; could you hook me up with a couple dozen pink roses, and give me a couple dozen or so loosies too?"

"Sure thing. How's your mama doing?"

"Good, good. You know how she is, though. She doesn't want to be in the nursing home, but she doesn't want me to hire a nurse to take care of her at home either."

Ruth arranged the flowers. "Didn't you try it anyway?"

"Oh yeah, I tried it for months. I went through practically every nurse available. She either fired them or they quit." Alan smiled; he loved his mom's fiery spirit. "She's such an independent thing."

"Well, the apple didn't fall far from the tree, you know?"

Alan laughed out loud, "That's the truth."

"How's Mrs. Brooks doing?"

Alan's first thought was of his mother, but then he realized she was talking about Angela. "Oh, Angela's fine. You know, same stuff, different day."

"I heard she was getting a new batch of horses from Brazil or something."

"No, ma'am. I made her send those suckers back! When I found out that they had to be quarantined for months, I put my foot down."

"Quarantined?"

"Yeah. It takes a long time, and is outrageously expensive."

"I'm sure."

"The trouble is she's got champagne taste on my beer budget."

Ruth laughed as she added baby's breath to the arrangement. "If yours is a beer budget, then I'll take beer any day!"

Alan returned her laughter. "Well, it is when she spends like she does. You know that old saying, 'if you have a thousand, it takes fifteen hundred.'"

"Oh and I suppose you don't spend money, huh?" she said jokingly to him.

"No, ma'am, not at all."

Ruth smiled a knowing smile, "Uh-huh, sure you don't. I seen that new car you're driving. What kind is that?"

"Oh! It's a Dodge Viper."

"American made, eh? It didn't *look* American made."

"I know, but you know my daddy would turn over in his grave if I bought something foreign!"

"Don't I know it! If we don't buy American, who will?"

"Yes, ma'am!"

"I heard you and Mrs. Brooks were separated."

"Yes, ma'am, we are."

"I'm sorry to hear that. It's a sad day when marriages die," she commented with a friendly smile. "Well, here you are. Tell both Mrs. Brookses I said hello and to take care."

"Will do." Alan paid for the flowers and returned to his car. His nerves remained on edge as he drove across town to the nursing home.

"Hi Miss Daria!" he greeted the head nurse.

"Why hiya, Mr. Brooks; how're ya doin'?" Daria asked him.

Alan leaned over the counter and gave her a kiss on the cheek. "This is for you, Darlin'," he said, oozing charm as he handed her a single, pink rose.

"Thank you. Your mama sure did raise you right! Such a shame you ain't single."

"There's plenty of me to go around," he said as he flashed his best, dimpled smile.

"You're just a mess and a half!" she said with a coy laugh, smelling her rose.

As Alan walked through the nursing home, he gave roses to every female resident and nurse he came across until he reached his mother's room. He entered singing, *Run for the Roses*, his mother's favorite Dan Fogelberg song.

His mother was sitting in a wheelchair near the television, watching *All in the Family* reruns. Her long, white hair was pulled back tightly into a bun on the back of her head. Her features were withered with age, but her eyes were still bright blue, the same as Alan's.

Alan adored her and doted on her as much as he could; Angela loathed her and could hardly stand to be in the same room. When Alan first started touring a lot, Angela and Fiona lived together in the main house. Fiona was convinced Angela wasn't good enough for her son, and Angela was flatly sick of hearing how everything she did was wrong and not "how we all do it."

"Junior!" Fiona said, enthusiastic to see him. She rarely called him by his given name; to her, Alan was his father, even though he'd been gone for many years. "Where've you been, boy?"

"Working, Mama." He softly kissed her on the cheek and then presented the flowers to her.

"They're simply beautiful, son!" Her face was aglow at his presence. "It's so good to see you. How're things going?"

"Fine. Where do you want me to put these?" he asked about the flowers.

"Put them up there on the table next to the TV. I want to be able to see them all the time. They are truly beautiful. Did you get them from Ruth's?" She pushed power on the remote control, turning the TV off.

"Yes, ma'am," Alan said as he followed her instructions.

"Come here and sit by me. It's so good seeing you. You been traveling a lot?"

"No, ma'am, not a lot. I've been writing and just finished up my next album."

"Then why haven't you been to see me more often?"

"I told you, Mama, I've been working..."

"I know why. It's that Angela, isn't it?"

"No, ma'am. Don't start with Angela again. She loves you; you know that."

"No, I don't. She's nothing but a conniving Jezebel! She only married you for your money," she grumbled her repetitive complaint. "Thank God you can't have any of the Brooks money until I die!"

"Mama, please don't talk like that!" He kissed her hand. "I don't want you getting all upset."

"You know, if you'd make that woman give you some children, that'd settle her down!"

Alan ignored her jab about no children; he was certain she had no idea how much it hurt him. If she only knew that there was a tiny grave out in the Brooks' cemetery, she'd understand how much her words hurt.

"How've you been? Have they been treating you well?" he asked trying to be a good son. His lips longed for a strong drink.

"No. I want to go home. Take me home with you, please!" she begged.

"You know I can't do that." He looked at her sympathetically. Telling her no again was like sending a spear right through his heart.

"They treat me like I'm a prisoner here!" she grumbled.

"What do they do to you?"

"They won't let me smoke."

"I know that; I told them not to."

"Now why would you do something like that?!"

"Because it's bad for you."

"It's my body, you know?" She started to go off on him, but

was suddenly distracted. "What happened to your lip?"

"Oh this? I told you about this."

"No you didn't," she insisted.

Alan was certain he'd told her the last time he visited. He worried about her memory. "Oh, well I didn't do anything. I just cut it."

"Doing what?"

"Nothing. I heard Selma Beck passed last week," he said with an obvious attempt to point her toward the local gossip. The last thing he needed was his mother's chastisement added onto Mary's rejection and the issues with his music.

"Yeah, I heard that too. Paper said she had cancer."

"Cancer? The paper didn't say that."

"Well, it didn't come right out and say it was cancer, but the obituary said in lieu of flowers to send donations to the American Cancer Society. That usually means she had cancer."

"Do you know what kind?"

"I don't know. I'll ask Agnes. You know how she is, she knows everything." Fiona's brilliant eyes gave him a skeptical once over. "You've lost weight. Aren't you eating? That fancy chef Angela insisted upon having isn't feeding you right, is he?"

"He's doing fine. I've just been too busy to worry about eating much lately."

"You've got to eat. Have you been drinking?"

"No, ma'am."

"Come here. Let me smell your breath."

Alan grinned and closed his eyes. He was glad to be completely sober as she performed her breath test.

"All right. You haven't been drinking today, but I can tell you've been drinking. A lot too."

He softly chuckled. "How do you know?"

"I can smell it on you."

"How can you smell it? I haven't had even a sip today. Just coffee."

"A mother knows," she said with a confident grin. She didn't give him a chance to change the subject again before she returned to the topic of his lip. "Now tell me what you did to that lip."

"Nothing, Mama, I cut it is all."

"I know that, son; *how* did you cut it? You weren't sky diving again, were you?"

"No, no. I'm not sure how I cut it; I just did."

"Were you drinking?" She looked at him with a knowing look on her face.

"Yes, ma'am." Although he'd often tried to get away with lying to her, he never could, so most of the time he could only reconstruct the truth to suit his needs. Out-right lying to her only produced negative results.

She smacked him on the back of his head with a nearby magazine she'd rolled up. "What did I tell you about that? You know alcoholism runs rampant in our family; why would you do that to yourself?"

"I didn't mean to."

"Oh hogwash! Of course you meant to! You're going to sit there and lie to me telling me you didn't *mean* to get drunk?" she asked incredulously. "Or are you saying you didn't mean to get *that* drunk?"

Alan only hung his head. It was tough being around someone who knew him so well.

"Where was Marcus during all of this?"

"I don't know where he was," Alan answered as if he were a child.

Fiona frowned. "You need to get rid of that boy! He's nothing but an overpaid nuisance! He's supposed to be taking care of you and keeping you out of trouble."

"He is."

"It doesn't seem like it. Julia seems to be doing a better job than Marcus. Why isn't Angela at least taking good care of you?"

"She is...," as soon as the words left his lips, he knew she'd know it was a lie.

"Hmm, I find that hard to believe. You look like you haven't slept in a week; you're losing weight again, and I know you're still drinking a lot more than you're letting on. Why don't you tell me what's got you so down?"

"It's nothing," he said, *that I can talk about right now*, he thought.

"How much have you been traveling?"

"Not much lately. I've been at home a lot the past six months or so."

"How are you and Angela getting along?"

"Fine."

"You're lying through your teeth again." She smacked his shoulder with the same rolled-up magazine. "You're still gallivanting all over the place for your football games and your crazy attempts to kill yourself, aren't you?"

Alan scoffed. "Of course!" he said, as if any other option was totally ridiculous.

"Junior, how are you ever going to give me a grandchild if you're never home and you're always fighting?"

There was her low-blow again about children. "I promise I'm home more now than I've ever been." He didn't mention that Mary was the main reason he was home so much.

"Uh-huh," she said with disbelief.

"Mama, I have to work. Even Daddy would say that."

"I know you do." Fiona placed her frail hands on either side of his face. "Junior, I know you're trying, but don't forget the importance of keeping your wife happy, even if she is someone as impossible as Angela."

"I know, but it's hard when I don't know what to do to make her happy."

She took her hands off of his face. "Well, traveling all the time and running away isn't the answer."

"I know, and I really have cut back a lot. But now Angela's the one who's always gone."

"Is she cheating on you?" Fiona's blue eyes stared right through him.

Alan felt like someone had just knocked the breath out of him as he struggled to answer. He stood up and moved to the window. The view of the pond near the nursing home was framed by Fiona's window. How could he answer her? After all this time of hiding it, he realized he wasn't completely sure he cared if Angela were cheating.

"I asked you a question, boy!" Fiona said, impatient for a response.

"I-I-I don't know," he finally sputtered out.

"I think I'd be finding out if I were you." She leaned on her elbow. "If she should get pregnant, you'd want to be sure that youngin's a Brooks! You need to call ole Sonny and have him hire someone to follow her."

"No, ma'am, we've been through this enough already. Sonny is Chief of Police now. He doesn't do that kind of work anymore."

"I'm not trying to meddle in your business, I'm just saying, you need to know."

"I'm not so sure I want to know," he whispered.

"Speak up, son, I can't hear you when you mumble!" she exclaimed as she tapped her hand on the armrest of her wheelchair.

"Yes, ma'am. I said, 'I will.'" He sighed. "I just finished my album, so I'll be going on tour soon. I'll call Sonny when I get back."

Fiona gave him a look out of the corner of her eye; she knew he was only placating her, but she wasn't going to let on. "Son, I'm not going to tell you how to run your life. You're a grown man, now. But, you better find out what's going on before then, huh?"

"Yes, ma'am."

"Have that new lawyer – what his name?"

"Earl Forsyth."

"Yes, Forsyth. Have him do it. Is he still your attorney?"

"Yes, ma'am."

"I still don't understand why you stopped using Adamson Fouche. He always took care of our business. I don't know anything about this Forsyth fella or any of his kin. He's not from here is he?"

"No, ma'am."

"Humph," she puckered her lips as if she'd bitten off of a sour lemon. "Your daddy would never use some outside stranger."

"Mama, Adamson retired; I couldn't use him anymore. Earl's not so bad. He took over Adamson's practice."

"So Adamson knows him?"

Alan didn't know if Earl and Adamson knew each other on any other level than business. "I don't know."

"Well, he had to have known him some."

"I think Earl just bought Adamson's practice and all the clients Adamson had."

"Yeah, well," Fiona grumbled. "Did you write all the songs on this new album?" she asked, trying to change the subject to something that wouldn't make him so obviously uncomfortable.

"Yes, ma'am," he replied with a smile.

"Why don't you sing me some of it?"

Alan was apprehensive. "Well, we haven't…"

"Oh come on, boy, I'm not going to be around forever. Sing for me."

"I don't have my guitar with me."

"Stop making excuses."

"Yes, ma'am." He breathed in a deep breath and began singing one of the songs he'd written long before he'd met Mary.

"That's a nice song, Junior. Is that going to be your first single?"

Alan didn't feel necessarily proud of any of the songs he'd written before he met Mary. "I don't know. I guess that will be up to Ben and Josh," he said about his agent and producer. *They have all the power anyway*, he thought.

"How're things going at the farm?"

"Fine. Everything's just fine."

"Johe still around?"

"Yes'm, she's still around."

"She still chasing the fellas like she's some 20-year-old hussy?"

"Oh come on, she doesn't do that!" he said with a heart-felt laugh.

"Uh-huh. You're just too blind to see it is all. You need to watch that one; she's a cougar! Mark my words."

"You don't even know what a cougar is."

"You think I don't know? I watch TV; I know things. It's about all I can do around here."

"Whatever." He picked up the remote control but didn't turn the television on. After a marked moment of silence between them, Alan asked, "Mama, why was I an only child?"

"What?" she said shocked by his question.

"How come you and Daddy didn't have any more children?"

"'Cause we didn't want any more. You and your daddy were handful enough!" She smiled as she thought of the two of them, "Y'all were like two peas in a pod."

"I…," he started, but stopped.

After a long respite, Fiona asked, "Why do you want to know?"

"I don't know."

"Yes you do, or you wouldn't have asked."

He drew in a sharp breath; disclosing the pressure he felt to have children wouldn't help. "No, it doesn't matter." He picked up her tiny hand and kissed it gently.

"You're the spitting image of your daddy," she said with a sweet smile.

"Thank you." If that were true, was the love he felt for Mary the same self-sacrificing love his dad had felt for his mom? He'd thought so often about the situation between him and Angela, and it never felt as noble as his father's love for his mother. More often than not, Alan's situation made him feel resentful and hateful toward Angela.

But with Mary, he felt powerless to resist her. His mission in life seemed to be to protect her, provide for her, and be with her. He wanted nothing more than to spend the rest of his life holding her hand.

"I don't feel like I'm anything like Daddy."

"Of course you are, son. You and Alan were like peas and carrots. You had your own ideas, and your daddy had his, but in the end, there were no two people on this earth more alike than y'all. I guess that's why y'all butted heads."

"Yeah, I guess. It's just that Daddy was such a good man. I just don't measure up."

"Of course you do! He'd be so proud of you if he were still alive."

Alan sharply exhaled a scoff through his nose. He wanted so badly to be more like his father – strong, noble, faithful – yet, he never felt that way. Mary at least gave him hope that he could be. Angela never gave him the chance.

Looking at his mother's ocean blue eyes, his conscience begged him to confess everything to her and ask for her wisdom and guidance. "Mama?" he asked. "What if me and Angela divorced?"

Fiona sighed deeply. "You know we don't believe in that kind of thing."

"I know. But how bad would it be if I just admitted I made a mistake and walked away?"

She shook her head and looked down. "You know how I feel about Angela, and it pains me to say this, but you've got to honor your vows. You made them before God."

"Well, not really. We got married in Vegas. I'm not sure God frequents Vegas." Alan tried to make light of the situation.

"Still, you promised to love her forever."

Alan didn't respond.

"You do still love her, don't you?"

Alan sat silent. He wasn't sure he ever really loved her. Love wasn't anything with which he had honest experience – except how he felt about Mary.

"I asked you a question."

"I don't know. I'm not sure I ever loved her. The real her. You know?"

"I understand. Still, you made a vow; you're a Brooks, and Brooks men are men of their word." Fiona's request that he honor his vows seemed almost the same as saying he could never see Mary again. His heart felt like it was imploding at the thought. He didn't like himself very much when Angela was around, but Mary – she was a different story – she made him feel alive, virile, and most of all, needed.

"You thinking about divorcing her?"

"Yes, ma'am."

Fiona sighed deeply. As much as she hated Angela, she believed in familial pride, too. "Then let me ask you something."

"Yes, ma'am?"

"Is there another woman?"

Her words felt like rocks bouncing off his head. How could he answer? If he lied to her, she'd know he was lying. But if he told her about Mary, he feared she'd never accept her as her daughter-in-law. So he did the one thing he hadn't done since Ted's arrival in Georgia, "I think Angela is having an affair." The words weren't nearly as hard to say as he thought they would've been.

"Really?" Fiona shifted her fragile body in her wheelchair. "I just asked you that earlier. Why didn't you tell me then?"

Alan returned to the window. The trees outside clapped their hands in the gentle breeze, as if even they were cheering that he'd finally admitted it. "I don't know."

"Are you sure there isn't someone else you've got your eye on and you're just now saying you think Angela's cheating on you so I'll approve of the new girl?"

He softly sighed. She knew him so well. "We haven't been getting along for a long time. We're separated now. Things haven't gotten any better."

"Make that woman give you a child!"

"Mama! I can't do that! Besides, I wouldn't want to bring a child into the mess we have made of our marriage. It wouldn't be fair to the kid."

"Hogwash! A woman changes dramatically after she has a

youngin'.'"

"No, Mama. I don't want a child with Angela," he said as he turned to look at his mother. In that moment, he let go of his and Angela's the child. The truth was, he didn't *want* a child with Angela. Even that child would've been a disaster. For the first time, he felt relieved that Angela had had a miscarriage. A child with Mary would be a completely different story.

"Tell me about this girl."

"What girl?"

"You know what girl. I'm not dumb. Sit down over here and tell me her name," she demanded.

Alan grinned, shook his head, and did as his mother instructed. "Her name is Mary."

"Mary, huh? Where'd you meet her?"

"She works on the farm."

Fiona's lips pursed, on the edge of disapproval. "Who are her kin?"

"She's not from here."

"Where's she from?"

"Arizona."

"Is she a Mexican girl?"

"No. She's white."

"That's good," Fiona said.

"I wouldn't care if she was. I wouldn't care if she was purple with green polka dots."

"You're in love with her, huh?"

Alan nodded. "Yes, ma'am. I am."

"So that's why you want to divorce Angela, huh?"

"No. Our marriage was over long before I met Mary. I've been holding on just for the family's sake, but I'm miserable with Angela."

"And this Mary makes you happy?"

"Yes, ma'am. Happier than I've ever been in my life. It's just Angela. She's the problem."

"Is she a gold digger, like Angela?"

"Definitely not."

"But how do you know?"

"I just do. She won't even let me buy her anything."

"Nothing? No gifts or anything?"

"Nope. Nothing. We spent Valentine's Day together going

muddin'. How many gold-diggers would do that?"

"Did you get her something for Valentine's?"

"No, ma'am. She told me not to, and said she doesn't celebrate it. She said if someone loves her, then every day should be Valentine's Day."

"Good girl." Fiona noticed the happy look on his face that thoughts of Mary brought to him, yet somewhere behind it, she saw a hidden pain. With a deep breath, she said, "Then, son, walk away. If you don't love Angela enough to have children with her, walk away. Sometimes you have to be man enough to know when to quit. There are times when no amount of effort is going to make a marriage work, which makes a divorce inevitable. Sounds like this is one of those times. Let me know what you need, and I'll help you."

Alan smiled; his dimples embraced his lips. "Thank you," he said as he knelt before her. "I couldn't do it without your blessing."

"Of course you could! You're a grown man."

"I know. But I still have a healthy respect for my mama. I don't want to disappoint you. You're the only family I've got left."

"You've got Aunt Kymber out there in Washington state."

"I haven't seen Aunt Kymber since I was a little boy."

Fiona chuckled. "Yeah, she still isn't speaking to me ever since I disapproved of her new man. I still say that man is as slick as eel snot!"

Alan didn't want to hear the whole story again, so he changed the subject as quickly as he could. "Daddy really loved you, didn't he?"

"Yes, he sure did. Ours was a love like none other! We could just look at each other without saying a word and he knew everything I wanted to say. Not many folks can do that these days."

"That's the kind of love I want."

"That's the kind of love everyone wants! But it doesn't just fall out of the sky. You have to work for it. You have to fight for it day in and day out. It doesn't just happen."

"All Angela and I do is fight."

"Don't you think me and your daddy fought our fair share?"

"I never saw y'all fight."

"We didn't fight in front of you. He used to drink like a fish! And my goodness would we fight about it!"

"I don't remember Daddy drinking."

"You wouldn't. He quit when you were still young."

"What made him quit?"

"Junior, don't make me go into it."

"Please? I need to know," Alan begged as he moved to the seat he'd sat in when he first arrived.

Fiona's kind eyes relented. "You were just a toddler. Your daddy and his friends would be at the house all the time drinking, smoking, shooting pool, picking guitar, and whooping it up! This one time, you picked up one of the fella's glasses of moonshine. And you drank some of it. I don't know why you did; the stuff tasted just like kerosene to me, but there you were, little Alan drinking homemade shine. I was so angry! I packed our bags that night and moved out!

"Since Alan was rip-roaring drunk, he barely noticed we were gone. After a spell, he sobered up and realized what had happened. Wait. That's not right. I think Gus sobered him up and told him we'd left. Julia insisted upon going with us, and I'm sure Gus wasn't happy having his wife gone." Fiona chuckled lightly before she spoke again.

"To hear Alan tell the story, he'd tell you Gus smacked his face until he came to so Alan would go get Gus's wife back. But, Gus tells quite a different story. No matter. The point is when Alan realized you and I had gone, and why we'd gone, the drink suddenly wasn't quite as appealing to him anymore.

"Gus said he tore out of there like he was running the Daytona 500! But I wasn't coming back so easily. I wanted all that booze gone from the house. Every drop of it – including the shine! As it turned out, he went even one step further. He tore down the bar, sold the pool table, and poured every drop of hooch down the drain. I'd always wanted a grand piano, and he bought me one. He had it put right there where his pool table was. It's the same piano Miss Dawn used to teach you how to play."

Alan thought of the piano. Mary had sat on the bench and watched him play the way Miss Dawn had taught him the day it snowed. He wished every day could be as good as that day was.

"Alan was a proud, stubborn man, but I never doubted his love for us."

"Did he ever drink again?"

"Not at home. But then one day, he said he was walking into

the ABC Liquor store to get himself a fifth when suddenly it just hit him. He couldn't take another step into the store. He turned around, got back in his truck, and never touched another drop."

"Wow. How come you've never told me that story before?"

"I don't know. I guess I thought I had. Or maybe I just didn't want you to know about your daddy's drinking problem. He was an alcoholic. He knew it, so he never touched another drop."

"But it sounds like he beat it."

"Yup, he did. And you can beat it too. You just have to *want* to beat it!"

"I'm not an alcoholic, and I don't drink that much," he said with a smile.

"Mm-hmm," she said disapprovingly. "I'm betting you drink more than you realize."

"Nah. Not much. And not every day. Just every once and a while."

"Junior, I know you're lying. The troubling this is that you're not only lying to me, but you're also lying to yourself. You've got to get a handle on your drinking."

"It's not a problem."

"Yeah? How about that cut on your lip? You said yourself you got it while you were drinking. Every time you look in the mirror, I want you to remember that drinking has permanently scarred you."

"I'm not saying that I haven't done things that I'm not proud of while drinking." He looked at his mother's knowing face. She didn't have to say anything; he knew what her look meant. "Hell, most of the things I regret happened when I was drinking." His thoughts went to Mary. How would he ever win her back?

"Nothing good has ever been found at the bottom of a bottle," Fiona wisely told him.

Slowly, Alan's head began to nod. "I know."

"Is there something else on your mind? 'Cause you know I'm always going to lecture you about the evils of drinking."

Alan hung his head.

"Is it this Mary girl?"

"Yeah."

"Is she pregnant?"

His head shot up to face her. "No! I haven't slept with her even once!"

"What is it then?"

"She told me she doesn't want to see me anymore."

"Why?"

He reached up and touched the scar on his lip.

"The alcohol?" Fiona asked.

Telling his mother what he did to Angela made him realize Mary's point of view. His heart broke. Why couldn't he see this before? "I've lost her..." The big man placed his head in his hands and muffled a quick series of sobs.

Fiona wheeled her chair over to him and stroked his blonde hair. "Nothing is lost, son, that can't be found. If you love this Mary, don't let her go without a fight. Surely she knows how sometimes a man makes mistakes."

"It's over," he said without looking up.

"Nothing is completely over until it's chiseled in stone. You've got to show her the man inside you. The man I know. Sure you're flawed; your daddy was flawed too. But it was those flaws that made me love him even more. You've got to show her that inside you is as fine a man as ever lived. Show her that, and she'll come back. She won't be able to resist you."

Alan ran his hands through his hair and looked up at her. His bloodshot eyes glistened as he looked adoringly at his mother. "I hope so."

"I know so," she said with a smile.

"I love you so much, Mama," he said as he gently kissed her hands.

"I love you too. You're my pride and joy."

"Thank you," he said with a weak smile and sniffle.

"Now pull yourself together and go get her."

Alan's cell phone indicated he had a text. His heart skipped a beat as he hoped it was Mary. He pulled the phone out and looked. It was a message from Felix: *I need to meet with you and Johe in the trophy room asap.*

"I've got to go," he told Fiona.

"So soon?"

"Yeah. That was Felix. He needs to meet with me." Alan breathed in a cleansing breath. His lips yearned for a drink. "Is there anything I can do for you before I leave?"

"Take me home. Please! I hate it here. Your daddy would

never leave me here!"

"I know," he said as his face contorted to one of painful sorrow, "but I don't have a choice." He stood up, then leaned over and gently kissed Fiona's cheek. "We'll talk more about that the next time I visit."

"Ok. But you didn't even get to see Janet." Janet was Fiona's mother's best friend.

"Yes, I saw Miss Janet on my way in. I gave her a rose." His smile reassured Fiona.

"Did she remember you?"

He frowned. "I don't think so."

Fiona shook her head, "Her memory gets worse and worse."

"It's so sad."

"Just shoot me if I get to that point."

"No!" Alan exclaimed. "I'm sorry, but I've really got to go."

"All right then. I'll be praying for you." Fiona tried to put on a brave face at the idea of her son's leaving.

He smiled a contented smile. "Thank you. It always helps me to know that."

"I'm always praying for you, Junior. You know that. I just want you to be happy." She looked up at him with a worried face. "And it's obvious to me you're still not happy right now, are you?" She reached out her hand to him. "I guess my advice wasn't quite what you're looking for, huh?"

Alan hung his head briefly, then looked at her and smiled. "It was just what I needed to hear. If you need something, let me know." He moved toward the door as if he were intending to leave. "Is there anything you need before I go?"

"I already told you. Take me home with you, *please*. I want to go home." Her eyes begged him. "I feel like a prisoner in here," she reiterated.

"I know, but you can't go home." As it did every time, his heart broke telling her no. What would his daddy think of how he was taking care of his mother? In so many ways he felt like a gigantic failure. "There aren't any more nurses I can hire to take care of you."

"I don't need a nurse!" she scoffed at the thought.

"But I can't be there to take care of you. I have to work."

"Of course you do, Junior! I can take care of myself." She pressed her mouth into a definite frown. "It's that Angela! She's the reason you put me in here! Lousy white trash!"

"I don't want to go through this again." He turned to leave. "Is there anything you need?"

"Yeah, I want to..."

"Besides going home," he interrupted her – it was a vicious cycle.

Her frown intensified; she crossed her arms across her chest. "No. I don't need anything," she said with a humph.

Alan leaned over and kissed her gently on the cheek. "I love you, Mama," he whispered in her ear.

"I love you too, son."

Alan smiled at her and patted her hand. "Thanks. You let me know if you need anything, ok? Call me or tell the nurses."

"Well, I'd really like to have a pack of Salems."

"Mama! No! No more smoking; you know that!"

She smiled. "I know, but it doesn't mean I want to less. Behave yourself, now."

"You behave yourself, too." He kissed her hand, waved goodbye to her and left.

He felt like he was going in a thousand different directions. His tongue felt like it was on fire – a fire that could only be quenched by a good cold beer.

On his way out, he stopped at the nurses' station. "Take good care of her, Miss Daria. I'll be in and out of town for a while. You've got my numbers, right?"

"Yes, Mr. Brooks," Daria said, reassuring him.

"And if she needs or wants anything, except cigarettes, get it for her and send me the bill, ok?"

"Of course. Don't worry, she's in good hands."

He nodded and left.

Alan made a bee-line for the nearest convenience store and bought two 44-ounce beers. Sitting in his car, he left the engine running as he twisted off the cap, and poured the sweet nectar from one of them down his throat. He loudly belched as he finished off the first bottle. "Ahhh, that's good stuff!"

He opened the second one and took just a quick sip from it. Knowing he had his mother's support in his decision to divorce Angela and pursue Mary felt like he was a bird let out of a cage! It was more than he had expected. Still, her other words haunted him.

He took another swig from the beer bottle, hoping to drown them out.

His thoughts immediately went back to the picture in his head of Mary and Ted riding. Ted had already stolen Angela from him; was he now moving onto Mary? He had to figure out how to get Mary back as soon as possible, but any plans he could think of were immediate thwarted when he heard the chirp of a police siren and saw blue lights flashing behind him.

"Damn."

CHAPTER 15

Alan leaned forward and pulled his wallet from his back pocket. He knew the routine well, and he was going to be ready before the officer approached his car.

The officer shook his head as he looked at the opened bottle of beer between his legs, and then Alan. "Well if it isn't Alan Brooks," the officer said.

"Wes? Is that you?" Wesley Green – his worst enemy since high school. Wes had slept with Alan's girlfriend, Wendy, when they were in high school. Alan had brutalized him on the football field every chance he got and kept him from getting the football scholarship he'd pinned his hopes on.

"Yes, it's me. What do you think you're doing?"

"Nothing. Just sitting here."

"With an open container."

"Well just because it's open doesn't mean I'm drinking it."

"Oh yeah? Shut your engine off and step out of the car."

"What for? Here's my license for crying out loud. I haven't done anything wrong."

Wes shifted into cop-mode. "Shut your engine off and step out of the car, sir."

"Oh, now it's sir, huh? Fine." Alan put his opened beer bottle on the passenger's side floorboard while tucking the empty one under the seat. He towered over Wes when he stood erect. "This isn't some kind of vendetta, is it?"

"No. This has to do with the fact that you're sitting in a running car while consuming alcohol."

"Did you see me consuming it?"

"No, but I'm going to get my Alco-sensor and test for the presence of alcohol."

"Wes. Come on. Really? Do you have to do all that?"

"I can smell it on your breath. You've been drinking it."

"So I had a sip. That's no crime. I'm not drunk. Not at all."

"It's illegal to drink and drive."

"I wasn't driving! The car is in neutral," he said as he reached into the car and wiggled the loose gear shift. "How can I possibly be driving if I haven't even shifted it into gear?"

"You have the engine running. You have the potential to drink and drive."

"You've got to be kidding me! That's like saying a loaded weapon has the potential to shoot people because it has bullets in it, even though no one is touching it!"

"It's called drunk while in charge of a motor vehicle."

"That sounds made up. You just made that up, didn't you?"

"So are you submitting to the Alco-sensor test?"

"Sure. Whatever. It's just going to show you that I'm nowhere near drunk and that you're an insane cop with a penchant for a vendetta!"

Wes offered up the Alco-Sensor for Alan to blow into, which he did as instructed.

"Hmm, .07."

"See, I told you I'm not drunk."

"Alan Brooks, you're under arrest."

"What?! I told you I wasn't drunk! The legal limit is .08!"

"You're under arrest for giving false information to a law enforcement officer."

"You've got to be kidding me! What false information did I give you?"

"You said you hadn't had but one sip. You obviously had more than that if you're blowing this high."

"Out of that bottle. I'd only had one sip out of that bottle!"

"Put your hands behind your back."

"Wes. Come on. You're being ridiculous!"

"I'm going to count to three, and if you don't cooperate, I'll add resisting arrest to your charges. One."

"You do know my family is good friends with Sonny Williams – your boss – right?"

"Two."

"You can arrest me, but you're going to regret it."

"Three. Now I'm adding resisting arrest."

"Then you better add assaulting an officer to it too because I'm about to mop up this damn parking lot with your face!"

Alan lunged toward Wes, but in a quick maneuver Wes had learned in the police academy, he dodged Alan and quickly dropped him to his knees and then flat on his face in the parking lot.

"Kiss it! Kiss the damn pavement!" he demanded of Alan.

"Hell no!"

Wes pulled out his night stick and held it behind Alan's neck as Wes's knees pinned Alan's shoulders to the ground. Wes grabbed Alan by the back of his hair and forcefully, repeatedly smashed Alan's face into the asphalt. "I said kiss it!"

Alan quickly flung the much-smaller Wes off of his back as if he were a ragdoll. "I'll have your badge, asshole!" he exclaimed as he spit blood out of his mouth.

But before Alan could move to the end of his car, Wes hit Alan with all his strength across Alan's buttocks with his night stick.

Alan swung around and landed a punch that began in China and ended up on Wes's nose.

Wes was swept completely off his feet and landed with a thud on the pavement.

"I don't have time to mess with you today! Now get in your damned car and take your stupid ass to the hospital to get your nose fixed!" Alan shouted as he picked Wes up by his collar and utility belt and stuffed him into his patrol car.

Alan flung his right hand a few times. It had just healed from his fight with Cliff; had he broken his knuckle this time? The swelling was increasing rapidly; he went inside the convenience store to get some ice for it.

Wes leaned over his shoulder and radioed, "Code 8" before his head limply fell onto his cruiser's seat.

Before Alan could exit the store, four more police cars showed up. Given the ice pack he had on his hand and the scuffed marks on his face, they immediately drew their weapons at him.

"Put your hands up!" the lead officer commanded.

"What the hell??" Alan put the bag of ice on his car's hood and put his hands up as he was instructed.

"You're under arrest," a young officer commanded him.

"Oh really? What for?"

"Assaulting a police officer and whatever else he says happened."

"Yeah? What about his assault against me? Does he get to go to jail for that?" Alan was more amused at their ridiculous claim than he was worried about being arrested.

"You have the right to remain silent...," another officer began reading.

Upon hearing those words, Alan realized the cop was serious. Wes hadn't mentioned those words even once. His eyes squinted to little slits. "I'm not through with you, Wesley!" Alan growled as the young officer tried to handcuff him. "I'll have your badge for this when I'm through! You think I won't! But I will!"

"You're under arrest, asshole. Now you're going to jail where you've belonged for a long time," Wes venomously said as he stood before Alan. A white handkerchief dotted with red blobs caught the blood coming from his nose.

"Yeah, you're a real tough man while I'm in handcuffs, aren't you!" Alan lunged toward Wes, who jumped back. "You coward! You don't even deserve to wear a badge."

"I've got news for you, Brooks. Assaulting a police officer is a felony with real jail time, real fines, and a real criminal record. Who's going to buy the CDs of a criminal? Huh? There goes that good-old-boy image – poof – up in smoke!" Wes said as he dramatically fanned his hands out before returning his hand to his nose.

"Watch your head," the senior officer said as he put Alan in the back of his squad car. As soon as the door was shut, he turned to Wes. "You realize it's not likely these charges are going to stick, right?"

"What the hell are you talking about? I'm standing her with blood gushing out of my nose!"

"The whole county knows you two haven't gotten along since high school. Chief's liable to drop the charges based on the fact that y'all were probably both out here beating the shit out of each other just for old time's sake."

Wes glared at his fellow officer.

"You think I don't see the scuffs on his face? Now's the time to come clean. If Chief catches wind of any inappropriate behavior, you're the one that's going to have to pay for it. I can hear him now 'Boy, what in blazes do you think you're doing bringing Mr. Brooks in here like this? You can't drag someone in here just 'cause he whooped your butt! Turn him loose, and you best go out there and apologize 'fore I chain you to a desk for the next century!'"

Wes wiped blood from his nose.

"Now, what happened?"

"He was sitting in his car with the motor running drinking a beer."

"Ok. Did you Alco-Sense him?"

"Yeah."

"And what did he blow?"

"A .07."

"So under the limit?"

"Yeah."

"Then how did all of this get to this point?"

"He lied to me. He said he'd only had a sip of beer. You and I both know it takes more than a sip to blow a .07."

"Did you test him again? Perhaps he'd just had one sip shortly before you Alco-Sensed him."

"No, sir. I didn't."

"You see what you did wrong there? Let me warn you, Alan Brooks has Earl Forsyth fighting his battles. Do you really want to start a fight with Alan? Hell, with Earl? And to make matters worse, Chief and Alan Brooks, Sr. went to Georgia together, pledged together, served in Vietnam together. Do you really want to stir the pot?"

"He broke my nose!"

"Yeah? You go sit down over there and let me talk to the other officers."

Wes did as he was instructed. His gaze was glued on Alan. "You're going down!" he mouthed when Alan looked at him.

Alan nonchalantly nodded up as if to say "Yeah, right."

Wes leaned his head back while he held the handkerchief on his nose.

By the time the bleeding had stopped, the senior officer came over to Wes again. "So, from what they gathered from witnesses, you never once read Mr. Brooks his rights, and you commanded Mr. Brooks to kiss the pavement. You even shoved his face into the ground with your nightstick behind his head." The senior officer had a grave look on his face. "Is that what you want the Chief to hear? You lost your cool and picked up where y'all left off in high school? You treated Mr. Brooks, a fine, up-standing citizen, like y'all were on the football field again?"

"He was resisting arrest!"

"Nobody said he was scuffling with you until you started it."

"He said he was going to mop up the parking lot with me!" Wes stood up trying to defend himself.

"Maybe so, but that ain't nothing but words. You know better. Once you had him subdued, you should've cuffed him and transported him to the station for processing. But no. No, you had to rub salt into an old wound, didn't you? Now, I'm giving you one more chance to do the right thing. Do you want to continue with these charges against Mr. Brooks and face Chief Sonny Williams, or do you want to shut your damned mouth and pray to God you don't have to tangle with Earl Forsyth on a police brutality charge?" the senior officer told Wes as he sternly glared at him over the rim of his glasses. "It's your decision. I'm not gonna tell you what to do here. I'm just advising you as someone who's been around the block a time or two."

Wes thought for a few moments, drew in a deep breath, and sharply released it. "Fine! Release the bastard! I'll arrest his stupid ass the minute he pulls his car onto the road."

"For what?"

"DUI!"

"I'm sure his alcohol level is quite a bit lower by now. And besides, he wasn't at the legal limit when you tested him. Are you sure you want to do that?"

Wes's eyes squinted; his breaths quickened as irritated anger overtook him. "Do whatever the hell you want with him then!"

"You've got to make the call."

"Release the bastard! But I want to impound his car first. Let the bastard walk home."

"Wes. Really? You have no grounds to impound his car."

"Fine. Just released him. But I want to talk to him first."

Wes walked over to the squad car where Alan was sitting with his hands cuffed. "I want you to know I'm releasing you. Not because I like you. And not because you're not guilty as hell, because we both know you are. I'm releasing you because you'd probably get off the charges anyway, and then I'd look bad. But you listen to me, if I see you so much as buy a beer and get in your car with it, I'm going to be on you like white on rice!"

"Yeah, yeah, yeah. I'm not afraid of you. If you had anything on me, you'd be holding me, but the truth is, you don't. I defended myself from a very angry cop. Perhaps you should go into anger management or something. Maybe it's something I need to speak to Sonny about."

Wes gritted his teeth. "Just keep talking, asshole. You mess with the bull, you get the horns."

"Take these damn handcuffs off! You ain't no bull, and you definitely ain't got any horns. You're more like a cow – just like you were in high school."

"You know I can hold you for 24 hours without ever processing you with any charges," Wes leaned in and angrily whispered.

"Go ahead and do it. I'll have your ass riding a desk so fast it will make your head spin! Sonny doesn't like his officers treating the voting citizens of this county without respect. And boy, you better learn some!"

"I've got your boy, right here! Let's go!" Wes shouted as he balled up his fists.

"Are you two through?" the senior officer asked.

Wes pressed his lips into a straight line and stepped back from Alan.

"Come on, Mr. Brooks. Let's get these cuffs off of you. I'm really sorry about all of this."

"No worries, sir. It's what I would expect from someone like Wes," Alan said as he rubbed his sore wrists. "He needs help with that temper of his."

"My temper? I don't think so! You broke my nose, you…"

"Simmer down!" the senior officer interrupted Wes. Turning back to Alan, he said, "Perhaps you should have your hand seen about."

"There's nothing wrong with him! He's just a pussy!" Wes shouted at Alan.

Without waiting for Alan to respond, the senior officer barked out orders to Wes, "Shut up! And I'll tell you what you're gonna do. You're gonna escort this fine gentleman all the way down to Chandler and then make sure he gets home safely, you understand?"

Wes's face and body language clearly displayed his displeasure at having to follow orders from a higher-ranking officer.

"That won't be necessary. I'll have my personal physician see to it. Thank you, though." Alan started to extend his right hand, but pulled it back and extended his left hand. "Sorry. Don't want to hurt it any further."

"Yes, sir," the officer said as he firmly shook Alan's left hand. "You be careful now. And, Mr. Brooks, toss the beer. Ok? You can quench your thirst when you get home."

Alan smiled and winked at the cop, "Yes, sir."

CHAPTER 16

After a quick visit to Dr. Sabia's office to have his hand bandaged, Alan showed up in the starkly white trophy room. Inside sat Johe on the white leather sofa. One of Angela's original sculptures served as a white marble and glass table in the midst of a conversation area, which contained even more white furniture and sculptures.

During the original design of the second-story room,. Angela insisted that the two longest walls be nothing but pure glass, and the two shortest walls on either end of the room be equipped with built-in, white trophy cases. One side of the windows overlooked the indoor training arena, while the other side over looked a grove of century-old pecan trees.

Initially, Alan had asked to display some of the Brooks' family livestock awards in there, but Angela refused. She claimed the room was for her use to entertain clients and show off her success. She didn't want to confuse clients with awards she didn't win.

However, her dreams of filling the cases with trophies and ribbons hadn't quite been realized as much as she'd hoped, and there had never been a client entertained in the room. Still, Alan let her have her way without complaint. Most of the time, the room sat empty or was used as a comfortable place for Angela and her friends to lounge while they waited for their horses to be saddled.

"Ok, I'm here," he said as he sat down in one of the backless S-shaped white chairs. "This better be quick. Where's Felix?" The beer he'd consumed wasn't quite doing it for him. He longed for a good shot of bourbon.

"He's on his way. What happened to your hand this time?" Johe asked.

"Pretty much the same thing that happened the first time."

"Yeah? You and Cliff go at it again? Looks like he got in a couple jabs to your face too."

"Ha ha. No. Wes."

"Oh damn. What's he up to?"

"Just a pompous-ass cop."

"You hit him?"

"He started it."

Johe shook her head. "That explains your face, huh?"

Alan rolled his eyes at her.

"When are you two ever going to grow up?"

Alan shook his head. "Never!" he proclaimed.

"Sadly, you're probably right. I'm just thinking maybe you need to do something different. Punching people isn't the best way to solve problems."

"Whatever."

Felix entered the room. "Thank you both for coming."

"You're welcome, but why are we meeting here? No one comes in here, so everyone's going to notice that we're here."

"Good. I want them to see us in here." Behind Felix's dark eyes contained the seriousness of their meeting. "I called you both here to discuss the security of the farm. First, I've ordered several of my men to try to break into Babbling Brooks, and they have done it – fairly easily from what I can tell."

"Really?" Alan asked, appalled by such a finding.

"Yes. So I'm recommending a complete reworking of the security..."

"It hasn't even been two years since I spent millions on the last security system!" Alan interrupted. "You said then that it was the best available."

"I'm aware. And at the time, it was, but technologies change. And if my men can get through, so can others, like Danielle," Felix said of Alan's stalker.

Alan drew in a breath, but pressed his lips closed and said nothing.

"Nevertheless, I've investigated further into the goings on

around the farm, and what I found disturbed me," Felix continued. "Apparently there were two sizeable insurance policies taken out on Biscuit; one just months prior to his death."

"Sizeable? As in how large?" Johe asked.

"Two and a quarter million dollars total."

"What?! Who would do that?" Alan inquired as he moved to the edge of his seat.

Felix produced a manila file folder and tossed it on the glass table between them. "There was a policy with Excalibur Insurance for a quarter of a million dollars with the beneficiary as Mrs. Angela Brooks."

Alan scooted back in his chair and crossed his legs. "So? I'm sure there's an insurance policy for her on most of the expensive horses. That's not real evidence."

"Let me finish," Felix instructed him. "And there's a two-million dollar policy taken out with the beneficiary a corporation called Ansun, Inc."

"Who the hell is that?" Johe asked.

"I've never heard of them," Alan added.

"Not surprising, so I did some searching, and apparently this is a New York company started by David Eastwood in the late 1990s that is an exclusive distributor of Mexican pottery."

"I don't know a David Eastwood," Johe stated.

"I don't either," Alan said.

"I thought you might not, but I'm willing to bet that you do know David Eastwood's brother, a Mr. Theodore Eastwood."

"Who the hell is that?!" Alan asked as his interest in Felix's story increased.

"That's Ted," Johe answered him. "Why would Ted take out a two-million dollar policy on just Biscuit payable to his brother's company?"

"I wondered that, too, so I dug deeper. What I found made me very concerned."

Alan uncrossed his legs and leaned forward again with his elbows on his knees while he listened intently to his head security guard's report.

"Apparently, this David Eastwood's company hasn't filed a tax return in the past 10 years. In addition, the company is beneficiary to insurance policies on every single horse in this barn."

"All of them?" Johe asked with growing concern. "Even Old Gem?"

"Yes. Every single equine in this building – including a Sun's Shine with the largest policy."

"We don't have a horse named Sun's Shine," Johe corrected him with disbelief in his findings. "You've made a mistake."

Alan stood up and started pacing. The room's only sound was his boots on the white marble floor as they walked from one end to the other. Neither Johe nor Felix said a word, both knowing that silence was best while Alan thought.

Once he stopped and ran his hands down his face, Johe stated again, "We don't have a horse named Sun's Shine."

"Yes we do," Alan said matter-of-factly.

"Who?"

"He's Mary's horse."

"Sun? You don't think…" Johe started to say but then darted her brown eyes to Felix before she spoke.

"You can say it. He knows," Alan instructed her.

"You don't think Ted and Angela know about you and Mary, do you?" Johe could feel Alan's growing irascibility. The questionable relationship between Angela and Ted was something she sensed Alan suspected. It was a situation that was never discussed, but implied as if they both assumed, yet neither knew for sure or stated definitively. She could almost smell Alan's asperity growing toward Ted.

Alan stood staring out the window overlooking the indoor arena. Below he could see Mary riding Rascal; Ted stood in the middle instructing her on her jumps. Ted's eyes glanced up from watching Mary and locked with Alan's. The two men glared at each other through the massive picture window.

"I don't have any evidence showing their knowledge of the situation between Mr. Brooks and Miss Mary," Felix answered Johe. "However, the sizable insurance policy on Sun's Shine makes me concerned for the horse's safety. I'm of the mindset that Ted killed Biscuit first in an attempt to cover his true target, which is Sun's Shine."

"Why would he do that, though?" Johe asked.

"Spite? To hurt Alan? Money? I don't know. I just know the policy on Sun's Shine was taken out at the same time as the policy on Biscuit," Felix added. "The others were added ten at a time each month until all horses were covered."

"How much?" Alan asked without turning from the window.

"Fifty-seven million total."

"On Sun. How much on Sun?"

"Ten million dollars alone on Sun's Shine."

"Holy shit!" Johe exclaimed. "Ten million dollars?! What insurance company would do such a thing without evidence of the horse's value?"

"I asked the same question. So I did some digging on Sun's Shine's background. Apparently he was quite a champion free-style reining horse. He and his rider, a Mary Franklin, were pioneers of the sport. After providing the company with this sort of evidence, I'm sure they had no problems insuring him for such a large sum."

"You don't think he plans to kill Sun, do you?" Johe asked

"Yes, I do," Felix answered.

Alan turned from the window. "Then get rid of him."

"You can't do that! He's Mary's horse!" Johe said.

"Ted. I meant get rid of Ted," Alan added.

"That doesn't completely solve the problem, Mr. Brooks. With the holes in the security, his closeness with Mrs. Brooks, and the knowledge he has of the farm, it wouldn't be hard for Mr. Eastwood to break in and take care of any unfinished business," Felix informed them. "With such hefty insurance policies on the equine lives, it wouldn't surprise me at all if the end result of his termination was a grand attempt on killing them all for the insurance money."

"You don't really mean that, do you?" Johe asked in complete shock.

"I do. Barn accidents happen all the time, and think of all the flammable items around here. He could break in, start a fire in the hay room, and leave before anyone detected he was here," Felix explained.

"Oh my gosh!" Johe exclaimed with a gasp.

"So terminating him at this time may produce quite drastically negative results. If we keep him here and watch him carefully, it's far less likely his behavior will escalate to that point."

"Ok. So, if his target is Sun, wouldn't it be a better plan to remove Sun?" Johe tentatively asked.

"And what do you propose I say to Mary?" Alan shot back at her.

"I don't know. But I guarantee you if she knew Sun was in danger, she'd do anything and everything possible to protect him."

"It's my theory that he's planning to use the holes in the security to blame this situation on Danielle. As you suspected, Johe, the idea that Danielle could be after the palomino horse Alan has been seen riding with could set Danielle up for such an attack of jealousy," Felix explained.

Alan's jaw clenched as he thought. He remembered his promise to Mary: *I'll do my best to protect him and you.*

"Granted, the added security in the barn has probably deterred him from doing anything immediate. However, I would wager he's biding his time until he can do the exact same thing to Sun."

"Wherever Sun goes, I can assure you, Mary will go, too," Alan stated.

The whites of Felix's eyes starkly contrasted against his dark skin and equally black eyes. He'd been head of Alan's security team since Danielle's first infiltration into the farm. Felix was the best, and Alan believed he deserved the best of everything. "Yes, I would think that would be the case. So perhaps our best course of action would be to terminate her employment," Felix said.

"Removing Mary and Sun is not an option," Alan firmly stated. "I don't want it mentioned ever again. I'd sooner get rid of Angela, Ted, and burn the entire barn to the ground myself before that would ever be an option."

"However, anything else will prove to be costly," Felix advised.

"Fine. How much money do I need to throw at this to make it go away?" Alan asked.

"This isn't about money," Johe answered. "It's about your security. Our security! Good grief!" Johe could see the fiery anger Alan was trying to hide behind his crystal eyes. She turned to Felix, "If your guys can get in, who else can? And I don't mean just Danielle."

"Anybody that did a little bit of work could figure out how to get in," Felix answered. "Don't get me wrong. It's not like my men just waltzed in without a modicum of effort, but the fact that they got in at all is the issue. At least we can be moderately assured that the attack wasn't targeted at you," Felix said to Alan.

"Yeah, but it might as well have been. If his plan is to do the same thing to Sun, I can assure you, it's the same as attacking me,"

Alan said.

The desire to take Mary and Sun and disappear repeatedly overwhelmed Alan's thoughts. *Damn Angela!* he thought. "I don't care what it costs; I want this place secure. I want Sun secure. The rest of the horses don't mean a damn to me, but he does," Alan firmly stated.

"My team is working to secure the farm, and we'll continue to look for holes. In the meantime, though, you need to decide how you want to handle Mr. Eastwood," Felix stated.

"Fire his ass!" Alan said with determination.

"Even though such an action could be disastrous? What grounds would we use?" Felix asked.

"He poisoned one of our horses!" Johe added.

"We have no definitive proof of Mr. Eastwood's involvement in Biscuit's poisoning. So far, no one has found any evidence that he ever possessed the tools to poison him. So you see, having the insurance policies doesn't necessarily mean he has malicious intentions, or that he was for certain the one behind Biscuit's poisoning."

"It doesn't mean he doesn't have malicious intentions either," Johe said.

"True. But having a motive doesn't prove guilt. We can't act so drastically just out of suspicion. It seems to me the best thing to do is to keep your friends close and your enemies closer, at least until we can get the farm secure. And while he's here, we can monitor his activities, and if he acts again, this time, we can catch him," Felix said.

Alan's mind flashed images of Mary's worried and terrified face when they'd previously discussed Sun's safety. If she knew about any of this, would she change her mind about hiring security guards for Sun? On the other hand, if she knew, what measures would she personally take to protect Sun? Would she leave? "And what good would that do? Mary's horse would be dead. That's not a risk I'm willing to take," Alan stated. His throat ached for the soothing feeling he could only find from a strong drink.

"I know. But it's a small price to pay. We're not talking about human life here…"

"Yes we are! There are few things in this world that Mary truly loves, and her horse is the main thing. We're not risking him. Period," Alan decisively stated. "Find another way!" He began pacing again.

"Then what do you suggest we do?" Johe asked.

"I'm not head of security here," Alan responded.

"Felix? What do you suggest?" Johe inquired.

Felix drew in a deep breath. "If we can't terminate Miss Mary, can we move her horse to an undisclosed location?"

"No. I already said that. Where he goes, Mary will go," Alan answered with a deep sigh. "I need a drink."

"How's that supposed to help?" Johe snidely inquired.

Alan's eyes scorned her for such a comment.

"Then what I suggest we do is search all of the cabins for any kind of evidence, while paying close attention to Mr. Eastwood's. In addition, we'll put in place round-the-clock security for Sun's Shine," Felix recommended.

"Won't that cause suspicion?" Johe asked.

"I don't give a damn what anyone thinks! I'm so sick of this shit! I'd like to take that asshole and rip him apart with my bare hands!" Alan exclaimed as his fists balled up in rage.

"Yeah? Like you did with Cliff and Wes?" Johe crassly said.

"Fuck you, Johe!" Alan blasted her.

Johe regretted her chastising remark about his desire for a drink. Perhaps he *did* need a drink.

"Calm down, Mr. Brooks. I think this is the best approach," Felix calmly stated. "This plan may show Mr. Eastwood that we're closing in on him, which might deter him from acting on any premeditated plans he may have."

"Ugh!! I just want to live a normal, happy life! Why can't I?? Why can't things be normal?!" Alan spouted in frustration.

"Mr. Brooks, few celebrities live normal lives. Security is almost always their biggest issue."

"Then I quit! Call Josh and Ben and tell them I'm through! I can't do this anymore. I want my life back! My! Life!"

Johe stood to join Alan. "Alan, Sweetheart, this isn't a time for you to have a meltdown. We all need you to be strong here. We can talk later about the rest, ok?" she used the same soothing voice she used on the high-strung horses.

"You're right," Alan said as he breathed a cleansing breath. "Yes, let's follow that plan. It's best to keep Ted around where we can watch him."

"Good. I'll start implementation. There's one more thing I haven't mentioned," Felix stated as both Johe and Alan turned to face him. "Mr. Eastwood recently applied to purchase a .38 snub nose Ruger."

"What the hell is that?!" Johe asked.

"It's a gun. A short-barreled pistol that is easily concealed. He also applied for a concealed weapons permit," Felix informed them.

Alan stood stark still.

For a moment, the room was so silent that even the sound of a pin dropping to the floor would have sounded like a high-speed car crash.

Alan broke the stupor by pulling out his cell phone. "This is Alan Brooks calling for Sonny Williams. Is he in?" he asked with a faux sense of politeness. "Yes, ma'am. I need to talk to him immediately."

"This is Sonny Williams," the Chief of Police answered.

"Sonny. It's Alan Brooks."

"Oh hell, Alan, come on. You know you and Wes go way back..."

"Wait. This has nothing to do with Wes," Alan interrupted him.

"Ok. What do you need then?"

"I know a Theodore Eastwood who has applied for the purchase of a weapon with a concealed weapons carry permit. I need you to put the kibosh on both of those. Do you know someone in the Probate who can stop it?"

"Yeah, I think I do."

"I'd consider it a personal favor if you would."

"I ain't gonna pry into your business or anything, but what's he got to do with the price of tea in China?"

"He's causing some problems, and I need to have this taken care of."

"All right, I'll look into it. But you have to do a favor for me, too."

"Ok. What do you need?"

"I need you to forget about the whole Wes police brutality thing."

"Sure thing. You take care of Eastwood, and I'll forget all about Wes."

"Good deal. How's your mama doing?"

"She's great. Stubborn as ever," Alan said with a chuckle.

"Seems like a prerequisite for the Brooks family name," Sonny said with a wry snicker. "You let her know I said hello and that I'll be stopping by to look in on her as soon as I can, ya here?"

"Yes, sir. She'll be glad to see you. She always says how nice it is having you as Chief of Police now."

"Good. Look, don't you worry about this Eastwood thing. I'll make a few phone calls, and I'll make it to where he won't ever have a gun permit in this state!"

"You're a good man, Sonny. Talk to you later." Alan hung up the phone.

Alan turned to Johe and Felix. "The gun thing will be taken care of. Now you take care of the rest," he said to Felix.

"Yes, sir," Felix replied.

CHAPTER 17

Angela sat in her bedroom at her vanity mirror brushing her long hair, while Ted paced back and forth behind her. Her silky pink robe hung on either side of her as her naked body peeked through the black trim.

"I'm tired of messing around! I had Vince all lined up, and now you want to cancel? What the hell, Angela?!" Ted asked with heaping amounts of aggravation. His boots made alternating sounds as he stepped from the rug to the hardwood floors and then back again. "I want the fucker dead!"

She put down her brush and looked at his reflection in the mirror. "Ted. We can't just kill him if he's finished his CD. Think of all the money we'd be giving up. Besides, he'll have to go on tour to promote it, which will mean we'll have all the time in the world together without worry."

"I don't worry anyway. And money? Puh! Don't you worry yourself about money."

"Yeah? Did you have a rich relative die?" she snidely asked.

"No. Let's just say I've got my ways." His boots continued – clomp, clomp, nothing, nothing, nothing, nothing, clomp, clomp.

"Yeah, sure you do," she incredulously said. "Besides, I'm not parting with $50,000 for your guy to kill him. That's just too much money."

"Well, we could always poison him," Ted suggested.

"No. No way. I've already tried that, and you see what it got me."

161

"Yeah. But at least it got the old bat out of your house."

"True. Still, it would've been better if she'd just given up and died. Then Alan would've inherited more money than I could spend in my lifetime. Stupid stubborn old woman!"

"Well, we could always take care of her too, you know?" His boots stopped behind her.

Angela turned to look at him. "Kill Alan and his mother? Don't you think that would cause a lot of suspicion? No. It's not an option. I'm not playing around with poison anymore. It's obvious that the Brookses are immune to it or something! Besides, if I get pregnant, she's sure to pony up some money for the kid. So shut up and get me the drug!"

Ted stared at the wall. "I wish you'd just let me kill him. I'm going to have a gun soon. I could kill him and dispose of his body before anyone knew he was missing. I know how to dispose of a body."

"Good grief, Ted! People would miss him immediately! We'd have the GBI and every other police task force crawling all around us, not to mention the news media. No. I still say my plan is better."

"All you'd have to say is that he went on another one of his trips, and you haven't heard from him. He could've died in a rock-climbing accident where his body can't be found."

"Yeah? And how did he get there? Fly? Orville would say something differently," she said of Alan's pilot. "If he flew commercially, we'd need for him to actually purchase a ticket and use it. He's not going to do that either. Drive? We'd have to get his vehicle there without fingerprints. There'd be too much covering we'd have to do for that idea. No. We're doing my plan, end of story."

"I don't like it, Ang. Every time I think of him touching you...." Ted fumed at the thought. "I want him *dead*!" He clenched his fists in anger and pounded one fist into his opposing hand. His boots started their alternating sounds again.

"I've told you plainly, if my plan doesn't work, then we'll shift to yours. End of story."

"No! It's not the end! You winding up pregnant with his kid doesn't make it end happily for me. When do I get to win? Huh?! How does that make me end up with you?"

"Teddy." Angela stood up from her plush stool and moved in

front of him. He placed his work-worn hands on her silk-covered hips. He loved it when she called him Teddy. "I'll always be yours. But you and I both know you can't afford me, and Alan can."

"I've got connections, you know? I'll be able to afford you." He leaned down to kiss her, but she pushed him away.

"Oh yeah?" she said mocking him. "You've got millions I don't know about?"

"I have my ways. Do you trust me?"

"Yeah, but I trust myself more. Just get me the drug!" Angela demanded as she backed away from him. "Have you even checked into it yet?"

"Yeah. I've got a guy in Macon who says he can get it for me."

"Good. Then get it."

"He also said he could get me some ricin."

"And what's that going to do?"

"I saw on TV that it would make him get sick like the flu and kill him in a few days."

"Uh-huh. I think you've been watching too much TV."

"It would work."

"Oh, I'm sure it would work. But when the police found out he died of ricin poisoning, guess who they're going to point the finger at."

"You?"

"Exactly! After the botched job with his mother, they'd start looking deeper into my activities. I'm not risking it."

"Still, it would work. Or we could use antifreeze. It's sweet. We could mix it in with his bourbon, and he'd never know he drank it."

"Antifreeze is completely traceable."

"But his blood alcohol level would be high, too. They'd probably think he just drank himself to death." He advanced to her again, this time determined to get a kiss from her.

She placed her hand on his chest, indicating her refusal. "'Probably'? I can't risk it. If I get accused of killing him, then there won't be any inheritance. I'll be left destitute. Is that what you want?!"

"I told you I've got money."

"Puh! Your measly salary would be cut off! Without Alan paying the bills, you'd be out of a job, and I'd be homeless. You've got to think this completely through."

"I'm not talking about my salary. I've got other money coming. Besides, they wouldn't know to check for ricin or antifreeze."

Angela moved back to her makeup mirror and pulled out a porcelain jar of moisturizer. "He's Alan Brooks. If he should die, they're going to perform a thorough autopsy. His fans would want to know why he died. And even if they don't detect the ricin or antifreeze, what would they think if I up and married you?"

"They'd think you're in love with me," he said as he stroked her wavy blonde hair.

"No, they'd think I killed him so I could be with you."

Ted chuckled. His hands rested upon her shoulders. "You give the public an awful lot of credit."

"Credit I obviously can't give to you."

"Are you calling me stupid?!" he shouted as he grabbed her long hair and pulled her head back to face him.

"Get your stupid hands off of me!" she venomously shrieked.

"Don't *ever* call me stupid!" He released her hair.

"Look, I want that drug!" Angela demanded. "I feel like I'm walking on egg shells, and I *won't* live like this!"

"I'm working on it. The guy said he'd get it, but it's not the easiest stuff to get your hands on."

"Why not?"

"Because people use it for bad deeds."

"I'm not using it for bad. I'm using it for good!"

"Good? Drugging your husband so you can trick him into having sex with you?" Ted scratched his auburn beard. "How can you call that good?"

She scoffed. "You make it sound so dark! I'm saving my marriage! We vowed forever, so why wouldn't I do everything in my power to preserve those vows?"

With a light chuckle, he said, "If that's what helps you sleep at night." Ted sat down on the opulent chaise lounge.

She took out a terrycloth headband and pulled her hair back from her face. "Look, if you were in this same situation…"

"I *am* in this same situation!"

"Don't interrupt me!" she snapped at him and pounded the vanity in front of her with her fist. "We're talking about millions upon millions of dollars here. If you were in the same situation, you'd do whatever you had to do to make it work."

"Well, my guy says it's going to cost you to get it."

"Ugh! It's always about money, isn't it?! How much this time?!"

"Don't worry about it. I've got it covered."

Angela laughed. "And just what money do *you* have?"

"I have twelve million dollars coming my way," Ted confidently said as he leaned back.

"Twelve million?" Angela stopped what she was doing and turned to him.

"Yes, ma'am. Twelve million."

"Really?" She parted her robe slightly to expose more of herself as she rose.

Ted reacted and sat up toward her. "I thought that would get you going."

Her hips swayed from side to side as she moved sultrily toward him.

"Oh damn," he whispered while his tongue licked his lips. In his mind, there was never a woman on the planet as sexy as she was.

"That's a lot of money, Teddy."

"Yes, ma'am, it is." He held his arms out to welcome her onto his lap.

"Where are you getting that kind of money?"

"Don't you worry your sexy self about it. Just trust me. I'll have it before the end of the year."

"End of the year?!" she exclaimed and shot up from his lap. "Why so long?!"

"Everything takes time. But I'll have it. You can count on me." He stood up and grabbed her in his arms and roughly kissed her. One of his hands ran down the slight opening in her robe, pushing past it's silky covering and finding her supple breast. Roughly he kneaded it and pinched her nipple.

"Get your hands off of me!"

His opposing hand smartly smacked her on the ass. "Stop it! You're going to get it one way or another."

She pushed fiercely against his chest, making him step back from her. "Not tonight."

He quickly grabbed the black tie from her robe and pulled it from its loops. "Yes, tonight. Nothing you can say will stop me," he hotly whispered in her ear.

Before she could move, he overpowered her and swept her arms behind her back. Nimbly, he tied he wrists tightly with her robe sash, which caused her soft nakedness to be completely exposed to the coarseness of his work clothes.

"What the fuck do you think you're doing?" she venomously growled.

"You're mine. Don't forget it," he said in a husky voice he knew she couldn't resist.

"Untie me, you fool!"

"Shut up!" he commanded. "I'm not your precious Alan." He slung her upon his shoulder as if he were picking up a sack of horse feed.

Angela kicked and squirmed against him, but there was no escape. She was completely at his mercy. And as much as she acted like she didn't like it, she was soaking wet with anticipation.

He tossed her onto the plush bed and watched her milky white skin writhe, trying to escape while he took his clothes off. "Just where do you think you're going?" he growled as his warm nakedness climbed on top of her. "You're not going anywhere." In a swift instant, he impaled himself into her.

Angela gasped. She loved being in his control. The gritty, dirty, harsh power he had over her was something Alan never had. She closed her eyes in ecstasy.

"Don't you dare! Open 'em!" His big hand pulled the hair on the top of her head, forcing her head back. "I don't want you thinking about that stupid Alan. This is me. Ted. Look at me!" he stopped and commanded.

Angela opened her lust-filled blue eyes.

With renewed vigor, he hammered his hips against hers. The headboard slammed against the wall. "Don't you look away!" he demanded. He pounded into her causing her teeth to rattle against each other. Placing his hands on either side of her shoulders, he continued to ravage her. He was a soon-to-be millionaire – he deserved nothing less than the aggressive, lustful sex he wanted.

She thrashed against her restraints, working up to a climax that was unlike any she'd had with Ted or anyone. "Oh god, Teddy!" she shouted. Her eyes lost focus; her teeth chewed on her bottom lip. Their sex grew more violent as her moans increased in volume. "Don't stop!" she begged.

His steely grip moved to her shoulders, pinning her in place as he ravaged her. Sweat dripped from his glistening brow onto her perfect face. From deep in his chest, he growled as his climax shot deeply inside her.

Angela panted and kicked as her orgasm overtook her. With a primal scream, she shrieked in complete exquisite pleasure.

Roughly, his hands grabbed both sides of her face. "You're mine. You understand that? Mine!" His fierce words spit upon her.

Eagerly, she nodded. "I'm yours," she breathlessly repeated.

CHAPTER 18

The morning was already sweltering. Mary wasn't even finished dressing for work, and there were already noticeable beads of sweat on her face. When she was finally ready and emerged from her cabin, the air outside sat stagnant, heavy; every breath took inordinate effort. Dreary clouds hung in the sky threatening rain but not releasing a drop; the sun shined powerfully onto them, heating the thick air. "I miss Arizona," she muttered to herself as she walked toward the barn.

She hadn't seen Alan but a few times since she'd thrown him out of her cabin, and not at all for a week. It had been over three weeks since she'd felt his lips on hers. Her heart ached. She lived somewhere between extreme regret and knowing she'd made the right decision. Neither seemed like a livable existence.

"You won't believe what I just saw on the way in this morning," Ginger gushed as she walked into Johe's office. The other stable hands were clocking in to begin their shift.

"Ok. I'll bite. What did you see?" Johe asked.

"The sexiest thing I've seen in a while!"

"Do tell!" Aja added. Her big doe eyes sparkled in anticipation for Ginger's story.

"Well, I was driving past that new apartment complex they're building just down the street from the Georgia Southern campus, and right out there was the sexiest man I have ever laid eyes on."

"Go on," Johe encouraged her.

Ginger told her story as she acted out his every action. "He was dressed in blue Levis, a tight T-shirt, and a hard hat. His safety harness strapped all around him just seemed to accentuate all of his features. And his sweat-soaked shirt left nothing to the imagination. As I was sitting there at the red light, he started climbing up this steel frame. I nearly came on myself right there on the spot!" Ginger said as she clutched her heart.

The women laughed at her dramatic performance.

"I couldn't move! All I could do was sit and stare at his rippling muscles through his shirt as he easily pulled himself up this steel structure. That safety harness cupped each ass cheek as if to say 'come on, take a bite!' I'm telling you, girls, I've got to find out who he is. He's my destiny."

"Destiny, huh? Yeah, I find that hard to believe. He's nothing more than an extremely fun fish..."

"Have you ever done it with a truly muscular fish like that?" Ginger interrupted her.

"Yeah," Johe answered.

"I mean a completely buff guy with rippling muscles."

"Yeah!" Johe answered again.

"Well, I haven't. I want to see every muscle in his chest and abs flexing as he pounds the hell out of me! Don't ruin it! I'll get him. You wait."

"What if he's married?" Aja asked.

"I doubt it. He wasn't wearing a ring," Ginger added.

"How could you tell from so far away?" Mary asked.

"Trust me. I analyzed every detail about him. "

"Just how long was this red light?" Johe questioned.

"Not long enough, I assure you. The damn idiot behind me honking at me to move broke my trance. Goodness, I can just imagine this guy in his harness hanging from my ceiling as he..."

Johe sternly cleared her throat. "That's enough ladies. Let's get to work."

"He's just lucky I didn't park my car and get out to talk to him."

"I'm sure the big sign saying 'hard hat area' was a deterrent. Now come on, we have hungry horses anxious for their breakfast," Johe said as she herded the women toward the feed room.

"You'd think so, wouldn't you? But it just added to the thrill – the danger of it all. Mmmm. I've got to have him. I won't rest until I do. My God! He's burned into my memory! How could God make such a fine specimen of man and not let me have him? That just seems cruel."

"What about Sean?" Aja sweetly inquired.

"Sean? You mean married Sean? Screw him. Freakin' liar. I don't need that kind of mess in my life, that's for sure," Ginger said but struggled to mean. Sean resided in many of her thoughts. She often searched for anyone to take him off her mind.

"But you did like him, right?" Aja continued.

"Yeah, I did. The sex with him was unlike anything I've ever had! So uninhibited. So in control. So over with! He gets to do all that shit with his wife. I'm sure she loves the smell of his farts under the covers too!" Ginger explained as they entered the feed room.

As Mary turned off from the women to go get her horse ready to train, she spied Alan standing next to the tack room. He looked just as heart-stopping sexy as he did the first time she'd laid eyes on him. Even the hair on her body stood up to take notice.

Her eyes inconspicuously scanned him up and down.

His head leaned down slightly with his black Stetson shading the bedroom eyes she knew were watching her from just under the brim. Flaxen locks of hair escaped and curled slightly at the base of his Herculean neck.

His burly shoulders – powerful and protective – were outlined by his vintage snap-down western shirt, which wasn't completely snapped to the collar. A few tufts of blonde curly hair shown through the unbuttoned buttons.

His brawny chest was highlighted by a light blue embroidery edge skimming right along the rim of his steely muscles.

His waist was trim; an impeccable complement to his thick chest and shoulders.

His ripped arms filled out every available bit of fabric in the long-sleeve shirt.

Tight Levi jeans showed off just how tempting every aspect of his body was.

Mary's eyes stopped for a moment to gaze at his package just before scolding herself for such tawdry behavior.

Even though nearly every square inch of him was covered, Mary could still feel the details from memory. She felt so safe in his arms – how could he be such a contradiction, both dangerous and safe? It was as though he were trying to tempt her, and as much as she was afraid of his efforts succeeding, they were doing just that!

Subconsciously her tongue ran along her velvety pink lips.

She noticed red wounds that were on their way to healing on his right hand. *What happened?* she wondered. Still, she tucked her hat down, closed her eyes, and held tightly to the fortress of strength she hid behind as she walked past him into the tack room. She couldn't let him know how much he affected her. How could she even speak to him without demanding he sweep her into his arms and find her lips with his? Or take her and make dominating, passionate love to her, just as Ginger had been describing?

No. The best thing to do was to pretend he didn't exist. She had to get over him, and giving him any sort of attention wasn't going to help her achieve that.

As she walked past him into the tack room, her lungs filled with the delightful smell of saddle leather, yet her heart was bursting with desire.

"So you're not even going to speak to me?" Alan's voice split the silence in the tack room. His boots made their distinct advancing sound on the wood floor indicating he was following her.

"What do you want me to say?" she heard herself reply.

"How about how you love me and you've come to your senses."

"Alan," she said implying he knew better. "How'd you injure your hand again. Cliff?"

"No. Remember Wesley Green?"

"Yeah. The one who slept with your girlfriend in high school, right?"

"Yeah. Well, last week we got into a little tiff."

"Aren't y'all a little old for that?"

"You'd think so. He's apparently a cop now."

"Oh really?"

"Yup. A cop with a very big chip on his shoulder!"

"Hmm. And I'm guessing the chip on his shoulder and the chip on your shoulder butted heads, huh?"

"Pretty much. But don't worry, Honey, you should see him."

Mary shook her head. "I'm sure. I saw what you did to Cliff."

"That was nothing."

"What'd you do to Wesley?"

"I'm pretty sure I broke his nose."

"And I'm guessing you're proud of that, huh?"

"Hell yeah! The rat bastard thought he could pull some police brutality on me. I'm not putting up with his shit!"

Mary exhaled sharply and shook her head. "You're only confirming what I've been saying."

"And what's that?"

"That you're just as dangerous now as you were a month ago."

"How on earth can you still think that?"

This time, Fear wasn't the one controlling her. Nevertheless, Fear had had plenty of time to win her over to his view of Alan. "If you're capable of such things to Angela, Cliff, and Wesley, then what else are you capable of doing to me?" She left out the part about Roger; there was enough evidence to justify Alan's danger without including Roger.

Alan moved to stand in front of her, so close she could catch whiffs of his outdoorsy, masculine scent mixed with the distinct aroma of aged Kentucky bourbon. Why was he tempting her so? Why couldn't he just walk away?

"You're being ridiculous. I wouldn't harm a hair on your head. As far as Cliff and Wes are concerned, they started the shit. I simply finished it. And Angela, I see now how I was wrong. And I'm deeply sorry. But I want you to know I didn't harm her in any way or put even one bruise on her.

"So why don't you tell me what this is really about? I'm smart enough to know there's more to it than you're letting on. One minute everything is perfect, and the next minute I'm scum under your boot," he said as he leaned his arm on one of the saddle racks.

Mary stood silently; her eyes glued to the floor. She wanted to tell him about her rape. About Roger. About everything. But what good would it do? The fact remained that he's capable of such things. And even though part of her was thrilled by the idea of being sexually dominated by him, the other part of her couldn't let go of her fear.

Besides, if he knew about Roger, what would happen then? Would he seek Roger out like what happened with Cliff? Could she trust him with such a secret? If she disclosed that information to him, he'd possess the power to single-handedly destroy her, even if he thought he was protecting her. Loving him and letting him love her required revealing all of her secrets, and regardless of what Tunda had said, Mary couldn't buy into revealing any of them to him.

Doing so was far more precarious a situation than she ever wanted to be in again.

"It doesn't matter, Alan," she quietly said. "I just can't," she whispered, barely making a sound.

"Can't what? Can't be with me? Can't love me? Can't what exactly?" he said a little irritated.

"I can't do this. Any of it. I'm sorry."

"Bull shit! What are you so afraid of?"

"You! Ok? I'm afraid of you!" she blurted out.

"I haven't done a damn thing to you! How can you possibly be afraid of me?? I love you, for God's sake!"

Mary's heart skipped a beat. It was the first time he'd said he loved her. She suspected he did, but he'd never actually said it. Her heart jumped up and screamed inside *I love you too!*, but her lips made no sound.

"What is it about me that makes you afraid of me? That's the point I'm trying to get to," he asked.

"Everything about you."

"You weren't afraid to go out on the boat with me. You weren't afraid to go muddin' with me. You weren't afraid to go to Tybee with me. So what is it that makes you suddenly so afraid? It's got to be more than the Cliff and Angela thing."

"They're part of it. But it's mainly you."

"Are you afraid I'll break your heart? I promise, I won't."

"No. It's just I had no idea you were capable of such things."

"What such things?"

"Like what happened with Angela," she said as she touched her own bottom lip. "And now Cliff and Wesley."

"Oh good God! What man isn't capable of such things??" he angrily asked.

"Please keep your voice down. I don't want everyone to hear us arguing."

"Let them hear!" he shouted.

"Please, Alan, be quiet! I'll leave if you don't keep your voice down."

"Kiss me then."

"No."

He moved closer to her, causing her to back up. "I said kiss me."

"I said no."

"Is there no love in your heart for me at all?" he asked as he looked down at her. "I just told you I love you, and you said nothing back."

Mary's heart was pounding. Her entire body felt like quivering pudding. The fire in his startlingly cerulean eyes caused her chest to physically ache. The dimples that remained hidden on his chiseled cheeks reminded her of the fireworks that went off inside her the first time he smiled at her and shook her hand. Did she love him? Of course she did! But being with him was a completely different story.

"Say," he commanded as he put his hands on her hips.

"Al-Alan, you know how I feel."

"If I knew, I wouldn't be asking," he said as he brushed her cheek. "Tell me you've struggled to breathe. Tell me your every thought is intermingled with thoughts of me. Tell me you feel a huge hole in your heart without me."

Her instinct was to let her face fall into his massive hand. She wanted to feel his caress once again. She not only loved him, but she also wanted him with a burning desire that frightened her very core. Her heart shouted that she felt all of those things he described and more. But her head told her every second that having him was impossible – *right?* she thought.

"Please don't. Please," she weakly begged.

"Don't what?"

"Don't make me say it."

"I want to hear it from your lips. Say it."

There was no Fear there to keep her from saying everything in her heart, and as if she had diarrhea of the mouth, she closed her eyes, and out came the words she'd been hiding: "You're in my heart. You're in my every thought, even when I'm asleep. You're a part of my soul that I don't ever want to let go of. But I have to. I want so badly to believe that we can be together, but I know we can't. I'm no good for you, and you're too dangerous for me. There's no way we can make this work. You're who you are, and I'm who I am. Those things are never going to change. It's best to just walk away while we still can."

Alan held her face firmly with both of his hands. "I don't care about that. I only know that I love you, and I can't live without you."

He leaned down to kiss her.

"Don't make me bite you, too," she said firmly. She was determined not to cry.

He released her and backed away. "So this is it then?"

"I guess it is."

"You guess? Does that mean there's still hope?"

Mary's mind was caught somewhere between the mind-blowing freedom of saying what was in her heart, the utter attraction and arousal she felt for him, and the desire to run from him. As hard as she tried, she couldn't make her voice work. Loving him was one thing, but being with him, was a death sentence. What he so obviously wanted was completely impossible. He didn't even know who she really was! Even if she had the ability to put aside what happened with Angela, the fact remained that no matter where they went or what they did, there would always be the threat of Roger lurking in the shadows. She'd never be free. How foolish she was to hope she could be.

"I don't think so," she finally said.

"You don't think so," he reiterated.

"How can you say you love me when you barely even know me?" she asked as she tried to escape him, but his hands were quickly on her shoulders to keep her in his presence.

"You think I don't know you? Are you crazy? I know you far better than you think!"

"You only know what I've let you know, which isn't that much."

"Honey. You think you hide yourself so well, but really, I know more about you than you realize."

A wave of panic washed over Mary. How much did he indeed know? Did he already know she was in fact Mary Franklin? "I can only quote the movie *Titanic*: 'A woman's heart is a deep ocean of secrets.'"

"And I want to spend a lifetime getting to know all those secrets. Please. Don't do this to us."

"You go on and be you; and I'll go on and be me. Anything more is far too dangerous to consider."

The door to the tack room opened, which caused Alan to turn away from her, and Mary to pick up the nearest bridle.

"What's going on in here," Ginger asked.

Mary made a face that displayed exactly how ridiculous such a thought was, "Nothing. Why?"

"Because the tension in here is so thick, I could literally cut it with a knife!"

"Pah! That's just this awful humidity," Mary replied as she maneuvered past Ginger and out of the tack room.

Ginger stood looking at Alan, who still had his back to her. "You're in love with her, aren't you?" she knowingly said.

Alan immediately turned to look at her. He nodded as he spoke, "Yes. Yes, I am."

Ginger shook her head. "I don't know how I missed it. All this time I thought you were the long-suffering husband, but really, you've been shacking up with one of the help. At least now it all makes sense – Cliff's firing, her training to take his place, and all."

His face turned scornful. "If you were a man, I'd kick your ass for saying such a thing! Instead, I'm going to give you only one warning – keep your idiotic mouth shut! You don't have a clue…"

"Hey! Hey! Cool your jets! I'm not gonna say anything. I'm just saying."

"I know what you're just saying, and it's not true."

"Look, if you want to bump uglies with the help, just let me know."

"I've never laid a hand on her."

Ginger looked shocked. "Never?"

"No. It's not that kind of relationship."

"Then what is it?"

"I love her. I love her spirit. I love her soul. I love how she so logically thinks things through and uses her head instead of her heart. I just wish she'd give me her heart instead of her head."

"Uh-huh. So you love her, but she doesn't love you back?"

"I don't know. Everything says she loves me, but she won't say the words. Instead, she says she doesn't want to be with me."

"Forgive me for pointing out the obvious here, but you *are* still married. Right?"

"Earl said he'll have my papers ready for me tomorrow."

"Again? And you're actually going to sign them this time?"

"Absolutely."

"Really? It's gotten that serious, has it?" Ginger incredulously asked.

"I haven't even told Mary. She won't talk to me. She says I'm too dangerous. What the hell does that mean?"

"Dangerous? She used the word 'dangerous'?"

"Yeah."

"Interesting."

"If you say so. Look, you speak girl code. Translate, please!"

"Oh it's a double-edged sword for sure. Perhaps she's afraid of Angela."

"She said that's part of it. But the main thing she's afraid of is me," he said as he touched his bottom lip. Surely there was more to it than just that.

"You, huh? Well maybe what she's really afraid of is *who* you are instead of you specifically."

"What the hell does that mean?!" he asked, exasperated by even her ambiguity.

"Who are you?"

"Alan Brooks."

"Exactly. Alan Brooks. Country music star, Alan Brooks. Exceedingly successful and wealthy, Alan Brook. Incredibly sexy and influential, Alan Brooks. Celebrity Alan Brooks. You're not just some guy off the street at a construction site wearing a sexy safety harness as she imagines sweaty, nasty sex with you."

Alan stood stark still with a dumbfounded look on his face. "Umm, TMI."

"Yeah. Sorry. Look some women can't handle all that. If you say she's always thinking with her head, I'm sure she's observed how hard it's been on Angela being married to you. Months of touring, the massive entourage who follows you everywhere you go. Days, weeks, months of Angela being alone while you take trips all over the world, adventures to the nether regions of forbidden countries in the search of some death-defying thrill..."

"Ok. I get it," he said as he scratched his head. "I guess it's true. You can't have a successful life and a successful relationship."

"Bingo. And I'm betting she's not willing to risk her heart only to have it end up alone and broken."

Alan scratched his goatee. How had he missed all of that?

"That's not easy for any woman to take, you know?"

Alan nodded. "You're right." He'd heard those same things from Angela a thousand times, but it never hit home as hard as it did coming from Ginger's lips.

"I don't know for sure all of that is what's bothering her, but my guess is that it's probably up there around the top. Especially if you want more than a wham-bam-thank-ya-ma'am with her."

He nodded more. "Perhaps you're right. Look, keep all this under your hat, ok?"

Ginger smiled. "You know, if you're done with her, I'm still single," she said with a wink.

Alan laughed and placed his hands on either side of her cheeks, causing her legs to go weak. He bent down and kissed her square on the forehead. "I'll keep that in mind."

CHAPTER 19

Later the same afternoon, Alan sat in his basement domain with a full bottle of bourbon in his hand; his thoughts were entirely wrapped up in Mary and his earlier conversation with Ginger. His mother's story about his dad's struggles with alcohol made the temptation of the bourbon less inviting than he'd hoped. Part of him wanted to drown out his thoughts, but the other part was determined to find a different solution.

All day he tried to get Mary's attention again, but she wouldn't even glance his way. All she did was practice with Ted and Angela, which meant he couldn't talk to her. But what cut him most was that she wouldn't acknowledge his existence. Except for the brief moment in the tack room, her tumultuous green eyes never looked his way, never once glanced in the same universe he was in.

Was Ginger right in her definition of what dangerous meant?

"Angela," he thought. He drummed his fingers on the piano keys. "Maybe that's it," he muttered, "she's scared of becoming like Angela." The same five notes repeatedly sounded from the massive instrument.

He twisted the cap off of the bourbon and held the bottle to his lips. "And where does that leave you, buddy. She's scared of *you* and everything you represent." He turned the bottle up, but didn't enjoy the normally delightful warmth it gave his insides.

His mother's words rang in his ears: "Nothing good has ever been found at the bottom of a bottle." He put the opened bottle on the piano.

"If there was only a way I could show her that I'm exactly like anyone else."

In a place he hadn't consciously accepted was a twinge of worry that maybe she really *didn't* love him. She didn't actually say the words.

"I should've quit. I should've told Josh to kiss my ass. I should've…." If he had quit, who he was wouldn't matter. *Would it?* There would be no touring, no wild trips, no anything where she couldn't be right by his side. Maybe then he wouldn't be so dangerous.

He looked at the bottle on the piano and began playing a melancholy tune. His instincts told him he should be rehearsing for the impending release of his CD, but his mind was too caught up in Mary to think of much else.

His fingers delicately danced along the ivory and black keys; he closed his eyes. His music was tender but with a tortured rawness – much like his spirit. The underlying notes were dark, revealing the depth of his dissatisfaction with everything. He often played the same piece when he was feeling depressed. Never had there been appropriate words to go with the notes; the song was simply a reflection of his despair. Yet, this time, he didn't finish the song. He knew where playing it was heading, and the bottom of the bottle sitting on the piano was a place he was trying to resist going.

He thought of the original song he'd written – *Butterflies in the Storm*. Every time he'd tried to remember, he'd struck out. Quietly, he sat at the piano and thought again, trying once again to recall anything. "Shit!" he exclaimed. "Stop overthinking and just go with it," he told himself.

His fingers sat motionless on the piano keys; the bottle of bourbon tempted him.

Just play… something! he thought. One note at a time, he started; within no time, he added in additional notes. Before long, his fingers began playing a tune; his soul simply sang about his Mary:

What happens to butterflies in a storm?
Who is there to keep them warm?
I'll be your shelter,
your shield from all harm.

I see the storm raging
In those eyes of yours.
Tears you won't cry
Fear you ignore.

I feel your skin tremble
When I touch your hand.
Even though you just smile
I understand.

Don't ever stop reaching
for a love that is true.
But when dark clouds start formin'
And winds push 'gainst you.
I'll be there to protect you
Keep you safe and warm
I'll come to your rescue,
my butterfly in the storm.

You don't have to tell me
All you're going through.
I just wanna love you
When the storm starts to brew.

You can never stop reaching
for a love that is true.
But when dark clouds start formin'
And winds push 'gainst you.
I'll be there to protect you
Keep you safe and warm
I'll come to your rescue,
my sweet butterfly in the storm.

I know it's hard to fly
When the storm weighs you down
No matter how hard you try.
Just fly my way,
Don't be afraid...

You can never stop reaching
for a love that is true.
But when dark clouds start formin'
And winds push 'gainst you.
I'll be there to protect you
Keep you safe and warm
I'll come to your rescue,
my sweet butterfly in the storm.

We're both butterflies in the storm.

Alan played the final note. It was the first song he'd written without the assistance of profuse amounts of alcohol in years. He sat frozen for a moment. The back of his neck prickled in excited anticipation. He clicked the record button on his nearby recorder, and he replayed the song. This time, he added some of the raw notes from the dark song he often played when he was depressed.

Chills formed on his legs as he played and sang. It had been ages since he'd felt such exhilaration. He hit stop on the recording. That was it. That would be his next single. And he would produce it exactly as it was recorded – just him and his piano. Not so very country, but precisely like Mary had suggested. None of the complicated arrangements. None of the additional instruments. Just him and his piano. The way it used to be.

He played and sang the song one more time. "Wow," he whispered in awe. It was the perfect combination of him and Mary – in musical form. Getting back to his musical roots made him feel ecstatic. It was a better feeling than any drink he'd had, and almost felt as good as kissing Mary for the first time.

Sitting on the back edge of the bench, he thought about when he would play the song for Mary. Should it be a surprise? Or would it be just the thing he needed to woo her back?

"No," he answered the idea of using it to bring her back, "she'll be expecting something like that. You've got to think outside of the box. You'll have to go deeper."

He transferred the recorded file to a flash drive and then moved it to his computer. "Let the song be a surprise for her," he told himself as he worked. "What she needs is more from your soul and less from your inspiration."

He emailed the recorded file to Josh with instructions that this would be added to the CD and his first single. "If Josh gives me one single suggestion to change it, I'm outta there," he said aloud to no one. "I'll produce it and promote it myself under another name if I have to." He closed his laptop and returned to the piano.

Just as he lifted the bottle of bourbon to his lips, an idea struck him like a bolt of lightning! Of course! He didn't have to be Alan Brooks the country star. He could reinvent himself using another name. Alan Brooks could just drop out and be the man so feverishly in love with Mary.

But how could he show her his heart when there were so many things still standing in the way? How could he show her that he wasn't some fly-by-night man who would only end up hurting her?

He put the bottle back on the piano without drinking a sip. His fingers instantly played a chord and then another. "When you strip it all down, I'm just a man, in love with a woman," he said aloud only for his benefit. "But how do I show her that?"

The notes resonated through the piano as he stopped to think. "Hmm…" He played a series of notes, and then stopped again with more thoughts. "And what happens if it all goes to hell?" He picked up the bottle again, but didn't drink. Instead, he screwed the cap back on it. "What if she gets the wrong idea?"

He stood up from the piano and started pacing with the bottle of bourbon in his hand. "She's going to think I'm a nut!" He turned back and forth, but before he knew it, the butternut squash colored walls of his hallway surrounded him. There were several options from the hallway: the bar, the recording studio, the residence, and the garage. Each direction offered a different option.

He stopped, and looked at the pastoral picture hanging on the wall. Off in the distance, his imagination could see his great, great, great granddad's cabin – the first Brooks' homestead. Even though it wasn't part of the picture, he always imagined it there. He thought of how much he opened up to Mary then. He'd shown her parts of him that he hadn't shown anyone – told her things he hadn't even told Johe. Doing those things had brought Mary closer to him. Could doing something similar bring her back to him? But should he use the cabin again?

"No. Go somewhere neutral." He placed the bottle on the floor and took long, determined strides down the hallway and straight to the garage.

CHAPTER 20

Mary sat alone in her cabin. After training all day and her interlude with Alan in the tack room, her soul longed for him. Every part of her wanted to text him and beg him to come to her, but no matter how many times she typed the text out, she couldn't make herself press send.

She read and then re-read the old email from Tunda:

> *Honey,*
> *Loving someone means giving him the ability to hurt you, but trusting him enough to know that he won't. If you love him, you know what you've got to do – tell him about Roger. Tell him the truth. Give him the chance to understand and love you anyway. Alan will protect you. I just know it.*
>
> *Love,*
> *Mother*

"How can I do that?" she asked as she wiped a wayward tear from her eye. "If he knew all about me, I know this 'love' he claims to feel for me would be gone."

She wondered exactly how different things would be in that regard. She didn't have him now, so there wasn't much of a difference.

"True. But then he'd know you're Mary Franklin and not Mary Stephenson. Would he use it against you?" She thought for a moment. "Doubtful. But, still…"

She clicked back on her browser. "Dammit! I'll never figure out this stupid new Yahoo mail." But before she clicked the mail icon again, a news article flashed before her news feed with an all too familiar face – Roger. The heading on the article chilled her to the core: **Bail Set for Prominent Tucson Attorney**.

"How is that even possible??" Mary asked as panic began to bubble beneath the surface. She wanted to click on the article, but she was afraid of knowing. Yet, her fingers had a completely different idea as they moved the cursor and clicked on the article:

Bail Set for Prominent Tucson Attorney

TUCSON, AZ (KOLD) – Pima County Supreme Court set bail for prominent local attorney, Roger Donavan Franklin, who is accused of murdering his wife in Tucson.

Franklin will be released from prison if he can post $1,500,000 surety bond, meaning that he or someone will agree to pay the full bail if Franklin breaches any of his court-ordered conditions. Ten percent of the bond amount in cash or property is required for his immediate release.

Conditions for release in these type cases generally include not carrying a weapon, not being allowed to leave the state, and reporting to a bail supervisor.

Franklin, 38, has been charged with the second-degree murder of his estranged wife, Mary Elizabeth Franklin, 25.

A date for his trial has not yet been set.

Mary Elizabeth Franklin's body has never been recovered. The Tucson Police Department's Crimes Against Persons Division found evidence that led investigators to accuse Franklin of her disappearance and subsequent murder. No word from Mary Elizabeth Franklin has been established since her disappearance September of last year.

The knowledge that Roger's bail had been set permeated her thoughts. All the comfort and safety she'd developed at Babbling Brooks since his arrest seemed to barely exist.

"Surely he doesn't have that kind of money," she whispered. Yet at the same time, she knew he kept an undisclosed amount of cash in a large safe deposit box at the bank. Was there enough in there to cover his bail? And even if it was, could anyone with the key have access to it? Her mind flashed back to the safe deposit key she kept on her car key ring. "Maybe the police have confiscated that as evidence."

Nevertheless, sitting alone in her cabin felt as though she were sitting in wait for his attack. Every creak and groan of the old structure made her jump and scan the room frantically. It felt like she was right back to the beginning when she'd just arrived at Babbling Brooks. Nothing was safe, and Roger was hiding in every dark space.

She walked around the cabin and turned on every light inside. If there was even a remote chance of Roger being there, she wanted to see him before he got to her.

"I wish Alan were here," she said aloud to the light. She missed herself around Alan. She missed the freedom and happiness she found with him. The freedom she'd found with him was infinitely better than the tension she felt without him; on the other hand, Alan's very existence in her life was more precarious than being away from Roger alone. The paradox the whole situation created frustrated her.

The lights did nothing to soothe her nerves.

Mary grabbed her iPhone and left the anxiousness of her cabin to be with Sun for a little while. There was at least security there, which made her feel safer.

The faux-summer heat still hung heavy in the evening's air as the sun hung onto the tiny edge of sky left. Even though it was after dinner time, the sun continued its prowess and kept the air stifling hot. *How can it be this hot and humid when it's not even summer yet?* Mary thought as she wiped her brow with her sleeve.

Sun perked his head up when he heard Mary's familiar whistle. With an excited whinny, he greeted her. "Hiya fella," she said with a smile. "I know it hasn't been very long since I left, but I missed you."

She grabbed a soft brush and went inside. Casually she brushed his golden coat. Sun returned to nibbling hay.

"How're you doing, Miss Mary?" the security guard on duty asked.

Mary startled at the unexpected intrusion. "Oh! Hi Mark. I'm well; thanks for asking. How are things around here?"

"Quiet as a tomb. The orange cat caught a big rat, but that's about the most exciting thing happened," he said with a laugh.

"A rat?! Eww!"

"Yeah. He ate every bit of it, except the tail."

"Eww! Disgusting! I don't need details," Mary put her hand across her stomach.

"Sorry about that."

"Well, have a good night," he said before he began his rounds again.

"You, too." Mary returned to grooming Sun. When she was sure that Mark had moved far enough away, she leaned against Sun's head and whispered, "Bail has been set. I don't know what to do. Run? Stay? If he gets released, he's going to be like a roving lion searching for me!" Her breath actually felt cool compared to the surrounding heat.

"I want Alan," she said with a sob. Sun's chewing resonated in the ear she pressed against his face.

"I want him to hold me. I want to feel like nothing in the world ever could, ever would hurt me because he's there. Oh Sun. What have I done? How could I have let him go so easily? Why can't Roger just disappear?! I need Alan! I need him like I need air! I've never needed someone like this!"

Sun took another bite of hay.

"Tell me what to do," she begged.

Her cell phone vibrated in her pocket and made her jump nearly out of her skin. As she tried to read it, she nearly dropped it into the shavings. She knew it was Alan. He was the only one who ever texted her. As bad as she wanted him, the idea that he was thinking about her too made her anxious.

Her heart skipped a beat when she read it. The message didn't give any details; it just read *If u think I'm dangerous, meet me at the Econolodge off exit 104. Room 103.*

Mary wasn't sure what to do. Should she meet him? What did he want?

She held her cell phone in her hand trying to think of how to reply or if she even should. With her mind preoccupied, she gave Sun one last hug and walked back to her cabin. There were no definitive thoughts telling her what she should do, instead her thoughts were intertwined with what she wanted to do – see Alan and get lost in his embrace. She wanted to feel safe, and that feeling only came when she was with him.

What time? She could hardly believe her fingers had typed out and sent a message before her brain had time to consider what she should say.

Moments later came his succinct reply: *ASAP.*

She paced, suddenly feeling very nervous.

Another text message came: *Give me the chance to prove why you can trust me, why I'm not dangerous.*

The scar on Alan's lip will always remind her that he was as dangerous as any crazed man. But then there was Roger – no scar, no warning, no nothing to tell her that he's the monster he is.

She sighed. "There he is again, always lurking in the background, tormenting and taunting me with all these memories and threats of destroying my future," she said about Roger. "When are you ever going to take away his power?" she asked herself.

Immediately, her forehead creased as she thought. Closing her eyes, she took a deep breath, picked up her purse and keys, and without another thought, she found herself driving away from Babbling Brooks.

The fact was she missed Alan; there was no denying it. Seeing him, smelling him, feeling his touch in the tack room only intensified it. The idea that she could at least see him alone again was too appealing to resist. If they were away from the farm, they could really talk things out. Maybe he would hold her for a little bit and put her fears to rest like he could so easily do.

Tunda's advice rattled around inside her mind: *Loving someone means giving him the ability to hurt you, but trusting him enough to know that he won't. If you love him, you know what you've got to do – tell him about Roger. Give him the chance to understand and love you anyway. Alan will protect you. I just know it.*

Her hands shook when she pulled into the Econolodge parking lot. Before she even knew that she'd moved from the truck to the hotel, she was standing outside room 103; her entire body trembled with nervous tension. Still, as if she were drawn by an unknown force, she knocked on the door.

"You can still leave," she whispered to herself. *Too late,* she thought when the doorknob turned.

Alan had an expressionless look on his face when he saw her. He always greeted her with a smile, but not this time. He seemed solemn.

Mary wasn't exactly sure what to make of it. The room had only one lamp on, and in its light, he looked somewhat pale. What was going on? Was he drunk? *Great*, she thought, *I get to deal with drunk Alan.*

"Thank you for coming," he finally said.

"You're welcome," she croaked, then cleared her throat and repeated louder. She sniffed the air for the tell-tale scent of alcohol. *He's sober?* she questioned.

"I know you're wondering exactly what's going on here, right?"

"Yeah," she said with an apprehensive smile.

"I can't lie to you, Mary, the idea that you would think I am dangerous or that I would ever harm you has consumed me."

"Alan, you just…you just don't understand…," she started.

"Shhh. Just listen, ok? I think I *do* understand much more than you realize. So, I want to show you," he paused, seemingly a little nervous himself, "I want to show you me – exposed, open."

He pulled his boots off and started unsnapping his western shirt.

"Are you drunk?" she finally asked while still smelling the room's air. There wasn't a modicum of alcohol aroma anywhere. The overpowering smell was cheap, marginally clean hotel room where someone had obviously smoked a time or two.

"No. I want you to understand how serious I am about this," he said. While he was waiting for her, it surprised him that he was able to forgo the drinks he so desperately craved. "This isn't about me. It's about you," he said as he unsnapped the sleeves on his shirt. "You deserve all of me. I want you to see me for who I truly am. No ego, no put-ons, no alcohol, no nothing." He took his shirt off exposing his bare, magnificent chest, which was lightly dusted in blonde curly hair.

"Just me – the man, not the image. I've often wondered what it was that kept you from jumping at the chance to live the kind of life I can offer you – from living the glamour and popularity that people with my kind of money and status have. I finally realized your reluctance. To you, life is so much more than money, popularity, and glamour. It's freedom. It's a depth in the heart that I've never experienced." He removed his Levis.

"Uh, keep your pants on," she said as she backed away from him.

"I promise I won't touch you unless you tell me it's ok."

Mary turned her head. *If he's not drunk, just what on earth is he doing?* she thought.

"No, please don't; I *want* you to *look* at me…to *watch* me…to *touch* me. T-to feel the projection of my love for you. I've never experienced anything like this. I've never done anything like this. But you're different. I thought I could woo you with my stardom – dazzle you with my usual bull shit. But I was wrong. Dead wrong."

She turned back to him again.

"I thought your abusive past was what was keeping that wall up between us, but then you forced me to see that I'm no better than your ex…," he said and closed his eyes. The words were difficult to say. He forced himself to open his eyes and look directly at Mary's bright green eyes. "…i-in my treatment with Angela, you're right. I'm no better than your ex-husband. I didn't understand how wrong I was when it came to Angela. The gravity of it all continues to reveal itself to me the more I think about it. I was frustrated, and I did things that I'm ashamed of."

"So you're going to go back to Angela?"

"No. I don't love her. I never have, really."

She could only look at him as his words bounced off of her. Her mind wanted to believe what he was saying. Her heart wanted desperately to convince her mind that all of this was possible, but memories of Roger permeated her thoughts and maintained a strong fortress. Alan's words were just pretty words. But then there he was continuing to remove his clothes. *What is he up to?* she wondered.

"I've never needed someone the way I need you. The idea of losing you has been too difficult to take. So, this is my way of showing you that you have nothing to fear." He took off his socks.

"All too often I hear 'you're the love of my life!' from fans, and I always wonder how they can say something like that when they don't even know me. The real me. And then there was you. You made me see that even I didn't know the real me anymore. You made me work harder for something I wanted than I ever have. I had to be patient, kind, giving, and self-sacrificing, which are all the things my mama taught me about love, but I'd long since forgotten. That's the real me. The me I was raised to be.

"You made me get to know myself again. I could never understand why we seemed to take two steps forward and one step back. I thought it was all your doing, but that was wrong too. You simply demanded that I be real not only with you, but myself. So this–this is my way of showing you – I'm real, a-a real, deep, heart-felt person, just like you."

He took his boxers off and stood before her totally naked.

The look on Mary's face was complete shock.

"I know you're scared. I can see in your eyes that you're terrified right now," he gently said.

Mary closed her eyes and nodded slowly.

"Don't be afraid. I'm not going to touch you or do anything you don't ask me to do. I've often wondered just what it was about your past that kept you from completely accepting me, and then it hit me. It's not you, it's me. I've never shown you the real me. The me that I live with every day. The me with no put-ons, no arrogance. The vulnerable me that falls down, gets hurt sometimes, feels sadness, feels love, puts on a plastic smile and then sings and dances like the sock puppet I am up there on a damn stage just for more money. The me that forces a smile even when I'm in the midst of a broken heart. The me who sticks his head in the sand or a bottle of whisky until whatever storm is blowing passes by. The me that is sure his wife has been cheating on him with her trainer for at least a year now." His heartbeat increased at the confession. It felt good to actually say it to someone else.

She opened her eyes and said, "So you're doing this because Angela is cheating on you with Ted?"

"No. I'm doing this because I don't care if Angela is cheating on me with Ted. I'm doing this because I want you to know that I'm not hiding anything from you. What you see is what you get."

She looked away, having a difficult time looking at naked him looking at her. The woman in her wanted him. *Good God go get him!* her desire shouted at her.

His voice continued, always soft, soothing. "I want you to know I have secrets, too. I have failures and vulnerabilities that are much like yours. Even though I'm a man, and that comes with all the nuances of strength, protection, power, and such, I'm still not perfect. People put me up on this pedestal all the time, and I let them because it's fun being up there sometimes, but most of the time

I'm constantly aware of just how far it is to fall off of it!

"I still face everyday problems. I-I trip over my own damn size 15 feet. I have a mole above my left ear that nearly gets combed right off every time I get my hair cut, which is why my hair often grows longer than it should. And if you look, my bellybutton is as close to being an outtie as it can be without being one. I say and do stupid, impulsive things. I rarely suffer the consequences of those impulsive things because Marcus and Earl clean up my messes and have for years. Several times in my life I've forgotten to zip up my fly. I've even gone on stage with my fly down! Which is why I wear button-fly jeans only. And I have moments where I feel like I'm going to explode if I don't have a strong drink. But even with all my goofiness and weirdness, the truth is I want nothing more than to walk away from it all and be that safe hiding place you so obviously need.

"The problem is, I don't know if I'll ever be good enough. All of those shortcomings make me afraid of failing you. They make me try to overcompensate for them. To make matters worse, everything I do seems to make the tabloid pages. I have to spend obscene amounts of money to ensure my safety simply because there are some serious crazies in this world. I think that my stalker is out of jail now, and there's no telling what kind of shit she'll be up to. But, I want you to know that I'm never more my true, awkward, simple self than when I'm with you. I feel like I'm at home – at peace. I haven't had such a feeling since sitting on the banks of the lake fishing with my daddy."

Mary drew in a breath to speak, but Alan gently said, "Shh. Don't talk. Just listen. My chaotic world stops when we're together. When we're apart, everything is a mess. I can't wait to be by your side again. This time apart has given me clarity beyond compare. Everything I can foresee in my future requires you. I don't want the rat race anymore; I just want you. And in order to have you, I need you to see that I have nothing to hide. I need you to see me stripped down and open – like I am now."

He took a deep breath and silently let it out. Standing expressionlessly before her, he hoped some stillness would encourage her to be more comfortable. He wanted his words to sink in.

The blank look on Mary's face didn't change.

So, he started speaking again. "I'm just a man, Mary. I'm a

flawed, natural, red-blooded man. I made a mistake when it came to Angela – a mistake in marrying her; a mistake thinking we could actually have a relationship; and a mistake thinking she was ready for make-up sex. Please don't hold any of that against me."

"Alan, you don't understand…"

"I do. I truly do. I've beat myself up a thousand times for what happened. I regret so much. I would give anything to go back and change it. But I can't. I can't lose you because of my stupidity. I'll spend the rest of my life trying to win you back." His blue eyes stayed glued on her in the air-conditioned room.

"You're my angel," he whispered, "you saved me."

Mary scoffed.

"What you don't believe me?"

"That's so cliché, so over used," she told him.

"Maybe so, but that doesn't make it less true. Would you look at me please?"

Mary turned her head, but immediately looked at the floor, which made her blush.

Alan didn't smile or react in any way. "You forced me to understand it's ok to lose the mask I've hidden behind. For the first time, I want you to understand who I am behind every façade. I want you to know without a shred of doubt and that this love I feel for you is pure. I want you to see that the *man* in me is totally in love with the *woman* in you."

Mary's gaze strayed from him again, toward the door. She couldn't look at him; his entire naked body was stunning. It aroused her more than she wanted to admit. It made her thinking feel hazy, muddy. Yet, she didn't feel afraid. The feeling was instead something she lacked experience handling. She wasn't sure she was totally in control of it as he appeared to be.

"Please don't turn away. Look at me; I want you to see how beautiful and-and wonderful you are to me." His voice was gentle and coaxing. "I've loved you from the second I laid eyes on you. There was something there, a mystery, a-a storm brewing behind those incredible eyes of yours. I-I-I was captivated right there. I thought I could woo you by being the quintessential Alan Brooks, sock puppet extraordinaire, but I was wrong. You made me reach much deeper than that. You made me put away this carefully sculpted image and get back in touch with the man behind it."

Mary closed her eyes. "You don't even know me."

"I would if you'd open yourself up to me. Your heart is a place no man has ever truly explored. I want to be that man! I can't *wait* to be that man!! If I have to wait a thousand years for you, you're worth every second."

"I mean, how can you say you love me when you don't even know me?"

"I've gotten to know you better than you think over these past several months. What I know, I'm completely in love with. I can't wait to get to know more and love that even more. I just need you to let me into your heart."

What does he want from me? she questioned as her uncomfortable thoughts were a swirling soup of confusion. *If he wants sex, why didn't he just do something? Should I take my clothes off, too?* She turned back to him and opened her eyes; he simply stood before her, his hands by his side, his breaths shallow. "What do you want from me? Sex?" she loudly whispered, trying to hide the indignation rising inside her.

Alan didn't answer; he could feel the sting from the daggers her words threw at him.

"That's it, isn't it?" She started unbuttoning her shirt. "Fine. If that's all you want, fine! Just take it!" She was cold and defensive as she took her shirt off and climbed onto the bed behind him. "Just hurry up and get it over with!" she growled in anger with her eyes clinched shut. Her body was a rigid board as she prepared to feel his warmth press her against the bed.

"Not a day goes by that I don't think about or dream about sex with you, but this isn't about sex. I haven't touched you or even attempted anything, have I?" His eyes matched the tenderness and sincerity of his words.

"It's always about sex with men, *always!* Don't stand there, naked, with a raging hard on, and lie to me!"

"I'm not lying to you. He has a mind of his own, and when you started taking your shirt off, well, he gets thoughts in his head that I don't always agree with."

"Yeah, right," she sarcastically said.

"Listen to me; you have to understand, I never realized what *true* love was until you. You made me explore the depths of my soul that I didn't know existed. This is about getting inside your heart; not inside your vagina!"

"Bull shit!"

"It's about knocking down the walls between us. I don't know about your past, and honestly it doesn't really matter." His words were merely a whisper. How was it that this seemed like such a good idea in his mind? "None of that matters. I'm glad it happened…"

"Glad it happened?!" Dressed in her jeans and bra, she shot up to her knees on the bed. "Glad it happened??!! Why on earth would you be *glad* it happened??"

"Because it's what brought you to me."

"What brought me to you was… was…." She stopped. "I can't believe you'd say you're glad my husband beat the shit out of me!! That-that he had me…" She stopped herself again. It amazed her how close she came to telling him about her rape. Where was her self-control?

"Don't do this. That's not what I meant," he said with a clear desire to take those words back. "What I meant was, I'm glad I found you. I'm sorry he did that to you. If I could change it, I would. But if he never did that to you, you wouldn't have left, and I never would've found you."

Mary's stance softened; she understood his point.

"Can't you see I love you? Not just your body, but your heart, your soul, your spirit, your mind?"

"You don't know anything about those things."

"What I do know, I love. Won't you let me in so I can know them better, and love them more?"

"And what if I told you I was an award-winning physicist? Would you believe me?"

"I would. I know you're not just an average person. You are far more intelligent than most people. I would be a little surprised to know you are a physicist, though."

"Why?"

"That just seems pretty boring for someone like you."

"Hmm, interesting." She picked up her shirt and put it back on. "So you're saying this isn't some begging attempt to have sex with me?"

"I don't beg for sex. I can get that anywhere, anytime I want," he stated with an offended scowl.

"Oh yes. How could I forget about all those panties thrown on the stage for you?" she said as she buttoned her shirt.

"Ha ha," he said wryly. "Mary, this isn't a joke. Please look at me and understand how defenseless I am right now. How many men would do something like this if all they wanted was a piece of ass?"

"Parade around naked? Most."

"No! Don' t you get it?? Look closely at me!" he commanded.

She did as instructed. His body trembled noticeably as he maintained control of his carnal desires.

"I stand before you, completely open – not a star, not Alan Brooks the performer, not Alan Brooks, Jr. son of Alan Brooks, Sr., not what you perceive as a rapist, not a man with money, not anything but a man – *me* – trying to love a woman – *you* – like no one has ever loved her before. I want to be the only man in your heart; to be the one who gives you everything he can; to grow old with you and rock in rocking chairs on my front porch when we're old and gray."

His compassionate blue eyes never changed their stare. He wanted desperately to touch her, to feel her skin beneath his fingers. Resisting temptation took every muscle in his body.

"Alan...I...can't..." The tone of her voice changed. "You can't..."

"Shh. No negatives. It's just me and just you. My heart loving yours. No put-ons, no nothings."

Mary moved closer to him; she could feel his warm aura.

"I love you, Mary. I love you more than I've ever loved anyone; more than I love even myself. I never thought it was possible. I never knew how to love someone more than myself, like my daddy loved my mama, but you changed that. I never understood any of it until you. I don't know how, but you did. This time away from you has made it crystal clear to me that nothing in the world matters to me but you. If the rest of the world melted away, I wouldn't care as long as you were beside me. My only desire in the world is to know that you love me too. Nothing else," he whispered.

His words were deliciously tempting. She looked up at his cerulean eyes; they seemed to glow in the dimly-lit room. "I-I-I don't...I-I-I can't...," she stuttered trying to escape her mind's inhibitions. Tears welled up in her eyes.

"Just take a deep breath. It's ok." He earnestly wanted to soothe her by holding her, but he knew he couldn't. He'd promised not to touch her.

"You once told me that the most attractive thing about a man was his scent…," he whispered, encouraging her to move slightly closer to him so she could hear him.

Mary let out an apprehensive giggle; it was just like Alan to listen too intently to something she said.

"Breathe me in. You don't have to touch me, just take me in. Don't question, just do it," his words were soft.

She wasn't exactly sure why or how she allowed herself to do it, but she closed her eyes, moved closer to him, and breathed in deeply – and there it was – the scent that was the very essence of Alan. It was delectable – intoxicating – the combination of the way the air smelled when it rained mixed with the wonderful woodsy smell of a Georgia pine forest. The only thing it was missing was the spicy aroma of bourbon.

Again and again she breathed in his scent. She'd caught whiffs of it before, but never like this, there was something different – something stronger, more alluring. As she opened her eyes to gaze into his, she could feel her mind's resolve weakening. There were stones crumbling around her feet as the wall protecting her quaked.

"I only want you to see me for who I am. Not the image, but the man."

"And who is that?" she asked without breaking her stare with his beautiful eyes.

"I'm just an average Joe who is hopelessly in love with you. I only want you to love me, too."

She wanted to tell him everything, to talk and talk telling every tiny detail about Roger, the rape, Tucson, Tunda, and the whole frantic cross-country escape. But she couldn't be certain he'd still love her, if he knew the truth. Couldn't she just hold onto that moment knowing he loved her with the purest love she'd ever witnessed?

Tunda's advice roared in her mind.

With every word he continued to say, she could do nothing but listen and hope beyond hope that somehow, someway this could all be true. She silently prayed she could find a way to be with Alan without having to face the past.

"My heart belongs to you, Mary Stephenson. I stand here before you promising that I will do everything in my power to be everything you need. I am confessing to you that every part of me is forever yours," he continued to say. "For so long I've been empty. Music was my safe haven. In my own musical world everything made sense and the entire world could kiss my ass. And then you came along. You changed everything. I realized I've sung a lot of stupid, uninspired, heartless songs that I see now were more about dogs dying than real love felt between a woman and a man.

"I never realized any of it until you. You came along and showed me life from a completely different point of view. You inspired me and believed in me in a way no one ever has. You showed me what love is all about."

"I don't know what you're talking about," she said modestly.

"You changed me. Before you came, I thought my life was over – an endless sea of mediocrity. But then there was you. You brought out the real me, the one who's been hiding behind a mask even within my own skin. The me who's been pretending to be happy when really I haven't been happy in years! You brought the light back into my life. You brought the hope back. You're the air that I breathe! You're the music that I write; the lyrics that I sing every day!" His dimples appeared on his cheeks.

Mary was surprised at how much she missed his smile. "I didn't do anything," she whispered.

"You think that, but you did…just by being you. Just by breathing, by your very being you have changed me. Now it's my turn." His eyes never moved from their constant gaze upon her. "Let me take away the fear you live with."

"But, Alan…" A silent tear escaped its captivity. "I…," she couldn't finish her thought.

Alan gingerly lifted his hand to wipe her tear away, but stopped, remembering his promise not to touch her. "Shhh. It's my turn to save you…to offer you freedom from your cocoon. Let me be the man who sets you free. I'll protect you 'til the end of the earth! You'll never hurt again."

Her finger tips trembled as she delicately brushed her fingers along the softness of his chest hair, not allowing herself to touch his skin. Could his promises actually be real? And if they were real, could she allow herself to accept them? They were so delectably tempting.

Alan's breaths quickened, but he remained steadfast. His heart rattled hard against its confinement. He silently gripped and twisted his fingers trying to ward off the temptation to touch her. He wanted her badly; resisting his natural instinct was one of the hardest things he'd ever forced himself to do. When he planned this whole thing, he thought it would be simple not to touch her, to resist her incredible appeal; he had *no idea what he was thinking.*

He breathed deeply, trying to soothe himself and inhale her essence at the same time. She was far more intoxicating than all the alcohol he'd drank in his entire life!

Mary's touch went past his hair to touch his warm skin; she didn't know what she expected to happen – an electric shock? When nothing happened, she let out a relieved sob.

"It's ok," he whispered, his voice wavering much more than he anticipated.

Her entire hand was then upon his chest, above where his heart was. "Your heart is pounding," she said.

Alan smiled, but didn't say anything. He didn't want her to know what a struggle it was for him to keep from touching her – from caressing her in his arms – from ripping her clothes off.

She lifted her hand up and gently pressed her lips upon his heart, feeling his pulse quicken at the touch of her velvety lips. From the pit of her soul she wanted him. She wanted to feel him completely encapsulating her, entering her, loving her. But her past. *Oh why must he tempt me so aggressively?*

Pulling herself back from him, she suddenly shouted at him angrily, "Why, Alan, why are you doing this?!"

"I-I-I told you why," he struggled to say, shocked by her sudden change.

"But why? You're making...," she stopped. "I don't understand the importance."

"Put yourself in my shoes. Y-y-you haven't talked to me or looked at me in over three weeks!"

"This doesn't change anything! You're still just as dangerous now as you were then!"

"How?! I'm standing here as defenseless as I've ever been in my life; how can I possibly be dangerous to anyone? The fact that I haven't lifted a finger to touch you should tell you how benign I am! And I want to tell you, it has been very hard!! "I want you so badly! Everything about you makes me want you more and more..."

"But when I said you were dangerous to me..." She sighed and paced the room in frustration. She desperately wanted to tell him who she really was and why saying he was dangerous had dual meaning. But when she stopped and looked at those incredible blue eyes that trusted her so intently, she couldn't do it. She couldn't tell him that everything he knew about her was a bold-faced lie. That the woman he was professing his love for didn't even exist. "I've got to go, Alan." She picked up her purse.

"Please don't go. Share with me what's going on inside your mind. Your eyes just closed off from me. For a moment there were no walls between us. Please don't block me out. I can't be the only one who's vulnerable here! I know you're scared, but I'm here. I'm never going to let anything happen to you, *ever!* I've just opened myself to you entirely. Please, I can't be the only one that's done that."

She looked at his confused face. Her heart wanted her to stay and talk to him all night long, to expose herself to him as he had to her, but her head kept flashing images of Roger's impending wrath before her eyes like a category five hurricane.

"Oh God, Alan, I just can't. You have to understand it's not you!" She was back in front of his naked body again. "You are wonderful, perfect! You are *everything*…it's-it's-it's… so much more than that." She was pacing again; it was obvious her thoughts were running more rapidly than her mouth could communicate. "This…this is all so dangerous…"

"But why?" His brow furrowed in confusion. "I don't understand."

"And you wouldn't."

"Then explain it to me, *please*. I'd do anything in the world for you. I'll be anything you want me to be."

"That's just it – you can't be anyone other than who you *are*, and I can never be anyone other than who I am. Because of that, we'll never be able to make it work." The tension was palpable, forcing her to leave as quickly as possible. Her footsteps led her directly to the door.

Things were spiraling out of control. "No! Don't go!" He followed after her.

With the delicate, pleading eyes of a deer, she briefly stopped at the door.

"I promised you I wouldn't touch, and I'll keep that

promise. But I want you to please stay and talk to me. Even if it's just hypothetical. Tell me what is so dangerous about our being together. *Why* won't it work? We can *make it* work."

"Goodbye, Alan."

His face became stern, angry with himself. "It's all because of Angela, isn't it?? It's all because of this!" he shouted as he touched his lip. "Earl said he'd have the divorce papers ready for me to sign tomorrow. As soon as I can, I'm signing them. I've had enough of her." He pulled off his wedding ring and threw it across the room.

"No! There's so much more to it than just her. Don't you understand; if you knew everything about me it would endanger you and Angela. You need to just stay away from me!"

"Why?? Are you a criminal or something? An escaped convict? What are you hiding?!" he demanded.

Placing her hand upon his chest as if to signal stop, she stood on her tip-toes and gently kissed him a salty, tear-filled kiss. With a soft sob, she turned from him and hurried down the hallway as the door divided the space between them.

CHAPTER 21

It was dark when Mary returned to the farm; her mind was a whirling tornado. "Alan, Alan," she mumbled repeatedly under her breath. Her thoughts were convoluted and confused. She wanted to get away to some peace and quiet where she could think.

Running from her truck, everything around there reminded her of Alan, images of his naked body flashed before her – she wanted him so badly – probably more than he wanted her. Just being near him made her want him; being near him – naked – made things even worse!

She didn't bother with a bridle for Sun. Looping the lead line around to the other side of his halter, she made make-shift reins, hopped onto his back, and galloped wildly into the moonlit night. Once the darkness overtook them, she put her hands into the air and let the wind whisper between her fingers; her heels dug into Sun's sides forcing him to run faster and faster. Her chest was on fire. Tears streamed down either side of her face. Her hat clung for dear life on her head.

When she was far away from any place where people were, she screamed out in agony. "Oh God it burns so bad!!" she cried out. "I *hate* you, Roger!!"

Why couldn't she just be with Alan? "Why? *Why*? **_Why_**?!" she screamed. "Why are you here messing things up? Go away!!" she shrieked at an imaginary Roger.

Sun galloped faster and faster until he was laid out running at top speed.

Mary leaned upon his neck, holding onto his mane. Her tears streaked her face; the wind whisked them away quickly. Over and over again in her mind contrasting pictures flashed – Alan: honest, kind, loving, naked – Roger: menacing, dastardly, cruel, deadly.

The wind stung her eyes as much as her tears, but she could hardly feel anything.

Sun bolted through the fields. He was sweaty when they reached the farthest part of the Brooks farm. It was where Mary finally slowed him, slid off of his back, and collapsed in a weak, crying heap.

"Oh Alan," she said as she lay hidden in the tall dry weeds. Looking up at the black night sky with its diamond-like stars, it wasn't the desert or the constellations she thought of, it was Alan.

She heard his voice resonating in her ears, "I love you, Mary. I love you more than I've ever loved anyone; more than I love even myself. I never thought it was possible. I never knew how to love someone more than myself, like my daddy loved my mama, but you changed that. I never understood any of it until you."

She analyzed his words.

"How can he love me like that? How? I'm...I'm...unlovable!" she cried out. "I'm nothing more than Roger's...," she wept bitterly at the memories.

Sun grazed casually nearby.

"You're my angel; you saved me," she heard Alan say again in her mind.

"Alan deserves someone better than me. I didn't save him. He saved himself. If he knew the truth about me, he'd see who he really loves doesn't even exist! He doesn't really love *me*. He doesn't even know me!"

Alan again filled her thoughts: "Your heart is a place no man has ever truly explored. I want to be that man! I can't *wait* to be that man!! If I have to wait a thousand years for you, you're worth every second."

The tears rained from her eyes into her ears; she wanted so badly to tell him the truth to see if it was possible for him to love her still, but the awaiting explosion was too much to risk. "Why didn't I just kill Roger? Why?" She stood up, angry at herself for not following Tunda's original plan.

"I've got to get away from here...," she said as she manically plotted. "But how? Oh God, the idea of leaving Alan..." She clawed at her chest; the fiery feeling intensified. "Agh!! It burns so bad!!" How had she allowed herself to fall so far in love with him too?

She thought of him standing naked in the hotel room. "Mmmm," she moaned at the thoughts of what could've been.

Her mind raced feverishly back and forth, straddling both sides of a contradictory fence – every tiny part of her wanted him in the most desirable way, and yet, she knew she couldn't have him. *If he knew the truth, things would be different*, she thought.

"Tell me what is so dangerous about our being together. *Why* won't it work? We can *make it* work," she heard Alan's voice in her mind again.

If only I could tell him why without jeopardizing myself..., she didn't finish the thought.

You're in love with him just as much, if not more, than he is with you! her heart told her.

Be realistic. If you succumb to your temptations, how are you going to keep things from going too far? her head told her heart. *How can you assure your safety? Secrets are best kept as secrets.*

She began pacing broad and thoughtful steps along the fence edge.

Seeing Alan's vulnerability and witnessing his incredible ability to resist even his own obvious desires encouraged her to eradicate the idea of him as a rapist. *Roger never would've done something like that*, she thought, *ever!*

She hung her head and turned back to the other direction. "Roger," she said aloud. It was Roger who always smacked her in the face with reality. No matter which way she turned, she always ran directly into Roger.

"If Roger knew about any of this, he'd kill us both!" She pulled the top part of a tall weed off and twisted it in her fingers. Mindlessly, she began plucking the pieces off of the weed and dropping them to the ground.

Images of Roger roaming the earth searching for her flashed before her. Her knees became weak at the thought. "On the other hand, if anyone can protect me from Roger, it's Alan." The more she thought about Roger, the more fearful she became.

"I've got to not think about Roger right now." She tapped the fence post and turned back. "Poor Alan. I can't imagine what he's thinking."

Alan was the single light of hope for a future. He was the light at the end of her tunnel, but on the other hand, he could also be the train that runs over her.

Still her heart clung to the hope that somewhere in the darkness she'd faced for so many years, the modicum of light Alan offered was a bright future and not destruction. She would be a fool not to partake in that light even if for just a moment.

Frustration with herself was settling into her psyche. "If you don't at least do something, you'll always wonder what might have been."

She stared up at the stars and thought quietly about the future. *He said he didn't care about my past, but if he knew, I bet he would care,* she thought. The truth about her past enveloped her like the darkness consumed the night; she winced as she faced it.

Alan's words filled her ears: "It's my turn to save you…to offer you freedom from your cocoon. Let me be the man who sets you free. I'll protect you 'til the end of the earth! You'll never hurt again."

She stood stone still. If only she could be certain Alan loved her, the true her, did it matter if she died tomorrow? Did life really matter? She could at least die knowing she was loved with a purer love than she'd ever find anywhere else. "And that's all that really matters," she whispered.

Tunda's words of advice whispered in her ears: *Loving someone means giving him the ability to hurt you, but trusting him enough to know that he won't.*

She reached in her pocket and pulled out her cell phone. She typed out: *Meet me at ur granddad's cabin.* Throwing caution to the wind, she pressed the send button.

Oh God! What did I just do?! her analytical mind screamed. *Are you stupid or something!?*

Her heart rebutted with, *No, it doesn't matter. Just go. He has to know. This double life is killing you! You can't go on like this. If he rejects you, then just leave. Don't use names.*

She whispered her heart's instructions, "Don't use names."

Without another thought, she was a woman on a mission. She whistled for Sun, who trotted up to her. Hopping onto his back, they were once again at their same break-neck speed toward the Brooks cabin in the woods. She wasn't sure what she was going to do or say; she only knew she had to see him again and do – *something*.

Sun quickly carried her to the cabin; sweat reappeared under his golden coat.

Mary slid off of his back and tied him to a nearby tree. Her mind raced, but her heart blocked any attempts at a cohesive thought.

She walked inside the dark cabin; the outdoorsy smell overwhelmed her. Thoughts of her father flooded her mind. It was like a wave of safety and security enveloped her, soothing her tattered emotions; was it possible this was the right thing? Did she, in some macabre way, have her father's blessing?

Closing the door behind her, she blindly made her way through the timeworn, pitch-black cabin. "Ow! Damn it!" she shouted when she accidentally kicked something on the floor.

Feeling her way more intently now, she found a stump chair and sat down on it. The moon was almost full, but its light was not in a position to illuminate the cabin.

"I should've used my cell phone for light, duh!" She took it out and slid her finger across the screen. The tiny amount of light it offered only slightly lit up the cozy space.

Alan had not texted back.

"Maybe it means he's on his way," she whispered.

As time passed, she reflected on how miserable she'd been even when she first came to Georgia; things were so different now. There were moments of bliss. "Many moments," she said aloud. Hope had carried her higher than she could've dreamed. And everything was because of Alan.

Smiling, she thought of how much he'd changed things. She recalled sitting in Cracker Barrel questioning just who Alan was behind closed doors; seeing him so completely unmasked in the hotel room spoke volumes. He had single-handedly shown that he was as genuine as anyone she'd ever met.

Her thoughts continued over the past months. How had she missed seeing how gradually he'd proven her first image of him as the egomaniac incorrect? He simply was Alan – a man who wanted nothing more than the purest desire of all: to love and be loved. The more she sat and thought, the harder she fell for him.

"He's totally opposite of Roger," she whispered as she checked the time on her cell phone. An hour had passed since she'd texted him.   Impatiently, she crossed her legs, swinging the top leg animatedly, anxiously.

She took her hat off and began the arduous process of unbraiding her hair. If Alan could expose himself to her, maybe she should show at least some of herself to him.

When she finished, she combed through her loosed hair with her fingers. "That should've killed some time."

She roused her phone again, another 30 minutes had passed. A dagger slowly began to pierce her heart.

Fear began to torment her: "He's not coming."

She fidgeted with a few locks of hair lying gently across her chest. Why hadn't she considered his not showing? If he didn't, what did that mean? How long was she going to wait? She texted him again: *Are you coming?*

She paced the cabin using her phone for light and thinking about what she would say. Would she use names? Part of her said no, and then the other part told her to come completely clean with him. He needed to know who she really was. Then any decision he made would be legit. Then she would have peace.

Another hour passed, and he failed to reply to her text messages.

Fear berated her over-confident heart. "What the hell were you thinking? He's through with you!"

Get your stupid ass in gear and go. He's not coming; there's nothing to wait for, she thought.

It felt as though a heavy weight had been dropped upon the dagger that now stabbed fully into her heart. She wrapped her hair up and tucked it back under her hat.

The moon had shifted enough to light up most of the cabin. *Don't you cry, you idiot. Don't do it! You got exactly what you deserved!* she chastised herself harshly. *You put him up on a pedestal; what did you expect?*

Sun appeared to be asleep standing next to the tree where Mary had tied him. "Hiya, fella," she said gently as she caressed his head; he rubbed it against her.

"At least *you're* still here." She untied him. "But then again, you've always been here." She swung herself upon his back. Slowly, they walked through the field; every part of her felt confused, hurt.

"At least I didn't do anything stupid, fella," she said to Sun.

CHAPTER 22

Mary and Sun made their way gradually through the moonlit night. When they were at the top of the hill overlooking the barn and the main house, all was quiet below. Her mind naturally wondered where Alan was.

She snorted to herself. *He's probably in there screwing Angela,* she thought. She felt a twinge of jealousy come over her. She immediately scorned herself for such stupidity. *He's her man, for crying out loud, and don't you ever forget it again!*

She clucked to Sun. "Let's get out of here. I'm sick of all of this! I should've stopped it all before he wiggled his way so deeply into my thoughts," she said, trying more than anything to talk some sense into herself.

Sun picked up the pace, but soon after lazily slowed down to another stop and grabbed a mouthful of grass.

Mary hardly noticed; her mind was elsewhere. She laid on Sun's back while he grazed. The moon shining brightly in the sky made all the dark parts seem visible with a gray light.

"Life's been good, hasn't it? I don't need him, do I?" she said aloud to Sun, who was eagerly looking for another bite of grass. She sighed. "Well, life's been good. We can agree on that." She gazed back at the diamond-studded sky. "But what happens now?" she whispered.

"Hey." Sun jumped out from under her at the sound of Alan's voice.

Mary instantly fell off, but immediately grabbed the reins and soothed Sun back down.

"What the hell are you doing here??" she asked as she remounted Sun.

"Come here."

Mary urged Sun over to Alan.

"I got your messages."

"Yeah, well, sorry for those. I wanted to...," she said, but stopped. It irritated her how she couldn't hide the quivering disappointment in her voice. "I-I-I don't know what I was thinking." Her gaze fell to Sun's mane.

Alan gently placed his hand on her leg. "We could've talked things out. Why'd you leave?"

"I left because I was c-c-confused." That word seemed to sum up why she left. "I didn't know what to say or what to do."

"And you do now?"

"Why didn't you show up?" she asked, purposely ignoring his question.

"I got word from Felix. He's discovered possible evidence against his suspect in Biscuit's poisoning, so I needed to see what he had to say."

"Oh my gosh! Who?" she said with concern.

"We'll talk about it later. Now back to your texts. So you know what to say now?" he asked again.

"I just know...I mean...I think.... I don't know." Her voice warbled as tears welled up in her eyes. "I thought I needed to talk."

"But you don't anymore?"

"I don't know. Maybe..." She sighed. "I don't..."

He didn't let her finish speaking before he swung up onto Sun behind her, taking the reins from her hands.

"What the...," Mary asked astonished.

"Shhh!!" He clucked to Sun, who trotted, and then loped through the pasture.

Mary acquiesced and leaned against Alan's chest as he maneuvered Sun through the darkness. There wrapped in his sheltering arms returned the feeling of complete safety. The same scent she'd enjoyed in the hotel – that incredible masculine scent – surrounded her; she became intoxicated all over again by his presence. Even with all her inner turmoil, there was no doubt; he was exactly what she needed. And in his arms was precisely where she belonged.

Before long, they were on the top of the hill overlooking the lake near the Brooks family cabin; the moonlight reflected brightly off the water. Alan rode straight for the cabin, dismounted, and tied Sun up to the same tree Mary had tied him to.

He held Mary's hand as they entered the rustic space. Without a word, he shut the door behind them. The moon's light showed the outlines of items inside the tiny room.

Alan stroked her cheek as he spoke. "I told you your past didn't matter; I let you down. I'm so sorry. It didn't occur to me how it could feel like incredible pressure on you."

"It did," she whispered.

"I understand that now. I'm-I'm ashamed of myself." He hung his head just before he looked at her again. His eyes were filled with deep regret. "It's just I know you're holding back from me. I can sense it. And I want you to let go. I want you to trust me enough to let yourself be vulnerable, and I failed. I'm so sorry."

"It's ok." She pushed his hand from her. "If I don't do this n-n-now," she stammered, "I-I-I'll never be able to." She drew in a deep breath. "Don't say a word or I'll never be able to say it all." Tears immediately pooled at the edge of her eyelids. She was glad it was nearly dark in there; it made it easier to talk. She was almost able to pretend she was standing outside of her body as she confessed.

Alan only nodded in the dimly lit room. He sat on one of the stump chairs and crossed his long legs.

"My past surrounds me like a dark, destructive storm hindering any escape attempts. It swirls my thoughts with its wind, shatters my hope with its impending doom, and makes my mind so muddled that I can't find my way. You've been the only light in all of the darkness. You've come to symbolize any hope I might have for a normal existence. But I can't cling to that."

"Yes, you can,"

"Shh. I can't because it's all a lie. I've been lying to you since day one. I-I-I'm not who you think I am. I've told you a little about my husband, and to put it bluntly, he was a monster. He always threatened me. He said if I ever left him, he'd hunt me down like a dog, take me into the desert, and kill me in the most painfully slow way possible, and then leave my body for the coyotes to eat."

She paused as she waited for a reaction from Alan which didn't come.

"He would beat me without mercy. I became very adept at applying makeup to cover up the bruises, red marks and swelling. I wore turtle-neck shirts and long-sleeves in the middle of 100-degree weather. I hid everything. From my family, friends, colleagues – no one knew about the way he was behind closed doors."

She struggled to keep the tears from falling. "He was my dream man; I didn't want anyone to think any differently about him.

"He could be the most charming man you'd ever met. When we first met, he would tell me we were just friends and he didn't like me any other way. To an 18 year old, this was equal to a challenge. But the truth was quite different. He used reverse psychology to lure me into his web. My dad said he was so oily he could slide uphill. Now, I don't know about that, but he *was* a smooth talker. So smooth that in just a couple of months, I agreed to elope with him, even against my parents' wishes. He was 31, and so exciting, so in control, and so unlike the other boys I dated. Marrying him seemed like it would be a fantasy! It was as if I was Cinderella marrying her Prince Charming! So, when I had the chance to marry him, I did. I jumped at it!

"It didn't even matter that I hadn't finished college or that my parents didn't approve; I did it anyway. We went off to Mexico and got married on the beach in Veracruz. I moved into his house and expected life to be so perfectly perfect from then on. And at first, it was.

"I lived the picture-perfect life – on the outside. I had everything any woman could want, except a life lived without fear. I had a litany of masks in which I wore to make everyone believe our perfect life. Yet behind those masks, I lived in constant terror. I never knew what was going to set him off. He could go from laughing and jovial to breaking my ribs in a moment's notice. And the threats…. He could look at me with those cold, black eyes of his and easily terrify me or thrill me, depending on the situation. When he looked at me like he wanted me, I never felt sexier or more desirable. At the same time, he could cause me to crawl inside my shell and simply tremble waiting for the storm to pass.

"I have been slapped for crying, for having my period, for studying for my classes, for calling my parents to chat, for washing laundry while he was in the shower, for having lunch with a colleague he didn't approve of, for having an opinion different from his –

especially if I voiced it in public. Oh! That was cause for the worst beatings. But of course, he never struck me in public. He would just flash his hate-filled eyes towards me and shut me up cold. I knew all too well there would be hell to pay when we got home.

"In public, most of the time, he was perfect! He was everything everyone expected him to be. I loved him so much when we were in public. He was every bit of the strong, virile man who with one glance across the room had me completely in the palm of his hand. He would hold me in his powerful arms and make me melt! I was completely in his control. I'm not really sure how I let myself go to him so easily, but I did.

"I was awestruck by him. He was so handsome. So perfectly poised and in control. I was still such a mess. I graduated with my bachelor's in three years. Afterwards, I only wanted to be his everything. To give my life completely to serving him and making him happy. The trouble was, I was a colossal failure at it, which he pointed out with frequent 'corrections,' as he called them. And even though I thought I could correct myself enough to stop him, the beatings continued.

"Once I started working, he started to stalk me. I know it seems weird and impossible – how does a husband stalk his wife? But he did. I would have lunch or dinner with friends, colleagues, or even a client, and he would show up or he'd already be there when we got there! It was unnerving having him join us and then monopolize the conversation. He always picked up the check, so there wasn't much my guests could say, but still, it always put me in such an awkward position. I didn't know what to do. Once, I asked him to stop." She sucked in air through her teeth. "But it only resulted in overblown accusations, which then caused a huge fight and ended with me getting a broken nose and a black eye. I didn't ask again. Instead, I started turning down lunch and dinner invites.

"And then there was the sex. In the beginning, when we were dating, our sex was fun, exciting, and very passionate. Unlike anything I'd ever experienced! As I look back on it now, I don't think we ever achieved the point in our relationship where our souls communicated through sex or where, uh, we were one with each other. It was more about satisfying the wild, carnal urge, you know? I naïvely thought we had everything and more, but when you're really young, that's what you think," she said nervously. "But once we got married, then the sex started getting weird."

"Weird? How?" Alan's voice was smooth, level.

"I don't know. Just weird. First with exciting and different positions, which were pretty fun, and I admit, I probably encouraged him because I did enjoy them." Her hands shook as she spoke. She wasn't sure what the repercussions of telling him about Roger would be, but somehow, she knew she *needed* to tell him. It was as if having someone who knew and truly cared, mattered. Sure, Tunda knew, but she didn't know it all, and that wasn't enough.

"Then with crazy toys – and I do mean crazy! Then public places, which, again, I probably encouraged," she said, ashamed of her contribution at the Governor's Masquerade Ball for the Betterment of Arizona Children.

She stopped and practiced breathing for a few moments before she continued. "He said it was for me – for my 21st birthday. He brought another woman home for us to 'share.' I couldn't do it." Her eyes welled up again; this time the dam holding back the flood was worthless as tears spilled over her eyelids. "I couldn't share my husband. He tried getting me rip-roaring drunk, but the only result he got was me puking in the bathroom all night. I'm pretty sure he ended up screwing whoever she was while I was throwing up. I couldn't swear to it, but I'm pretty sure."

"Jack ass," Alan whispered.

"Something inside me started to die after that night. Yet, if that were all, I think I could live with it, but there's so much more." Her tears continued their silent march down her cheeks. "He'd get wasted and bring home a friend and expect me to take Ecstasy and have sex with his friend while he watched." There was a venomous undertone to her voice.

"Did you?" Alan asked.

"I didn't want to! A few times he beat me until I willingly took the drugs. Other times he would force feed them to me; his different friends would hold me down and help. I'd wake up the next day not remembering much but feeling insanely sore and broken. I hated him more every time he did it! We would argue a lot, and he would hit me a lot, until I eventually learned to just shut up and stop fighting him."

"So you went along with it?"

Mary hung her head and stifled a sob.

Fear cackled loudly. "I told you he wouldn't understand."

"He'd beat me to a bloody pulp! What choice did I have?! I can assure you absolute hysterics occurred during and after every beating. I would have done anything imaginable to avoid them! Yet, I couldn't. I couldn't do anything right! For some asinine reason, I couldn't stop myself from making wrong moves, asking wrong questions, or provoking him.

"Yet through it all, I always found ways to justify his behavior. I wasn't paying close enough attention; I wasn't meeting his needs; I wasn't sexually adventurous enough; I wasn't sexy enough; I had gained two pounds; I had forgotten to purchase his beer; he was stressed at work; I was distracted. Oh, I could come up with a gazillion different excuses for him. And in my head, they all justified his horrific behavior. I kept telling myself when he became more successful things would change. But the problem was, when he made partner and became more successful, things did change – they got worse." Mary wiped her tears on her sleeve.

Alan's eyes were glued on her dark silhouette, sickened and shocked by her story.

"Nothing was ever enough for him. No matter how much I would give in to him and try to please him, it was *never* enough." The words, which had been so difficult to find before, poured out over her lips like her tears over her eyelids. "Right after my parents' deaths, he lined up what he called a gangbang."

"What?! And you did this?!" Alan regretted the amount of disgust accompanying his tone. He didn't want to pass judgment on her, and yet his voice was filled with derision and the judgment he wanted to withhold.

"No. I flat-out refused. I'd had enough. I packed up a few things and moved to an apartment across town. I had been accepted into graduate school at the University of Arizona, and he refused to allow me to attend. My parents were both professors, and after they died, I wanted to do something with my life. I wanted to follow their legacy. So, I accepted the offer of admission and left him. Life was finally moving in the right direction for me. That is, until he found me…"

Her entire body began to noticeably shake.

Alan stood up and placed his hand on her shoulder, which caused her to immediately yank back from him as she'd done many times before. She moved several steps away and clung to the fireplace mantle. The agony and terror she thought she'd gotten over revealed themselves to Alan in the form of gut-wrenching sobs.

He wanted nothing more than to hold her – comfort her. Nevertheless, the idea of upsetting her further made him resist the urge. He reminded himself – if he were going to be effective in comforting her, she would have to come to him. Quietly, his heart broke as he listened to the tiny woman cry. All he could do was insinuate himself near her so his calming aura could communicate to hers without any words or physical contact.

She breathed in a deep breath and reminded herself – although she'd never be safe, she wasn't afraid of death. Facing death was something she'd already experienced.

Fear cringed at her bravery.

"H-h-he nearly killed me that day," she calmed her sobs enough to say.

Mary wiped the tears from her cheeks and stood firmly erect next to the stone fireplace. Her back remained to Alan. She had to be strong.

"You're safe here, you know?" Alan softly whispered.

She turned around to face him, surprised at how close he was. "Am I? I thought I was safe there, too." She stepped back a few steps to the very edge of the fireplace mantle.

"I don't remember every detail about what happened, but I know he nearly choked the life out of me and then dropped me from my second-story balcony. It took months before I recovered – before I could even walk again. During all of that, I met Tunda Bailey, the woman you think is my mother. And in many ways became my surrogate mother.

"Tunda volunteers at the Tucson Battered Women's Shelter. My doctor in the hospital called her in since he suspected there was more to my story than met the eye. Tunda protected me. She picked up on my husband's dark side pretty quickly. Even still, I defended him. I don't know why. Embarrassment? Love? Stupidity? I don't know! It took Tunda pointing out the obvious to me. His 'corrections' weren't corrections; they were all-out beatings!"

"Why didn't you call the police?" Alan asked.

Mary nervously laughed through her tears. "Police? What were they going to do? I can't tell you how many times I called them and they did nothing! Most of the time they wouldn't even respond to the call. They're his friends, so it was far easier to ignore it and deal with the 'real' crime than their buddy beating his wife up."

"How could they ignore something like that?"

"It's Tucson, Alan. A big city with real big-city crime. Even if they had responded, my husband was buddies with enough of them to make them resist interfering. They just walked away. Remember, he was as smooth as any man – a real man's man."

"What about going to a doctor or counselor?" Alan asked as he hung on her every word.

"I never went to the doctor alone. And when I did, he did all the talking. I didn't dare talk over him or contradict him. I wanted to live! A counselor? There was no way he would ever consider counseling. I never mentioned it. If we had sought counseling, I'm sure the counselor would've just pointed out how I wasn't good enough. I'm already aware; I certainly didn't need a professional confirming it!"

"But you are good enough. You're perfect in every way."

"No I'm not. I'm flawed in every way possible. There were times when I would try to fight back, but I think they just encouraged him, so I stopped. I simply tried to defend myself or reduce the amount of damage he did."

"Why did you stay with him?"

Mary turned to look directly at Alan. "Because I loved him. I knew he *could* behave, he just didn't. I believed for so long.... I believed I provoked him. I was the reason he hit me. If only I could behave, he would behave. He'd proven so many times at various events he could be everything I believed him to be. And then I'd open my mouth and all hell would break loose."

"You can't control someone that much, you know?"

"I know." She turned back away from Alan. "At least now I do. But I was young. Unaware of how a marriage was supposed to work on the inside. I looked at him as a father-figure. Someone who corrected me when I was wrong. It wasn't until...," she started to say, but breathed in deeply and stopped short of mentioning the rape. "In a lot of ways, I think my situation was a lot like yours."

"How?"

"I didn't want to admit defeat. I didn't want to admit I'd made a mistake by marrying him. I wanted to prove to everyone how the man I married was one in a million, like they all thought when we were dating. So, I did like you said you do. I put on a plastic smile, danced around like the pathetic sock puppet I was, and did all the things everyone expected of me. I suffered the beatings in private. When I was too banged up, I didn't go out. I'd stay inside until the swelling went down.

"Even still, once I was here in relative safety, there were countless times I wanted to run back to him. To run into his arms, kiss his amazing lips, smell his intoxicating smell, see the sexy desire for me in his eyes, and know for one moment everything was good.

"But I know that's impossible. I can't. *I can't.* He won't change. He'll *never* change. I was lying to myself when I thought he would. For years I clung to a pathetic strand of hope that maybe someday he would. But one day, I realized he never would." She sobbed as she thought of the rape video. "I wanted so desperately to please him! And all I did was make him hit me and-and-and do... unspeakable things!!" she sputtered.

Alan placed his hands on her shoulders, turned her to face him, and pulled her frail, defeated body to him.

Mary was too weak to resist. She buried her face into his chest and sobbed while Alan placed his hand on her hat, keeping it on her head.

"Listen to me. You did *not* cause him to hit you. You understand that? He's a trailer-trash bastard!"

She pulled back from him and wiped her nose on her shirt. "That's just it. Everyone assumes all battered women are poor or uneducated, or their husbands are some low-life, dirty T-shirt wearing, uneducated idiots, but the truth is, it can happen to anyone."

"What do you mean?"

"My husband isn't some trailer-trash, low-class, low life. He's an attorney. This past year, he ran for election as the Arizona State Representative. He's a powerful man with means. And me? I was just one step away from finishing my doctorate."

Alan's mouth gapped open. "Exactly, who are you?"

Mary sniffled as she pulled herself together, closed her eyes, and prepared herself to say the words she swore she'd never tell a soul: "My name isn't Mary Stephenson; it's Mary Elizabeth Franklin. My husband's name is Roger Donavan Franklin. I staged my disappeared from Tucson on September 15th just last year, and made my escape here."

CHAPTER 23

Alan stumbled back, shocked by this revelation. He found a stump chair and sat down; his jaw remained upon his chest. In his mind, he had an entire therapy session with himself, soothing the insecurities he had fostered by her one-step-forward-two-steps-back approach to their relationship. Everything she'd said explained her reactions – her jerking away from him, her openness and then sudden reticence. The silence in the cabin was unnerving; the musty air hung still as if it were holding onto the words she uttered. Even the chirping spring peepers were quiet with the revelation of such news.

Mary wasn't sure what to do or say – should she say anything? She wanted to run. She clung to the edge of the fireplace like it was her only lifeline and quietly sobbed. She knew she needed to tell him about the rape, but she wasn't certain she could. Was her resolve strong enough to go that far? She wasn't sure. The reality of her past shook her very foundation. And articulating it was almost as bad as reliving it.

Mary sniffled. She had to be strong. "I don't think I ever pleased him." Walking away from the fireplace, her tear-filled anger flared again. "He always wanted more – more perversion, more violence, more submission from me, and more power for him! He wanted to have total control over me! He wanted me to be like him – no inhibitions whatsoever. But I couldn't! I love sex, but not like that!!" Telling him about the rape paced back and forth behind her teeth.

Alan didn't say anything or make any moves.

The silence between them was deafening.

Fear filled the silence with his taunting, "Runnnnnn!"

Still, Mary remembered how bravely Alan stood before her, naked and completely vulnerable. "If you would've asked me this time last year where I saw myself, the last thing I would've said was here, longing to be in your arms."

She began unbuttoning her shirt. Her eyes never leaving his.

"Everything I am right now is nothing like I thought I would be," she said with her voice noticeably shaking. Would all of her lies make him reject her?

Her shirt dropped to the floor next to her.

"Letting go of people and places I thought I couldn't live without only to find an entirely different world I now can't live without would've been a ridiculous thought last year. Yet, here I am."

She unfastened her jeans.

"The mask is gone."

She pulled her boots off.

"The sock puppet is put back in the drawer."

She kicked away the crumpled pile of jeans.

"The dance is over. I can't hide anymore."

She unhooked her bra.

"No more secrets. No more lies. Just me."

She dropped her bra next to her jeans.

"So now, all I'm left with is feeling so very exposed, n-n-naked just as you were in the hotel room."

She slid her panties down to her ankles and then kicked them to her jeans.

"All that's left, is the real me."

Tears returned to her eyes as she thought of the tell-tale scars on her breasts. Alan would know she hadn't told the entire truth. What would she say if he asked? She hoped the darkness kept them concealed.

Alan hadn't moved or changed his stare. What did that mean? Had she made a grave mistake? Were her lies too much for him to take?

Fear ran his icy fingers along her naked arms making chill bumps prickle her skin. "He won't love you after all of this," Fear whispered in her ear.

Yet she remained steadfast. Nothing could make her run from Alan.

Fear cackled in her ear as he had done many times before. "He thinks you're a whore!"

Mary remained rigid.

Fear murmured, "Because you *are* a whore! Who could love a whore like you?"

Mary's soul spoke to Alan's without Fear interrupting.

Fear continued, "Look at him! He doesn't love you. He looks like a stone!"

Alan could hardly believe his ears. The idea that the reasons for her actions were something other than she didn't love him felt like the world had been lifted off of his shoulders.

His entire body trembled. He tried to stand, to go to her, but his legs betrayed him. He could only kneel before her. Placing his head against her belly, he clung to her, pulling her hips against him. "I thought I'd lost you," he whimpered as he tearfully spoke.

She left her arms weakly by her sides. How could he love her still? She didn't even love herself. *I'm a whore*, her mind repeated what Fear had told her. She'd confessed she was a liar – a lying whore who was nothing more than Roger's punching bag slut. How was it possible for Alan to love her still??

"I was so easily captivated by your beauty that all I knew was I wanted you. I had no idea you went through all this. I can't even fathom everything you've gone through to become the beautiful, strong woman you are," he tenderly told her. "My God! How can you ever be with someone like me?!" He allowed deep sobs to shake their intermingled bodies. His hands ran around to the small of her back. He'd been on the edge of falling apart, and now was struggling to keep it all together.

He needed her. He needed her like he needed oxygen to breathe. He gulped the air scented with her presence into his lungs.

Mary gently smoothed his hair. "So now do you understand why you're so dangerous?" she asked him. "If my husband finds out where I am, he'll kill me. He'll kill you. He'll kill everyone here!" Mary sobbed – a terrified, dreadful sob. Her knees were weak. It was the sheer strength of Alan holding onto her keeping her standing.

"It's a good thing you divorced him," he said softly,

encouragingly.

She collected herself the best she could, but she couldn't help but gasp for breath between words. "I I-I-I don't know for sure if I'm divorced."

"Why not?" Alan asked as he looked up at her.

"Because I just left. I escaped. Does desertion mean I'm divorced?"

"I don't know. We'll have to ask Earl."

"Roger always threatened he'd kill me if I left him. He's–he's tried before. So-so when I found…," she stopped herself and took a couple deep, cleansing breaths. Would telling him about the rape be crossing the line to telling too much? "When I found a video im-implicating him in-in something very serious, I-I-I'd had enough, I ran! I ran like a fugitive! Tunda and Johe arranged everything for me to come here. I took nothing with me, and I ran away!"

"And he doesn't know what happened to you?" Alan asked.

"No. I staged my own disappearance. I changed my name and ran as far away as I could." She failed to mention Roger was being charged with her suspected murder. "Johe and Tunda were college roommates. They worked together to make everything possible."

"Does Johe know the truth about you?"

"N-n-no. At least, I don't think so. Tunda told her I was her daughter. The plan was to get me somewhere safe away from Roger. I never intended to hurt you or anyone," she quietly said. "I never meant for all of this to happen between us. I only needed somewhere to hide…"

"I don't care. I can't lose you." He pulled her tighter. "I won't lose you again."

"No, Alan. Any relationship between us won't work. You're Alan Brooks, and I'm a pathetic loser who's constantly on the lam."

"You're not a pathetic loser!"

"But, you've made a life for yourself. Just your association with me could tarnish it."

He stood up and cupped his hands behind her ears. "Fuck that life! I haven't been happy in it for years. I hate I wasted so much time building what I thought I wanted, only to find out it's all just a mirage forcing me to keep reaching for something I can never grasp. Right here—right here with you is where I'm happy. It's the only place I've been happy, ever!"

"But…"

"I've never met someone as strong as you. Don't you know what you've accomplished?"

A loud sob escaped from her lips. "I'm not strong. I ran away instead of facing it all, like you would've done."

"Yes you are. You've held onto the same thing I've held onto for years – hope. I know what kind of strength it takes to cling to something so intangible, so—tenuous."

Mary could only stand and tremble.

"No one will ever hurt you again. Not as long as I have breath in my body." The moon reflected the intensity of his ice-blue eyes.

Gently, Mary shook her head, her brow furrowed. She wanted so much to believe him, but how? "I can't do that to you – to the Brooks family."

"What makes you think you're doing anything bad to the Brooks family? I'm the last of it. And you're not doing anything bad to me."

"What about your mother?"

A broad smile graced his lips. "I've already told her about you…"

"You what?" she incredulously interrupted.

"Yes, ma'am. And she can't wait to meet you."

New tears trekked down her face. Tears of hope. "Why would you do that?"

"Because I love you."

"But, I lied to you. Everything I've told you about me has been a lie."

He wiped them away with his thumbs. "Not everything. There are things where no matter how hard you try to hide them, you can't. Just because you changed your name, doesn't change who you are on the inside. With you is the only place where the world makes sense. When I'm with you, I am complete. I *am* a Brooks. Everything I was born to be, I am when I'm with you. You're my missing puzzle pieces."

Mary released an anxious whimper. "Why? Are you insane or something??"

"Because you're still you, regardless of everything you've been through, you're *still* beautiful, incredible, wonderful you. You complete me. I've never been able to be me with anyone else but you. I only wish…"

Alan looked directly into her stormy green eyes. The tempest she hid finally made sense; his heart grieved because of the terror she'd been through. He wanted to sweep her away from every painful memory and protect her. "I wish I could've prevented all of that. I wish I was the first man to ever love you, to ever touch you," he said as he gently stroked her cheek with his thumb.

"How can you want to have anything to do with me after everything I've done?" she asked with a noticeably warbling voice.

"Because I don't care I'm not the first man to ever love you. You see, the only thing I care about is making *damn sure* I'm the last."

"But...," she said, struggling not to be caught up in the ecstasy of his touch, "but what about..."

"I don't care about any of the past. It's over. He's gone. I'm here. And I love you even more now than I did five minutes ago. Nothing else matters to me." He pressed his warm lips against her wet cheek. "Everyone has made mistakes in their lives; I'm not perfect either." He touched the scar on his lip. "Remember?"

Mary sobbed. Now was the time to tell him about her rape. But could she? Should she?

The words struggled to free themselves from her lips.

He kissed the tears on her opposing cheek. "Don't cry. Just having you here with me makes everything right in my world. The storm clouds following me around seem to disappear when you're here. Why wouldn't I want you here with me all the time? I don't care what happened in your past; it is what it is – the past. Besides, what kind of person would I be if I judged others based solely on their past?" He smiled down at her.

Her tears glistened down her weakly grinning cheeks in the moonlight; Alan gently wiped them away. Maybe he didn't need to know about the rape. It was in the past – did it matter now?

"You see, I love you... *you*, just you, warts, past, ex-husband, and all. Nothing will change that."

Inside, Mary was torn – how could he be real? Alan's caress was so gentle and unlike Roger's. Every part of her screamed at her to give into Alan, but she felt uneasy. She wanted him desperately, but was it even possible?

She felt the warmth of his breath upon her cheek. His lips grazed her face until they delicately touched hers.

His very existence filled her heart with more love than she'd felt in her lifetime. The fact that he didn't turn and run from her or pull out his cell phone and report her told her more than words could ever say. It was as though her gaping wounds were healed by his gentle acceptance, his tender smile, his intense eyes, and his unwavering love.

She looked up at him; his eyes were gentle, patient. "But…"

Alan put his finger to her lips. "No more buts. I'm here now. And I promise, I'm not going anywhere. Let me be your safe hiding place."

She tossed her hat to the floor causing her hair to tumble down around her. The fire within her soul flamed beyond control; there was no holding anything back anymore. She was emotionally and physically naked.

He kissed her with a pent-up passion he'd reserved only for her.

To Mary's surprise, she met him with equal desire.

Alan picked her up and gently lowered her onto the antique bed. He didn't speak a word; there was no doubting she'd be his. He was drawn deeper and deeper into her as he continued to kiss the sweetness from her lips.

Mary unsnapped his shirt and didn't flinch at all when his hands smoothed across her bare skin. She was hungry – starving for something her soul had longed for but hadn't found until she'd found him. Her desire for him was evident as she arched her body allowing his hands to caress the small of her back and embrace her entirety. She suckled gently on his bottom lip, responding eagerly to his touch.

Alan leaned over her as his shirt fell silently to the floor.

Her hands immediately found his familiar muscular chest and felt the dewy softness of his chest hair once again. Her craving was stronger than it had ever been; she felt as though she would explode with anticipation.

The air surrounding them was filled with nothing but love and desire.

Alan cradled her breast and licked the tip of her nipple before encompassing it with his warm lips. He unfastened his jeans.

His breath was searing upon her delicate skin; he exhaled timorously as he gently entered her.

Mary gasped. She hadn't expected it to feel as good as it did, and yet, it was everything she believed it would be.

"I love you so much," he whispered to her and kissed her tenderly. His strokes were slow, purposeful – loving.

Tears fell from her eyes into her ears; she'd never known what love making was all about. Every sense in her body tingled and savored the sensations.

His brilliant eyes were glued on hers as he gently caressed her luscious hair.

"I love you, too," she whispered. Inside her heart, she knew those words were as true as any she'd ever uttered. Her mind and her heart reconciled. Fear disappeared; love had won. Every part of her was his.

Alan kissed her again; his strong arms embraced her.

She was totally lost in his unspeakable rapture – returning his kisses with her own uncontrollable blaze. Although the world outside may be falling apart, in that moment, everything was right.

CHAPTER 24

They spent the entire night making love and cuddling each other beneath the moon's careful watch.

When the sun replaced the moon, Mary woke up in the safety and comfort of his arms. Alan Brooks breathing softly beside her was a thrill; the fact that he was naked beside her only poured fuel on the flame!

As unobtrusively as possible, she snuggled against him; the heat from his body made her sweat, but his intoxicating aura only drew her closer and closer to him – until she was on top of him. Her hair created a canopy around them.

Alan opened his azure eyes. "Good morning, beautiful," he said cheerfully. "And just what are you doing up there?"

Mary said nothing. With no prompting, she leaned down and kissed his warm, steady lips.

He wrapped his arms around her, with his hands intermingled in her hair. Gently, he laid her back and planted himself on top of her. Her arched body passionately pushed against him; their lips parted slightly as they kissed.

She smoothed her body along his and nibbled on his bottom lip, ignoring the obvious scar. Her grip on his muscular shoulders bordered on clinging to them. Her hips autonomously raised in anticipation of feeling him inside her.

Goose bumps appeared all over her body when he entered her.

Alan gently, methodically moved in and out of her.

Mary met him with every thrust. Her entire being was

228

enraptured by the intense feeling of their bodies fitting so perfectly together. The heat rising inside her made her pull herself up by his neck, place her lips next to his ear, and zealously whisper, "Faster."

His response was immediate, exactly the way it had been when they rode in the Viper.

"Oh God, don't stop," she moaned softly as her fingers dug into his powerful arms. Burning adrenaline thumped through her body, and she felt there was no one else in the world but Alan. Ecstasy overtook any thoughts of fear, and her ultimate climax triumphed over any guilt.

With a primal growl and deep groan, Alan slammed his hips against her deeply penetrating her. He too reached his climax.

While still inside her, Alan exhaustedly collapsed on top of her. "What an awesome way to wake up!"

Mary giggled. "Your heart is racing," she said with a delightful smile. It had been years since she'd felt so womanly. It felt good—amazingly good. Every part of her tingled and internally quivered in sensational pleasure.

"Yeah? Well that was a lot more than I was anticipating," he breathlessly said as he slid out of her. "Damn. That was hot. I swear, anytime you want to wake me up like that, you have my permission." He rolled off of her and welcomed her against him.

"Duly noted," she agreed. "I like morning sex. I guess I had forgotten how much."

Alan sharply exhaled a breath which was in fact a quiet chuckle.

"What?"

"Nothing. It's just nice to see you letting go some."

"Well, you're certainly a contributing factor to it, I can assure you."

He kissed the top of her head. "I could stay like this with you forever."

"I could too," she breathlessly whispered.

"Can I ask you something?"

"Of course."

"When I mentioned Mary Franklin to you on the boat, why didn't you tell me then?"

"I couldn't. I-I guess I wasn't ready."

"I would have reacted the same way, you know?"

"Still, the whole situation is extremely precarious. Just your knowing is as dangerous a risk as I've taken since I left."

"And you just up and left without telling anyone?"

"Well, Tunda knows, but that's all. I left all my friends, colleagues, educational pursuits, everything behind."

"Wow. That must've been really hard."

"It definitely wasn't easy."

"I can only imagine. Roger must be going crazy!"

"You obviously haven't read much of the news about my disappearance, huh?"

"No. I've heard just scant information about this woman missing from somewhere out West. I don't know anything else. I don't have time to sit and read the news, you know?"

"Yeah, well, don't. I don't want you reading anything, ok? I-I-I don't want to go there. I want to, uh, I want to leave the past where it belongs."

"Ok. I won't."

"Promise?"

He ran his fingers through her long hair and kissed her forehead. "Yeah, I promise. But you have to promise to talk to me. If you don't want me to get my information elsewhere, you have to promise to answer my questions. No more mystery woman."

Mary thought in silence for a few moments.

"Well?"

She looked up at him; he returned her gaze. "Ok, but you've got to promise *me* whatever I tell you won't cause you to lose it and do something very stupid."

"Stupid? Like what?"

"Like trying to get revenge, like you did with Cliff and Wesley. I got my revenge. I don't need you to get it for me."

"Ah come on, Mary, that's not even fair!"

"Promise me." Her eyes locked on his.

Alan gently kissed her on the forehead. "All right."

Mary snuggled into the nook between his neck and shoulder.

"What made you finally leave him?"

"It took a long time for it to reach the point it was when I left. I look back now, and I should've left a long time ago, but I kept saying the timing wasn't right. There were so many things standing in the way, and then finally, I'd had enough. The last straw happened, and I decided the timing would never be truly perfect."

"What was the last straw?"

Mary shifted uncomfortably. "I-I-I don't, I don't want to talk about it."

"It's ok. I'm proud of you." He kissed the top of her head. "I don't think I could let go of you so easily, if I were him. I'd be hunting all over creation for you. It took a lot of courage to do what you did."

Who's to say he's not? she thought. *Change the subject!* "What made you fall for Angela?"

"What, Honey?" He was so completely caught up in his thoughts that he hadn't expected her to say anything.

"I asked you what made you fall for Angela. Remember, out on the boat, you asked me what made me fall for Roger; I'm asking you the same thing."

He laughed. "I also remember you not answering me directly. In fact, you danced all around it as much as you could."

"True enough."

"Still, I'll try and set the example here. I don't know exactly what made me fall for Angela. I guess because she was there and because…." Alan paused.

Mary could sense he was a bit embarrassed. "Come on," she said with an encouraging voice.

"Because I was horny as hell, she had big boobs and was willing."

"All of those equal marrying material in your mind, huh?" she asked with a giggle.

"Hell, I don't know. I was stupid. The sex was amazing; she mentioned something about getting married. At first, I said no way. But then she cut me off – completely! She wouldn't talk to me, let alone have sex with me unless we were married. Little did I know things wouldn't change very much after we were married," he said with a scoff. "Thank God Mama had sense enough to make her sign a pre-nup."

"And she still married you?"

"Yeah. It was a very generous pre-nup. I guess it's what made me think she married me for love." He sighed. "What a fool I was, huh?"

"Nah. No more than I was."

Alan's strong arm kept her snuggly against him.

They lay quietly listening to their hearts beating before Alan spoke again. "What made you fall for Roger?"

"I don't think there was just one thing really; it was a thousand little things." She traced little paths through the blonde hair on his chest.

"He was very attractive and amazingly sure of himself. He was so certain what he wanted out of life, which was totally opposite to the way I was. I was still trying to grasp the whole concept of *not* going to class if I didn't want to."

Alan laughed. "I miss college days, don't you?"

"Oh, yeah. I was just an innocent freshman – still wet behind the ears and fresh out of high school when I met Roger. He was a third-year law student."

"How'd y'all meet?"

"I first met him at a Phi Gamma Delta party." She laughed as she thought about it. "It's all very silly and girly."

"So, I want to hear it."

"I'm warning you, it's the stuff teenage girls sit around and giggle dreamy-eyed incessantly about."

"I'll keep a tight hold on my man card. Continue."

"Well, Roger was much older than most of the people at the party. Yet, I noticed him right away. Something had shifted. I was like a wolf sniffing the air, and he was my prey. He was so overconfident, but oh so handsome...." She stopped and put her hands over her face. "It makes me blush to tell you about this kind of stuff."

"Why? Angela rubbed her bare foot up and down my crotch!"

She giggled. "I'd forgotten!"

"Yeah, so go on. Nothing you can say can be as bad as getting a boner at an awards banquet!"

"I can't believe I'm telling you this. Well, anyway, he'd just been on vacation in Mexico and was tanned and sharp looking. I've always had some weird weak spot for dark-haired, tanned men..."

"Hmm, kind of makes me screwed, huh?"

"Oh come on, it's not like you're an albino. You're tan and blonde."

"Yeah, but not quite your weak spot, huh?"

"Oh good grief. There's more to life than just looks, you know? If we were to use that as judgment, then I would say I'm not your type. Look at Angela? She's tall, blonde, and has beautiful curves. I'm short, brunette and more like a twig."

"Touché. Continue."

"Well, like I was saying, I noticed him the minute he walked in the room," she said with a nervous laugh. "Then again, I don't know, maybe we noticed each other. I'm not exactly sure who pursued who, but it didn't take either of us long to hook up. He...," she thought back to being with young Roger, "cleverly challenged me to get caught into his web, and before I knew it, he just took over. It was unlike anything I'd ever experienced."

Her nervous, school-girl giggles bubbled over. "I never knew what hit me. I-I had a boyfriend at the time; I have no idea what it was about Roger. He made me totally forget myself, but I literally *had* to have him! He taunted me, tempted me. After I danced with him at the party, I broke up with my boyfriend, and chased Roger until I got a date with him."

Alan laughed. "A woman who knows what she wants; I can appreciate that!"

"I couldn't get enough of him! Now, I realize he was chasing me too, but it wasn't as obvious. He cleverly sculpted my actions into exactly what he wanted. He was like a drug or something! Before I even knew what hit me, we were engaged. I don't really remember him asking me; it was more like a command."

"Guess that should've been a clue, huh?"

"Yeah, I guess so. Roger – he took care of me and always seemed to know what was best."

"Was he your first?"

"My first what?"

"You know, your first lover?"

"Oh! No, but it's not like I was some kind of slut or something. The boyfriend I broke up with to date Roger was actually my first. I think sex was one of the reasons we didn't last. What else is there for teenagers to do after sex? Nothing but either get married or more and more sex." She paused waiting for some kind of comment from him. When it didn't come, she continued. "Was Angela your first?"

"God no."

"Don't lie."

"No! I told you who my first was, Wendy."

"Oh yeah, I forgot about her."

"So people didn't know about the abuse?" he asked quietly and calmly.

Mary was a little irritated when her attempts to turn the conversation back on him didn't work. "Well, mostly. After the first abuse incident, remember the one I told you happened in front of DeNay and Milo?"

"Yeah. When he broke the wine glasses into your arm, right?"

"Yeah. That one. Anyway, my parents were the next ones to know there was something drastically wrong in our marriage. Everything had healed, and Roger and I were well on our way to a happy marriage, that is, until I mistakenly lost my debit card. When Roger found out, he smacked me across the face, really hard. It gave me a black eye."

"What did you do?"

"I moved out. I went home to my parents. I thought my dad was going to kill him! Roger came over and begged for me to come home. He apologized and called out for me, but I didn't want to hear his mess. Hitting me once was bad enough, but hitting me twice was too much."

"Yet, you went back."

"Yeah. I was a fool. He bought me flowers every day. Bought me things I'd said I wanted, but I didn't think we could afford – jewelry, designer clothes – everything! Sadly, I fell for it. I thought it meant he really did love me. Within a couple of weeks, I went back, which was against my dad's wishes. After I went back, I hid future fights from them. I didn't want them to know I'd made a mistake. And besides, my dad's reaction to Roger was always volatile, and all I ever wanted was peace.

"Once my parents died, a lot of things changed for me. They left me more financially stable where I could survive without Roger if I needed to."

"That's good!"

"You'd think so, wouldn't you? But he seemed threatened by it. His attacks got worse and even more mind-twisting. It wasn't long before most of the money had all but disappeared."

"Where did it go?"

"I don't know. I guess Roger spent it. Whenever he'd hit me or misbehave, he'd buy me something – a dress, a negligee, a bracelet, whatever – always trying to buy my forgiveness. I guess he used it for that."

"So that's why you wouldn't let me buy you anything, huh?"

"Yeah. I don't want anyone buying my favor."

"It makes sense."

"The best way to show me you love me is to love me from your heart. I don't need things. I've already had things, and I've proven I can live without them. Besides, they're all just representations of his dark, evil side."

"Still, I'd like to make you happy."

"And you do. Right here. Just being with me."

"It just seems so little and insignificant."

"To you, maybe, but to me, it's huge."

Alan smiled. "As long as you're happy, I'm happy."

She kissed his neck. "And I'm perfectly happy."

They both got quiet again before Alan broke the silence. "You think you'll ever get married again?"

"I doubt it."

"Why not?"

"What about you?" she asked, pointing the subject back at him.

"I'm already miserably married, remember?"

"Yeah, but what if you were to divorce Angela, would you marry again?"

"I'd planned on marrying you," he said and squeezed her tightly.

Mary laughed. "Oh yeah!"

"Yup. The months I've spent with you have been happier than all 10 years combined with Angela."

"Really?"

"You bet! I'd love nothing more than to spend the rest of my life with you."

Mary euphorically smiled. "Really?"

"Can't you ask anything else?" he asked with a laugh.

"Yeah, of course I can."

"You're avoiding my question."

"I don't believe you actually asked me a question."

He became suddenly more interested in her answer. "If I was to divorce Angela, and I asked you to marry me, would you?"

"Ummm, I don't know, Alan. There're a lot of difficulties in my life. I'm not officially divorced from Roger, you know? And you lead a very public life. How would it all work for me? Roger is only one slipup away. Marrying you just might equal a death sentence for us both."

"You don't think I can protect you?"

"No, I know you can. I'm just saying, any marriage with all my baggage isn't exactly the prescription for a happy life."

"What if we got you officially divorced from Roger, would you marry me then?"

"Alan. You have to know if I filed divorce papers against Roger, he'd know I'm still alive and where I am."

"True. But again, I can protect you."

"You can't be with me 24/7."

"Yes, I can. And when I can't, I'll hire body guards to protect you."

Mary sighed deeply. "That's no way to live."

He rose up onto his elbows, which caused her to move from her comfortable nook.

Mark looked at him and said, "Ok, see, this conversation is stupid and moot because you're married with no intention upon leaving your wife, so it has no purpose whatsoever. My mother always told me anyone who stays in a bad marriage must be getting something out of it…"

"Oh come on, you know what I'm getting out of it!" he interrupted her.

"And what's that?"

"Shit!"

"Oh yeah? You must be getting something or you're enjoying the shit she gives you."

Alan looked at her befuddled; then with a clever smile, he said, "Nice try, smarty pants! You're trying to dissect my marriage so you don't have to answer my question!"

"I can't believe we're having this conversation!"

"Why? What's so wrong with it?"

"One night of sex and you're thinking about marriage?"

Alan's face displayed how shocked he was at her statement. "That wasn't just sex!"

"I know, I know. I'm just saying."

"That was out-of-this-world love making unlike anything I've ever…"

"I'm sorry." Mary kissed him sweetly. "Can we just not talk

about it anymore?"

"I'm divorcing her, you know?"

"For sure?"

"Yup. Earl promised to have the papers ready today."

"Oh. Wow. I didn't know. Why?"

"You know why."

"It better not be because of me."

"Damn right it is."

"No. I don't want you to do that. I don't want to be the reason you do anything. I want the reason to be because it's what you want."

"It is what I want. But it's still because of you."

Mary leaned back against the headboard and quietly growled. Her hair draped around her like she was a mermaid.

"Just say yes."

"Yes to what?"

"Say yes you'll marry me."

She smiled. "You don't even have a ring."

"Oh, I can get you a ring!" He started getting out of bed.

"No! Don't leave!" She pulled him back against her.

"Say you'll marry me."

"Oh Alan," she said with an ethereal, happy smile, "you're positively incorrigible!"

"Say yes," he playfully demanded as he pulled her over his shoulder and held her in his lap. "Say yes, or I'm never letting you go."

"Good thing I'm not trying to leave, huh?"

His lips were instantly upon hers as he laid her back upon the bed.

"Again?" she hotly whispered. Her eyes closed; she was easily lost in his ecstasy.

"I can't get enough of you," his deep, lustful voice softly breathed upon her skin. His lips teased her, taunted her.

Their hearts beat in unison while butterflies of anticipation fluttered throughout their veins, yearning for the freedom they found in each other.

Mary breathed in deeply as her fingers determinedly danced along his muscular arms and up to his shoulders.

With his startlingly blue eyes looking directly at her, he

whispered, "Say it."

"Huh?" she asked as she opened her eyes.

"Say yes." His hips aroused her further as they ground against her; each time she expected to feel him penetrate her, but didn't.

Her reply came from the deepest part of her soul, "Yesssss, oh yes!"

She gasped in the frenzied release of suspense as he entered her again.

Her head reminded her, *No one tells Alan Brooks no.*

"No one...," she moaned in desire.

CHAPTER 25

Silence filled the small cabin as the two lovers lay together.

Alan softly nodded off.

Mary's thoughts ran laps inside her head. *Is he sleeping so I'll wake him up again?* she thought with a silent laugh. She rolled over with her back to him, ran her fingers down his arm, and entwined their hands. *Oh Alan. If you only knew how perfectly perfect you are to me.* Raising their hands together, she quietly kissed each of his fingers.

She thought about how she'd agreed to marry him. Was she signing her own death warrant by such an agreement? "Just shut up," she told herself aloud.

He lightly stirred and placed his opposing arm across her, and then buried his face into the back of her head with tender sweet kisses. "Did you say something?"

A blissful smile immediately graced her face as a contented sigh left her lips. She kissed his other hand. "No. Did I wake you?" *If only we could stay like this forever*, she thought.

"I wasn't sleeping," he said as he stretched his entire body, spreading his toes out.

Mary could feel his muscles tense and then relax against her. *If only there was no life outside of this old cabin, life would be perfect. But,* she chuckled to herself, *life just doesn't work like we want.*

Her thoughts wandered down through the pastures, past the images of her and Alan walking hand-in-hand through the tall grass, and down to the barn. It was then that reality hit her. *What will people think about all of this?* She shifted and released Alan's hand. *If Johe knew, she'd fire me on the spot!*

The sun gleaming through the window only reminded Mary how the morning was slipping away, which also meant the work day was passing. *The last thing I need is wagging tongues at the barn.*

As gradually as possible, she tried to wiggle free of Alan's embrace.

To her dismay, he asked, "Where do you think you're going?" His arms tightened around her.

"I have to go."

"Why??"

"Because I have to go to work."

"Fuck work."

"That's all fine and good if you're Alan Brooks, but I'm not, am I?"

"You're better than Alan Brooks, you're his woman!"

His woman? she replayed in her mind with a tender smile. "What would Angela say?" she asked with an amused smile.

"I don't give a damn what Angela would say!"

"Whether you care about her or not, she's still there." She wormed her way out of his embrace, stood up, and stretched. "But, we'll talk more about her later." She sat on the edge of the bed and tried to run her fingers through her tangled hair; her prized locks fell down to rest on her thighs.

"Come here, gorgeous," he commanded as he lifted her up and gently placed her on top of him; her hair poured onto his chest. "You are the sexiest thing alive!"

"Oh please," Mary said with a scoff.

Alan planted his lips onto hers. "Shut up and kiss me," he commanded without removing his lips.

"Alan, we can't do this again," she said, resisting him.

He seemed confused. "I think it's a little late for regrets."

"No, I don't regret anything. I meant we've got to get going or people are going to talk." She climbed off of him and out of bed. The first thing she found was his shirt; she draped it over her shoulders and slid her arms in the sleeves, but didn't button it.

Alan leaned on his elbow, watching her.

"What?" she asked with a nervous smile.

"Let Victoria have all of her secrets; there's nothing sexier in the world than seeing you wearing my shirt."

"Well, I'm not going to parade around here naked, so I put on your shirt. I hope you don't mind."

"Mind? Hell, you can have every shirt I own!" He stopped and thought for a moment, "On the other hand, if you'll promise to parade around naked, I'll do the same."

She laughed. "You're a horn dog!"

"Shut up and get back in bed. I want to do stuff to you."

"And just why would I do something like that?"

"'Cause you know you want to." He stood up from the bed and moved behind her. "You know, I never knew you had all this hair tucked underneath your hat," he finally said.

"Pht!" she commented as she smoothed her hair out and worked on braiding it back.

"No, leave it down."

"Have you lost your mind?! You want me to walk around with my hair down when no one has seen it like this except, now, you? You're crazy!" she said and continued to braid it.

"I don't care." He put his hands on hers. "Leave it down."

He buried his nose into her hair and inhaled deeply; her fragrance filled his senses. "You know, I never really thought about it until you said something, but you're right! The unique smell someone has is just about the biggest turn on ever!"

He breathed in deeply again.

"God, I could get high just off you!" He wanted to be drunk – drunk on the very essence of her. She was better than any alcohol he'd ever had!

His hands caressed her delicate curves. "I want to remember everything about you right now; don't change a thing. Just come back to bed. I'm not finished loving you yet." His face clearly displayed his level of arousal. "We've got all day to work, but we'll never have this moment again. Come back to bed."

"You can't possibly be ready for another round," Mary lightheartedly said as she continued braiding her hair.

"Oh yeah? Wanna make a bet?" He shifted his hips side to side, swinging his erect penis against her back.

She smiled sweetly at him. "Later. I have to work."

"Work?" He eagerly kissed the nape of her neck. "I think I've proven before I can get you out of work. Now get your gorgeous ass back in bed!"

She playfully frowned at him. "I don't do well with orders." She moved across the room to one of the stump chairs.

Alan smiled at her little game. "Miss Mary, when I'm with you, I've never felt so alive in my life! Your coy smile – mmm – it makes my world completely stop. Do you have any idea what you do to me? Please come back to bed and make love to me again," he said with a much more respectful tone, but keenly playing along.

Mary only shook her head; she wondered if he knew what he did to *her!* There were a thousand little things about him that thrilled her from her head to her toes.

The confinement she'd lived in for months – for years – was finally gone. She felt free. Truly, unequivocally free. And Alan was her savior.

He stood behind her. "Being here with you – whoa," he said as he caressed her hair, "it-it-it's not like anything I've ever experienced. Nothing else matters but how you feel in my arms, and how good I feel in yours. Don't deny me that!"

"I'm not denying you anything. I'm just saying, in order to keep all this quiet, we have to at least pretend to continue life like normal."

"It won't be so quiet when we get married, now will it?"

Mary sighed deeply. "Yeah, about that…"

"Oh no! You said yes, and I'm not letting you change your mind!"

"I wasn't going to. I was just going to point out the importance of keeping all of this quiet. You *are* still married to Angela, and she *is* still here at your farm. If people knew about us, it would make life very difficult for me, so please, let's keep it quiet."

"I'm going today to get you a ring. You want to come?" He nuzzled himself into her hair again. "Stop braiding your hair," he said and stuck his fingers into her work and started unraveling it.

"Damn it, Alan!" she teasingly complained. "No. I can't come with you. I have to work."

He growled low in his chest. "No, you have to come back to bed," he commanded. "I want you to come over and over again until the only word you can say is my name."

When she stood up, he eagerly moved back onto the bed, propping his head on his crossed arms.

Seductively, she swayed her hips from side to side. His unbuttoned shirt hung too big from her narrow shoulders, yet covered only the edges of her nipples as she slid over to the bed. "You mean like this? You want me back in *this* bed, do you?" she purred.

"Oh God, yes, Baby, you know I do!" The corners of his lips curled up in a delighted smile.

Once she was close enough, he swept her tiny body into his virile arms and laid her where he just was. His mouth danced upon hers, while his hands gently smoothed the loose strands of hair back.

"I don't ever want to be away from you," he whispered just before kissing her deeply.

"Well, we're leaving for the show in July, which is only a couple of months off," she reminded him after he'd kissed her.

"Shh. Don't tell me things like that."

Mary laughed. "But it's true."

"Then I'm going with you," he said just before he kissed her again.

She giggled and pushed him back. "No you're not! I think you can survive for a little while without me."

"Nope. Either I go with you, or I'll get you out of it." He breathed gently on her skin as his lips tip-toed down her neck and to her barely-covered chest.

Delicately, he brushed back her partially braided hair and one side of her shirt. Abruptly, he stopped.

"What the hell happened to you?!" He shot up from the bed and uncovered the rest of her, which exposed similar scars on the outside of the other breast.

Mary immediately pulled the shirt across her in an attempt to hide the tell-tale scars from her rape. How could she have forgotten about them? "Nothing! Nothing happened!" Forcibly, she scurried out from under him and from the bed.

He pulled at her arm. "No, *something* happened! Nobody gets scars like that from *nothing*."

Mary yanked hard against him.

"It's that rat bastard Roger, isn't it?!" His anger flared.

She continued to pull against him; her face stricken.

At first, he held fast, but as she became more animated and determined to get away, the look on her face made him relent and let her go.

She hurriedly picked up her clothes and put them on as quickly as she could.

"What the hell happened?!" He began to fire off demands in short succession: "Who did this to you?! It was Roger wasn't it?! I'll *kill* that son of a bitch!! Talk to me!! Stop getting dressed!! Talk to me!!"

Alan was next to her; his demanding and irate face frightened her. His eyes were burning pools of liquid.

How could she explain what happened without him wanting to know more and more? Wasn't her confession last night enough? Would he do the unthinkable and hunt Roger down like he did Cliff?

Looking at the floor, she whispered, "Stop. Please. Stop."

"I need to know what happened."

Mary closed her eyes. Her body trembled. Flashes of Roger's hours-long interrogations flickered before her like an old movie.

"Say," Alan demanded.

She could only turn away from him and move toward the door.

Alan could sense he was being overbearing, yet he couldn't stop himself from moving quickly to the door and holding it shut.

Her body became a motionless shell housing her soul.

Alan had seen this look before. He changed tactics and compassionately said to her, "I don't want you to leave." His tone of voice was more calm but still clearly assertive. "We're going to talk about those scars, ok?" His eyebrows were raised in alerted concern.

"I don't want to," she meekly told him, her eyes incapable of looking at him.

"No secrets, remember?"

"It's something I'm not ready to talk to you about, yet," she whispered.

His voice became tender. "Ok." He nodded. "I trust you, and I trust you to talk to me about them when you're ready."

Mary's lips barely moved as she said, "Thank you."

He moved from in front of the door and slowly, calmly put his clothes back on. All of his moves were smooth and deliberate, as if she were a scared animal. "I want you to know I'll be here to catch you when you're ready. I'm here with my arms open wide, if you'll just trust me enough with all of your secrets; I'll keep them and you safe, I promise."

Given the opportunity to leave, he was surprised when she didn't jump at the chance. Instead, Mary stood in silence; she wasn't exactly sure what to make of Alan. Roger would've reacted so differently. Anytime she'd tried to escape from him, his fists always made it abundantly clear there was no chance at freedom. He would beat her for trying to leave, and then beat her more to get the information he sought.

"Are you leaving?"

Mary remained stoic.

"Mary?"

She couldn't move or respond.

"I'm sorry. I didn't mean to be so forceful." He ran his hands down his face. "I-I wasn't expecting the scars."

She said nothing.

"So you're not talking to me anymore?" he gently asked as he softly caressed her cheek.

She jerked back from him.

"Oh, hell, we're back to this again," Alan muttered and hung his head.

"No, it's just I thought I knew you…"

His heart had mixed emotions from finally hearing something from her. "Of course you know me. Nothing's changed. It's just going to take me time to learn, you know? I'm still a man, and men are passionate about the women they love. I'm still the same person." He worked hard to keep his voice as calming and soothing as possible.

Mary closed her eyes. "Are you?" she timidly let the words fall from her trembling lips. Her thoughts were wrapped entirely in questioning if she should tell Alan of her rape.

"Yes. I'm still the man who is madly in love with you. Nothing has changed, or ever will change. We know each other on a different level now, which means there are things which are different, too. I know there are secrets still yet to reveal – secret pains we haven't disclosed. And I can't always promise my first reactions will be the right ones. What I can promise you is I love you. And because I love you, hearing bad things happened to you are hard for me to swallow at first. I'll get better, ok? I promise."

"How do I know you won't turn back to Angela again?" It was lame, but it was her only defense.

"What?" he incredulously asked with an almost laughable scoff.

"You know what."

"Well, I have a secret of my own I haven't told you. I've already told Angela I'm divorcing her."

"You told Angela?" she said with a super-sized amount of surprise.

"Yes. I did. I don't love her. I haven't loved her for a very long time. It took loving you for me to realize what true love is. So, see, isn't that proof enough? There's no Angela conversation worth having."

Her heart grinned as a warm glow began growing inside her. She was glad to hear of the impending divorce, but she was very happy she'd successfully steered the conversation away from the scars on her breasts and right back to Alan. Still, as much as she tried to change the subject, she knew the question about her scars and the rape would remain like the constant smell of manure in the barn – no matter how clean the stalls were, it still hung heavy in the air. "Yeah," she softly said.

She noticed the white tan line on his left hand; her mind flashed back to images of the revolting veterinarian, Dr. Williams, who the stable hands had nicknamed Dr. Willie due to his philandering. Was Alan truly different than other men, or was she lying to herself? Was he sincere? Or was he just adding another notch on his bedpost? When the papers did arrive, would he indeed sign them this time? Or would he destroy them like he'd done many times before?

"I'm ready to build my future with you beside me." He cupped her face in his hands. "I love you, Mary. With all that I am, I love you. You have to trust me."

"I was raped," Mary blurted out. It felt as if God Himself had reached into her soul and pulled a demon out through her mouth.

"What?" Alan hardly knew what to make of what she'd said. His hands instantly dropped from her face.

"I was raped." The second time she said it made her legs weak. She sank into one of the stump chairs.

"When?"

She pulled out her cell phone and quickly did the math. *Fourteen months, twenty-four days, ten hours, and 21 minutes ago*, she thought. "Over a year ago," she said.

He stood dumbfounded by her confession.

Mary instinctively buried her face into her own hands. Why couldn't she stop the words? *He's going to think you're worthless now*, she thought. An unworldly sob boiled over from her soul.

His immediately desire was to wrap her into his arms, but when he reached for her, she jerked away. He retreated to the wood chair across from her. "He did it, didn't he?" he asked about Roger.

For several moments, Mary could only cry. The walls inside feverishly tried to rebuild themselves.

Alan quietly let her, not demanding a response or any interaction with him. It surprised him when she spoke again, "N-n-no, not directly. He didn't do it himself. He...he...," the words dangled on the tip of her tongue, and yet, saying them felt like she was reliving the betrayal again.

"He what, Honey?"

"I can't do it," she whispered. The thought of Alan beating Roger to a bloody pulp, like he did Cliff, worried her. Yet, an unnerving desire for relief compelled her onward.

"If you can't, it's ok," he tenderly whispered. "But if you talk about it, you might feel better." He wanted to touch her and bring her peace, but he knew better. It was best for her to come to him. "It's ok; I'm right here. I'm not going anywhere." Silently, anger simmered inside him as he fought to keep it under control.

"He...he...," she started in an almost screeching voice, but stopped herself. *No, no, it doesn't matter now. He already knows,* she thought as she tried to soothe herself.

"You're safe here," he gently whispered.

Moments ticked by as Mary cried and tried to gather the guts she needed to tell him what happened. Finally, she whispered, "He...he... had someone...rape me."

"He what?!" Alan could hardly believe his ears. His insides quaked; somehow he hoped he hadn't heard her correctly.

"He had someone rape me."

"Are you sure he was behind it?"

Mary nodded. "Yes, I'm sure."

"W-Why-How?" The indignation brewing inside was an experience he hadn't felt before. Seeing Wes with Wendy or haring about Cliff's assault were nothing compared to this startling revelation. He wanted to kill Roger Franklin! But hiding that burning desire was paramount.

"I don't know. I-I-I didn't know he was behind it at the time." She wiped her tears off on her sleeves, but they were soon replaced with more bitter, frightened tears.

Her soul was a deep, gaping chasm, and at the bottom of the chasm was a tiny, whimpering, beaten spirit who felt defenseless and exposed. Everything she had done to protect her spirit was gone. Even as naked as she had been just the night prior when she confessed her real identity to Alan was nothing compared to the vulnerability she felt now.

Could she trust him? Would he use her fragility against her as a way to coerce her into kinky sex? Would he try to have sex with her as a way to make her feel better? Would he look at her as merely a sex object like Roger had? Yet, her heart insistently refuted such thoughts. A war raged inside her, while Alan sat quietly.

Somewhere, Mary expected Alan's harsh judgment. She expected his coarse rejection. She expected him to blame her and tell her she'd brought it on herself. But none of those came. Timidly, she looked over at him. His careworn face showed only his heartfelt sympathy. "I-I-I didn't know about his involvement until much later. I thought he was my hero. I thought he was going to avenge me, until...," she tucked her knees to her chest, "one day, I found the video."

"The what?!" He leaned forward with his elbows on his knees.

"The video made of the attack."

"He was there?! And-and he did *nothing*??" Alan asked as his ire got the better of him. His muscles tightened and released over and over as he struggled to contain his anger.

"I-I-I don't know if he was there, but I know the whole thing was videotaped, and he had the video with its threatening message from the rapist. I found it in his office."

"What did the message say?" he demandingly asked.

Mary rocked back and forth with her face pressed against her knees.

"What did it say?" he asked again with a far gentler tone.

With her eyes clenched shut, she looked up and recited what was written on the cover: "'You're wife sure is a sweet treat! Let me know when I can enjoy her again. —ELF'." Her face was instantly buried back again between her tightly held knees. "He had me raped for his own perverted pleasure!" she shrieked.

"That sick bastard!!" He wanted desperately to annihilate Roger Franklin. Yet, his immediate concern was her – to hold her, to comfort her, to hide her in his protective embrace. He remembered her reaction to his behavior with Cliff; the last thing he wanted was to worry her further. But he wasn't sure he could hold her without her knowing what was bubbling beneath his skin.

Her tears wildly rained down as unworldly sobs were released from the cavernous chasm inside her soul. "I've been trying to get over it for what feels like centuries."

"You're the bravest person I've ever met," he sincerely said. His face was austere. "I'm so proud to know you…to love you."

An agonizing sob which had long been hiding inside her broken spirit clawed its way out of her body. How could he still love her? This pathetic, sniveling, unlovable spirit inside her – how could he still love it? She searched his eyes for the judgment she anticipated would be hiding behind the lies she was sure he was saying, but instead, she could only see steady love and patience flowing from his compassionate blue eyes.

"It's not your fault…," he started but couldn't finish. He needed her against him. He needed to hold her – to hold onto her. He reached for her hand, but didn't touch her.

She looked at his extended hand and then back up at him.

Patiently, his hand remained steadfast.

Like a defeated ragdoll she placed her hand into his. Sobs accompanied the tears marching down her cheeks; nevertheless, she was surprised what a liberating experience it was to confess and still feel his steady, warm hand holding hers. She'd only told Roger about the scars – even her therapist didn't know.

Gently, he tugged on her hand as if to signal for her to come closer.

Mary relented. With a myriad of wails, her spirit climbed out of the chasm it hid in and into his lap like a child. Her spirit clung to him as if he were the only source of strength available. The puppet strings Fear had fastened to her long ago were severed with Alan's accepting and loving embrace. The power Fear possessed had been negated. With a long shrill shriek, Fear melted from existence. His reign of terror was finally over. For the first time in years, her spirit felt genuinely safe.

The weight of the world fell off of Mary one tear at a time.

Alan's insides felt sick as he thought of what happened to her. The simple statement she'd barely had the courage to utter, enraged him. His insides burned with wrath. He hated Roger with a hatred he'd never experienced before.

The magnitude of the trust it took for her to share so much with him made his heart swell with the desire to protect her. He focused his thoughts on her in a desperate attempt to keep his temper under control.

He chewed on his bottom lip, running his teeth across the scar. It was at that moment when he deeply realized the gravity of his actions toward Angela. "My God, I'm a monster," he whispered, barely making a sound. The depth of his regret felt like a boulder had dropped upon his head and was slowly sinking its way throughout his body.

No wonder she thought I was so dangerous, he thought. He stroked her hair as tears welled in the great man's eyes. He hated himself. Burying his face in her hair, he clung to her as mournful sobs escaped his powerful body in the only way he knew how to articulate his profound regret.

CHAPTER 26

By mid-morning, Mary leaned against Alan's gleaming black Viper; the lights of the garage reflected in its shimmering paint. Alan's hands rested gently on each of her hips.

"What's wrong?" Alan asked.

"It's nothing."

"You know I hate that shit!"

She chuckled lightly. "I know. It's just, well, you know all of my secrets now."

He gently smiled and caressed her face. "It's a wonderful feeling to know you trust me so much. I'd break my back taking care of you from here on."

Her green eyes looked up at him with a trust that could only be produced from the unification of all facets of her being. "I know you would."

"I understand you on such a greater level now."

She sweetly smiled in relief. "I'm not sure what that feels like."

"It feels just like this…this bliss we have."

"Yeah, but you know it's only fleeting, right?"

"What do you mean?" His hand returned to her hip.

"There's still Roger. He'll always be an issue."

"I know. And I'll kill him before he ever lays a hand on you again!"

"That's not what I meant. I meant there's always the threat of him. My coming to Babbling Brooks was the only shot I had at freedom. I've been safer here than I could've been anywhere else.

251

It's like its own hidden paradise away from the world."

"I know. That's why I like it here."

"If we make waves, will I still be safe?"

Alan grinned and gently kissed her forehead. "I'd die protecting you."

With her head nodding, she said, "I know you would. But, things are more complicated than you realize. Roger's in ja…"

"Shh!" Alan put his finger over her lips before she could finish. "Do you trust me?"

She cast her eyes down and weakly said, "Yeah."

He tenderly pulled her chin up to make her look at him. "I asked you if you trust me. That wasn't a very convincing answer."

"Roger's in jail," she divulged.

"How do you know?"

"Tunda emailed me the news article."

"What's he in jail for?"

"The police think he killed me."

"Killed you?"

"Yeah. He obviously didn't." She hung her head with it still in his hands.

"Good."

"Good? He's accused of something he didn't do." She sharply looked up at him, surprised by his callous answer.

"So. At least he's getting what's coming to him."

"Being charged with something he didn't do??" she incredulously asked.

"He belongs in jail for what he did to you."

"But he didn't kill me. He doesn't deserve…"

"Yes, he does! He can rot there for all I care!"

"Yeah, I guess. Still. I'm afraid."

"If he's in jail, what do you have to be afraid of?"

"What if he gets out? He's going to be pissed…"

"Shhh. He won't get out."

"His bail has been set. What if he makes bail? He could already know where I am." She wondered about the broken window and about Biscuit's poisoning. Were those attacks pointed at her? And if they were, who would've done them. *Roger*, her mind answered.

Alan thought for a moment. "I'll make you a deal. If he makes bail, we'll leave. Ok?"

She cringed at the thought of leaving Babbling Brooks and Sun. How could she take him with them? "What about your mother? What about Sun? Your legacy? Running away from it all isn't all it's cracked up to be! You really have no idea all the things you have to give up. Are you sure?" Mary asked.

"Yes, of course. I can have the jet ready in no time. We'll run away to Europe, to one of those countries where people can really hide. We'll get married out there, once my divorce is final. What matters most is we stay together and stay safe. Leaving here would be our best chance."

Her breaths quickened.

"You ok?"

"Yeah…no. I don't know. What if…"

"What if what, Honey?" Alan's tender eyes searched hers. "You still worried about Roger?"

She could only nod.

"You've got to let go, and trust me. He'll never, ever harm you again."

"What if Biscuit's poisoning was Roger," she whispered. "And he's toying with us."

"It wasn't," Alan's reassuring voice sounded. He pulled her to him where his heart was quivering with concern. "Don't worry yourself. I'll light a fire under Felix, and he'll go ahead and get the bastard who did it, ok?" His attempts at firm words didn't help as much as he'd hoped. He took her hat off her head, placed it on the car's convertible top, and rested his forehead on hers. Her hair stayed securely hidden under a red bandana. "But you, well, you're going to have to trust me."

"You understand how hard it is, right?"

"What? Why?" he asked as he yanked his head back from hers.

"Because. I placed my entire life into the hands of a man once, and you know how it ended."

He cupped his long fingers behind her ears and crouched down toward her. "Listen to me. Are you listening?"

"Yeah," she meekly said.

"I'm not him. I'm Alan. Alan Brooks. And if I have to spend every penny I have, if I have to hide you away and destroy him myself, if I have to move heaven and earth, he will *never* touch you again!"

"You promise?"

A blast of tension-relieving air shot through his nose. "I promise," he said with a comforting smile.

"Promise you'll keep my secrets?"

"I promise. I'm surprised you even feel the need to ask," he said. His body pressed against hers; his mind reminded him of feeling her naked softness melting beneath him. The idea that she had ever belonged to an animal like Roger made him angry. Roger's allowing someone to rape her caused waves of molten adrenaline to shoot through Alan's body. He had to focus on something else.

"I know, but I had to know for sure. One wrong move and Roger would be here in a second. And you, well, you're a very public figure. If anyone finds out the truth about me, it would mean Roger's immediate release, without bail, and he'd kill us both!"

"Stop. Just stop. Ok? You don't have to worry your pretty little head. I've got an entire team of people who protect me and my image. All I have to do is give the protection order, and they'll protect you, too. So stop your worrying. I got this," he said as he tucked a wayward hair underneath her bandana. "You know, it's kinda thrilling knowing you're hiding all your hair under there just for me."

She nodded and chuckled lightly. "It's for me too, you know?"

"Yeah, but you can't see it like I can. It's just magnificent! I look at you, and I see this incredibly sexy woman standing before me. Like Venus!"

Mary blushed and hid her face briefly. "I probably shouldn't have recreated your whole naked scene, huh?"

"Are you kidding? It was perfect! But you can bet the image is what I see every time I look at you. So exposed, defenseless, stunningly beautiful, and, most importantly, all mine!" He growled deep in his chest. "Thoughts like that make me want to take you right here, right now."

"In the garage??" she said with a shocked, somewhat nervous giggle.

"Yes, ma'am! Right here. On the hood of my car," he said as he ran his hands down to her butt. He kissed her deeply, passionately.

Mary playfully pressed him back. "You're insatiable!"

"With you? Yup." He leaned back in for more, but was once again pushed back.

"Well, as fun as another round with you sounds, we've got to get to work. Johe's probably foaming at the mouth because I'm not there."

"I can handle Johe."

"I know. But handling Johe the way you're talking about would only make things worse. The last thing we need to do is walk around the farm proclaiming our love."

"Are you kidding? I want to climb to the roof of my house and scream it at the top of my lungs!"

Mary playfully kissed him. "I do, too. But we can't. Not yet. Ok? Promise you'll keep your mouth shut?"

He half-closed his eyes and sighed. "Ok. But I don't want to. I want to run mad through the streets shouting your name!"

She sweetly giggled. "I know. But you can't. Besides, think of how much more special it all is knowing our hidden secret."

"Like a secret hiding place, huh?"

"Exactly. A hiding place in each other's arms."

"Mmmm, indeed." He nuzzled and kissed her neck.

"You're going to have to stop that!" she said as she pushed him back again.

"Why?"

"Because. I just can't."

"Ok. I understand." He backed a step from her.

"It's not that I don't want you because God knows I do! It-it's that we've got to go."

"Ugh. Ok. You're just adding to it — making me wait and want you all the more."

"I'm making myself wait too, you know? It only adds to the excitement."

"You're going to wear my ring, aren't you? You're not going to hide it in the drawer like you do those pearls, are you?"

A laughable little scoff left her lips. *Just where did that come from?* she wondered. "I don't hide them. They're just special; I don't want them to get messed up."

"I want you to promise to wear my ring."

She stepped a step closer to him and sweetly kissed him. "I don't mean to open up a can of worms here or anything, but you haven't appropriately asked me, and I haven't officially said yes," she said with as coquettish a look as she could.

Alan threw his head back and laughed out loud. "So you're going there, are you?"

"I can't make promises until…"

He got down on one knee.

With an embarrassed, girlish giggle, she said, "No! Not here! You don't even have the ring yet!"

"I see how you are!" he jokingly said as he stood up. "You want to see the ring first, huh? I promise you, I'll get you the biggest diamond in the world!"

Mary scoffed in surprise. Did he really think like that? "There's no need for something so ostentatious! I would still marry you even if you proposed with an onion ring."

He smiled big. "But I won't," he whispered deeply.

"Well," she started with her eyes half-closed, "when you have it, then, I expect you to get down on one knee."

"You'll be lucky if I don't write it in the sky!"

"Alan! No! You promised to be quiet," she said while laughing. "Now, go to rehearsals. I'll see you when you're done."

He pulled her tightly to him and zealously kissed her. His entire body caressed hers.

Mary gasped when he lifted her onto the car. In the brief moment when she could catch her breath, she whispered, "Don't."

"Ok, I'm sorry. You just don't know what you do to me!"

"You've got to get going."

"Don't remind me."

She slid off the car and from around him. Her fingers quickly grabbed the brim of her hat and placed it onto her head. "And so do I."

"Ok, ok. Stay safe," he said as he looked at her. His heart ached when he thought of anything bad happening to her.

"I will. I'm not doing anything extranous today. Just the same old, same old."

"Ok." He pulled her to him for one last kiss, and then released her.

She quickly trotted out of the garage and walked casually toward the barn.

Moments later, the ground shook as the Viper went by with the convertible top down. Alan's cell phone was stuck to his ear; his eyes were covered with his black Wayfarer sunglasses.

Mary entered the feed room to get Sun's breakfast together. She could hear Johe talking nearby. Before she could get the second scoop of feed, Johe was there behind her.

"You're late," Johe informed her.

"I know," Mary replied.

"Why?"

"I don't know. I couldn't get going this morning." Mary scooped up more feed and then put the bucket down.

"You didn't clock in."

Mary sighed. "I completely forgot."

"Ok. Just don't forget."

"Ok."

Johe took one look at Mary and asked, "You ok?"

"Yeah, I'm fine."

"Your eyes look puffy. You've been crying, huh?"

"It's ok. I'm fine."

"So you were crying? What's going on?"

"Nothing."

"Well, whatever it is, I'm here," Johe said as she hugged her with one arm. Instantly, though, her nose picked up on a scent. She increased her hug to a two-armed hug. "Anytime you want to talk, I'm here, ok?" Johe breathed in deeply – sex! She smelled the strong scent of sex all over Mary. After hugging her, she raised an eyebrow and looked at her with her head tilted. "So, where have you been?"

"What do you mean?" Mary's brow crinkled at the implication.

"You know what I mean. You positively *reek* of sex." A mischievous toothy smile caused wrinkles in Johe's well-tanned skin.

"What? That's crazy!"

"Look, I think I've had enough sex in my day to know what it smells like. You've been doing the dirty with someone, and…," she sniffed again, "quite a few times, I might add," Johe said with a light chuckle. "And to think I was worried there was something wrong with you!" she said with a quick laugh.

It was as if Mary could see the realization wash over Johe when she put two and two together: Mary and Alan must have been having sex. She had to conceal this knowledge and its accompanying situation.

Mary nervously rolled her eyes at her. It was obvious – Johe knew. All Mary could do was deny it. "Come on, you're crazy! I've got to feed my horse." She picked up the bucket and headed out the feed room door. "It's not true, ok?" Mary said to Johe, who was following her.

"Uh-huh. I don't believe you."

"I don't care if you believe me or not, it's not true," Mary said as she walked toward Sun's stall.

Johe remained close on her heels. "Then who is it?"

"Nobody."

"Don't tell me it's Rob," Johe said with disgust.

"Please! I can't believe you'd think such a nasty thing!" Mary said, shocked by her words.

Johe's anger fired her next words out of her mouth, "It better not be Alan!"

Mary melodramatically stopped in the hallway, briefly threw her head back in frustration at Johe's persistent inquisition, and continued toward Sun's stall without a word.

"It is, isn't it?" Johe's blood raced through her veins. "Have you thought about how bad this looks? First Alan and Angela separate, then there's the picture of you and Alan at Churchill's, then Cliff says he's seen Alan coming out of your cabin – frequently – and at all hours of the night and gets fired, and now you come to work, late, and smelling strongly of sex. It all makes me suspicious," Johe said with a firm voice. *So their relationship has progressed quite a bit, huh?* she thought.

"You can be suspicious all you want, but it doesn't make it true," Mary said as she poured the grain into Sun's feed bowl. The hungry horse dove into his breakfast.

Johe shook her head. "Don't you remember what I told you? Do you really want to be another notch on his bedpost?"

Mary inhaled a sharp breath. "I know what you told me, and I'm telling you as plainly as I can – butt-out."

"What did you just say?" Johe asked with clear animosity.

"I said 'butt-out.' I respect you and care about you, but really, I don't need you butting into my personal life so much."

The hackles on the back of Johe's neck stood erect. "You listen here, you're here as a *favor* to your mother! If she even *is* your mother!"

Mary's head immediately snapped around to look at Johe. Terror was plainly written on Mary's face. Had Alan betrayed her?

"Yeah. That's right. You think I don't know what's going on with you? So I suggest you keep yourself walking the straight and narrow and stop playing with fire! People who play with fire get burned."

Quickly, Mary pulled herself together. "You're being overly dramatic, don't you think?"

"Look, you don't want to make me into your enemy."

"That's not my intention at all. I'm just saying, I want you to butt-out of my personal life."

Johe got in her face and shook her finger at Mary. "If you're fucking Alan, you'll regret it! I'll personally see to it you do!"

Stoically, Mary said, "I look forward to it."

Johe's eyes squinted at her. The last thing she expected was for meek, mild Mary to stand up to her. It was both suspicious and impressive. *She must be sleeping with Alan; where else would she get such nerve*, Johe thought. *And if she is sleeping with him, you better watch your step*, she told herself. "You missed training this morning. Ted's pissed," Johe said changing the subject and her tone.

Mary's courage stood down. "I'm not surprised."

"It doesn't help that Angela isn't here either."

"Where's she?"

"In Savannah or somewhere."

"Oh."

"He's going to make me reprimand you," Johe warned.

"I expected as much."

"What do you think I should do?"

"I don't know. Make me write 'I'm sorry' a hundred times?"

"Ha ha. Very funny."

"I don't know then." Mary's thoughts were mixed with concern that Johe knew the truth about her. Surely it wasn't Alan who told – right? Her face did little to hide the anxiety seeping into her psyche.

"Hey," Johe said with concern. "You ok? I'm just messing with you, you know?"

"Yeah, I-I'm ok."

"Just ok?"

"Yeah."

"Look, you're right. I shouldn't be sticking my nose into your private life. You don't do that to me, so I want to say I'm sorry."

Mary quickly grinned. "Thank you."

"You're welcome. But I have to say, I didn't expect such a feisty response from you. I'm glad to see you've got some spunk to you. Kind of reminds me of that night you kicked Mike in the nuts!" Johe said with a smile.

Mary nodded.

"But there's more you're hiding, isn't there?"

"No. I just need to get to work."

"It's Alan; isn't it?"

"No. It's nothing. I didn't sleep very well last night, that's all."

"Honey, they're all nothing but fish, including Alan. Flush him on down like a dead goldfish before he flushes you," Johe said, ignoring Mary's denial.

"Thanks. But, I think I'm going to go grab a shower. I thought maybe I could get away without a shower today, but since you said I stink, I should probably rethink that," Mary said.

"It's sex; I know it is. There's no doubt in my mind."

"Yeah, whatever."

"Well, don't forget, Dr. Willie is coming today. Felix had me schedule him to take blood and hair samples from Sun and two of your other horses."

"Oh yeah? Why?"

"I don't know. He just told me, and I'm telling you."

"What time is he coming?"

"About two."

"All right. I'll be ready by then," Mary told her.

As Mary walked toward her cabin, she texted Alan: *Did you tell Johe about me?*

His response came quickly: *Absolutely not! Why?*

No reason. Thanks. Mary sighed in relief.

I love you!

I love you, too.

CHAPTER 27

An hour had passed since Alan left Babbling Brooks and Mary. He stood on the rehearsal stage; he and the band had only practiced 7 songs, all of which were the worst songs he'd ever written, in Alan's opinion.

His nerves were like splintered wood. He felt raw, agitated. Seeing the anxiety and worry in Mary's eyes when she told him about the rape played over and over in his mind. He'd promised to protect her, but how could he when he wasn't with her?

Roger, the thought of his name made Alan's head burn.

The fact that she'd been raped shook him to his core. Knowing Roger had planned it and even videoed it made his insides blaze with fury.

Imagining her soft, delicate body being hit by Roger's fists made his nerves send electrical current shooting all through him. He wanted to obliterate Roger. He wanted to tear him apart with his bare hands!

What if Roger found her? What if her rapist found her? Would she be safe going to the upcoming horse show? His mind created a litany of scenarios, each more unthinkable than the first.

She's right. She can't leave the farm. But what kind of life is that? he thought. *If Roger were to find her, he'd kill her. And then I'd have to kill him!*

"Let's go with 'The Devil in White,'" Jon announced from behind his drum set. He tapped out the upcoming rhythm with his drum sticks, and at just the right moment, the band joined in.

261

Alan strummed his guitar and put his lips to the microphone. His thoughts continued to torment his tattered mind. The point where he was supposed to begin singing came and went. The band immediately repeated the bars to give him time to start again.

Even as he tried to force himself to focus, his attention wandered precariously away from what he was doing and right back to Mary. Thoughts of the holes in the farm's security made his imagination run rampant.

His innate desire to safeguard her triumphed over every thought or feeling. He wanted to get to Tucson immediately and destroy Roger Franklin! It was the only way Mary could ever be completely free.

The stage was littered with instruments, cords, and stands, while the band played the same two bars yet again.

Haphazardly, he blew into the microphone. "Sorry, fellas, I'm just not focused at the moment." The instruments slowly faded and then went silent.

"You wanna take five?" Jon suggested with a quick thump on the bass drum.

"Yeah. Everyone, let's take a five-minute break," Alan said into the microphone.

He grabbed a bottle of water as he stepped off the stage. *Mary, Mary, Mary...*, his mind repeated.

Listlessly, he flopped into his red director-style chair. Kicking his black snake-skin boots onto the table in front of him, he knew he needed to rehearse, and yet he also knew he wanted to be with Mary.

He'd never felt anything like this – everything was changing, nothing else mattered. He opened and clenched his fists, flexing and then releasing all of his muscles. The ire combined with mind-numbing worry created a potentially lethal combination. Despite all the times Angela had angered him, and the troubles he'd faced, he'd never felt like this.

He ran his hand down his face with a guttural sigh. His mind was busy plotting – scheming. His thoughts were filled with wondering how he could get to Roger Franklin, find the man who had raped Mary, and make damned sure the two men paid for what they'd done. But he'd have to do all this while making sure he didn't get caught. *How to do it all?* he thought.

He thought of Mary's words: "...my coming to Babbling Brooks was the only shot I had at freedom. I've been safer here than I could've been anywhere else. It's like its own hidden paradise away from the world." He contrasted those thoughts with Felix's claims of security holes. Was running to Europe the best thing to do? Or should they stay in the relative safety Babbling Brooks offered? How could he be certain he could find Roger Franklin?

Oh, I'll find him! his mind shot back. *And when I do, he'll beg for mercy! But there'll be none.*

"All right, what's up?" Jon said as he sat next to the silent Alan.

Alan stared at his mangled bottle of water and shook his head.

"Uh-huh." Jon pulled out a cigarette and lit it. Casually, he blew smoke as he spoke. "You want one?" he offered the pack to Alan.

"Nah, man," Alan said as he put his hand up.

"You want something a little stronger, huh?" Jon smiled and laughed lightly. He took a long drag from his cigarette, holding his breath momentarily. "Yeah, me too," he said as the small remnants of smoke slowly billowed out of his nostrils.

Alan opened the bottle of water; his thoughts repeated the sights of the scars on Mary's breasts, the words she'd said, and the fragile look in her eyes. Images of her defenseless body lying bloody and broken at the hands of Roger flashed before him and turned his blood to lava. The frenzy of his fury felt as if it would rip through his skin.

Tilting the bottle of water up to his lips, Alan sipped from it. In an instant, the bottle was hurled across the stage. "Isn't there anything better to drink in this place than that shit!?" he shouted. "Marcus!"

"It's Travis," his rehearsal assistant almost whined.

"Where the hell have you been?!"

"Right here, sir."

"Get me some tequila."

"Um, well...," Travis hesitated.

"What did I say?!" Alan growled as he jumped to his feet, towering above Travis.

"But Josh said he didn't want any alcohol at rehearsals," Travis practically quoted Josh's directive.

Alan menacingly advanced toward Travis, who cowered to Alan's prowess.

"I-I-I'm just f-f-following orders."

Alan picked up his chair and slung it on the stage with a primal growl. As he saw the chair destroying the stage set-up, he knew what he had to do. The sooner he could get to Tucson and annihilate Roger Franklin, the better. Without another thought, his footsteps trailed to the door.

"Wh-wh-where are you going?" Travis asked.

Alan didn't answer; he simply slammed the door behind him and loudly squealed his Viper's tires through the parking lot.

"Wh-what the hell is up with him?" Travis asked Jon.

Jon shook his head. "I don't have a clue. I'll give him a little bit to cool down, and then I'll talk to him." He turned to the rest of the band members, "Y'all don't think just because Alan's gone we get out of rehearsing. Let's get this shit cleaned up and get back at it!"

Alan's heart was racing. The thoughts of driving straight to Tucson swirled inside his head, clouding his judgment. He needed to focus his brain. With a quick jerk, he turned the car to the nearest convenience store and bought a 44-ounce beer. This time, he took the keys out of the ignition and drank as if he were thirsting to death. For some reason, it tasted terrible! His phone rang on the seat next to him. He glanced at the large display – Josh. "Fuck you!" Alan yelled at the phone, but didn't answer it.

He drank again from the beer, hoping it would taste better. It didn't.

As the beer spilled out of the bottle onto the ground, his cell phone finally silenced. "I need something stronger than this!" he said to no one. His mind immediately thought about the liquor store just down the street from Earl's office. Maybe Earl would have some suggestions for finding Roger Franklin. He could go to Earl's office, sign the papers, and talk about it for a spell. Alan dialed Earl's phone number as he sped away from the convenience store.

"Earl Forsyth," he answered.

"Hey…"

"Peg is printing off your divorce papers as we speak; I was just about to call you."

"Good. I'll swing by and sign them," Alan said with solid resolution.

"No trepidation in signing them?"

"Nope. Not at all."

"Great. Once you sign them, do you want me to have Angela

served, or are you going to give them to her?"

"I'll give them to her. Look, I need to talk to you..."

"What about?"

"A situation I can only talk to you about in person."

"Ok. I have court in just a little bit; is it urgent?"

"Yeah, it kinda is."

"Is it really urgent, or are you just being impulsive?" Earl asked with a knowing tone.

Alan sighed. His tongue burned for something strong to drink. "I suppose it can wait for a little bit."

"Good. By the way, I wanted to thank you again for your help with my friend. He's out on bail now, all thanks to you."

"I'm proud to do it," he said without much thought. Out of the blue, Alan remembered Earl's talk about a hunting trip. "Didn't you say you're friend lives in Arizona?"

"Yeah. Tucson."

"Tucson, huh?" A devilish smile formed across Alan's face. "I also remember you mentioning a hunting trip in exchange for helping your friend out."

"Yeah."

"Is it hunting season out there?"

Earl chuckled lightly before he said, "The Indians don't have to abide by the same laws and rules that we do. They can hunt whenever they want to. It's their land, after all."

"Sounds good. I have some business to handle in Tucson tomorrow, and it would be great if I could get some hunting in while I'm there." *Hunting will at least explain any gunpowder residue on my hands after I waste the fucker!* Alan thought.

"Well, that might be a problem."

"Why?"

"Part of his bail agreement precludes him from carrying a weapon."

"Well, we can carry it for him," Alan said with a tone indicating he didn't care if he was breaking the law.

"I don't know about that. The last thing he needs to do is go back to jail. And then you'll have to pony up the entire 1.5 million."

"But – wait – what? 1.5 million for bail?? You didn't tell me that!"

"You didn't have to pay all of it, just 10%."

"Oh. All right. How about this, I'll bring my own guns so if he gets caught carrying one, we can tell the police he was just holding it for me."

Even though Alan couldn't see him, Earl shook his head. "You know that's not going to work, right?"

"I'm just saying, I really need to get in some hunting and relax. Josh has been pushing me like there's no tomorrow! I just walked out of rehearsals. I-I can't do this. I've got to clear my head!"

"Yeah, I know you did. He called me right before you did."

"The man has no shame."

"No kidding. All right, look, let me call Roger and get back in touch with you. Maybe he can bow hunt or something."

What did Earl just say? Alan thought. "What'd you say his name is?"

"Roger. Roger Franklin."

The hair on the back of Alan's neck stood on end as his skin erupted into flames! *Surely they're not one in the same – right?*

"What did he go to jail for again?"

"I told you; he's accused of killing his wife."

"Who's his wife?" *Surely it's not my Mary*, he thought, but braced himself. He wasn't sure he could stand to hear Earl's next words. The idea that he had single-handedly released Mary's tormentor made him want to violently puke!

"Mary Franklin. Didn't I already tell you all this? I know you've heard about it on the news."

"N-no," Alan managed to mutter.

"I'm really surprised you haven't heard about this. Good grief. Isn't that just like the media? A wealthy white woman goes missing, and they cover it constantly. But let a woman of color go through the same thing, and we never hear a word..."

The car instantly decelerated. Alan couldn't breathe. He felt like every drop of blood in his body had just sunk all the way to his feet. He had to speak, but what could he say? He couldn't let on to Earl that the two Marys were the same people. He had to get off the phone with him as quickly as possible, or should he stay on the phone and pump him for information? His mind screamed for a stiff drink. "Yeah, I hear you. Tell me about his wife's disappearance. What happened?"

"You know I can't talk about the specifics."

"I know. Just give me the general info."

"Ok. From the information I've been able to gather, the police have very little to go on. They have some tiny amounts of blood evidence and some shit she wrote in her diary, but that's about it. Her car was found abandoned in the University of Arizona parking lot. Her purse was found sitting on the floor with just a few items missing. From the scant amount of evidence, it looks like she just disappeared into thin air! There are no fingerprints, foreign DNA, or any other evidence. They don't even have a body or clear motive. Roger has an iron-clad alibi. He was in Phoenix at a fundraiser. It's preposterous to think he'd kill his wife!"

"What's your connection to this fella?"

"We went to law school together and run in some of the same circles."

"How? He's there, and you're here."

"Well, we're both part of a very exclusive club."

"What club is that?"

"We're swingers. And let me tell you this, his wife sure is a sweet treat! I would love to enjoy her again."

"Again?" The words bounced around inside his mind and lighted on familiar words coming from Mary's lips.

"Well, uh, Roger and I made a deal and swapped wives for a night."

Alan felt sick. Was Earl Mary's rapist?? "When was this?"

"Valentine's Day, last year. It was awesome! I flew out there, and Roger flew out here. The rest is history."

"So you had sex with his wife, and he had sex with your wife?"

"Yeah."

"What kind of man whores his wife out to his friends?" Alan acerbically asked.

"Come on. You make it sound so sordid. Natalie was all for it," he said about his wife.

"What about Roger's wife? Was she all for it, too?" His head started to question if Mary was telling the truth, but his heart told him otherwise.

Earl chuckled before he said, "Not exactly. But she was ok by the end."

The rage Alan had felt while at the rehearsal hall was nothing compared to what was bellowing inside of him now. "So you raped her?" he blasted him. The temptation to speed straight to Earl's office and pound him into the ground was nearly overwhelming! His entire body trembled; he had to have a drink right away.

"That's a pretty strong allegation there; don't you think?" Earl's voice stiffened up as he turned from Alan's friend to an attorney.

Alan quickly realized he was in imminent danger of losing the one lifeline he had to Roger – and Mary's freedom. He immediately changed his tactic. "I'm-I'm," the word was stuck in his throat, but he had to push it out, "sorry. What did she look like?" he asked in an attempt to change the subject.

Earl returned to his stance as Alan's friend. "Oh my, she's a stunner! A tiny thing with long beautiful hair and piercing green eyes that could tear through hardened steel."

Alan's heart ached. His stomach churned. Earl was talking about his Mary, and there was no doubt in his mind – Earl was her rapist! How would he keep from killing him when he saw him next?? He had to get a strong drink in his system and fast! The beer he'd poured out in the convenience store parking lot seemed to laugh at him.

Alan swallowed hard. "Wow! She sounds beautiful!" he struggled to exclaim and sound natural. "With a beautiful thing like her on his arm, why on earth would he possibly want to kill her?" His hands shook and his head pounded. The ABC package store came into view. He had to get a drink – now!

"Exactly what I said! I think the judge who signed the indictment has a personal vendetta against Roger. In any other case, an indictment would never have been issued on such flimsy evidence."

"Look, I'm going to swing by ABC and then come sign those papers, ok?"

"All right." Earl looked down at his Rolex watch. "Oh! I've got to get to court. I'll leave your papers with Peg. Be sure to sign all four copies. We'll talk more about the hunting trip afterwards."

"Sounds good." Alan hung up the phone before he even heard the rest of what Earl had to say. He left the engine running as he swung the door open wide and jumped out. With strong, determined strides, he burst into the liquor store. The impending assault on Earl could only be curtailed by copious amounts of alcohol. If not, he was liable to beat the life out of Earl, and then how would he get to

Roger?

"I need a bottle of your strongest tequila!" Alan demanded from the man behind the counter.

"What size?"

"I don't care! Big! I need it *now!!*" Alan's hands shook. Fury threatened to overtake him.

"We-e-ell, we have some Sierra Silver Tequila over there. It's about the strongest tequila I've got," the clerk said in his slow, southern drawl.

Alan immediately rushed to the tequila shelf, picked up the bottle with the little red sombrero on it, opened it, and began pouring it down his throat.

"Hey! You can't do that!" the clerk exclaimed. As quickly as his short legs would move, he came from behind the counter. He reached out to knock the bottle away, but Alan put his hand on the guy's forehead, which kept his reach from Alan.

"Put that down! You can't steal from here! I'm gonna call the cops!"

Alan finally stopped drinking, and released the little man. Over half of the bottle had been consumed. "Look, I'm going to pay for it. I just needed a drink right away."

"What are you, an alcoholic or something?" the clerk asked.

The words stung more than the strong alcohol. "No. I'm just thirsty!"

"Nobody drinks so much tequila at one time."

Alan didn't say anything. He simply turned the bottle back up, finishing it off. "I'll pay for this one, and these two big ones right here, too."

The clerk examined the empty bottle with ample amounts of skepticism. How could someone drink so much so fast? "You want me to throw this away?"

"Sure."

The bottle made a thudding noise as it hit the trashcan. With a sigh displacing the imposition Alan's disruption had caused, the clerk rang up his bill. "That'll be $104.29."

Alan placed two one-hundred dollar bills on the counter, collected the black plastic bag with the large bottles, and walked out the door.

CHAPTER 28

Later the same afternoon, Angela lay gently on a white plush chaise at her favorite Savannah spa.

Gillian sat across from her, chattering away about her pregnancy. "I've been so horribly sick I can hardly stand it! Although I haven't thrown up yet, I always feel like I'm going to any minute."

Angela's face tingled from her recent facial, and her fingernails and toenails were still wet with nail polish. The last thing she wanted to hear was Gillian blather about her pregnancy.

When Angela's cell phone rang, she was both relieved and annoyed by the disruption. "Hello?" The phone balanced carefully by two fingers.

Gillian never missed a beat with her story.

"Mrs. Brooks? This is Travis."

"Who?!" she grumpily asked.

"I'm sorry. I'm Mr. Brooks' new rehearsal assistant..."

"What the *hell* are you doing calling me?!"

"Well, you see, we've got a situation, and I'm hoping you can help me."

Angela's first instinct was to rip into this obviously clueless young man, but decided against it in the quest for the latest information about Alan. "What's going on?" she asked with as much fake nicety as she could muster.

"Mr. Brooks walked out of rehearsals today. Josh is livid!"

"He what?!" Angela faked shock.

"Mr. Brooks trashed the stage and suddenly stormed out of

rehearsals. We need to find him and get him back where he belongs. He's not answering his phone, and no one has been able to reach him…"

"And you called me?" Her mind immediately began wondering what Alan was up to. Were things really so precarious his team would reach out to her? And if things were extremely bad, what did it all mean for her?

"We've called everyone trying to find out where he is. I called his attorney's office twice. Once they said they hadn't seen him, and the second time they reported he'd already been there and left."

"What was he doing there?"

"The lady said she told him we'd called, but since she said he smelled like he'd been drinking, I doubt he'll…"

"Why was he at the attorney's office??" Angela demanded.

"Oh! The lady said he stopped by to sign and pick up some papers. Afterwards, no one's seen or heard from him since."

Angela shot bolt-up from the comfortable chaise. *Papers?* she thought. *Oh hell.*

"I thought maybe he might've called you."

She instantly turned on the helpful, sickening-sweet charm. "I'm sorry, but, no, I haven't heard from him either. Then again, it's pretty unlikely I would. I'm here in Savannah today. Have you checked with Johe?"

"Joe? Who's he? How would he know where Mr. Brooks is?"

"Johe isn't a he, she's a she. She's the manager of the barn, and she and Alan are pretty chummy. Where's Marcus? He can usually find Alan when no one else can."

"Marcus had a family emergency and couldn't be at rehearsals today."

Angela scoffed. "Family emergency, huh? Knowing Marcus it means his mother needs her toenails trimmed! You should talk to Marcus first…"

"I was told not to disturb him," Travis interrupted Angela.

Listen here, you little shit, do you know who I am?! You don't interrupt me when I'm speaking, or I'll have you terminated! formed in her mind, yet her mouth clamped shut and refused to let her say. "Well, ok then. I'd check with Johe."

"Do you have a number?"

What do I look like, directory assistance?! she thought. "No. But you can call my assistant, Lena, and she can give you the number.

"What's Lena's num...." Before Travis could finish asking his question, Angela hung up.

So he stopped at the attorney's office and picked up papers, she thought.

Gillian continued to talk about how shocked she was to be in her second trimester and still feeling sick.

I wonder if those papers are the divorce papers he threatened. Angela tapped her red nail against her prominent chin. The last thing she needed was for Alan to be freaking out and hastening their divorce. Perhaps she'd need to put her date rape drug plan into action sooner than she'd thought.

Angela looked up at Gillian's thin face talking. The words which seemed to make little sense or hold any interest for her before, suddenly were the most important things she could hear. "So, Gills, when did you start feeling like this?"

"Um, I think I was about 6 weeks pregnant," Gillian replied.

"So there weren't any real ill effects before then?"

"Well, I was really tired and my boobs hurt like crazy. Didn't you have similar symptoms when you were pregnant before?"

"Did I? I don't remember."

Gillian giggled. "You've just blocked everything from your mind, haven't you?"

Angela didn't make a sound. She simply rose from the chaise lounge and walked on her heels with her cotton-separated toes in the air. She had to talk to Ted. Drugging Alan had to happen immediately!

"Hi Sweetheart," she said with her syrupy voice.

"Hi Angel. What can I do for you? You missed practice this morning."

"Never mind about that. Do you have the stuff?"

"Yes, ma'am."

"Why didn't you tell me sooner?!" she quietly snapped.

"Well, I don't actually have it in my possession, but it's just a quick ride to Macon to get it."

"I need you to cancel everything and go get it, *now!*" she forcefully whispered.

"What's the rush?"

"Alan's gone bat-shit crazy! If we don't watch it, our tiny window of opportunity will slam shut!"

"Ok. I'll leave right now. Where are you?"

"Savannah. As soon as they fix my makeup again, I'm leaving. I'll meet you in the garage, ok? I'll wait for you in the black Trans Am in the far corner."

"The one from Smokey and the Bandit?"

Angela sighed. "Yeah. It has tinted windows. Don't keep me waiting long!"

"I won't. I'll be back this evening as quickly as I can. When are you going to do this?"

"Tonight."

"You're not wasting any time, huh?"

"There's no time to lose. He's a loose cannon right now. If we don't act now, there may not be another chance. Hurry back."

"I love you," Ted sweetly said.

"You know I love you," she said with an incredulous scoff before she hung up.

It was dark outside by the time Ted met Angela in the black Trans Am. "I don't like this, Ang," Ted said plainly.

"I don't care what you like. This is about my survival – our survival. If he goes through with this divorce, we're through. You understand?"

"Yeah, I get it. I don't like it, but I get it." Ted handed her the amber vial of medication.

"This is the only way."

"I'd rather kill him, to be honest, but I agreed we'd try it your way first."

Angela leaned over and kissed him; his tongue filled her mouth as his hands ventured under her shirt to her smooth skin.

She pushed him back. "Ok, ok. Don't get me all worked up already!" she said breathlessly. "It's Alan I need, not you."

Those words were cleavers chopping Ted's heart into tiny pieces. "Do you have any idea how hard this is for me?"

"Hard for you?" She reached down to his crotch. "Hmmm, why yes, it *does* seem a little hard for you."

"Come on, just let me have a moment with you before you go to him."

"And go in there with your load inside me? Don't you think he'd notice?" she asked him completely aghast at such a request.

"Once you give him this stuff, he's not going to notice much,"

Ted said pointing to the bottle. "Come on, just a little?"

"No. No more sex with me until I'm successful with Alan."

Ted sighed deeply. The hatred he felt toward Alan only intensified each time Angela turned him down. The idea of Alan being so far superior to Ted ate at him like a moth on a wool sweater. Ted was convinced the world would be a far better place without Alan Brooks.

"I've got to go. Travis said he was already drunk, so he's probably completely wasted by now. I've got to catch him while he's still drinking. Otherwise, it will be tomorrow before I'm able to give it to him," she said. "Kiss me quick this time."

Ted obeyed and then got out of the car to open the door for her. "This better work," he said as she stood up.

"It will. There's no way it won't."

Ted put his hands on her hips. "Do you know how badly I want to bend you over this car and fuck your brains out?"

"Mmmm, there's nothing better than angry sex, but I promise you, once all of this is over with, I'll let you take out all of your frustrations on me," she said getting into her seductive character. She grabbed his penis through his jeans. "Oh yes! Feeling him take me from behind would be bliss," she hotly whispered. Her scorching, moist breath burned the skin just in front of his ear.

Ted flipped her around and pinned her against the car, pulling up her skirt.

"No! We're not doing this!"

He didn't hear her as he held her down while unzipping his pants. In a split second, he was inside her. Pounding hard against her curvaceous body and the car's fender, he pulled her hair and growled in her ear, "You'll fuck me first!" The idea of her having sex with Alan infuriated him and made him drill into her harder and faster.

"No!" Angela forcefully whispered and clawed at the windshield wipers.

But there was no escape. Steamy frustrations were slammed against the car and inside Angela. Ted wanted to destroy Alan. Angela didn't belong to Alan, she belonged to Ted. Depositing his seed inside her before Alan could was his way of displaying dominance.

Moments later, he felt the tell-tall signal of satisfaction stirring inside him. With powerful thrusts and a firm grip on her shoulders, he filled Angela with his semen.

He released a deep sigh while he kissed her neck.

She angrily pushed him away. His spent member fell out of her.

"I told you no! Didn't you hear me?? Now I'm filled with your junk before I can even get to Alan!"

Ted aggressively grabbed the back of her head, tilting her face to look at him. "You're mine. Don't you ever forget it," he hissed and released her.

Angela hardly knew what to make of Ted. Their sex had been increasingly more aggressive and domineering. The whole scene concerned her. Had she created a monster in Ted? As she adjusted her clothing, she quietly and with a sadistic smile said, "You dented the car."

He proudly beamed. "So."

"So, how am I going to explain it?"

"No explanation needed."

"Alan's going to notice this big dent."

Ted scowled at her. "Do you think I give a shit what he thinks??"

"No, but *I* do. And if you had any sense to you, you would, too."

"Well, I don't care what he thinks!" He zipped his pants. "I don't like this plan."

"I know. You've already said that."

He grabbed her hips and pulled her to him; his lips immediately found hers.

"Let's not get carried away, again," she said as she pushed him back. "Don't forget your place."

"My place is between your thighs."

"Yeah, well, not while I'm trying to save us. Desperate times call for desperate measures," Angela said as she admired the amber vial. She smoothed her clothes out and turned away from the garage and Ted. Her high heels clicked on the cement floor as she walked toward the door leading to the basement.

Ted watched her as she disappeared inside the house. The faint sound of piano music spilled outside until the door was closed. The gun in his pocket burned his thigh. He had to get out of there before he did something he'd regret.

CHAPTER 29

Ted stood in the darkness of his cabin's bedroom. His hands dissonantly rested on his mirrored dresser. The gun and silencer he'd gotten from his connection in Macon lay between them. The reflection in the mirror couldn't be seen, yet he knew it was there watching his every move.

His mind could only envision Angela. Over and over he saw her with Alan. His hands upon her. His body pressed against hers.

Ted's breaths were shallow, terse. *Alan Brooks*, he thought.

The first time Ted had seen Angela, he was awestruck. The sun shined on her golden hair like a goddess. The light reflected in her blue eyes as if they were fine topaz specially cut and placed there to gaze upon him. Her statuesque body with its delicate, soft curves tantalized him and drew him deeper into her. She would be his. Nothing would stand in his way.

Alan Brooks, his mind reminded him.

When Ted's lips first kissed Angela, he felt the soft warmth of a thousand suns. Her lips dripped with the sweetest honey.

Alan Brooks. He could see Alan's lips caressing them.

Could Angela ever understand the passion he felt for her? Could she see how much he didn't want to share her? What if this time he'd lost her forever? What if she found happiness with Alan instead of him?

He could see her sultry eyes burning for Alan. Everything Ted had ever wanted was there behind Angela's eyes. Heaven. Now his heaven was Alan's.

Alan Brooks, his mind seethed.

He remembered the many times he promised her he would be the one to love her and never leave her. How he would be the one to take care of her. How he would be the one to quiet all of her fears.

Alan Brooks.

Didn't she hunger for Ted the way he hungered for her? He'd done everything he could to be everything she wanted.

Yet, there was still *Alan Brooks*, his mind said again.

Angela, warm and naked under Alan's control. His thoughts wandered to the first time he'd ever touched Angela. Her flesh trembled beneath his fingers like the ground during an earthquake. Feeling her heart beat next to his told him they would be together until the end of time. Alan was feeling it now.

Alan Brooks, he thought again. Alan was the only thing standing in the way.

Damn Alan Brooks, his mind raged.

The temptation to take the gun and shoot Alan in the head burned inside him as it did just moments ago when he was in the garage. Would he lose Angela forever if he shot him? How would he get away with it? The force it took to make his hands remain steadfast on the dresser was more than he could bear, yet he stood stark still.

Meanwhile, Angela's high heels clicked on the hardwood floors as she entered the hallway between the recording studio and bar. Alan was exactly where she expected him to be. It was almost 10:00, which in Alan's world meant he was most likely inebriated enough where he wouldn't notice her slipping something into his drink. The challenge was how to get him to let her remain downstairs long enough to ensure he drank the spiked drink. Multiple times he had scolded her for leaving "her area of the house." Would this time be different?

Angela stood next to the bar, just out of sight from the piano.

Her hands shook.

The music stopped.

Her heart pounded.

She waited with bated breath for it to start again, but after several moments passed and it didn't, she thought this might be a good time to make him a drink and slip the drug in it.

Slowly. Quietly. She poured a generous double shot of bourbon into a thick glass sitting on the open bar. Her hands trembled as she poured the contents of the vial. "Shit," she whispered as a drop spilled onto the bar. *I hope this is still enough to knock him out,* she thought as she stirred the bourbon with a nearby stirrer. *Here goes nothing.*

Tiptoeing, she crept from the bar to Alan's recording studio. He was there at the piano with his head leaning against the lyre. A large bottle of tequila sat next to him; it was mostly empty.

Whew, Angela thought. *Maybe he'll drink this without a thought.*

The door creaked a loud screech which seemed to echo throughout the bar area when she pushed it farther open.

Alan didn't respond.

Good. He's probably already very drunk, she thought. "Sounds like you're having a tough time," she sweetly said. "I brought you a drink." She presented the drugged drink to him.

Alan listlessly turned his head without lifting it off of the lyre. His mind was filled with conflicting thoughts. While he wanted nothing more than to be next to Mary, the thoughts of Earl raping her made him sick. How could he face her knowing he'd so easily put her in harm's way? It made him want to kill both Roger and Earl even more.

And then his thoughts would consider what it would be like to kill someone – to see him draw his last breath; to know he'd died because of Alan. Could he live with himself knowing he'd taken another man's life? He drank directly from the bottle.

For Mary? Yes, he thought.

But on the other hand…

Angela's words ricocheted down the dark tunnel of his mind and finally brought him back to a sense of reality.

"I said I brought you a drink."

"I still have some, thanks." He turned the bottle up again, but didn't finish it.

"Ok. I'll just put it over here," she said as she placed the glass in front of where the bottle sat. "Why don't you play me what you've done so far?" she asked. Picking a fight with him would ensure he would drink anything within reach.

"Why do you give a damn?"

"Because you're my husband."

"Not for long," he placed the bottle back in its same spot.

"Oh come on, Alan. You and I both know we're made for each other. You're not going to leave me any more than I'm going to leave you."

Alan scoffed. "You'll see." His fingers played a series of notes which morphed into "Ding Dong the Witch is Dead" from the *Wizard of Oz* movie.

"Funny. Very funny. You're just trying to provoke me, aren't you?"

"No. I'm through doing anything with or to you."

"I don't believe you."

"It doesn't matter to me if you believe me or not. It's over," he said coldly as he grabbed the bottle and finished it off.

"You can't just give up on our marriage!" she forcefully complained. A little of Ted's semen seeped out of her vagina.

"Angela. You and I both gave up on our marriage long before now. We've just been too stubborn to let it go."

"But… but…"

"No buts. You go your way, and I'll go mine." He picked up the glass she'd brought him.

Angela's heart was racing. *Yes! Yes! Drink the pretty drink,* she thought.

"I picked up the divorce papers today from Earl's office."

"You what?"

"You heard me. They're in there on the bed."

"Did you sign them?"

"Yup!" He held the drink to his lips, but didn't drink.

The hair on the back of Angela's neck burst into flames. "I'm not giving up without a fight!" She had to make sure he drank every drop.

"For the love of God, Angela, just sign 'em! It really doesn't matter anymore, you know? I don't love you; you don't love me. There's no point beating this dead horse," he said as he waved the drink between the two of them, spilling some of the contents onto the hardwood floor.

"You know I love you."

"Honey, with love like yours, who needs hatred?" Alan put the drink down to the left of him on the piano.

"That's just mean-spirited! I've never done anything to make you think I don't love you!" she stood up and shouted.

"Where would you like for me to begin?"

"Wherever you'd like!" she demanded with her arms across her chest.

"You're not even worth my time." With those words, he picked up the glass of bourbon and shot it down his throat. With a relieved sigh, he placed the glass back on the piano, and continued to play the "Witch is Dead" song, hoping it would make her go away.

His heart ached. He wanted desperately to be with Mary, but he wasn't in a good enough place yet – knowing what he knew. Mary would undoubtedly see right through him. If he was going to protect her, he would have to figure out a way to handle things like he'd learned today a lot better than he was.

"You're just terrible – you know?" Angela whipped up some fake tears.

Alan stopped playing and sucked the remnants of her drink from the glass.

"I've done nothing but love you and support you in all of your crazy endeavors! I never batted an eye when you wanted to go on those death-defying, pointless, trying-to-regain-your-youth trips. I supported you while you traveled all over the world…"

Alan slammed the glass back on the piano. "Working! I travel for work!"

"While I was left here alone to run things in this big old house. And when you're here, half the time you're not here! You're at the piano working or drunk off your stupid ass!"

"You knew what you were getting into when you married me."

"Did I? I hardly knew you!"

"Oh, so you just married me because you liked my money, huh?"

Yes, she thought. "No, I loved *you*."

"You just said you hardly knew me, so how could you love *me* when you didn't know *me*?"

"I knew you. You were such a great lover…"

"There's more to a marriage than sex."

"I know. But it seems you only came home to have sex with me, and then you'd be right back to work again. I wanted more from you, but you weren't there."

"That's not even true."

"But it's what it felt like. Now after all these years of standing by you – and-and-and supporting you – you're going to divorce me??"

"Yup," Alan mumbled. His head felt woozy; the room seemed distorted. His body tingled all over. The delicious numbness he'd been craving since the realization about Earl slowly tingled around his body while a delicate warmth enveloped his skin.

Angela watched his motions intently. The edges of his mouth slightly drooped, which indicated the drug was beginning to take effect. "Who nursed you all those times you drank yourself silly?" She waited, mentally perched on the edge of her seat, for a nonsensical answer.

His head leaned heavily forward; his hands rested limply on the keys. He turned to look at her. In a hazy film, he could see her blonde hair cascading down on either side of her shoulders. She looked beautiful – in an ethereal, angelic sort of way.

"What are you doing down here??" Alan snapped. His tongue felt like it was sticking to the roof of his mouth. "I don't know how many times I have to tell you to leave me alone while I'm working!"

"I'm sorry. I was just coming down to see if you were ok. The music stopped, so I was worried something was wrong."

"Like you care…" He forced his head to balance upright on his shoulders.

"I do care!"

"Could've fooled me!" he said through clenched teeth. Why was the room spinning so fast?

"I wish you'd stop this. You once said you loved me. Don't you still?"

"What I feel for you, Ang, is not something I would describe as love."

"Well, you don't hate me, do you?"

His arms felt like they weighed 100 pounds each. "No. I don't hate you. I wish I *could* hate you."

"Well, if you don't hate me then at least we've got something."

"Yeah, well, I can assure, it's not enough to make me change my mind."

"I know." Angela pouted slightly. "I still care about you, though."

"Sure you do," he said sarcastically. "The only person you have ever cared about was you. Everything in this world revolves around you. Heaven forbid if it doesn't." His head fell limply to one side.

Angela wanted to light into him for saying such a thing about her, but instead, she watched him closely. The medication was obviously taking its effect. "Are you feeling ok?" she asked as if she really cared.

"I'm fine."

"You sure? You don't look so good." She arose and moved behind him and gently kissed his cheek. Her hands roamed down his chest.

"C-c-cut it out, Ang," he mumbled and flopped his arms toward her in a feeble attempt to push her away.

"Mmm," she moaned, "you know what I want."

"Ob-obthiously I don't."

"You want me to show you?" she asked using her most enticing voice.

Alan firmly and lucidly grabbed her arm. "What are you doing?!"

"What do you mean what am I doing? I'd think you'd know by now!" she said to him, half disbelieving his coherent reaction.

He shook his head again. Why were the lights so cloudy? Why did Angela's voice sound like she was talking into a tin can? Why did he see two – no wait – four pianos?

"Come on. Let's go in your room."

"I've got – I've got – something…"

Angela held Alan's hand and helped him stand up. Her hips swung lustfully as she led him down the hallway. Like a sheep being led to the slaughter, Alan followed her.

CHAPTER 30

By the time Angela got Alan to the bed, he passed out on it. "Shit! Now what?" she muttered.

"Alan," she said as she shook him. "Alan!" she called to him and shook him harder. "Wake up! You've got to wake up!"

Nothing.

"I'm not messing with you! Get up! Come on, help me take your boots off."

Nothing.

A flash of panic shot through her: *I killed him.*

She felt his skin.

Still warm.

She grabbed his wrist and felt his pulse.

Although it was beating, it seemed off.

"At least it's beating," she whispered while looking at the face-down man. Lying next to him on the bed were a packet of papers which were stapled in the upper left-hand corner.

"What the hell is this?" she questioned as she picked them up. Once she read the top of the first page, she immediately flipped to the back page to see if Alan had actually signed them.

There, in blue ink, was his cursive signature just above the printed block letters "Alan Foster Brooks, Jr."

"My God," Angela said aloud as she sat down on the edge of the bed. "He actually did it!" Fury boiled inside her soul. "But he's not going to get away with it!" Each individual page she tore into small pieces and piled them neatly on the bedside table. "You shit head!"

she yelled at him and punched his arm as hard as she could. "How could you do this to me?! After all I've done for you! I hate you!! I've always hated you!" Her aggressive fists flailed upon his limp body. "You'll pay for this!"

When beads of sweat popped up on her forehead, her assault stopped. She flung her hair back and glared at him. "I guess it's time to get this party started."

With considerable effort, she tugged on his cowboy boots. "Grrrr!!!!" she growled continually as the first one finally slid off. "Whew! That was harder than it needed to be."

Alan only lay as limp as a rag doll.

Again, she struggled and tugged on the second boot.

Alan's massive foot fell lifelessly to the bed.

God, I hope getting his clothes off won't be quite so hard, she thought. Since he had collapsed face-first on the bed, rolling him over was necessary to remove the rest of his clothes. Using her feet and the floor as leverage, she groaned loudly as she tipped him over. He landed in the middle of the king-sized bed.

Eagerly, she climbed back up and straddled his groin. She chuckled to herself. *It's been a while since I've been in this position,* she thought. A glob of Ted's semen seeped from her vagina, through her panties and onto Alan's jeans. "Damn, Ted!" she grumbled and pushed her panties up into the folds of her labia.

Quickly, she returned to the work at hand. Her fingers nimbly unbuckled his belt and made hasty work unfastening his vintage button-fly Levis.

She grunted and pulled, groaned and yanked on the waistband of his jeans. The previous beads of sweat on her face merged into droplets dripping from her delicate face. *This is ridiculous! Please tell me all this will be worth it,* she thought. The jeans had only moved a few centimeters. *If I can get them off of his butt, the rest will be easy.*

She climbed back on the floor and tried pushing him over again. But as she strained and struggled to get the proper leverage, the thought occurred to her: what if she flipped him all the way to the floor? *If he lands on the floor, the whole thing is over,* she thought. *Maybe I can prop some pillows behind him enough to get his butt up off of the bed.*

She sat on the edge of the bed and using all of her strength pulled Alan's hip with one hand and stuffed a pillow under him with the other. Alan's large body crushed the Eiderdown pillow beneath him.

Again, Angela went to the other side of the bed and tried the same thing with the other hip, which garnered the same results.

"Damn feather pillows!" she growled. "I need cinderblocks to hold him up!" Climbing back off the bed, she firmly grabbed the left pants leg and tugged and yanked with all of her strength while using the footboard for leverage. The only result she got was another big glob of Ted's semen seeping past her panties to her thighs.

"Why does he have to wear his Levis so damned tight?!" she complained.

Standing at the foot of the bed with her hands on her hips and breathing harder than she anticipated she would, she contemplated her next move. "It shouldn't be this hard!"

Trotting off to the bathroom to clean herself up, her thoughts were filled with various ideas.

She pulled down her soaked panties from Ted's invasion and sat on the toilet. "Damn, Ted," she grumbled while wiping the moisture from herself.

The toilet water swirled as she washed her hands. There on the side of the sink were Alan's personal grooming scissors. "Of course! Scissors!" she said overly excited. "Yes, I'll just cut his clothes off. He'll never know the difference any way," she told herself as she hurried down the hall with the scissors in her hand.

Moments later, she was back in the bedroom. Alan lay in the exact same position she'd left him. Using big scissor cuts, she unsuccessfully sawed against the fabric at his button-fly.

"You've got to be kidding me! What are these jeans made of??"

Determined to ignore the discouraging voice inside her head, she moved to the foot of the bed and started cutting the jeans around Alan's ankles. Cutting became considerably easier once she'd made it to the pants leg. The scissors easily zipped down Alan's shin, until she reached his knee. "Shit!" she exclaimed when she saw the blue denim turning dark. "I must've nicked him."

Nevertheless, she pressed onward, maneuvering her cuts along the thinner denim between the pocket and button-fly, until she came to the waistband. By the time she cut through the waist band, her delicate hand was sore. "This is ridiculous!" she exclaimed as she sat back on the bed. The dark spot on the denim had increased in size, so she pulled back the fabric from his knee. Sure enough, there was a small gash on his knee cap.

"Stupid jerk!" she shouted as she slapped his numb face.

Angela reached over and pressed the jeans fabric against the cut and held it tightly. *If he bleeds all over the bedding, I'm toast. There's no way I can change the bed linens with him on it,* she thought.

Eventually, the bleeding stopped and was contained entirely by his jeans. "Whew!" she said. "I've got to be more careful with the other leg."

She continued cutting his jeans until his lower half lay completely exposed, save for his boxers. Quickly, she cut them off as well. There was no point wasting energy trying to remove them when she had her handy-dandy scissors.

With considerable force, she pulled one of his arms until he sat limply upright. In a split second, she moved behind him and pulled at his T-shirt. "Don't make me cut it off too, you bastard!"

His floppy arms made it nearly impossible. His head rested heavily upon her shoulder. "Oh forget it!" She dug around on the bed for the scissors and cut up the back of his T-shirt. After she'd moved from behind him, he collapsed back on the bed. Angela pulled his shirt from his chest.

Climbing off of the bed, she dropped the shirt on the floor and grabbed a full handful of jeans and began to pull.

Alan's lower body slid sideways slightly as she struggled to remove the ruined jeans. "Oh *now* you move! This is ridiculous! I don't know how people can be accused of using this drug to rape anyone when you have to go through all of this shit to get their clothes off!" she complained.

Lodging her backside against Alan's body to hold him in place, she pulled harder on the jeans. This time, it worked. Alan stayed on the bed, and the jeans and boxers slid out from under him.

"There!" She stood back and marveled at her work.

What are you going to do when he wakes up and finds his clothes destroyed on the floor? she thought as she took her clothes off. "I'll deal with these later," she answered herself. Without another thought, she stuffed his shredded clothes between the mattress and box springs.

"Now, let's get him going," she whispered. "Alan. You know you want me," she purred into his ear.

He made no response.

Angela kissed his limp lips. "Come on, sleepy head."

There was no response.

She kissed down his chin. To his chest. To his abs. Still nothing.

Carefully she took his limp penis in her hand. "Hello, Mr. Yummy. Don't you want to play with me?" she asked his penis and then kissed the tiny hole.

There was no response.

Angela put more of his penis in her mouth.

There was no response.

"Don't tell me even when you're passed out you don't want me," she muttered.

She put his penis back into her mouth and ran her tongue around it.

It grew slightly inside her mouth.

"Ahh, yes! Now we're getting somewhere."

She rubbed up and down the shaft. "Come on, Alan, you know what I can do for you. You've just got to get Mr. Yummy awake." She put his entire member in her mouth and seductively moaned, "Mmmmm."

Nothing happened.

She spit out his penis and moved to his head. "I can't wait to feel you inside me again," she whispered in his ear, all while moving her hand up and down on his mostly limp manhood.

Climbing on top of him now, she rubbed her naked body against him. With a firm grip on her breast, she shoved her nipple between his lifeless lips. "Come on, Alan. You love my tits!"

There was no response.

"You're just determined to not make this easy, huh?"

Seductively, she moved down his completely naked body back to his penis. Her tongue caressed it up one side and down the other. "Yuck! It tastes like Ted's junk!" she spit out to the side. She took the sheet and wiped Alan's penis clean before her mouth enveloped it again. Her tongue swirled the mostly flaccid member around her mouth.

Nothing happened.

Angela moved to his testicles and carefully sucked one into her mouth. Alan usually loved this, but there still was no response by his penis.

She spit out his ball. "What the hell?! You *love* that!"

She sat next to him and thought. "It's nasty, but it's bound to work," she said as she stuck two fingers into her vagina and produced them below his nose.

Nothing happened.

She shoved the goo-covered fingers into his mouth.

Again, nothing happened.

Angela climbed on top of him and tried to stuff his only slightly stiff manhood into her. Surely just feeling her would wake it up. She tried rocking her hips back and forth, but it slid out.

Frustrated, Angela flopped onto the bed beside him with her head upon his arm. Was he dead or something?

For a split second, she wondered if whatever she gave him had killed him. Panic lay in the bed beside her, taunting her as she intently listened for his heartbeat. Faintly, she could hear it.

"Whew. At least he's not dead."

Panic told her if his heartbeat was so faint, he could die.

"I don't guess we're going to have sex then, huh?" she whispered to the unresponsive Alan. As she laid her head back on his chest to listen to his heartbeat, her mind concocted a clever plan – a plan which was even better than her original one.

All I need is for Alan to think he had sex with me. Then I can claim I'm pregnant long enough for him to get rid of Mary and never sign those divorce papers again. It takes months before I would start showing, so I could keep this going for a good while, she thought.

She got up from the bed and ran naked through the basement out to her car, where she'd left her purse and her cell phone. Quickly she Googled "fake pregnancy." Immediately, a site came up entitled: "How to Fake a Pregnancy."

Angela excitedly read through all of the instructions, skipping over things she didn't think pertained to her or she didn't want to hear.

"Yes. This is the answer." She closed the web page and confidently strode through the basement back to Alan. She laid her head back on his chest and listened for his heartbeat.

He was still alive. "Good. When you wake up, you'll be in for the surprise of your life!"

She placed her cell phone on the bed-side table and curled up beside Alan.

CHAPTER 31

Alan felt as though he were drifting somewhere in an atmosphere he wasn't entirely sure existed. In the darkness, he saw differing shades of emptiness dancing and swirling before his eyes. His head ached, yet he wasn't completely sure he had a head. He felt down his naked body, but he was unable to feel anything or to be absolutely aware he even had a body.

As if through his pores, his body tingled while bits of reality seeped into his psyche. His thoughts began to make some sense.

Visions played out before him. His mother sat next to the grand piano as he played Chopin. The music played loudly in his head – Chopin's *Military* polonaise. He'd learn to play it at 9 years old and swore he'd never play it again. Why was he playing it now?

"Forte, Junior. That means louder. You have to display strength in this work," his mother lectured him.

He began playing again, this time louder and more dramatic.

"Not *every* note needs to be louder. It should be a booming performance with soft notes, too. Look at your sheet music." There was clear disapproval in his mother's voice.

The sheet music looked like a garbled mess and seemed to morph continually into various songs. He felt panicky. How could he play like his mother wanted when he couldn't distinguish the notes? The harsh chords of *Military* resonated inside his head as his right hand pounded them out, but his left hand began playing Ray Charles' version of the sentimental blues song *The Snow is Falling*.

"Stop goofing around, or I'll get your daddy's belt!" his mother's acerbic words tore into his mind like the threatened belt would into his flesh.

Alan tried to speak about the sheet music, but his words sounded like his mouth was filled with marshmallows.

With his eyes closed, his fingers began playing by memory.

But when he hit a wrong note, his mother scorned him again with her words, "Fine! If you're not going to play seriously, then you can practice your fingering until I tell you to stop!" She arose from her chair and left.

Alan's eyes opened to see his childish hands moving across the white and black piano keys. His soul longed for his demanding mother's approval, yet the music became garbled as the scene turned into more shades of darkness.

As if he had simply blinked, he was transported to a John Deere tractor with his dad ahead of him on a Caterpillar bulldozer. They were planning to clear out a piece of steep, low-lying property. Alan, Sr. wanted to expand the size of the lake and create a good fishing area.

Alan, Sr. called to him, "Hey there, boy! It's about time you got here!"

Alan tried to say something to him, but it only came out as mumbled moaning. He drove his tractor to rest directly beside his dad.

"So you finally figured it out, huh? She only wants you 'cause you're Alan Brooks," his dad said plainly.

Again, Alan tried to answer but was incapable of forming his thoughts into words. All he could do was nod his head.

"Good. I'm glad you've come to your senses. You've got to follow your heart. What're your plans now?" Alan, Sr. put a chaw of tobacco in between his cheek and gum.

Alan mumbled louder this time.

"I just want you to be happy. Are you happy?" his father asked him.

Alan could only shake his head.

"Mm-hmm. Your main problem isn't her. Don't get me wrong, she's a big problem, but, the biggest one you need to deal with is the booze." His father's hazel eyes could scorn Alan with just a glance. Alan, Sr.'s strong, calloused hands removed his own ball cap and scratched his wavy blonde head. "I know all too well about the drink's dangers. What I found is all very simple." He spit out brown tobacco juice from the left side of his mouth and wiped his mouth on his sleeve.

"You've got to decide what's most important in your life, and focus on it. For me it was your mama and you. Nothing else matters except what's important. Somewhere along the way, you got lost, boy. Just like when you got lost on the camping trip with the Boy Scouts." Alan, Sr. chuckled and spit again.

Alan, Sr. watched Alan as he fumbled to speak.

"She's pregnant, huh?" A broad, extremely pleased smile came across Alan, Sr.'s face showing dimples that nearly mirrored Alan's. He took off his work glove and shook Alan's hand. "I'm so proud of you! You need to fill the big old house with the sounds of children's laughter. Don't let the Brooks name die."

Alan tried to explain to him there was no baby; Angela had had a miscarriage, but he couldn't form the words. It was as if his lips were sewn shut.

"With a baby on the way, it seems to me it's time you got your life together." Alan, Sr. slid his hand back into his leather work glove and adjusted the fingers as he continued to speak. "From what I can see, the root of all your problems is tied up in one question: are you happy with the *man* or the *image*? When you can honestly answer and own it, you'll be able to walk away from the bottle, just like I did. Then you can focus on your family."

Alan, Sr. started the engine of his bulldozer. "Time's a wasting! Your boy's gonna need his daddy, just like you needed me. Just remember, the man or the image..." The growl of the bulldozer's motor drown out the rest of his voice.

Daddy, don't!! Alan tried to shout, but instead he could only whimper as he again helplessly watched the bulldozer flip over and crush his father to death. The image faded to black, and Alan felt like he was sinking into quicksand. Only his father's words remained and echoed inside his mind, "The man or the image..." Alan's mind was filled with the bouncing sounds of his father's words.

Blurry pictures of Mary flashed before him. She was surrounded by what Alan thought was a snow storm in the darkness of night. In his hallucination, he moved closer to her; what appeared to be snow was in fact millions of butterflies swirling around her as if being blown around by hurricane-force winds. Mary's entire body was wrapped in a thick dark covering.

Alan tried to touch her, but he couldn't reach her.

She struggled against the clay-like entrapment; her eyes begged him for help.

Nevertheless, he felt as incapable of offering any as he ever had. His heart pounded in his chest as he tried with all his might to grab ahold of her, but he was always just centimeters away.

Her green eyes glowed brightly against the fluttering wings surrounding her. Her gaze burned through him to his soul. "The man or the image…," her lips moved, but it was his dad's voice.

How did she know what his dad had said? He lunged toward her, but he felt as though his legs were made of gelatin. His fingers stretched out to her, through the butterflies; their wings tingled along his limbs. Just as his hand touched the very tip of her glorious hair, his body slammed him back to utter, lonely darkness. "What the…?!" Alan called out.

The room was pitch black, yet he wasn't sure if any of it was real. Was his mom scolding him for taking his music so blasé? Was Mary wrapped in a cocoon? Was his dad really there or still dead? Why was he talking about Angela's miscarried baby? His dad's words echoed inside his head: "Your boy's gonna need his daddy, just like you needed me. Just remember, the man or the image…"

"Daddy?" he whispered. Alan wondered if he were dead too.

No one answered.

Oh God! I'm in hell?? he questioned, terrorized at the thought. The darkness was suffocating. The sense of utter loneliness petrified his mind. He couldn't make out shapes. Where was he? Was he in his own body or was he just a spirit? His eyes began to flash imaginary lights before him. His ears heard the sounds of breathing. Was it his own?

Frantically, he felt around him until he felt warm flesh. He rubbed his hands up and down his naked body, which made him realize he was without clothing.

I can feel that, he thought. *I must not be dead.*

He fumbled around feeling everything around him. When his hand landed on a warm lump, he felt all over it. His mind frantically tried to determine what it was. Was it the devil? Maybe it was Mary. Was she still wrapped in the cocoon? Determinedly, he began ripping back the covering – trying with every bit of his resolve to free her.

"What the hell are you doing?" Angela's sleepy voice snapped at him.

Alan's mind quickly flipped through his memory files – whose voice was that? "Angela?" he asked.

"Yeah?" she sleepily replied.

He reached out with the other arm and felt the edge of the bed. Pulling himself to the edge, he swung his feet to the floor. Things were beginning to feel familiar to him. Objects he couldn't see before, he could see with his mind's eye. *Light. I need some light,* he thought.

Fumbling now, he reached for the bed-side lamp, which instantly banished most of the darkness from the room, revealing his bed partner.

"What the hell are you doing here?!" he shouted at Angela. His disappointment in Mary's absence was palpable.

Startled awake by Alan's outburst, Angela grabbed the comforter and pulled it to her chin. "What?!" For a split second, she wasn't sure what was going on, but just as quickly, she began to put on her act. "What do you mean what am I doing here?" She flipped the down comforter off of her, revealing her nakedness. "Don't tell me you don't remember."

Alan rubbed his forehead. "I don't remember anything."

She smiled as she slid her body against his bare back. "Well, let me refresh your memory." Her lips quickly found the small patch just in front of his ear that she knew drove him wild.

"Get the hell off of me! What's your problem??" He flung her away from him.

"Nothing. I just thought…," she said while she pouted.

"You thought what??"

"I thought after last night, we were getting back together."

"What gave you such an insane idea?!"

"You did, of course. We made some of the most beautiful love we've ever made last night. Don't you remember?"

Alan closed his eyes, rubbed his hands down from his hair to his goatee, and tried to think. He could only remember his dad's troubling words. "No."

Angela smiled. "Well, we did. You told me you loved me. You even tore up the divorce papers," she said. Briefly she wondered if she was pushing things too far, but decided to go for all or nothing. "See," she motioned toward the pile of white paper shreds, some of which had fallen to the floor when Alan searched for the lamp. "Those are the divorce papers. You tore them up last night."

"I didn't…. I don't remember much from last night."

Angela frowned. "I guess it was all a bunch of lies, huh? I don't understand you, Alan. I love you. Last night, you said you loved me too. You *wanted* me. We made love several times. I can't believe you can't remember."

"I don't remember *any* of this."

She sighed. "Well, you were drinking, so I guess that's not so surprising."

"I was drinking?"

"Yeah. Quite a lot too."

He felt horrified! Had he cheated on Mary with Angela? Had he really torn the papers up? What would Mary think of him?? *The man or the image…* rattled inside his mind. He hated himself. Hated himself for drinking. Hated himself for cheating. Hated himself for not living up to the man his father raised him to be.

"I guess they were-were…" She began to whip up some fake sniffles. "Were just some-some drunken, thoughtless, meaningless words, huh?"

Alan could only look at her with his mouth gapping open. Had he actually done those things? He immediately felt guilty.

"I don't remember anything from last night. Whatever I said and did, I obviously didn't mean."

"You mean you're st-st-still di-di-divorcing me?" Angela asked with a liberal peppering of sobs.

"Y-y yes." He hated how unsure his answer sounded. "Yes," he said more firmly.

"You said you wanted to make a baby last night!" Angela exclaimed with a super-sized helping of faux sadness.

He questioned just how he could've made such a mistake. Was that what his father meant about the baby? Should he reconsider the divorce? *Surely not. Surely he meant the baby Angela miscarried,* Alan thought. "It was a one-time thing – an accident."

"An accident??" Angela said, nearly screeching. "That's all I am to you – an accident??"

"I didn't say…"

"You told me over and over you loved me last night! Was it all just some ploy to get me to sleep with you??"

"I don't remember any of it. Whatever happened last night…. Look, it doesn't change the future. Did you really think it did?"

"Of course! You told me you loved me! I believed you!" This time she was able to produce an actual tear.

Alan sat on the side of the bed with his back to her. He closed his heavy eyes and rubbed his head. What would Mary think of him? His heart ached. How could he tell her?? The room seemed to be spinning out of control. "Please get out of my bed now," he coldly said.

"No! Not until you agree that what we shared last night was-was beautiful!" She was pissed when he missed the delightful tear she'd squeezed out. It had already snaked its way down her cheek by the time he looked at her again.

"Get out now before I throw you out!" he angrily said as he tried to stand up, but instead leaned on the edge of the bed. Balancing himself with one arm, he pointed toward the door. His arm trembled, and he wasn't at all sure he was going to remain standing much longer.

Angela climbed out of the bed, bent over, collected her clothes, and held them over herself as she left his room. At first she was going to put her clothes back on, but since the servants were probably already working, she decided to cover her nakedness with only her disheveled clothes and walk through the house. She wanted them to see her leaving Alan's basement. She needed them to know she'd been with him – naked – so that when she announced the pregnancy, no one would question who the daddy was.

Once the door closed behind Angela, Alan fell into the bed. He felt worse than he'd felt after Angela bit him. He turned the light off; the room returned to its windowless blackness.

Did you really have sex with Angela? he thought. He strained to remember what happened the night prior – nothing came to his mind.

His stomach was in knots. He wanted to go back to where his mom, dad and Mary were, but he didn't know how to get there. His arms wrapped around his aching stomach. Vomiting seemed to be the only way to receive any relief, yet the vomit seemed determined only to torment him.

How could he tell Mary about what happened with Angela? She deserved to know. Would she leave him?

"Daddy," he whispered, "what do I do now?"

CHAPTER 32

Alan stayed in bed for two days before Julia went against Alan's wishes to leave him alone and convinced Gus to intervene.

"Sir?" the loyal butler whispered as he gingerly entered the unlit room.

Alan was pasty white. His lips were chapped. His eyes were sunken in and dark. His naked body laid wrapped in a fetal position around a vomit-stained pillow.

Gus touched Alan's neck to see if he had a pulse. To his relief, there was the indication of life. "Sir. I'm going to call Dr. Sabia to check on you. You do not look well."

Within the hour, Dr. Sabia flipped on the light in Alan's bedroom.

Alan's eyes winced at the intrusion.

"At least you're not dead," Dr. Sabia said. "Tell me what happened."

Alan lay motionless and speechless.

"Gus, do you know what happened?"

"No, sir. I know he's been this way for a couple of days."

"Does Angela know?"

"I don't know."

"Hmm. I know things have been volatile between them."

"Yes, sir."

Dr. Sabia immediately started an IV in Alan's hand, took several vials of blood out of it, and began giving him fluids.

"They have resided in separate parts of the house. I believe Mr.

Brooks was planning to divorce her. Julia said she heard him informing Mrs. Brooks of this."

"Mm-hmm," Dr. Sabia said as he pulled a chair next to the bed and stood on it to hang the fluid bag from the bed post above Alan's head. "You don't think she had anything to do with this, do you?"

"I can't speak for sure, sir, but if there is anything I have learned is that anything is possible."

"I'd like to talk to Angela," Dr. Sabia said as he examined Alan.

"I'll retrieve her for you," Gus stated as he quietly and courteously left the room.

"Hey. Alan," Dr. Sabia said as he shook Alan lightly.

Alan didn't respond.

"Come on, buddy, I need you to talk to me. Tell me what happened."

Alan barely shrugged.

"Ahh, so you're still with me, huh?" Dr. Sabia sat in the nearby chair.

Alan blinked slowly and stared at the opposite wall.

"You know you've got to stop the drinking, right? You can't continue down this self-destructive path. You're going to end up killing yourself."

Alan's eyes slowly blinked once.

"I'm not going to stand by idly and watch you. You've got to do something different. Do you want me to send you to rehab?"

Alan's face scrunched and his head moved slightly side-to-side.

"So no rehab, huh? You want to join the ranks of all those other stars who've killed themselves before they reach their full potential, huh? Well, if that's what you want, you're well on your way!" Dr. Sabia adjusted the speed in which the fluids were entering Alan's body. "Are you thirsty?"

Alan's head gently shook.

"You should be. You probably drank so much booze that you're missing most of your fluids. I see you've been vomiting, huh?" Dr. Sabia said as he noticed the stained bedding.

Alan didn't respond.

"It's a good thing Gus called me when he did. People die like this, you know? I mean it. It's not really hard."

The two sat in silence for a few moments before Gus returned with Angela in tow.

"I don't know what you expect me to say. I don't know what the hell is wrong with him. He drinks too much. This isn't anything new. What do you expect from me?" Angela complained loudly.

"Angela. I'm glad you're here. How long has he been like this?" Dr. Sabia asked.

Angela scoffed. "Who called you?"

"Gus. Now answer the question," Dr. Sabia said, determined not to take any of Angela's lip.

"How would I know? We're separated, remember? He's not my responsibility," she said indifferently.

"Ok. When is the last time you saw him?"

"Two nights ago."

"What happened?"

Angela closed her eyes; her face crinkled up like she was about to cry. Eagerly, she began fanning herself. "He told me he wanted to make up – he promised we were getting back together. He duped me into sleeping with him. Then when we woke up, he claimed he must've been drunk because he didn't mean any of it," she said while noticeably choking back tears. "So I'm sure you can understand my situation."

"Yes, I understand. Do you know what he was drinking?"

"Probably his usual, bourbon. But I did see a tequila bottle, too."

"Hmm, thank you."

"He's been out for a couple of days. There's no telling what else he may have ingested!" she added. With Dr. Sabia there, she had to find a way to cover her tracks, just in case.

"Ok. Thanks." Dr. Sabia took one of the vials of blood and wrote *Drug Test* on it.

"Are you through with me?" she asked.

"Yes. Thank you. You've been very helpful."

Angela left the room; Gus remained.

"Dr. Sabia," Gus whispered once he heard Angela's high heels clicking on the stairs.

Dr. Sabia rose to join Gus away from the door.

"I should have told Mr. Brooks, but I didn't. I wasn't sure how correct the information was, so I kept it under my hat."

"Don't worry about it, Gus. What happened?"

"Well, a little over a month prior to this happening Julia,

overheard Mrs. Brooks on the phone with someone. Julia said she thought she overheard Mrs. Brooks say something about a date-rape drug. Julia didn't know the context of the conversation, so I told her to drop it."

"Did Mrs. Brooks mention what kind?"

"Not that I'm aware of, sir. Julia said she barely heard the words, and since she wasn't completely sure, she agreed to take a wait-and-see approach."

"Probably the best thing to do."

"I'm not sure why I'm mentioning it now except that the story Mrs. Brooks just told you doesn't make sense to me. Julia has told me on more than one occasion she and Mr. Brooks have talked about a new woman he's been seeing."

"New woman, huh?"

"Yes."

"So the story about them making up is pretty implausible, huh?"

"Exactly."

Dr. Sabia pursed his mouth. "Don't worry, Gus. I'm sure he just drank himself into another stupor. Only this time, it's quite a bit worse than before. I'm going to try and get him to go to rehab, but if he won't go, I'm going to admit him into the hospital for a couple of days for exhaustion. He probably hasn't been sleeping, too, which he knows is bad for him."

"Ok. I apologize if I was out of line."

"No, no. Giving me any information is the right thing to do. If it'll make you feel better, we'll run a full drug screening on his blood just to be sure. I'll check for all of the common club drugs. Anything's possible. Relationships can get really ugly when they begin to dissolve, and when you mix big money into it, you get ones as volatile as this one is." The two men looked knowingly at each other. "Thank you for the information. Let's hope nothing of the sort has happened."

"Yes, sir."

After two bags of fluids, Alan's color had somewhat returned. He was more alert and able to respond to Dr. Sabia's questions.

"This was as close to death as you've ever been. Listen to me carefully; if you don't clean up your life, I'm going to be called out to pronounce you dead. Do you understand? "

"Yeah," Alan unenthusiastically muttered. His heart ached. In his mind's eye he could see Mary's trusting green eyes looking right into his soul. How could he have betrayed her? He almost wished no one would have found him so he could've died. How will he ever face her again? Yet, how could she be safe without him? Especially since Earl had unfettered access to the farm.

"Do you want to die or something?" Dr. Sabia asked him.

Alan only slightly shook his head.

"That's where you're heading."

Alan lay still, unresponsive. He didn't want to hear anything Dr. Sabia had to say. His arms clung to a feather pillow; his mind filled with thoughts and images of Mary. *How will she ever forgive me?* he wondered. *How will she trust me again?*

"Alan! Listen to me." Dr. Sabia shook Alan's shoulders hard. "Have you ever had a reaction like this before?"

"No! Get your hands off of me!"

"Did you take any medication?"

Alan barely indicated a negative response.

"Are you sure?"

"James…" Alan warned in a weak voice.

"I'm just asking. I'm not trying to get you thrown in jail. Did you take any recreational drugs?"

"No. Stop!" Alan turned away from the doctor's face. The last thing he wanted was for Dr. Sabia to ask any more questions. His heart ached for Mary. He wanted to run to her and beg her forgiveness, but if she knew what he'd done with Angela, he felt certain she would reject him.

"These are all standard questions."

"Just leave me alone," Alan said into the pillow.

"Not this time. I'm going to have to involuntarily admit you to a drug and alcohol rehab facility."

"What?!" Alan weakly slung his head over toward Dr. Sabia. "I'll kill you first!"

"You're not going to kill anyone but yourself like this. It's my professional opinion you're a danger to yourself. It's for your own good. You're going to kill yourself if you don't stop."

Listlessly, Alan lay in bed and stared at the wall. Was death such a bad thing? At least then he could be with his daddy again. But what about his mama? Who would take care of her? And what about Mary?

His daddy's words came back to his mind: *From what I can see, the root of all your problems is tied up in one question: are you happy with the <u>man</u> or the <u>image</u>? When you can honestly answer and own it, you'll be able to walk away from the bottle, just like I did. Then you can focus on your family.*

"I can do it on my own," Alan said.

Dr. Sabia scoffed. "You've been a heavy drinker for as long as I've known you. Do you really think you can just up and stop?"

"Yeah. I was doing good."

"*Was*, is the key word there."

"I don't drink every day," he said with more determination and gusto than he'd shown since Dr. Sabia's arrival.

Dr. Sabia smirked in discontent. "Maybe so, but when you drink, you go all out. Nothing is left when you're done. You're like a swarm of locusts on a field."

Alan thought about how he could have devoured the entire ABC liquor store when he made the connection about Earl. His heart ached at the memory. He wanted a drink to drown out the pain.

He was completely sober the night he'd spent with Mary. It was the best night of his life! Living more nights like it would definitely be a welcomed change. But how? Would he think of Earl every time he touched Mary? Every time he saw those scars?

Alan began nodding. "Ok," he quietly said.

"Ok what?" Dr. Sabia asked.

"I'll go."

"You'll willingly go to rehab?"

"Yeah."

Dr. Sabia jumped up from his chair. "Gus, get a car, get Mr. Brooks' bag packed, and have someone pour every drop of alcohol in the house down the drain. And I want you to have the plane on standby ready to take off as soon as we arrive. I'm going to call the clinic and see if I can get him immediately in there. We have to act quickly before he changes his mind. Where are his clothes?"

"I don't know," Gus replied

"We'll need someone to dress him," Dr. Sabia ordered.

"I'll get Marcus here." Gus immediately left to put things in action. Alan's seeking help for his alcoholism was an answer to prayers.

Dr. Sabia returned to Alan. "You do understand, if you allow yourself to reach this point again, you may not come back, right?"

"Yeah."

"This isn't going to be easy, but in the end, it will make things a lot easier. They'll help you work through getting dry and such."

"I know."

"Good. You can't go on like this." Dr. Sabia decided to do a little investigating. "Angela deserves better."

"We're getting a divorce," Alan said plainly.

"Oh? She said you wanted to get back together. I heard y'all were separated, but I didn't realize it had escalated to divorce." Dr. Sabia wondered if maybe Gus was right: Angela *had* drugged Alan.

"Yeah."

"I'm sorry."

"Don't be. It's long overdue. Besides, I found someone."

"Who?"

"It doesn't matter. She'll never forgive me."

"Did you ever think the alcohol has had a negative effect on both your marriage and relationship?"

"Maybe."

Dr. Sabia raised his eyebrows. "At least you're coming to a clearer understanding of things."

"I think I've been living a lie."

"Exactly. And the truth is what?"

"That I drink too much, Angela doesn't love me for me, and the one person in the world who does will never forgive me for what I've done."

"I'm sure she'll forgive you," Dr. Sabia said as he removed the IV from Alan's hand.

"Not for this. I think I cheated on her with Angela."

Dr. Sabia looked at him with his mouth gaped open briefly before he said, "Well, Angela is your wife."

"But I told her I was serving Angela the divorce papers. She trusted me."

"People forgive."

"You don't understand. She already has really bad trust issues."

"You can't expect yourself to be perfect."

"No. But I can expect myself to not fuck it up!"

Dr. Sabia put his hand on Alan's shoulder. "It'll be ok. I promise."

Within the hour, Dr. Sabia helped Alan dress and left the room to make all the arrangements for his detox. Marcus knocked lightly on the bedroom door. "You in here, buddy?"

"Yeah, come on in," Alan answered.

"Dude! You look terrible!" Marcus said at first sight of him. "You're as white as a ghost!"

"Thanks. That's just what I wanted to hear," Alan said with a nasty look on his face.

"I meant, I'm here to help you. What's going on?" Marcus corrected himself.

Julia presented a tray of food for Alan, who sat down at the table to eat. It surprised him how ravenously hungry he was.

"I'm checking myself into rehab." The words were difficult for Alan to say. Did they mean he was weak? What would his mother think? What would his father think, if he were alive? "Get my suitcase packed," Alan said as he shoved a large bite of pancakes into his mouth. He thought of the pancakes Mary had made them when it snowed. His heart ached.

"All right. Do you want the big one?"

"No, just get the medium-sized one. I don't plan to be there for long."

"Pack the big one," Dr. Sabia poked his head in the room and insisted.

Marcus left the room to retrieve Alan's suitcase. Once he'd cleared the doorway, Alan's maid, Julia, returned to the room carrying a laundry basket.

"It sure is good to see you up and eating, Mr. Brooks," she commented. "My goodness this room is a wreck!"

"I know, Jules. I'm really sorry. But I'll be out of your hair for a little while," Alan politely told her.

"You're never any trouble. We'll miss you around here," she said as she began stripping the bed of its linens. "When are you going to be back?"

"I don't know yet."

"You take care of your...," Julia stopped as she pulled clothing out from between the mattresses.

"What were you saying?"

"Um...," she said as she held up the shredded clothing. "What happened here?"

"Damned if I know," Alan responded while his eyes scanned the tattered clothes. "Those are my favorite Levis!" he complained.

"They were shoved under the mattress here," Julia pointed out the location.

"Marcus!" Alan called for him. "I don't have a clue. Maybe Marcus knows."

Marcus walked into the bedroom. "Yeah?"

"Do you know how these clothes got stuffed under the mattress?" Alan asked.

"No, why would I?"

"There's no need to be smart. I'm just asking if you know anything about them," Alan said with a stern face.

"I told you I don't know."

"Julia was changing the sheets and found them. I want to know how they got there."

"I'm sure I don't know," Marcus said as he examined the clothes. "Aren't those your favorites?"

"Yeah, they are. I'm pissed as hell! They're destroyed!"

"I don't know anything about it. Have you asked Angela?"

"No, I'm asking you."

Mentally, Marcus rolled his eyes. "I told you, I don't know anything about them."

"Fine. Whatever. Just get me packed."

Julia shoved the clothes into the laundry basket with the soiled sheets.

Dr. Sabia walked into the bedroom. "All right. I have you booked to enter the Betty Ford Center."

"Isn't that in California?" Alan asked.

"Yeah. What's wrong?" Dr. Sabia countered.

"Nothing. I just didn't want to be so far away from home."

"Look. You need to be very far away from here. You need to focus on yourself for a while. Once you've got a handle on your addiction, you'll know more about how to handle your life. You can then start putting the pieces back together."

"I need a shower, and there's one more thing I've got to do first before I go," Alan said.

CHAPTER 33

Alan's black stretch limousine was parked next to the main house, awaiting his eminent departure. Marcus carried a large suitcase out of the house and placed it in the trunk.

Mary, who had felt so exposed to Alan just a couple of days ago, stood at the barn doorway wearing the pearl necklace he'd given her. Feeling confused, she stood motionless.

He's leaving without so much as a goodbye? she thought as she ran her fingers slowly along each pearl around her neck. *What happened? What did I do?* Her heart was heavy. She hadn't spoken to him at all since the night they'd spent together making love. Even her repeated texts to him had gone unanswered. Now he was leaving? Her heart ached.

Was she just like the fish he caught out on the boat? He caught her, got what he wanted, and now he was finished with her? Was John right? Was she just another notch on his bedpost?

She slowly blinked her eyes. Surely that wasn't the case.

Alan stepped out from the house and without looking up or toward the barn, climbed into the back of the limo.

"He's leaving?!" Mary's words softly shrieked. She covered her mouth to hide them. "Where's he going?" Her soul wanted to run after the shining car, but her body stayed steadfast. "You're nothing more than a damned fish," she muttered. "That's what you get for thinking otherwise!"

The dust particles settled from the limo's early-morning departure. Mary's head throbbed. How could she have exposed herself so openly to him? She reached around her neck and found the diamond clasp holding the strand of pearls together. What was she thinking wearing them anyway? *I shouldn't have told him about Roger. I shouldn't have let him in.* She shook her head at herself for not resisting him.

I should've known better than to trust him, she scolded herself. *You're just a fool – a stupid pathetic fool.* She removed the necklace. *Idiot!* she thought as she stuffed the delicate strand into her pocket. *Now what? He knows all your secrets. Ugh! Get back to work, you romantic sap.*

While saddling Rascal, Ted approached her. "Today, we're working relentlessly until you successfully jump three feet. No excuses. Understand?"

Rapidly, Mary nodded her head.

"Good. I'll meet you in the arena. I'll have Rob set the jumps to the appropriate height."

"Ok," was the only word she could squeak out. Yes, jumping would take her mind off of Alan. Anything was better than thinking about his desertion of her.

She finished saddling Rascal and led him down the aisle to the indoor jumping arena. Rob was still busy setting the jumps.

Mary tightened the straps on her helmet, collected the reins, mounted, and began warming the horse up on the outer edge of the arena. The six-bar jumps loomed in her future as Rascal trotted past each one. How many times would she fall off today?

With a slight kissing sound, Mary urged Rascal into a canter. The controlled, three-beat gate carried her faster past the jumps. Her body braced itself for the inevitable crash.

"Don't think about it," she whispered to herself. "You can do this. Just trust Rascal. He knows what he's doing. You just hold on."

"All right, Mary, I want you to take the red and white jump. It's set at two-and-a-half feet."

Mary maneuvered Rascal around a big circle and then set him up for the smaller jump. Her body trembled as she anticipated biting the dirt.

Rascal tucked his front legs under him and easily cleared the jump, successfully landing with Mary still in the saddle on the other side.

"Not very elegant, but successful. Good job," Ted said. "Now circle back and do it again. This time, I want you to be sure you're putting yourself in the two-point position."

"But when I do, that's when I fall off," she complained.

"Trust me. Ok? Use his mane for security and your legs for balance. Don't drop your reins."

"Ok."

Mary turned the horse back in a big circle.

"Keep your hands quiet and your lower legs underneath you. Press your heels down to keep your weight balanced there. Guide him to it, but let him do the work."

As best as she could, she followed Ted's directions. This time, the jump was much more successful.

"Great! Much better. Now do it a few more times, and we'll try one of the bigger fences," Ted said.

Again and again, Rascal and Mary successfully jumped the smaller jump. "Now try the bigger one."

Apprehensively, Mary approached the bigger jump. Her entire being prepared to taste the dirt beneath Rascal's feet. "Here goes nothing," she whispered to her mount.

As if they were flying, Rascal did everything he was supposed to do. Mary clung to his mane for added stability, but focused on pushing her heels down in the stirrups to keep herself straight. Two hooves landed, and then the last two landed. "We did it!" she shrieked in excitement. She reached down and patted Rascal's arching, powerful neck.

Ted held up his hand, indicating for her to stop. "Let the horse have a quick breather. How'd that feel?"

"Surprisingly exhilarating! I didn't think I could do it! I can't wait to do it again!"

"I knew you could do it. You just had to get it in your head that you could. But it's not enough to do it once. You have to do it over and over again. Soon, you'll get there. Walk him around a bit to cool him down some. Damn! It's hot in here!"

"Will do." The reins hung down slack as she encouraged Rascal back to the arena's railing. After four laps, Ted spoke again, "Ok. Let's get going. I want you to try the same jump again."

By early afternoon, Mary and Rascal were easily clearing most of the three-foot jumps in the arena.

Ted proudly stood in the middle with a keen eye on Mary's

performance. "Good! That's very good. Now circle back and take him over the barrel jump."

She did as he instructed, and just as Rascal's hooves landed on the ground, Mary's eyes spied Alan. *He hasn't left!* she thought. Immediately, she pulled Rascal to a stop, jumped off the horse, and ran to the edge of the arena.

"Are you ok?" she asked when she took one look at the pale man. His tired eyes lit up when they saw her.

"I'm fine. We need to talk," Alan gently said. He knew he needed to tell her about Angela, but one look at her trusting, loving face made the words dry up in his throat.

"What the hell do you think you're doing?!" Ted shouted from the arena. "Get your ass back on...," he stopped cold when he spied Alan. The hair on the back of his neck stood up. Images of him with Angela flashed before his mind's eye.

Alan scowled at him, but didn't say anything in her defense.

"Um, ok, but can it wait? Ted and I have really made good progress today," Mary said to Alan. "I am finally jumping!"

"I saw! I'm so proud of you," he said with a weak smile.

"I saw your limo. Where'd you go?"

"I had a few errands to run. But I've got to go again."

Her bright jade eyes pulled him into her, making him want to stay and be lost in her arms. Everything he'd ever need was there with her. Did he really need to go to rehab? He could easily tell Frankie he wasn't going, yet what he'd done with Angela pushed him where he should go. He couldn't bear even considering such a thing ever happening again.

Mary's eyes dropped.

"Please don't give me that look. I'm not strong enough to resist it. I came to say goodbye."

"Where are you going?"

"I-I'm going to rehab. I wanted to tell you before I left."

She looked up at him with an understanding smile.

"Gosh you make me want to stay so bad. Just your smile makes me want to."

"No, I understand. You've got to go."

"I'm checking myself in. This whole thing has got to stop," he said, skipping over the Angela part. "You deserve a whole, sober man."

Mary nodded with a happy, trusting look. "Good. I'm really glad to hear you're taking care of yourself."

"I'll have the divorce papers served on Angela while I'm gone. Before I left, though, I wanted to give you this," he said as he produced a black velvet box.

"Right here? Right now?" she apprehensively asked with a nervous but gleaming smile.

"I'm not so sure I could get back up once I got down on one knee, so you'll have to let me just slide it on your finger. I'll ask you the right way when I get back, ok?"

Mary eagerly produced her left hand.

Gingerly, thoughtfully, Alan reached between the arena railing and slid the 4-carat diamond ring on her finger. "Now, this isn't the final ring. I'm having the real one custom made for you, but I wanted you to have this before I left. When I get your real ring, I'll ask you the right way."

She admired the colorless, sparkling ring. "So much for keeping it quiet, huh?," she breathlessly asked.

"It's just a tiny pebble."

"No, it's perfect," she said with a contented smile.

"Nah. This one isn't much of anything. You just wait." He leaned against the arena's bars. "I love you so much," he whispered with an obviously exhausted face.

"I love you, too," she whispered back. "I'd kiss you, but Ted would crawl all over my ass if I did."

"I don't care what the bastard thinks!" For all Alan knew, the last kiss he'd had on his lips was from Angela. His heart ached at the thought.

Mary smiled. "Ok. Let me come out there and kiss you properly." Quickly, she flitted out the gate and over to Alan. His arms were immediately around her.

"I don't deserve you," he said as he stroked the edge of her face.

"You're wrong there, Mr. Brooks. It is I who doesn't deserve you."

His rough chapped lips gently found her sweet, soft lips. His heart swelled. Everything about her drew him deeper into her aura. With her was his peace. She held his heart right in her tiny hands. How could he have betrayed her? He hated himself. He hated alcohol.

"I'm going to miss you so much," he gravely said.

"It'll be all right," she replied with a happy smile.

"I hope so. I'm terrified I'm going to miss something." His crystal eyes burned with tears he couldn't cry. He had to tell her about Angela, yet her precious, trusting face kept the words behind his teeth.

"Like what?"

"One of your breaths, a sigh, or a single beat of your heart."

"You're being silly."

"No, I'm serious. I want you with me every second. I'm afraid one day you'll figure out I'm not so great and leave." His voice cracked as he spoke as if the words he should say were strangling anything else.

Mary smiled a comforting smile. "You're the one who has shown me how to live again. But most of all, love again," she whispered. "You've shown me true, unselfish love, and restored my faith in its existence. Why would I ever want to leave?"

Alan squeezed her hand tightly. "I don't know. I guess I'm just afraid I'll lose what we have."

"I'll be right here when you get back."

"Promise?"

"Promise."

"Good. I've got to go. They're already pissed at me for making them wait so long. When I come back, we're getting married, ok?"

"Ok," she said with trusting eyes. "You take care of yourself. I promise, I'm not going anywhere," she assured him again. The look in his eyes made her wonder what was going on in his head.

"They probably won't let me talk to anyone while I'm in there."

"Oh. Yeah. I didn't think of that."

"If they do, though, I'll call you every chance I get."

"I know you will. Focus on you, ok? We'll be together when you get home."

"I promise." He leaned down and kissed the ring on her finger. "I love you."

She gently smiled. "I love you, too."

Gleefully, she returned to Rascal and climbed back into the saddle.

Ted instantly noticed the sizeable stone on her finger. *Oh hell, Angela's going to be pissed*, he thought. Inside, he did a little victory dance – Alan was indeed going to divorce Angela. It meant Angela would unequivocally be his. He looked at Mary in a different light than he did before. She had single-handedly made it possible for Angela to finally be his.

He watched Alan leave; hatred toward him still burned. "Now where were we?" Ted asked Mary with ample amounts of frustration.

Alan moved down the corridors of the barn like he'd been beaten with a baseball bat. Briefly, he stopped at Johe's office. "Hey, Johe," his voice said lacking any sort of emotion.

"Hey. Damn! You look like hell! What's going on?" Johe asked with just one look at him.

Alan entered and sat in the old school-house chair. "I'm going to be gone for a while. I want you to take care of Mary for me, ok? Have Felix hire whoever he needs to, but I want to know she's safe and secure while I'm gone. Under no circumstance is Earl to step foot on this farm. Understand? I've already informed Felix too."

"Ok. What's going on?" she asked with a quizzical look. "I thought Earl was your attorney. Banning him from the farm is a little odd, don't you think?"

"I don't have time to explain it all; just do what I said, ok?"

"Ok. Sure thing. Is everything ok? Do I need to be alarmed?"

"No. I'm checking myself into rehab…"

"Oh thank God! It's about time! What made you change your mind?" Johe interrupted him.

"Mary."

"Good for her!"

"She's precious to me, Johe. I'd die if something happened to her."

Johe sighed. "I know she is."

"It will put my mind at ease knowing she has you to watch over her."

"Don't worry. I've got this. You take care of yourself; everything else will be just fine here," she assured him.

"I don't know how long they'll keep me, so I'm telling you as plainly as I can – I don't want Mary going to the show with Angela."

"I don't think you have much of a choice. Ted said he wants her going, and he pretty well gets what he wants around here," Johe said as her office chair creaked loudly when she nonchalantly leaned back in it.

"I don't want her going, period." Alan's face displayed the gravity of his words.

"You're not going to offer up at least some justification for your proclamation?" Johe asked.

"Because I said so, and that's enough."

"Well, Mary's in training; Ted wants her there so she can learn more training techniques. It's not your decision if she stays or goes," Johe said as she moved the mouse around on her computer, rousing it from its slumber.

Alan's cell phone rang – Marcus. He quickly clicked ignore. "I don't care what Ted wants. I don't want her going. This is my farm, and what I say goes," he said more forcefully.

Johe sat up and looked at him suspiciously. Her elbows rested on the paper-covered desk. "And you have no other argument to make other than this?"

"Don't give me your shit; you know why. Besides, Angela's a raging bitch. I don't want Mary exposed to her brand of bitchiness."

"She's tougher than you think; she can handle herself," she said of Mary.

In a swift, foxlike move, Alan was in Johe's face, domineering, forceful. "She's not going, and that's final!" he demanded with a snarl that lived in a place where anyone against Mary was the enemy.

"Ok, ok! She's not going!" Johe peered up at him in utter disbelief.

Alan stepped back from her and returned to his seat. His heart thumped hard as the adrenaline worked its way through his system.

"Who do you propose I send instead?"

"I don't care. Send Ginger or Aja."

"Aja is only part time."

"Well, then you go."

"So you'd rather have me cooped up with the wicked bitch of the east, huh?"

"You've got more experience handling Angela than Mary does. Just do it, ok? I don't want Angela filling her head with shit that doesn't matter anyway."

"What kind of shit?"

Alan rolled his eyes. "Why must you continually ask questions? Just do it. And make sure you keep her fuck toy away from Sun. The security guards know to keep a special watch, but I'm telling you to be watchful, too."

"I'll definitely keep Ted from Sun, but even Felix said it was unlikely anything would happen this close to Biscuit's death, especially if Ted is behind it. Have you talked to him?"

"Ted? Hell no!"

"Felix."

"Oh. Yeah. I talked to him earlier. He said they've uncovered some evidence that he feels certain points the finger right at Ted. They're waiting for fingerprint analysis to be certain, but that can take up to a couple of months."

"Yeah? I hadn't heard the latest. What did they find?"

"Of all things, the idiot didn't get rid of the syringe he used. Felix thought maybe he kept it to use it again, but I'm not so sure about that."

"Where did they find it?" Johe asked.

Alan shook his head and laughed before he answered, "In the kitchen drawer of his cabin."

"What? I don't know if Ted is *that* stupid, do you?"

"I don't know. His elevator certainly doesn't seem to go all the way to the top, if you know what I mean."

"Yeah, but still. You'd have to be flat-out stupid to leave evidence so easy to find."

"That's what Felix said, too. After the lab report came back positive for copper-laced ethylene glycol, just like what was found in Biscuit's bloodstream, Felix insisted we send it out for fingerprints. If Ted's fingerprints show up on it, then we'll know for sure."

"And Ted's already given you his fingerprints?"

"Not willingly," Alan said with a deceitful smile.

"You stole them, huh?"

"In a round-about sort of way. Felix said one of his guys observed Ted drinking out of a water bottle. When Ted threw it away, Felix's guy picked it up and bagged it for evidence."

"That's pretty slick. Did you also get my fingerprints that way? You know, you could've had them if you'd just ask me for them."

"Oh come on, Johe! I know it wasn't you."

"Ok. Just making sure. So what are you going to do?"

"I'm not sure yet. I wanted to fire him on the spot, but Felix encouraged me to not rock the boat just yet. And now with this rehab thing, I'm not sure what to do."

"What do you want me to do while you're gone?"

"Stay vigilant. If he makes even a slight move toward Sun or any of the other horses, fire him. You have my permission. If Felix says anything, you tell him you're operating under my direction."

"Will do."

"And there's one other thing you should know."

"What's that?"

"When I get back from rehab, Mary and I are getting married."

Johe noticeably gulped. "Oh really? What about Angela?"

"I've already signed the divorce papers."

"You actually signed them this time?"

"Yup. Without a thought."

"Wow."

"Yeah. Mary and I are engaged."

"You move fast, huh?"

"I love her, Johe."

"Have you thought of the implications of such a move?"

"I don't need you to lecture me."

"I know, I know. I'm just saying."

"I know what you're saying, and I'm telling you to butt out. I love her. Period."

"I wasn't going to say anything, but you've kind of pushed me into a corner."

Alan crossed his arms. "Go on."

"We don't really know who she really is. She claims to be my friend Tunda's daughter, but I know there's no way that's possible. She has green eyes. I know for a fact that Tunda and Bill both have dark brown eyes. Tunda's Native American! You can't get a green-eyed child from two parents with brown eyes, and one having dominate genes. It's simple genetics."

"Have you spoken to Tunda about this?"

"No."

"To Mary?"

"No."

"Good. Don't. You can rest assured; Mary's not hiding anything from me that I don't already know, ok? There are no secrets between us." A twinge panged inside his heart at the words. *No secrets? And look at you hiding what happened with Angela. You're going to have to tell Mary at some point*, he thought.

"Are you sure? You never know what you're getting yourself into."

"Johe." Alan leaned forward in the chair, resting his elbows on his knees. "I promise you, there are no secrets between us, ok? Stop worrying. I wanted you to hear this from me and not someone else. I don't need your judgments or suspicions. Ok?"

"Ok," Johe reluctantly said.

"Thank you." Alan picked up his phone and checked the time. "I've got to go."

"All right. Take care of yourself. Don't worry; I've got things here."

"I know you do. I trust you," Alan said with a smile. He gave Johe a friendly hug and then left.

Moments later, he climbed into the back seat of the waiting limousine. Longingly, he kept his eyes on the barn as the long car pulled away.

"You're doing the right thing," Dr. Sabia confirmed.

"I hope so. How long do you think I'll be there?" Alan asked.

"I'm not sure. I would think a month at least."

"A month? That's a long time, don't you think?"

"You've got to dry out. It might take longer than you think to get all the alcohol out of your system. Let's just play it by ear, for now."

"Ok. But get me out of there as quickly as possible. I swear, I won't touch another drop."

"We'll see."

CHAPTER 34

It was quitting time when Ginger noticed the ring on Mary's finger. "What the hell?!" she asked as she yanked Mary's left hand into hers. "Where'd you get that?!"

As elated as Mary was to receive the ring, she hadn't prepared an explanation for it. Should she lie or just tell the truth? Everyone would know as soon as Alan returned anyway, so why should she wait? Still, with Alan being gone, she chickened out. "It's from my fiancé."

"Fiancé? And who is he? He'd have to be pretty well off to afford a ring like this!" she said admiring the colorless stone.

"You'll find out."

"Has Johe seen it?" Before Mary could answer, Ginger called out for Johe. "Hey Johe! Have you seen the rock on Mary's finger?" Ginger wandered down the short hallway to the kitchenette where Johe was cleaning out the coffee pot.

"What?" Johe asked.

"I said 'have you seen the rock on Mary's finger?'"

"No. I can't say I have," Johe answered without looking up. *Dammit!* she thought. *Damn Alan! He never could keep things quiet.*

"It's a monster! I'd say three to four carats! I didn't even know she was seeing someone," Ginger stated.

"Well, apparently she was. You're not surprised are you?"

"Yeah, I sort of am," Ginger said, pretending not to know.

"Don't be. It all makes sense now, doesn't it? Every time we'd go out, she never went home with anyone. She didn't even dance

317

with anyone."

"Still. Who is he? Is it someone we know?"

"I suspect it's someone we both know very well," Johe casually said as she scrubbed the sink out.

"Cliff?" Ginger asked, even though she already knew it had to be Alan.

"Psh. Be real."

"Mr. Brooks."

"Bingo."

"Damn," Ginger profoundly said. "I mean, I suspected something was going on, but I didn't realize it was *that* serious. Does Angela know?"

"Probably not. Mary's still alive, isn't she?"

Ginger nodded. "Yeah, she is."

"I just hope he-uh-she knows what she's getting herself into." Johe placed the sponge on the edge of the sink.

"I know I wouldn't want to tangle with the likes of Angela."

Johe leaned against the kitchen counter. "Me either. But then again, she has Alan on her side."

"True."

"You know this is going to change everything, right?"

"I hadn't really thought of it, but now... yeah, things will be really weird."

"Exactly. We'll all be lucky to still have a job when Alan returns."

"Where's he gone this time?" Ginger asked as she sank into one of the dinette chairs.

"He's checking himself into rehab. I never thought I'd see the day, to be honest. But he claims it's all Mary's doing."

"She forced him to rehab?" Ginger asked.

"No, I don't think there was any force involved. From what I've been able to gather, he nearly died from alcohol poisoning. He probably is doing it to protect his precious Mary," she said with an undercurrent of asperity in her voice.

"Maybe. But I'm glad he's doing it anyway. He's a good man."

Johe sighed deeply. "True. The best of men." Silence filled the room as Johe contemplated how she'd once held Alan's affections and let them go. If only she'd known then what she knew now, perhaps things would've been different.

"Will Mary still work at the barn?" Ginger broke the awkward reticence.

"I seriously doubt it," Johe said. She turned, picked up the sponge and began wiping the counters down. "Do you really expect Alan's new wife to continue to do menial labor?"

"I guess not. But, what are we going to do? We're already down Cliff, and Rob – well, he's not exactly the best with the horses."

"I don't know. But if I were you, I'd start looking for another job, just in case."

"Another job?? Why?"

"Because when Angela's gone, I doubt there will be a need for all of these horses. Mary has her horse, and Alan has his. They're pretty much all they'll need."

"So they'll get rid of the rest of them?"

"Yup. That would be my best guess."

"Wow. I never would've guessed," Ginger blankly said. As much as she hated Angela, the thought never occurred to her what would happen without Angela. Ginger, Aja, and the rest would be out of a job.

"Yup. And with the horse show coming up, we're supposed to go with Angela instead of Mary."

"Is there even going to be a show?"

"I don't know. It's still two months away, and there's no telling how long Alan will be gone. I suspect any divorce will be a long, drawn-out event. No matter what Alan thinks, Angela's not likely to quietly agree to a divorce," Johe said.

"So, it's possible Angela will still be going to the show?"

"I don't know. All I know is I was told to keep Mary from going, period," Johe repeated Alan's words. "So now either you or I will go."

"Won't it be rather awkward?"

"I expect it will." *Damn it, Mary!* Johe thought. "Imagine how much more awkward it would be if Mary went with Angela."

"Ooooh. Yeah. That would be bad. I wonder what Angela will think when she finds out about them."

"I don't know. But I'm not so sure I want to be around when she does," Johe said as she returned the sponge to the edge of the sink.

Nighttime had fallen by the time Ted was done at the barn and could be with Angela again. He'd replayed over and over telling her about Mary and Alan kissing and the ring he'd put on her finger. Different scenarios ran through his mind, each of them ending with an irate Angela. Nevertheless, he planned to point out the good in it – it was a golden opportunity for them. *We can finally be together*, he thought. *Once I cash in at least one more time, everything will be perfect!*

Ted took the stairs of the north staircase two at a time. Anxiety to tell her the news pushed him quickly to Angela's bedroom. He sincerely hoped this news would make her give up on her crazy pregnancy scheme. Besides, if she were pregnant, in all likelihood the baby was his. He'd made it a point to get there first.

His knuckles rapped on the closed doors of Angela's bedroom.

"Come in!" a muffled, irritated Angela's voice sounded from behind the door.

"I don't understand why it is so hard to pick up my dry cleaning when I tell you!" she loudly complained from inside her expansive closet.

Lena, her assistant, stood with a pile of pink clothing in her arms.

"There's nothing in here for me to wear! I want the Versace pink dress!" Angela demanded.

"These are all pink; won't they work?" Lena asked.

"No!" Angela growled. "Are they Versace?"

Lena flipped through the clothing, looking at the different designer labels. "Here's a Versace," she said as she tried unsuccessfully to pull out a piece from the middle of the stack.

Angela snatched the hanger from Lena, causing the entire pile to fall out of her hands. Lena immediately began picking them up.

"Oh my God! You're useless! I want the pink and white twist front Versace. Not this piece of trash. It's from two years ago." Angela paused for a moment trying not to fire the girl. "Get out! Just get out!" she shouted with her finger pointing toward the door.

Lena scooped up the rejected clothing and scurried past Ted as he entered.

"And don't come back until you have the right dress!" Angela shrieked in frustration.

"Hello, Darling," Ted said as he brushed back her hair and kissed the back of her neck.

"What do you want?" she tersely asked as she turned to him.

"To bask in your presence? To awe at your unparalleled beauty?"

Angela sucked her gleaming white teeth. "I'm not in the mood."

"Well, you're not going to like what I have to say then, huh?"

"Ugh! Don't start your stupid childish games with me. Just say it!" she complained as she returned to the racks of color-coordinated clothes hanging along the closet's edges.

"Sweetheart, what I've got to tell you will probably make you angry, at first, but I think when you stop and think about it, you'll realize it's probably the best news ever."

She stopped, put her hands on her hips, and returned to him. "Ok. What is it?"

"I saw Alan and Mary again today. This time, he kissed her right in front of me."

"This isn't news, Ted," Angela said with her eyes squinted. "You already told me he has a thing for the tramp."

"Ah, yes, but this time, was different. Neither of them seemed to care I was standing there watching."

"Is he fucking her?" she asked with noticeable irritation.

Ted scoffed. "It's not like he threw her against the arena and started pounding her, but I'd be willing to bet there's more to it than meets the eye."

"What makes you say that?"

"He put a sizeable diamond on her left hand."

The ground beneath Angela's feet began to tremble as the words he'd spoken echoed inside her head.

"Apparently their relationship has taken a giant leap forward," Ted nervously continued. The cold stillness of Angela's reaction made him worry. All of his scenarios included an irate Angela. One who was screaming and throwing things. One he could handle. He hadn't expected this reaction. What should he do?

The 16-carat engagement ring Alan had given Angela sat motionless on her left hand.

"So, I'm betting you'll be getting divorce papers soon. And then we can finally be together. No more Alan, and no more need for you to be pregnant."

Angela didn't blink.

"I-I'm so relieved," he nervously continued. "Angela?" Ted gently asked.

There was no response.

"Angela. We'll be free from him. We can finally be together. No more plotting and scheming. It'll just be me and you forever," Ted said as he stroked her long blonde hair.

Feeling his touch yanked her back into reality. Her milky-white face turned blood-red. "Get your damned hands off of me!"

"What?! This is *good* news!"

"How do you get that?! This is the *worst* news possible!"

"Because, like I told you, we can finally be together."

"Ted. I've told you a thousand times – you can't afford me. Alan can. It's a simple fact." *I'll be Alan's pathetic ex-wife while his whore Mary steals my spotlight!* she thought but didn't say.

Her father's words bounced off the walls of her mind: "You won't amount to shit!"

The look of terror written all over Angela's face worried Ted. He wanted to protect her. The gun on his dresser called to him, begging him to rid her world of Alan Brooks. No matter what Angela said, it's exactly what *had* to happen! "You'll have to trust me when I tell you; I have a plan, and all of this will just disappear."

"Uh-huh. How? Are you going to kill his *whore*?!"

"You leave the details to me. Do you trust me?"

"Don't do this shit, Ted!"

"Listen to me. I can handle this, but you've got to trust me. Do you?"

"Yeah," she whispered.

"Do you trust me?" he firmly asked again.

She didn't respond.

"Angela. Do you trust me?" Ted asked more forcefully.

"Yes," she said loudly, and then followed with a quiet, "I guess."

"Good. Then just relax. I've got this under control."

"But what if he divorces me before you can put your plan in place?" her voice carried twinges of panic.

"Shhh. Don't you worry yourself. I've got this."

"You're not going to kill him are you?"

"I will if you want me to."

"If he's fucking her, have at it!" she angrily proclaimed.

"Since he's engaged to her, we can probably safely assume he is." His heart pounded in his chest. Finally, he had Angela's permission. Every day he'd been tortured by the gun's cries, begging him to shoot

Alan, and every night he could only stand before it and stare. But now things were different. He had Angela's permission.

Angela balled her fists up in rage. She thought of her plan to trap Alan in their marriage with a baby. It was without a doubt the perfect plan. No one else's plan was as fool-proof as hers. Even if Alan was engaged to Mary, he'd drop her like a rock when he found out about their baby. He'd never abandon a Brooks child. "Well, one thing's for sure."

"What's that sweetheart?"

"He's not fucking her right now. He's in California in rehab for the next month or so. So it'll buys us some time."

Ted sighed deeply. "You're not still going through with the same pregnancy plan, are you?"

"Yes, of course. Why wouldn't I?" she asked, aghast. Was he still doubting her plan?

"Because he's made a promise to marry Mary!"

"Promises are made to be broken. When he finds out I'm carrying his child, he'll forget all about his little trollop. Besides, I can't wait to see his little Mary squirm! Won't she be devastated when she finds out the truth about her precious Alan?"

Truth? Ted questioned. "No! No! This isn't the way to go!" Ted demanded. His hazel eyes burned into her. Hadn't she just given him permission to kill Alan?

"Cool it, Ted!" she commanded as she pushed past him to another clothes rack. "It's the way it has to be. If he's fucked her, it will all stop once I announce the baby. He'll instantly be focused back on me, and Mary will be a thing of the past. And then I'll make him pay!"

"I'd rather put a bullet in his head!"

"Stop!" she harshly demanded. "I don't want to hear your shit again!"

"I only act this way because I don't want anyone else to have you," Ted determinedly said. "I'd rather see the fucker dead than have to spend another night knowing he's touching you..."

"Stop it! Stop it right now, Ted!" Angela insisted and snapped her face back toward him. "You're not killing him, and that's final." She shook her finger in his face.

"But just a minute ago you said if he was fucking her I could."

"I was just saying. I still stand behind my promise, though. If my pregnancy plan doesn't work, we'll put your plan in place." She was confident her plan would work exactly as intended, so there would be no need for Ted to kill Alan. *On the other hand, killing Mary...*, she thought, but then recanted. *No. You can't forget, if Mary's killed, Alan will never get over her. The baby is the right move. Distract him. Give him what he's always wanted. He won't even remember her name when I'm through.*

Ted grimaced. The entire conversation hadn't gone as he'd thought. He could hear the gun's siren song. Perhaps it was time to stop listening to Angela and start putting *his* plans in motion.

CHAPTER 35

Alan hadn't been gone an entire week before Mary was startled awake by pounding on her cabin door.

"W-who is it?" she asked through the closed door. Her knees trembled. *Surely, if it's Roger, he wouldn't knock*, she thought. The quilt with the circular pattern wrapped around her shoulders to cover her night clothes.

"It's Johe. Get up! It's Sun!"

Immediately, Mary unlocked the door. "What's wrong?!"

"He's sick. Get dressed! I've called Dr. Willie. He's on his way," Johe barked out orders as Mary hurried back to her bedroom to change her clothes.

"What is it?" she asked while shoving her feet into her boots.

"The security guard said he's groaning and shooting diarrhea everywhere."

"Oh my God!" Mary barely had her shirt buttoned before she charged out the front door of her cabin. As if she were running to a fire, her feet carried her to Sun's stall.

"Eeeeeasy boy," she said at first sight of him. His stall walls were coated with loose green feces. The stench made Mary's lip curl and her stomach turn.

"I'm sorry to wake y'all," the security guard said, "but I was mighty worried about him. He just ain't right."

"No, no, you did the right thing!" Mary slid the stall door open. "Hiya, fella. What's going on?"

Sun looked skittish.

She clipped a lead line to his halter and tried to lead him out.

Sun earnestly kicked at his belly, but refused to move.

"Looks like he's colicky," Johe said.

"Colic? How? From what? He's been eating the exact same meal twice a day since he was young."

"I don't know. Horses colic for any number of reasons. Dr. Willie will be here soon. He'll know what's going on. Until then, all you can do is keep him moving."

"Absolutely." Mary pulled on his lead line again, but Sun threw his head up showing his determination not to cooperate with her idea. "Come on, boy, you know you need to get moving." She pulled on the lead line again.

Sun stood still.

Mary moved to just next to his halter, grabbed hold of it, and pulled with all of her strength. Sun took one step forward and then followed her out of the stall. With every other step, he kicked at his belly.

After many laps around the barn, Johe announced, "I think I hear Dr. Williams. I'll go get him."

"Ok," Mary replied as she and the sick horse moved slowly down the familiar corridors.

"Thank you for coming out so quickly, Dr. Williams," Johe said.

"No problem. Which horse has the problem?" Dr. Willie asked.

"It's Mary's horse, Sun. I'll walk you down there to him. The poor thing had diarrhea all over his stall and is now kicking at his belly."

"Sounds like colic, save for the diarrhea," Dr. Willie stated.

"I thought colic, too, but the diarrhea part is what threw me. What do you suppose is causing it?"

"I'm not sure. We'll check him over. One thing's for sure, diarrhea can be very serious in horses. How long has it been going on?"

"I'm not sure. The security guard noticed Sun wasn't well and alerted me to it an hour ago."

"Has he had any symptoms like this in the past?"

"I don't know. You'll have to ask Mary."

Dr. Willie approached Mary and Sun.

"I'm so glad you're here, Dr. Williams!"

"How long has he had the diarrhea?" was the first thing Dr.

Willie asked her.

"His stool has been a little loose for about a week or so, but not definitively diarrhea," Mary explained.

"What have you been feeding him?"

"Just his regular food. A mixture I mix myself: sweet feed, oats, and corn. And then he gets two flakes of hay twice a day."

"Good. Sounds good." Dr. Willie put his stethoscope in his ears and held it against Sun's belly listening for Sun's belly sounds.

"He was fine when I left him," Mary informed him.

Sun kicked at his belly.

"Eeeeasy boy. Dr. Williams is going to make you feel all better."

"I can't say for sure yet, but I'm thinking he's got colic. His gut sounds are definitely off."

"That's what Johe said, but how? He eats a very carefully prepared, special diet. And I've never heard of a horse having diarrhea with colic."

"Was there mold in the hay?" Dr. Williams asked.

"It's been too dry for mold," Johe responded.

"Has he been out in the pasture any?" Dr. Williams inquired.

"Yes, he has been in the pasture more than normal lately," Mary replied.

"Well, I'm thinking he's got the sand colic. It's not really common in these parts, but lately I've been seeing more of it because of the drought."

"Sand colic?" Mary asked with surprise.

"Yup. There's one way to know for sure." Dr. Willie went to his truck and returned with an arm-length glove rolled up to his shoulder. "Now hold him steady," he instructed her as he held Sun's filthy tail with one hand and put the pre-lubed gloved hand up the horse's anus.

Sun became antsy with the pressure against his sore bum.

"Easy, boy, easy," Mary talked soothingly to him while holding onto his halter as best she could. One wrong move could dislocate Dr. Williams' shoulder. "It's ok. Just a few seconds longer. Easy now." Her voice was always as calming as she could make it.

Dr. Willie pulled his arm out of Sun's rectum with a hand full of fecal matter. With his other hand, he pulled the glove off, inside out with the fecal matter remaining inside. "Get me a bottle of water, Johe."

"What's this test going to show?" Mary inquired.

"If he's got the sand colic, when I mix his manure with water, the sand will sink to the bottom while the rest of the manure floats to the surface."

"Huh. Interesting."

"Yeah, it's the only way I know to diagnose it. I only have to use it when there's a drought."

Johe returned with a bottle of water.

Dr. Willie poured the bottle's contents into the glove, sealed it off, and shook it. The water instantly turned green, and down in the fingers and well into the glove itself was the tell-tale amount of sand residing in his intestines. "You see this here?" he asked as he showed Mary. "That's sand and dirt. It's the worst I've seen so far. You can't feed him on the ground."

"I don't! He always eats from a feed bucket. How are you going to treat him?" Mary anxiously asked.

"We'll get a tube down his nose and pump some water and psyllium in him. But you're going to have to keep him moving and hydrated. Don't let him lay down even for a second. We don't want his intestines to get twisted. If it does, we'll have to put him down."

Mary audibly sobbed. "No, no! I'll keep him moving."

"We can take shifts," Johe added.

"Let me get my supplies," Dr. Willie said as he left. "Don't let him eat even a nibble of hay until tomorrow. He'll pass all this mess out of him, and then you can feed him his regular meal mixed with more psyllium. Do this at his morning meal for the next week. It should set him to rights."

After Sun's treatment, Mary thanked Dr. Willie, and began walking Sun.

By the time the sky was painted pink with the sunrise, Sun finally passed a normal bowel movement. Mary was exhausted, but nothing mattered more than her horse.

"How's he doing?" Johe asked.

"Better, I think. Thank you so much, Johe."

"Don't mention it. You want me to have Ginger or Aja clean up his stall?"

"No, I'll do it. I'm just relieved – Sun's ok."

"Me too! He sure gave us a scare," Johe said as she patted Sun's flaxen mane.

"I'm going to get him cleaned up before I work on his stall."

"Ok, but don't forget what Ted said yesterday."

"Oh yeah. Angela and I will be training together today," Mary said with an air of dread. Angela. In the time since Alan left, Mary hadn't had to face her, but today it was unavoidable. She looked down at the ring Alan had placed on her finger. How could she hide it?

"The show is getting closer every day, and from the last time I saw her practice, she still isn't ready."

"I know."

"Then you better hurry and get ready. Ted mentioned he wants to start at 9:00," Johe informed her.

"Ok. I'll have everything cleaned up and ready by then."

"You want some coffee?"

"No, thanks."

"How about a granola bar or something?"

"No, I'm good. Thanks. Sun is my main concern."

"Suit yourself," Johe said and walked back toward her office.

"How're you feeling, fella?" Mary asked him as she put him in the bathing stall. There was no time to clean him up until his bowels were noticeably better. "You ready for some breakfast?"

Sun rubbed his head against her.

"Yeah, me too, but it looks like you'll be the only one eating today. Let's get you cleaned up first."

Once his nasty white tail had been scrubbed clean, Mary returned him to his stall. One look at the mess remaining made her wish she'd taken Johe up on her offer for Ginger's or Aja's help. Globs of diarrhea were dried on the walls and in putrid piles on the floor.

"You know how to keep me on my toes, huh?" Mary said to Sun. The entire stall had to be stripped and pressure washed. Her stomach grumbled. "Neither one of us is getting breakfast until this mess is cleaned up. Maybe you'll think twice before you pull up the grass from the roots and eat it."

Sun looked at her with his ears perked up, his face looked as innocent as possible.

Mary laughed and caressed his precious face. "Yes, you did all the mess in there. And trust me, it's some foul, nasty stuff!"

It took over an hour to completely strip and clean Sun's stall. By the time the last load of wood shavings was poured inside, Mary wanted to lie down in them and sleep. "No rest for the weary, I guess." She turned to Sun. "Now don't you even consider laying down in here. I know you're tired, too, but you can sleep standing up." She tied his lead line short so he couldn't lay down, just in case. She still wasn't certain he was in the clear. If he were to lie down, his intestines could twist.

"You'll be all right," she said with a yawn. "I'll go get you some breakfast."

The hungry horse seemed to smile at her.

"I love you, you crazy boy," she said as she patted his head between the stall bars. Her feet felt like she was dragging cinderblocks attached to her ankles. The angst she had for Sun's health had carried her forward all night. but was now gone. Each footfall advancing toward the feed room was placed out of pure determination mixed with healthy amounts of exhaustion.

Inside the room was Ginger preparing breakfast for the horses she was assigned to. "Johe told me about Sun. You've got to be exhausted," she said to Mary.

"I'm ok. He needs to eat, and I'll be training with Angela today," Mary responded with a groan while she scooped up his specific grains.

"I'll take care of him; you go on home and try and catch a nap." Ginger placed her hand on the bucket. "His stall is right beside Wildfire's. It's no trouble at all to pour this in his food bowl."

Mary yawned. "I've got it. I don't want to upset him. He's been through enough."

"You've been up all night! You've got to sleep."

"I will. But not until he's taken care of."

Ginger shook her head. "And then you're going to bed, right? There's no point hanging around here. Even if Ted wants to train, you'll never stay in the saddle being so tired."

"I'm going home to take a shower, have a cup of coffee, and then I'll be back."

"Damn, you're stubborn."

Mary mixed the two grains and psyllium with the correct amount of sweet feed, which is a combination of protein-rich grains, pellets, and molasses. Her eyes hung heavily.

Sun whinnied shrilly when he spied Mary coming with his

breakfast.

"Aww, you're hungry, huh?" she gently told him as she slid the door open.

Sun dug his muzzle into the bucket before Mary could pour it into his feed bin.

"Good heavens! Let me at least pour it in the bin first!" she said as she pushed him away. "At least you've got a good appetite." Her hands stroked his well-groomed mane.

He dug into the food like he hadn't eaten in days.

"Don't gobble it down; you don't want to make yourself sick again."

Sun reached back with his head as if to thank her for the food while he chewed.

"You're a good boy. Slow down and at least chew it up. I put some extra good stuff in there to help you. Dr. Willie said you'll be all right in no time." Mary hugged him. "I've got to get my day going. Stay out of trouble, ok?"

"Trouble," she repeated and looked down at the diamond ring. Her heart wouldn't let her take it off, yet it was possibly the source of impending trouble with Angela. "Gloves," she said to Sun. "I'll just wear riding gloves." Alan had placed it on her finger, and wearing it meant she kept a part of him with her at all times. Take it off wasn't an option.

CHAPTER 36

For four solid weeks, Mary threw herself into her work, and taking care of Sun. After his first bout with sand colic, he'd had 3 additional ones. Dr. Willie's concern grew with each incident. Sun's weight had dropped significantly, which left Mary a nervous wreck about his health. She purposely made herself numb and became a stone to anyone who wasn't associated with getting her job done and Sun. Her nights were spent either walking Sun while he was sick, sitting in his stall with him, or sequestered in her cabin, ignoring all outside interruption. Even when the girls invited her to go out and celebrate her engagement, she begged out of it. Her immediate concern was Sun.

The Monday beginning the sixth week since Alan had left, Mary sat at her dinette table with a buttered waffle covered in syrup and an empty coffee mug. The coffee pot spit water as it completed the brewing process.

She nibbled on one bite of waffle, but had to force herself to swallow it. She felt sick. As sick as she did after drinking too much. Without any warning, she vomited in her mouth, barely making it to the kitchen sink to spit it out. "What the...?" she questioned just before she vomited again.

The smell of the freshly-brewed coffee seemed to be the most offensive thing imaginable. With the entire coffee maker in her hands, she scrunched up her nose and scurried outside the back door to place the appliance outside on the back stoop.

"Blech!" She stuck her tongue out in disgust with herself. With weedy legs, she went to the bathroom to brush the nasty taste out of her mouth. But before she could put any toothpaste on her toothbrush, she shot to the toilet and vomited again.

You didn't eat enough last night, she thought back to how little she had eaten. Missing Alan and Sun occupied most of her time, with food being the least desirable option. "Alan," she sighed, "even when he's not here, he's distracting me."

She remembered the weeks after her rape and in high school when she struggled to eat. Vomiting became a dreaded, albeit, regular habit; there was a slight twinge of worry – was she heading down the same path again? "You have to make an effort to eat something at each meal time," she told herself as she washed her mouth out with water. Again, brushing the vomit taste out of her mouth became her priority.

After brushing her teeth, she returned to the kitchen, scraped her waffle into the trash, and grabbed a piece of wheat bread. She forced herself to take small bites while walking into the living room. "You've got to eat, even if you don't want to," she reminded herself.

With only the upper left-hand corner of the bread missing, she sat down to her computer to read her email.

> *Dear Mary,*
>
> *How are things? I know you're busy, but I miss hearing from you. I assume everything is fine; I thought I would write and ask. The weather is heating up here as spring is coming to an end. The saguaro cacti are finishing up their blooming cycle, and the white-winged doves are back in abundance. The desert is so beautiful this time of year. I hate you missed seeing the saguaro blooms; they always take my breath away! I attached some pictures for you. I hope you enjoy them!*
>
> *How are things with you and Alan? It does my heart so much good to hear you've found him. I hope to meet him one day.*
>
> *I should close this message now. Scruffy is anxious to go on his morning walk. Take care, dear, and write soon.*
>
> *Love,*
> *Mother*

Before she could hit reply or look at the pictures, she felt sick again. "Dammit!" she exclaimed as shot down the short hallway to the bathroom. The vomit barely made it into the toilet. This time, it was mixed with little bread balls.

Leaving the bathroom, she went in the kitchen to find something to settle her stomach. Her hands shook as she poured herself a small glass of ginger ale and sipped from it. "I must have eaten something really bad."

The coolness of the glass felt good on her forehead, so she took out a kitchen washcloth and wet it under the cold water. After wringing it out, she placed it on her forehead and then neck. "I'm so sick of this puking business! I've got to stop and get to work."

She moved from the kitchen to the couch and lounged on it. The computer screen still showed the email from Tunda.

Slowly, the ginger ale disappeared down her throat until the entire glass was empty. For a few moments, she laid on the couch wondering if it would stay down. After fifteen minutes had passed, she felt better and was sure it wasn't coming back up. "Whew!" she audibly said as her feet slid into her boots.

Upon entering Johe's office, the aroma of freshly-brewed coffee smacked her in the face.

Ugh, Mary thought.

The first words Johe said to her were, "You look like you've seen a ghost!"

"No. I've just got an upset stomach today. It's probably something I ate. Everything smells a hundred times worse!"

"Then if I were you, I wouldn't go down to Sun's stall. He's got the runs again, this time far worse than before."

"What?! Again? Why didn't you come get me?"

"I know you're exhausted. I already called Dr. Willie; he's on his way. Ginger and Aja are down there about to clean up his mess."

"No, no, they don't need to be doing it. I'll take care of him." Mary immediately left Johe's office for Sun's stall.

Inside stood her thin horse with his flaxen tail coated in loose stool – again. Dark green, nasty diarrhea hung on the walls on the stall and coated the shavings.

"I've got this. Thank you so much for helping," she told Ginger and Aja who had brought the wheelbarrow and pitchfork to his stall.

"I don't understand what's going on with him," Ginger said. "Did you feed him anything differently?"

"No. Just his normal dinner last night," Mary informed them. She took one step into the stall and immediately vomited up the ginger ale she'd drank before she left her cabin.

"Oh my God! Are you all right?!" Aja asked as she placed her gentle hand on Mary's back.

Mary wiped her mouth on her sleeve. "Yeah, I'm fine. I guess I didn't realize how bad it would smell," she said as casually as she could.

"Get out of here, girl, before you faint!" Ginger commanded her. "You look like you're going to pass out at any moment."

"Yeah, come on, I'll help you back to Johe's office. You can lay down on her couch for a little while. We'll take care of Sun for you," Aja sweetly offered.

"I think I ate some bad soup last night," Mary volunteered. "I can't seem to keep anything down."

"The last place you need to be is here," Aja said as she walked with Mary down the aisle back to Johe's office. "You get some rest, and when you feel better, go home."

"I'll be fine. Dr. Willie is coming to take care of Sun. I need to be here when he gets here."

"Psh! We'll handle it."

"Sun doesn't like anyone else but me."

"But he knows us. He'll be ok," Aja said with a generous smile.

Before they made it to Johe's office, Mary heaved like she was going to vomit again. To her relief, nothing came up.

"Johe's going to make you go home. She's an extreme germaphobe when it comes to the pukes."

"I promise. I'm fine."

The two women entered Johe's office; Mary slowly and tentatively laid down on the black leather sofa. The coffee's aroma hung heavily in the air. Johe sat at her desk nursing a cup.

"You need to send Mary home. She's sick," Aja volunteered.

Mary scornfully looked up at her. "I'm not sick. It's just something I ate."

"Yeah, you said that earlier," Johe said with a skeptical eye. "Go get her a cool rag out of the kitchen," she instructed Aja. "If you throw up one more time, I'm sending your barfing ass home," Johe informed Mary.

"Yes, ma'am. I'm really feeling much better. I wasn't expecting Sun's stall to be such a mess. That's all."

Aja returned with the cool rag. "My mama always put it on my throat when I was sick," she said as she handed Mary the wet washcloth.

Eagerly, Mary placed it on her throat. She breathed deeply while focusing on keeping her stomach from shooting out of her mouth.

"I'm going to help Ginger with the stall. You rest," Aja told Mary with her sweetest voice.

"Leave it. I'll get it," Mary insisted.

Johe nodded, indicating it was ok to leave it as she pulled the old school-house chair up next to Mary. "What'd you eat last night?" Her coffee mug resided in her hand.

"Just some soup and crackers."

"Where'd you get it from?"

"Out of a can. Why?"

"Was the can dented?"

"No. It was just a normal can. Why? Is there any way you could put your coffee over there? It smells just awful!" Mary said while putting her arm across her mouth and nose.

"Of course." Johe moved across the office and placed the steaming mug on a pile of papers. "I'm just wondering what you could've eaten that gave you food poisoning. What did you have for lunch?"

"Umm, I had some of the sub sandwich Felix brought in for the guys."

Johe nodded as she returned to the chair next to Mary. "I had some of it, too. No one else has gotten sick from it. Are you allergic to anything?"

"No, not that I'm aware of."

"What did you eat for breakfast?"

"Everything I ate, I threw back up, so that's not it. I'm feeling much better now." She determinedly sat up.

"You don't look better. You're as white a sheet! Lay your ass back down."

"No, no. I'm much better."

A vehicle pulled up outside the barn. "It sounds like Dr. Willie's here. You stay put!"

"I need to help him with Sun," Mary said as she stood up. Her legs felt as if she were standing on waving blades of grass.

"Look, Alan instructed me to look out for you. How can I do my job if you're so rebellious? Don't make me fire your ass and ground you to your cabin," Johe sternly said.

"You'll fire me?" Mary incredulously asked.

"You bet your sweet ass! Now behave yourself. If you step one foot out of this office, it's curtains for you."

Mary lightly chuckled. "You can't fire me. He's my horse; taking care of him isn't even part of my job duties here," she unwaveringly stated.

"You're the hardest headed woman I've ever met in my life," Johe muttered as the two of them left the office to greet Dr. Willie.

"Thank you for coming out so quickly, Dr. Williams," Johe said.

"No problem. Is it Sun again?" Dr. Willie asked.

"Yes, sir. I don't know what's going on with him. He's never had problems like this before," Mary stated.

"You're aware how very serious this is, right? If he keeps it up, we're going to have to put him down."

"NO! No! Don't even say it's an option!" Mary passionately begged. "He was fine last night when I left him," she informed him. She stopped briefly, closed her eyes, and breathed deeply. Vomit seemed to be hanging onto her tonsils, and she didn't want to let it out again.

"Ginger takes care of the horse next to him, and she was surprised to find him sick again," Johe added while keeping a skeptical eye on Mary.

Sun looked noticeably rattled when Mary led him out of the stall. "Eeeasy boy," she calmly said. "Dr. Williams is going to make you feel all better."

Dr. Willie took his stethoscope and listened to Sun's belly sounds. "It's definitely the colic again."

"Has he been out in the pasture any?"

"No, I've kept him in his stall."

"Well, something's going on! He's getting it from somewhere. Do you feed him from his food bowl? Does he drop his food when he eats it?"

Her stomach rumbled and reminded her how precarious each one of her moves were – one wrong move could cause her to shoot vomit everywhere.

Before she could respond, Dr. Willie continued, "You can't feed him on the ground."

"I don't! You tell me this every time, and I tell you every time he always eats from a feed bucket. I haven't noticed him dropping any grain when he eats. Just make all this stop!" Mary fearfully demanded.

"All we can do is treat his symptoms with psyllium. The rest is up to him. You'll have to keep him moving again."

Mary audibly sobbed a sound of exhaustion. "I'll keep him moving."

"We can take shifts," Johe added.

"Let me get my supplies," Dr. Willie said as he left.

After Dr. Williams treated Sun with psyllium again, it was Mary's job to walk him. As weak as she felt from vomiting, she pulled all the strength she had together to care for Sun. All day and night she walked him non-stop. When others offered to take a shift so she could rest, she declined. Sun was her responsibility – her only concern. She and Sun walked around the barn until the orange light replaced the night's darkness.

When his manure fell like normal, she breathed a sigh of relief.

"You know you've got to stop this, don't you?" Mary asked him as she led him in the bathing stall.

Cleaning the nasty stall was another matter altogether. "I guess I'll sleep when I'm dead," she said with a weak laugh before she began the arduous task of cleaning such a filthy stall.

Her entire body trembled as she emptied the last load of clean shavings into Sun's stall. It took insurmountable effort not to collapse in them.

"Time for some breakfast," she said with a yawn. She dragged her heavy feet down the aisle to the feed room. It felt as if she could actually feel the world spinning.

Just as she entered the feed room, Ginger was leaving, pushing her cart loaded with horses' breakfast. "Go home! Go home right now!" she commanded. "If you don't leave now, I'm going to go get Johe, and she'll make you go home!"

Mary leaned against the doorframe and with a quick burst sobbed. "I can't!"

"Yes, you can. Go. Right now. I mean it! I'll feed Sun."

"H-he needs me."

"Yeah, but what good are you to him like this? I'll make you a deal. You mix up his food, and I'll give it to him. But then you go home and go straight to bed, ok?"

"I don't know what's wrong with me," she said with a defeated sob.

"You've been up for over 24 hours. You're exhausted. That's all. Come on," Ginger said sweetly as she put her arm around Mary and led her to Sun's feed containers. "I'll help you mix up his feed; you just tell me how much of each."

Mary relented. "He gets a scoop and a half of oats, a scoop of corn, and two scoops of sweet feed."

Ginger reached into the feed barrel and scooped out the correct amounts of each.

"Now mix it using the bucket over there," Mary instructed her.

"Ok." Ginger started to do as she was told, but stopped. "Hmm."

"What?"

Ginger looked carefully at the molasses covered sweet feed. It looked odd compared to the other horses' sweet feed. She looked over at Mary, who was leaning against the chalkboard with horses' feeding instructions. "It's nothing," she said with a comforting smile. "I'll get this taken care of. You go on to bed now, ok?"

Weakly, Mary nodded. Mustering up the scant amount of energy she had left, Mary left the feed room and walked straight to her cabin.

When Ginger felt assured she was gone, she took a scoop of Sun's sweet feed, poured it into an empty bucket, and then took a scoop of the other horses' sweet feed and poured it into different bucket. "Johe," she said as she entered the office with the buckets in hand. "I think there's something wrong with Sun's feed."

"What do you mean?"

"Look at it compared to the other," she commanded.

Johe looked at the two feeds. "They look the same to me."

"Look closer. There's something mixed in with the molasses. Does she give Sun supplements?"

"No, not that I'm aware of. It's probably the psyllium Dr. Willie has him on."

"I don't know. I've seen that stuff, and it doesn't look like this."

Johe reached into the bucket and pulled out a handful. Rubbing her fingers across the grain mixture, she said, "It's gritty." She put a piece of corn in her mouth and swished it around. "My God, it's got sand in it!"

"Sand? That sure explains a lot!"

"Yeah, but how did it get there?" Johe asked. Just as soon as the question left her lips, her mind answered it: *Ted.*

Her first thought was to do nothing. Mary had stolen Alan and completely disrupted the order she'd worked so hard to put into place. But then there was Ginger. Ginger knew, and would reveal any wrong doing on Johe's part.

"Don't feed it to him. Use some of our sweet feed. Let me figure out what to do next, ok? Until then, seal the barrel up, and don't use it."

"Will do."

"Thanks for bringing this to my attention."

Ginger smiled in agreement and returned to her chores.

Johe's office chair creaked as she sat back in it. Her mind alternated between two extremes as she tried to determine what to do. The right thing to do was to call Felix, but on the other hand.... "Damn, Alan and his stupid promises!" She picked up the phone and dialed it. "Felix, we've got another problem."

CHAPTER 37

Mary didn't awaken until the next morning. When the sun was shining through her bedroom window, she stretched and yawned under the wedding-rings quilt. It was the first time she'd deeply slept in what felt like weeks, yet she still felt an unmistakable malaise. After gently swinging her legs over to the edge of the bed, her stomach began gurgling.

You're just hungry, she thought and stood up to go to the kitchen and eat. She felt weak; her knees were shaky. Like the stumbling of a newborn foal, she crept forward, but held her hand against the wall as she took baby steps away from the bed. Before she could make it outside the bedroom door, vomit filled her mouth. On spindly legs, she ran to the bathroom just in time for the contents of her mouth to overflow and violently hit the back of the toilet.

In short order, she was covered in a cold sweat and felt genuinely terrible. Pulling a bright blue towel from the towel rack above her head, she dabbed her forehead. Her entire body quaked as she spread the towel on the cool tile floor and lay down with a roll of toilet paper as a pillow. *What's going on? Why am I so sickly and tired?* she wondered. Her right leg bounced hard against the toilet bowl.

The next thing she remembered was hearing Aja's gentle voice on the other side of the door. "Mary?" She lightly tapped on the door. "Are you ok?"

There was only silence from the other side of the door.

"Mary? You in there?" Aja's voice sounded again. "Are you ok?" Aja left the bathroom door and looked in the bedroom.

"Mary?" she called louder. "What's going on?" Her tone displayed her clear concern.

Again, there was silence. For a moment, Aja thought she could make out splashing water and heavy breathing.

When she heard the toilet flush, she returned to the bathroom door and insisted, "Let me in." Eagerly, she jiggled the handle indicating her attempt to open the door.

"I'm fine. What do you want?" Mary's weak voice quivered.

"Are you ok? Johe sent me out here to check on you."

"I'm fine. Just..." Before she could finish her sentence she heaved loudly this time, only yellow bile came up.

"Are you still sick?" Aja asked from behind the closed door.

Mary limply laid her head on the toilet seat. "No, I'm fine."

"If you say you're fine one more time, I'm going to call Johe down here to check on you, too. Now, what's going on?"

Mary heaved and spit again. "Please, Aja, just go away," she weakly begged. "I'm fine. I-I-I must have the stomach flu or something. I'm ok."

"Are you sure?"

"Yes. I don't want you to catch it." Mary unrolled some toilet paper and wiped her mouth. She clung to the counter and pulled herself up on frail legs. Looking in the mirror, she saw her ghastly reflection. Her face was pasty white, her eyes were red and swollen, and her lips puffed out in front of her. Her entire body ached.

She turned the cool water on to wash her face, but before she could even put the washcloth under the running water, she was back at the toilet bowl loudly heaving.

"You're not ok. I can hear you throwing up. I'm coming in!" Aja announced as she turned the doorknob and gingerly entered the room.

"No," Mary managed to reply before she vomited nothing again. Simply blinking her eyes felt like her eyelids were coated in sandpaper.

"I'm here," Aja announced.

"No, please. I'm fine."

Without another word, Aja timidly entered farther into the white tiled bathroom where a weak Mary forcibly heaved nothing but noise. "You're not ok. What's going on?" she looked around the room, spying the towel on the floor. "How long have you been in here?"

Mary didn't look up. "Just go away!" Her words echoed inside the toilet bowl.

Aja sat on the bathtub near her. "What can I do for you?" She gently stroked her back.

"Nothing. Just leave me alone." Mary's head lay wearily on the toilet seat.

"Can I get you a cool rag?"

"Ok." Mary heaved again. "I'm willing to try anything," she spoke into the towel she used to wipe her face.

Aja took a washcloth from the cabinet and drenched it with cold water. "Here," she placed the rag against her throat. "Just relax, ok?" Feebly, Mary leaned against her.

"I don't know what's wrong with me." A tear formed in her eye, but refused to go any further.

"I don't either. Do you want to go to the hospital?"

"No." Mary worried someone there might recognize her as the missing Mary Franklin.

"How about I call a doctor?"

"No. What will a doctor do? Tell me it's a virus and wait it out."

She nodded. "You're probably right. But you need to drink something."

"I don't feel like drinking anything. It'll just come back up anyway."

"When's the last time you ate or drank?"

"I don't know." Her heart pounded inside her ears; her head felt like she was wearing a hat two sizes too small.

"After all your work yesterday, your body is probably dehydrated. Your lips are chapped. I'm going to go get you some water. If you throw it back up, at least you'll have something to throw up."

With her eyes more than halfway closed, Mary nodded and took over holding the washcloth on her neck.

Aja left her for the kitchen. In a flash, she was beside her again with a glass of water. "Take a small sip." She instructed as she offered her the water. "I'm going to go get Johe."

"No. Don't leave me." Her tongue stuck to the roof of her mouth making the words difficult to say. Limply, Mary's head rested on Aja's knees.

Aja stroked her head gently. "You didn't eat or drink anything at all yesterday?"

"I-I don't…remember. I don't think so."

Aja pulled out her cell phone and texted Johe: *Mary's really sick. I think she needs a doctor.*

Before Mary could finish half of the glass of water, she was back at the toilet vomiting the fluid back up. Listlessly, she returned to clinging to Aja's knees.

Moments later, Johe's motherly voice echoed in the bathroom, "Hey. I've called Dr. Sabia. He's on his way."

"Please don't," Mary feebly begged.

"It's too late, Honey," Aja gently said and continued stroking her braided hair. "Try sipping a little more water."

"She's probably dehydrated. We'll let James look her over," Johe softly said to Aja.

"I hope he does something. The poor thing," Aja's worried, kind voice sounded shrill in Mary's ears. "With all this stuff going on with Sun, she's just worked herself to exhaustion."

The next thing Mary remembered was Dr. Sabia's gentle hand upon hers. "Mary," he firmly said in an attempt to rouse her. She could feel him pinching the skin on her hand, yet she didn't feel compelled to pull it back.

"Yeah," she moaned.

"You're dehydrated and your blood sugar is low. We're going to take you to the hospital and get you some fluids, ok?"

"Don't wait for her approval," Johe insisted.

Everything felt like Mary was floating through a fog. The ambulance ride to Candler County Hospital, the nurses talking to her, the needle going in her hand – all felt like a dream.

"Is there any chance you're pregnant," a nurse asked her.

Mary didn't flinch. The words didn't make much sense to her.

"Run a pregnancy test to be sure," Dr. Enoch, the emergency room doctor, ordered. "Mary, we're giving you fluid, a shot of adrenaline to bring your blood pressure up, and a shot of Glucagon. You should be feeling better soon." The doctor turned to one of his nurses, "Where's Dr. Sabia?"

"He's out in the waiting room with the others. Do you want me to go get him?"

"Yes, please."

"How's she doing, Joel?" Dr. Sabia asked the attending doctor with a hearty handshake.

"Her blood pressure was 70/40 when she got here, but we've given her a shot of adrenaline, and it's up to 80/50 now. Her glucose level was at 31. The Glucagon will bring it up pretty soon. I'd say we got to her just in time."

"Damn. I didn't do any diagnostics on her. I took one look at her and got her here."

"Good thing. As tiny as she is, we very easily could've lost her. We've got fluids going in her now. How long has she been vomiting?"

"Johe said just a couple of days, but her horse has been really sick, so she hasn't been eating or drinking like she should."

Joel shook his head. "In this heat?" he asked with surprise. "Someone like her doesn't have the fatty reserves to go so long between meals. We'll get her stabilized, but I want to keep her for observation at least overnight."

"She's a stubborn one; she's not going to like hearing that," Dr. Sabia said with a chuckle. "There's one thing you should know – she's very, very well connected with Alan Brooks."

"Oh yeah?"

"Yeah. So, keep all of this quiet, and go the extra mile, ok? I'll support whatever you recommend."

"Will do. Thanks, James."

"Anytime. I'll send Johe and the others home."

Dr. Enoch left the room to attend to other patience. Within an hour, he returned to Mary. "How are you feeling?"

"I'm better," she weakly said.

"Good. Those medicines are pretty fast acting." He patted her hand. "I'm going to admit you overnight for observation…"

"No. I've got to take care of my horse. He's been sick."

"I've already talked to Dr. Sabia. He assured me everything is under control. Johe will take care of your horse. You need to focus on taking care of yourself, ok? Which means you need to eat and drink regularly. I'm not going to release you until you prove to me you can keep down some food and water."

The nurse entered the treatment room. "Here's the blood work you ordered," she said as she handed him a piece of paper.

"Just as I expected, your electrolytes are out of balance and fluid levels are way down. We're going to keep pumping the fluids into you. And…. Oh! Well this explains a lot. You're going to be a mother," Dr. Enoch said with a smile. "Congratulations!"

"Wait… what?" Mary asked.

"You're pregnant. I take it this wasn't something you expected?"

The nurse changed out her IV bag and exited the room.

"No. Not at all. Are you sure? I haven't missed a period." *Or have I?* she wondered.

"Yeah. We ran a blood test; you don't have to miss a period for it to be accurate."

Slowly, Mary held her hand out for the paper.

Dr. Enoch handed it to her. "See, it says so right here. Pregnancy – positive." He pointed out the line she needed to read.

"How's that possible?"

"Miss Stephenson, I don't need to explain how a woman gets pregnant, now do I?" he said with a boyish smile.

Mary softly chuckled. "No, sir."

"Have y'all been using protection?"

With a gentle feeble smile, she shook her head.

"Well, there you go."

"What's this?" she asked as she pointed to a date.

"What? Oh, it's your approximate due date."

"February 14th?"

"Yup! A Valentine's Day baby," Dr. Enoch said with a happy chuckle. "How lucky can you get?"

Mary didn't smile. *Why does that day always come up?* she wondered.

"Alrighty. We'll get you something for the nausea. It'll help you keep your meals down. You're eating for two now, so be sure to eat up. Is there anyone you want me to contact?"

"No."

"Not the baby's daddy?"

"No. He's, uh, he's out of town. I'll tell him when he gets back." Weakly, she laid her left hand with the 4-carat diamond ring upon her flat belly. *Pregnant?* she thought with a genuine smile.

CHAPTER 38

Ted felt as if his feet were walking through a field of glue smeared all over the pharmacy floor. He didn't see why he had to be the one buying Angela's pregnancy test. The idea she could be carrying Alan's child infuriated him. The only thing keeping him going was the real possibility his swimmers got there first. "Anyone's but his fuckers," he muttered as he walked down the feminine products aisle.

"Can I help you, sir?" an older, heavy-set lady asked him.

"Uh, yeah. I'm looking for a pregnancy test."

"Surely you don't think you're pregnant, do you?" she jokingly said.

"No, no," he said with a smirk, "my gir—my wife. I think my wife may be pregnant," he said. He justified calling her his wife wasn't too far from the truth since as soon as Alan was gone, she would be his wife. Regardless of what Angela said, he was going to make sure to get rid of such a nuisance.

"Well then, when was her last period?" the lady asked him as they walked down an aisle.

He felt uncomfortable and nervously chuckled. "I don't know. You'd have to ask her."

"Well the reason I ask is some of these tests can test before she even misses a period. Has she missed one yet?"

"I-I-I don't…," he started, "I'm just doing what I'm told."

"Ok. Then let's try this one." She pulled out a white and purple box, handing it to him. "It's supposed to be good even if she hasn't missed a period yet."

"How do you use it?" he asked.

"Well, she has to pee on the stick with her first morning urine. If a plus sign shows in the window, she's pregnant. If there's only a line, she's not."

"Perfect." His feet shuffled as he moved to the cash register.

"Will that be cash or charge?" the cashier asked him.

"Cash." Ted pulled out his wallet. He paid for the pregnancy test and returned to the farm.

"It's about time you got back!" Angela scolded him.

"I skipped a meeting with Johe to get this for you."

"So. Focus, Ted!"

"I still say I don't like this."

"I don't care what you like. She took the white sack from him and disappeared into the bathroom.

"The lady at the pharmacy said you should use first-morning urine," he told her through the closed door.

"Huh? What does it matter?"

"I don't know. I'm just saying what she said."

"Let me read the instructions." She opened the box and pulled out the white piece of paper. *What if it's negative? Then what?* Angela's eyes read the instructions quickly. "For best results, use first morning urine," she read to him aloud. "Dammit! Couldn't you get one I can take now? I've already been to the bathroom this morning."

"Well, it just says 'for best results.'"

"Mm-hmm, true. I'm going to try it. If it doesn't work, you can go tomorrow and get another one."

Ted rolled his eyes. "Wouldn't it be more convincing if you went out and bought your own? People would at least talk about how you suspected you were."

"Good point," she said as her urine splashed into the toilet. The activated test sat on the sink counter while she cleaned herself up. "We'll know in about five minutes," she said when she opened the door.

"Oh goodie," Ted said with a super-sized amount of sarcasm.

"Look, I'm doing this for you, too. The least you can do is be somewhat excited about it!"

"The woman I love is knocked up by my mortal enemy? Yeah.

Forgive me for not throwing a party."

Angela's eyes dazzled. "Party? Exactly! I'll throw a party for Alan's return from rehab. At the party, I'll announce to everyone about the pregnancy, and I'll make certain his whore is there," she said with a diabolical look.

"Why don't you wait and see what the results are before you start planning your little soirée?"

"Alan comes home in three days. I'll have to throw it together pretty quickly. Get me my cell phone."

Ted sighed deeply and left to retrieve what she wanted. "Party. Great. Yeah, let's celebrate the drunk's return!" he mumbled.

Angela sat at her mahogany table writing a list of people she'd need to contact to put everything in place.

"Don't you find it a bit ironic to welcome him home with a drunken free-for-all?"

"Huh?"

"I mean, he went to rehab to dry up, and you're going to welcome him home with a flood of booze. Either you're crueler than I anticipated, or have some diabolical plan you haven't shared with me. So which one is it?"

She chuckled lightly. "I didn't even think of that."

"Don't get me wrong. The fucker can drink himself to death for all I care; I'm just worried about your image is all."

"Good point. I'll make sure to instruct the planners to include absolutely no alcohol. I don't want people to think I'm some out-to-destroy-him bitch." Angela started scanning through her phone for the appropriate people she should call.

Ted wandered into the bathroom. The pregnancy test lay lifeless on the counter, waiting anxiously to tell the future.

"Ted!" Angela called for him.

"Coming," he answered as he left the pregnancy test behind.

"Remember the website I found where you can buy fake baby bumps?" Angela asked.

"No."

"Well, I Googled it and apparently you can buy little strap-on bumps to make everyone think you're pregnant. So it won't matter what the test says; I'm going to be pregnant one way or another."

"Oh yeah? Well I guess it'd be easier, huh?"

"Definitely."

"Are you even going to check the test?"

"Has it been five minutes yet?"

"I'm sure it's been more than five minutes."

"Ok. Let's see," she said as she entered the bathroom and picked up the test. "Shit!"

"What?"

"It's negative."

"Maybe you should've used first-morning pee."

"Maybe," she thoughtfully said. "No matter. If I say I'm pregnant, then I'm pregnant, and nothing else matters. I'm going to announce it at the party in front of everyone. Alan won't have any choice but to be happy about it."

"Yeah, I guess so," Ted said feeling relieved – at least she wasn't really pregnant.

"Still, maybe I should take another one tomorrow morning with the first-morning pee. I wonder if it makes much of a difference."

"I doubt it." Ted rubbed her shoulders. *Not pregnant*, he thought with a relieved smile.

"I'm going to go down to the drug store and get another one. A different one this time. They're only 99% accurate. This one could be wrong."

"Angela, come on. It says you're not. Can't we just accept it and go on?"

"No. If another one comes back negative tomorrow morning, then we'll move on to plan B, but I want to know for sure. My boobs have been sore, and Gillian said hers were so sore she could barely wear a bra."

"But it could also mean you're about to start your period, right?"

Angela turned a scornful eye to him.

I just want to kill the fucker, Angela or no Angela! Ted thought.

"Just in case, though, I want you to order me the fake baby bumps."

"Why me?"

"Because I don't want the purchase traced back to me."

"Oh, but you want it to be traced back to me? Won't it be a little odd?"

"Just do it. Sheesh. You'd think you'd be more willing to help me," she complained and entered her closet to get dressed for the day. "I've got a lot of work to do today, so don't expect me down at the barn at all. I've got a party to plan, and everyone needs to see me excited for Alan's return. Oh! And be sure you let Johe know the horse show trip is canceled. We're not going. If I'm pregnant, the last thing I need to be doing is riding in a horse show."

"Whatever," Ted grumbled as he left her bedroom. A knock on the front door of the stately home caused him to scurry down the staircase and quickly out the side door to the outside veranda. Meeting with Johe was tops on his to-do list. *Ordering some stupid fake baby bump is at the bottom*, he thought.

"Come in, Mr. Forsyth," Gus greeted Earl.

"Thank you, Gus. I'm here to see Mrs. Brooks. Is she available?"

"Let me go fetch her for you."

"Thank you," Earl said politely.

"You can have a seat in the drawing room as I retrieve her. I'll have Lynn bring you some coffee." Gus slid the massive doors closed behind him. His immediate concern was how Earl had infiltrated Babbling Brooks. Alan had explicitly stated he was not permitted. Gus sent Julia to get Angela, while he made a phone call to Felix. Earl needed to be removed as quickly and quietly as possible.

Earl made himself at home. While he reviewed some of the art hanging on the wall, he remembered Lynn – a twenty-something girl who it was rumored was amazingly easy and preferred sex with older men.

A timid, young maid entered the room. "Mr. Forsyth, can I get you anything?" she asked.

This mouse can't be Lynn, he thought. "Are you Lynn?"

"Yes, sir."

"I've heard about you," he said as he moved around the room with cat-like maneuvers. His eyes remained glued upon her while he slid the room's doors shut.

"What have you heard?"

"You like older men."

"Yeah," she shyly answered.

"Mm-hmm. Caught you," he aggressively said as he pursued her.

"Mr. Forsyth, Mrs. Brooks would fire me in a second if I did something while on the job," she said with a coy, flirtatious smile.

"She'll never know," he whispered as he rubbed the back of his hand along the sleeve of her uniform. "You ever been with Mr. Brooks?"

"No, sir. Mr. Brooks isn't like that."

"Every man is." He leaned down and kissed her cheek; his words scorched her delicate skin. Encouraged when she didn't pull away from him, he let his hand wander down the front of her uniform where he cupped her breast as his fingers pinched her erect nipple.

She moaned when he found it.

"You like it rough, don't you? You dirty girl."

"Uh-huh," she whispered. Her nipple pressed hard against the cup of her bra.

"When I'm finished with my business here, meet me in my car."

"I can't. What if someone catches me?"

"I have tinted windows." He pushed a fifty-dollar bill into her hand. "Shh, it'll be our little secret." He slid his hand farther down her uniform, down her skirt, and then up inside where he found the wetness he hoped he would find. "Oh you *are* a dirty girl!" He slid her panties to the side and plunged two fingers inside her.

Lynn gulped and panted at the pleasurable intrusion.

"You like it don't you, you slut!" Earl growled in her ear. His other hand grabbed her around her neck and held her firmly.

Lynn clung to his manly arms. She could only whimper in response.

Approaching footsteps made him pull his fingers out and release her. With his sultry eyes glued upon hers, he licked his lips and then guided his glistening juice-covered fingers into his mouth. Slowly, deliberately, he licked them clean.

Angela flung the doors open, causing Lynn to flinch.

Lynn worried her swollen nipples would show through her uniform. She turned from Earl, kept her eyes down, and slumped her shoulders as she exited the room.

"What do *you* want?" Angela forcefully asked.

"I'm here to serve you divorce papers, Mrs. Brooks."

"What? Not this again! Alan already tore them up once."

Earl handed her a manila folder with the signed divorce papers inside. "If so, would he be serving you again? Consider yourself served. I expect your attorney will want to take a look at them, but I can assure you, he's being far more generous than he legally is required to be. If you agree to the terms outlined within 5 days, then you can have everything contained therein. But if not, the next offer won't be nearly as generous."

"I have news I'm certain will make those papers positively useless."

"What news?"

Angela nodded confidently. "I'm throwing a party for Alan's return from rehab; it'll be announced there. Tsk. What a shame I won't be inviting you to it."

"Not inviting me, huh?"

"Nope," she said with an air of superiority. "You think I want Alan's lawyer mucking up the fun? I don't think so. So, you'll just have to wait until Alan returns those papers to you in tiny shreds."

Earl rolled his eyes. "Whatever," he said. "I don't have time for your childish games." Thoughts of his planned rendezvous with Lynn superseded any Angela melodrama. He started toward the door.

"Good. I'm through with you anyway."

"Indeed." Earl slid the doors opened only to find the image of Felix's imposing figure.

"Can I help you?" Felix asked.

"Not this time. My business is nearly concluded here," Earl confidently said.

"Nearly? What else do you need to attend to?" Felix sternly inquired.

Earl squared his shoulders; was Felix hindering his access to the cute little filly waiting for him?

Felix's phone went off, but he didn't answer it.

"Don't you need to get that?" Earl asked.

"I will, as soon as I've seen you off the premises."

"Exactly!" Angela added, happy to see Felix coming to her defense.

"Let me escort you to your car, Mr. Forsyth."

Earl thought of the anticipated romp with Lynn in his car. "No thanks. It's not necessary."

"Yes, sir, I'm afraid it is." Felix's phone rang a second time.

"It's about time you did something around here for me," Angela told Felix.

Felix didn't respond to Angela. It was far more important Earl be removed as quickly and quietly as possible. It didn't matter if she thought his removal was for her.

"Damn-near impossible to hire good help these days," Earl said with a noticeable scoff when he spied his empty car.

Felix remained stoic and personally escorted Earl off the Brooks property without incident.

CHAPTER 39

Ted entered the barn, exasperated from his dealing with Angela. His mind was busy plotting the details for finally getting rid of Alan. Although the thoughts were the same ones he'd had since Angela had spent the night with Alan, they were more fervent and insistent. Every night the gun on his dresser called out to him – begging him to use it to end all the suffering. "Everything would be better without Alan Brooks," the gun would say.

"I could just shoot him before anyone knew who did it," Ted muttered as he thought of the silencer. If he did it at the party, the noise of the party would drown out any residual sounds. He could casually walk up to Alan, shoot him, and insouciantly walk away.

"Ted," Johe called out to him and trotted outside of her office. "I told you I need to talk to you. Where the hell have you been?"

"I had errands to run."

"You've been avoiding me for two days."

"I'm not avoiding you, Johe. I have things to do, and those things don't revolve around you, you know?"

"Whatever. I need to talk to you in my office."

"Now?"

"Yes, now." Johe entered and immediately picked up the phone.

Ted followed her inside with a disgruntled scoff. "Are you going to talk to me, or the phone?"

"I'm trying to reach someone."

The gun continued taunting him. In his imagination, he wondered what Johe would look like with a bullet between her eyes.

"He's not answering."

"I guess I can go, huh?"

"No. I still need to talk to you. Have a seat." She dialed the phone again and stood with one hand on her hip.

"Do I have to?"

"Yes! Sit!" she barked.

Reluctantly, Ted pulled the school-house chair out, but refused to sit in it.

Johe rolled her eyes, hung up the phone, and then dialed Felix's number again.

Ted paced circles around the chair before he remembered the orders from Angela about canceling the horse show trip. "I need to talk to you, too."

"What about? I said have a seat!" she said more forcefully as she once again waited for Felix to answer.

"What for?"

"Just do it," she said with ample amounts of irritation.

Ted did as he was instructed.

Johe waited with the corded phone against her ear.

"Yes?" Felix finally answered.

"He's here," was all she said.

"Who's that?" Ted asked.

"Felix. He wants to meet with you too," Johe replied.

"Whatever," Ted said with a blasé attitude.

"While we're waiting for him, what did you want to talk to me about?"

"We've decided to cancel the horse show trip."

"Why?"

"Angela said to. She didn't say why," he half lied.

"Good. There's no sense in her embarrassing the farm any further than she already has."

Images of Alan's lifeless body flickered before Ted's eyes the more he sat. Whatever words Johe continued to say morphed into the way he imagined the sound Alan's last breath would make. *If only Alan were here, I could go ahead and get it over with*, he thought.

"Are you listening to me?" Johe asked.

"What do you want from me? I have things to do," he said with an aggravated voice.

"We need to wait for Felix."

Ted sighed deeply. "Is it ok for me to get a cup of coffee at least?"

Johe sighed, and then said, "Fine."

"I didn't realize I was going to be interrogated this morning."

"It's not an interrogation. We have some questions we want you to answer."

"More? Didn't those goons get enough from me?" Ted asked as he walked into the kitchenette.

"Things change," Johe said while typing some information into the computer.

"Indeed, things change," he muttered. The fresh coffee smelled delightful pouring into his mug. "I took the last of the creamer," he announced and walked back into Johe's office. "So when is Felix supposed to be here?" Would killing Alan at the party be the right thing to do? Or should he catch him leaving Mary's cabin one night and drop him like a ten-point buck?

Just as he'd finished asking, there was a knock on Johe's office door.

"Come in," she said.

Felix entered with two security guards behind him. . "Sorry. One of my guys dropped the ball."

"How?"

"He let Mr. Forsyth onto the farm," Felix explained.

"Oh! Don't tell Alan."

"I had to see the situation was under control."

"Good."

"What's going on?" Ted demanded.

Johe turned her attention back to Ted. "It's come to my attention you've been behaving quite inappropriately at Babbling Brooks."

"In what way?"

"Felix?" Johe held out her hand.

Felix handed her a manila file folder containing several papers.

"We have evidence pointing to you playing an important role in Biscuit's poisoning. And…."

"What?! That's ridiculous!" Ted exclaimed, interrupting her. He moved to the edge of his seat.

"In addition, Felix's men have found evidence indicating you've been lacing Mary's horse's food with sand in an attempt to kill him, but make it look like he died of natural causes."

"That's preposterous! I would never do something like that!" he shouted as he stood up from the chair and snatched the folder from Johe's desk. "You have no proof I did those things!" he proclaimed without reading the folder.

"It's all written right there, Ted," Johe said. "When a search was done on the cabins, a syringe was found in your kitchen drawer. After tests, it came back positive for copper-laced antifreeze, which was the same combination used to kill Biscuit. We sent the syringe off for further analysis, and lo and behold, your fingerprints were on it. The analysis reports are included in the file. Also, there are copies of receipts from the hardware store where you bought 200 pounds of sand. We've tested Sun's sweet feed, and it is heavily mixed with sand."

"Is it a crime to buy sand?"

"It is when you use the sand to purposely harm an animal."

"What? I've been around horses my entire life! Why would I ever harm one of them?"

"I don't know. I've been asking myself the same question," Johe said.

Felix and his men stood silently by the closed door of the office.

"Someone framed me! No doubt it was that worthless Alan Brooks!"

"No, Ted. It's not possible."

"How do you know?"

Felix spoke up, "We have video surveillance footage of you loading the bags of sand into your truck at the hardware store. You used your credit card to pay for them…"

"All the more reason to believe me! If I were trying to get away with something, don't you think I'd have sense enough not to do something so blatant?"

"Ok, if that's the case, where's the sand?" Johe leaned back in her chair and asked.

"I used it."

"What for?" Johe inquired with her arms across her chest.

"For a flower bed for Angela. I turned the receipt into her for reimbursement."

"So, if we got Angela down here, she'd agree you used the sand for her?" Felix asked.

"Exactly."

"What about your fingerprints on the syringe? How do you suppose those got there?" Johe asked.

"I have to give the horses shots from time to time. Of course I touched the syringe! I bet if you tested every single syringe in the tack room, my fingerprints would be on them too."

"Actually, we did test all of the syringes. Your fingerprints weren't present on any of them. Nevertheless, we went a step further and tested the needle covers of all the syringes. And guess what – we found your DNA only on the one with the traces of copper-laced ethylene glycol. I'm sure you know how it got there. I've seen you do it hundreds of times."

Ted's facial expressions were blank, and he remained silent.

Johe continued, "You probably took the needle cover off with your teeth. Every time you give a shot, you do it the same way."

"Someone had to have used a used syringe! There's no other explanation for it!" he tried to defend himself.

"So what are you really saying here?" Johe asked with her elbows on the desk.

"I'm saying I've been framed! Someone planted this shit and is trying to frame me!"

Johe looked at Felix, who looked at her. They both knew the next step was confronting him about the insurance policies.

Felix nodded and closed his dark eyes briefly – granting Johe permission to bring them up.

"After further investigation, Felix uncovered insurance policies on the horses here with a beneficiary of Ansun, Inc., which is a New York based business owned by none other than a David Eastwood. Sound familiar?"

Ted's face turned sheet white.

"Do you have an explanation?"

His mind raced. "O-o-of course I do."

"Then how about sharing it with us."

"David's my brother."

"I know. But why does your brother have insurance policies on the horses of Babbling Brooks?"

"Just as insurance against anything bad happening to me."

"Happening to you?" Johe incredulously asked.

"Yes."

"You do realize how nonsensical you're sound right now, right?"

"So. It doesn't have to make sense to you. He does it at every barn I've worked at. It's just a hedge of protection for me."

"Really?" Johe looked up at Felix and shook her head. She looked back at Ted and continued, "You mean to tell me you can't come up with anything better? 'Cause, your explanation is just pathetic."

"I don't care if you believe me or not. I have work to do," he said as he stood up.

"Not today you don't," Johe firmly stated. "You're resignation is required."

"My what?!" Ted incredulously asked.

"You can either resign, or I'm going to fire you."

"You can't do that!"

"Want to make a bet? I'm acting on Alan's orders."

Alan Brooks, bounced around inside Ted's mind. His breaths quickened. "Well, then, I think you're going to have to fire me. Then you'll have to single-handedly explain it all to Angela," he confidently said in an attempt to call her bluff.

"Very well. Ted Eastwood, you're fired. These gentlemen will escort you to your cabin and assist you with removing your personal belongings. Please immediately vacate the farm. As for Angela, I'm not worried about her. I'm acting under Alan's orders. She can take your firing up with him."

Alan Brooks, seethed inside Ted's thoughts. "Fine." He stood up and placed his hands on the edge of Johe's desk. His breaths were short, nasally. The pistol on his dresser called out to him. His thoughts ran rampant about all of the implications losing his job would mean – no more training, no more horses, no insurance money, but most importantly, no more Angela. As much as the idea of killing Johe and everyone at the farm was appealing, Alan was his main target. *I'll kill the son of a bitch!* he thought, *And then everyone else and burn this whole place down!*

"Gentlemen, please accompany Ted to his quarters and then off of the property. I'll notify the staff."

"Yes, ma'am," they said in unison.

The two men grabbed each of Ted's arms and began pushing him toward the door.

"Get your damned hands off of me!" he shouted and swung

back at them. "I don't need Alan's goons treating me like I'm some kind of criminal!"

"Just be glad I'm not calling the police and involving them in this," Johe stated matter-of-factly. "You can thank Alan for wanting to keep it quiet."

Alan Brooks. Ted's eyes squinted at the mention of his name. "You'll be sorry for this! You'll all be sorry!" he warned.

"I doubt it."

Ted rapidly walked about ten steps ahead of the security guards, who followed behind him. "Angela! Answer the damned phone!" Ted shouted into his cell phone. He hung up right as the voicemail picked up and called again.

Voicemail answered.

He called again.

"What?!" Angela shouted through her phone.

"Johe fired me!"

"She what??!" Angela stopped cold on the staircase; the divorce papers remained tucked under her arm. Wasn't it bad enough having Earl serve her, and now this?

"Get over here!"

"I'm on my way," Angela said as she retreated back down the stairs.

It was only moments later when Angela burst through Johe's office door. "What the hell do you think you're doing?!" she shouted at Johe.

Felix bowed his chest up and moved between Johe and Angela. "Mrs. Brooks, calm down and have a seat."

"I will not! Ted said you fired him," she yelled at Johe.

"I did. The mess he's been up to are fireable offenses."

"Like what?" She was instantly concerned about how much Johe knew. Did she know about her relationship with Ted?

"He poisoned Biscuit, and he attempted to kill Mary's horse, Sun," Johe explained with an air of confidence.

Aghast by such revelations, Angela sat in the old schoolhouse chair. "What?!"

"Felix has been conducting an investigation into Biscuit's death. He found evidence implicating Ted as the mastermind behind all of the mysterious things happening around here."

"Ted? The mastermind?" Angela said with a scoff. "What kind

of evidence shows something as asinine as that?"

"We have DNA evidence," Johe seriously said. "And apparently, Ted took out insurance policies on the horses here at Babbling Brooks."

"Insurance policies?" Angela genuinely looked surprised.

"Yes. The insurance policies pay millions for the death of horses here. You wouldn't know anything about them, would you?" Johe looked at her skeptically.

"O-o-of course not!" she exclaimed astonished by such an implication.

"Because there are policies paying directly to you as well."

"What?!"

"Yes. So perhaps you have some explaining to do." Johe didn't mention the policies with Angela as the beneficiary were routine policies funded by Babbling Brooks.

"N-n-no. I-I-I don't know anything about any of this! Does Alan know?"

"Not yet. But he will as soon as he gets back."

Angela fidgeted in her chair. *I've got to get to Alan first*, she thought. "How much were the insurance policies for?" she asked.

"On Biscuit, two and a quarter million dollars total, on Sun, ten million dollars."

Angela placed her hand to her mouth. Her mind recalled Ted's conversation about twelve million dollars he'd have before the end of the year. Was he plotting behind her back? "I know nothing about any of this."

"Now you do."

"Still, having insurance on horses isn't a fireable offense."

"But killing one of them and attempting to kill the other one are."

"You can't prove he's responsible, can you?"

Johe held up the manila folder containing the evidence Felix collected. "Yes, I definitely can. DNA is irrefutable."

"It's preposterous! He's the best! If he feels he needs to do such things for money, then maybe we need to increase his salary!"

"Really?" Johe pretentiously asked with a scoff. "You're kidding, right?"

"Not at all. And who do you think you are firing him in the first place? This isn't *your* farm!"

"Alan gave me permission to fire him should I find the need to. The security guards are helping him pack his belongings and vacate the property."

"What?! I want to talk to him first."

"Be my guest. He's in his cabin. Felix will escort you there," Johe said. Her chair creaked as she leaned back in it.

Without another word, Angela and Felix left Johe's office, heading straight for Ted's cabin.

"I'd like to speak with him alone," she said to Felix.

"I don't think so, Mrs. Brooks."

"I don't need you to protect me from him!"

"I'm just following orders."

"And I'm ordering you to back off! I'm still married to Alan, and what I say trumps anything an overpaid stable hand says!" she nastily pointed out. "Get your men out of here. Now!"

Felix ordered the men out of Ted's cabin where they stood guard outside the front door.

Angela turned to Ted. "What. The. Fuck. Do. You. Think. You're. Doing?!" Her face was instantly red with anger. "Your plan is to kill off *my* horses and collect the insurance money?!"

"Don't be ridiculous! I didn't do anything! They've framed me! Can't you see?"

"No! They said they have DNA evidence against you! How do you explain that!?"

"Someone must've picked up a syringe I'd used on another horse. They used the same syringe to inject Biscuit."

"What about the insurance policies??"

"It's standard operating procedure for me. It protects me."

"Oh bull shit! Don't even try to sell me your shit!" she exclaimed and threw her hands apart at him. "You just said you were going to have twelve million by the end of the year. Did you think I forgot?! You're a fucking idiot is what you are!"

"How do you get that?" he asked soothingly, as if he were trying to calm a wild horse.

"When Alan finds out about this shit, he's going to try and point the finger at me too! What is wrong with you?! Where's your head?"

"I was only thinking about our future. You always say I can't afford you, so I've made the problem go away. I can afford you with twelve million dollars! When I'm done, I promise, you can walk away from Alan and never worry about him or money again. You've just got to trust me, ok?" He stroked her arms.

"Trust you? Trust *you*?? Look at the shit you've pulled me into!" She pushed his hands off of her.

"Just promise me you'll still invite me to the party. I promise all of our troubles will be solved. I've got everything under control."

"So, Johe firing you was all part of your plan?"

Ted thought for a second and then smiled. "Of course it was," he lied as he gently stroked her soft cheek.

"But you called me so upset!"

"I know I did. I had to make it all believable. Just promise me you'll invite me to the party. Then we'll be together forever."

Angela sighed deeply, blasting air through her nose. "I don't understand it all."

"But you don't need to. You just have to trust me, ok? I love you more than anything in the entire world. I only want to spend the rest of my life together with you."

"What about the baby?"

Ted pushed his lips into a straight line. "You and I both know there isn't any baby."

"Yes, but everyone will believe there is."

"True. So, we'll stick to the same plan where that is concerned. You'll announce you're pregnant, and I'll take care of everything else."

Angela sighed deeply and leaned her head into his hand. "Ok. As hard as it is, I'm going to trust you."

"Don't forget about my invitation."

"I won't."

CHAPTER 40

It was late Saturday evening when Alan's plane touched down at
Savannah International Airport. The paparazzi greeted him with
their flashing cameras snapping pictures of him and calling out to
him. In typical Alan style, he stopped and posed for their pictures,
answered their questions, and signed autographs until it was time for
him to leave.

"I sure have missed everyone, Frankie," Alan said from the back
of the limo.

"We missed you too, sir!"

"What's all been going on?"

"Not much of anything, really. The weatherman said we're
supposed to get some thunderstorms tonight. Shame it won't be
some good soaking rain, but rain is rain. I'm sure the farmers will be
glad."

"No doubt." Alan wanted to ask Frankie about Mary, but in the
name of continued secrecy, he didn't. "Hey, would you stop up here
at Anderson's Jewelers? I need to pick something up."

"Sure thing, Boss." Frankie pulled the limo to a stop outside of
the jewelry store.

Alan hopped out and walked inside. "Hiya, Larry. Do you have
my ring ready?"

"Yes, sir," Larry responded and went to the back safe. "I think
you'll be very happy with the results," he called from the back room.

"If you did it, I'm sure I will be."

"Here you are," he said as he handed Alan a sturdy black velvet box.

Alan's anticipation made his hands feel sweaty. He opened the box and inside was the gleaming 22-carat diamond and pearl butterfly engagement ring he'd had custom made for Mary. "Wow. Just wow. I have to say, you've simply out done yourself this time."

"Well, you know I aim to please. You'll notice the corresponding wedding band has the infinity symbols interlinking to set off the butterfly's wings, just like you wanted. I wasn't sure I could do everything in platinum, but you always find a way to challenge me. I think they turned out fairly well, don't you?"

"I'm simply awed! It's beyond perfect."

"You want me to send Greg the bill?"

"Absolutely. Damn, man, I'm speechless. It's more beautiful than I could have imagined!"

Larry chuckled. "She's going to love it then, huh?"

"Definitely. There's no chance she'll do anything but. Thanks again."

"Anytime. Let me know if we can help you further."

"Will do!" Alan put the box in his pocket, shook Larry's hand, and returned to the limo. "Frankie, get me home. I have some urgent business to take care of!" he happily said.

After a little over an hour of travel time, the sun had completely set when Frankie pulled the limo up to the front of the Brooks' home.

"I'll help you put the car away," Alan said.

"No, sir. You're finally home. I'll put the car the car away; you go on inside. I'm sure you'd like to shower and change, right?"

"Oh yeah! I should, shouldn't I?" His excitement about properly proposing to Mary had his mind otherwise occupied.

"Yes, sir."

"Good call, Frankie." As eager as he was to see Mary's precious face, he was equally anxious to make his proposal perfect, which meant he needed to clean himself up from his travels. His feet barely touched the marble steps of the Brooks palatial home.

Upon entering the foyer of the grand house, he was greeted with a collective "Surprise!" from a massive crowd of well-wishers.

Alan stumbled back in shock, but then immediately shifted into his public persona. "Well hot damn! What a way to come home! Thank y'all! I had no idea," he announced with a laugh as friends crowded around to shake his hand, kiss his cheeks, and hug him.

The one person he was looking for was Mary. Was she there? Had she planned it?

"Mama!" he shouted at the sight of his frail mother in her wheelchair. "Oh my God, Mama!" He hurriedly pushed through the well-wishers to get to her.

Angela was pushing her wheelchair.

Alan took one look at Angela and slightly squinted scornfully at her before his attention was returned to his mother.

"Welcome home, son! Angela told me you're coming home from rehab. I'm so proud of you for kicking the drink!"

Alan leaned down and kissed her softly on the cheek. "How good of you to come out and celebrate with us."

"It wasn't my idea to attend," Fiona said.

"It was mine," Angela added.

"Yours?" Alan looked up at Angela and questioned.

"Yes. I thought having her here would be a delightful surprise."

"And indeed it is!" Alan leaned into Angela and lightly kissed her cheek. "Thank you," he said. "This doesn't change anything, you know?" he whispered into her ear.

"We'll see," she replied.

Out of the corner of his eye, he spied Mary – an angelic vision in a white dress with a handkerchief hemline. Unassumingly, she stood with her hands nervously folded as she spoke with some other women. Her high heels made her feel practically as tall as Alan.

Instantly, he tore away from Angela and Fiona. "My God, I've missed you," was the first thing he said to Mary when he swept her off her feet. "Excuse me, ladies," he politely said as he whisked Mary away from them.

"I've missed you, too!" Being in his arms again felt better than she remembered – better than she'd hoped.

"I want you to meet my mama," he said with one of his dimpled smiles that made Mary's heart skip a beat.

"Won't it be awkward with Angela right there?" she nervously inquired.

"Mary. You've got to be prepared for this kind of stuff. I'm here. I'm not going anywhere. Angela has already been served the divorce papers. This whole party shit is her pathetic attempt to tempt me back, but it's not working. Nothing will work. You understand?" he asked as he held his face close to hers.

Mary nervously nodded.

"Now come on over and meet my mama. I know she's been anxious to meet you."

"Still," she said with worried eyes, "Angela…"

"Stop it. Ok?" he said with a determined look on his face. "There's nothing between me and Angela. Nothing. I promise."

Mary nodded as she acquiesced with a smile.

"There you go," Alan said and returned the smile. "I'll go get Mama and bring her to you, ok?"

"Ok."

Alan left Mary standing and returned to Fiona. "Thank you, Angela. I've got Mama from here," he firmly stated and took over control of Fiona's wheelchair, effectively pushing Angela aside.

Angela could only stand back and watch while brooding inside. "Don't get too comfortable, Mary," she muttered under her breath.

"Mama, this is my Mary," he said with a broad smile across his face.

"My goodness, she *is* beautiful isn't she?" Fiona asked as she extended her hand to Mary, who responded in kind.

"It's a pleasure to meet you, Mrs. Brooks," Mary politely said as she held Fiona's frail hand.

"Fiona, please. I can't tell you how much it pleases me to see the joy you've brought to my son. I can't remember the last time I've seen him so happy."

"The feeling is mutual," Mary replied.

Alan placed his hand at the small of Mary's back when a friend came over to talk to him and shake his hand.

Fiona smiled brightly when she noticed the large diamond on Mary's finger. She motioned for Mary to come closer to her. "When's the wedding?" she whispered.

"As soon as possible," Mary responded with a happy look. She could easily see Alan in the old lady's deep-set, cerulean eyes. It was evident where he got them from. Even her smile was reminiscent of Alan's. Mary readily returned her smile with her own glowing response.

"What do you think about giving me some grandbabies?"

Mary giggled lightly and hid her face – if she only knew. "The sooner the better."

"Good girl."

"Sorry, Mama, I haven't seen Mary in over a month. You can't hog her all to yourself," Alan playfully told his mother as he returned to Mary.

Fiona released Mary's hand, which allowed her to stand upright again. "You've done well, son. I'm proud of you. This one is a keeper!"

"Marcus will take care of you." Alan motioned for Marcus to join Fiona. Alan's strong arm embraced Mary's shoulders as they walked down the hallway toward the ballroom. "I need to get you in a closet somewhere so I can kiss you like I want to," he whispered to her. His hand was shook by several people as they walked.

"Thank you for not doing it in front of everyone. You know I'm not one for any kind of public display. I'm more of the quiet-nights-at-home-alone type."

"Mmm, I miss those nights."

"Me too."

"I love the pearls," he said as he slid a finger across the necklace he'd given her months ago.

Mary blushed.

"Good to see you, Alan!" a man shoved his hand into Alan's.

"Good to see you, too. How's your mama and them?"

"Doing good. I guess since you're dry now, we've all gotta be dry too, huh?" he said with a hearty laugh as he showed Alan the non-alcoholic beer Angela had ordered.

"Now surely we can do better than that." Alan turned to Mary, "Excuse me, Mary."

"No excuse needed. Go tend to your friend," she said with a gracious smile.

"Hell, bring her along! A lady as pretty as her shouldn't be left alone," his friend said.

"True enough," Alan said as he draped his arm across Mary's shoulders and led the two of them into the ballroom where the expansive bar was housed.

The grand piano his daddy had bought his mama to settle an argument sat on the edge of the room. Alan looked at it and remembered his mother's story. Still, he said to the bartender, "Hey, Mac, get us a few beers."

"No, no, I'm not drinking anything," Mary piped up.

"No? Ok, just make it two then," Alan said.

Mary cringed and pulled herself out from under Alan's arm, leaving the two men alone. *A month and a half he stayed away, and in just a few minutes he's back to drinking?* she sadly thought. *All this time away from him was for nothing.*

Mac produced Alan and his friend two bottles of non-alcoholic beer. "Mr. Brooks, Mrs. Brooks said no alcohol tonight. All we've got is non-alcoholic beer and Coke products."

"None?" Alan questioned

"No, sir. Absolutely none," Mac confirmed.

"So you mean to tell me every single person here is sober?" Alan asked.

"Yes, sir."

"What kind of party is that?" Alan's friend asked with a ridiculing chuckle.

"Hank, he's right." Alan drew in a deep breath; his eyes glanced over at the piano and then back to Mary, who had moved a good distance from the men. "I-I-I'm clean now," Alan told his friend.

"Good for you," Hank slapped Alan on the back and shook his hand. "I'm happy for ya, buddy."

"Thank you. It was time to get myself straightened up, you know?"

"Yeah, yeah, yeah. I get it."

"So, if you'll excuse me, I need to go make nice with Mary. She probably thinks I'm over here drinking."

"Sure thing, and, hey, good luck to you."

Alan grabbed the non-alcoholic beer from the bar, tipped it toward Hank and nodded. "Thanks." He took a swig from the amber-colored bottle.

"Hey," he whispered in Mary's ear.

"Did you get your beer?" she acerbically asked.

"Yup. My non-alcoholic beer tastes pretty much like watered down horse piss, but I'm drinking it."

"Good," she said; her heart filled with relief. "Good," she repeated.

"I've made up my mind about something."

"Yeah? What?"

"After this CD, I'm done. I'm quitting the business. I'm going to start my own record label and help upcoming artists be successful, the right way."

"What do you mean?"

"I mean producing the type of music they're good at and not forcing them to sell-out to what sells the most."

"What made you decide that?"

"Losing touch with my music is one of the things that drove me to drink. I had no idea, but it became very clear to me in rehab. I don't want others to go down the same path."

Mary looked up at him with an adoring smile.

He turned his bottle up to his lips and drank. "Besides, I want to make damn sure you don't end up like Angela."

"What do you mean?"

"Unhappy. Vindictive…"

"You don't really think that I would, do you?"

"Probably not, but still, I'm now very aware of my contribution to Angela's behavior. I won't do the same thing to you." He reached down and encapsulated her tiny hand inside his large hand.

"You couldn't…," she started, but the crowd drowned out her words as they cheered with gregarious joy when Angela took the stage. Mary and Alan both looked up to see what was happening.

CHAPTER 41

"Speech, speech, speech," the crowd chanted.

"Quiet down everyone," Angela said, oozing charisma.

The audience did as instructed.

"As most of y'all know, we're here to support my precious husband, Alan Brooks, on his successful completion of rehab. But that's not the only reason we are celebrating. Alan?" Angela held the silver microphone to her perfect ruby lips and motioned for him to join her. Her eyes scanned the crowd looking for her husband. "Will you come up here? Bring Mother Brooks, this is for her, too."

Alan squeezed Mary's hand just before he released it and quickly leaned down to whisper, "I sure hope it's the signed divorce papers." He then wheeled his mother to the edge of the stage, and in a single leap over the stage steps, stood next to Angela. A well-trained entertainer's smile graced his bright-eyed face as he waved to his cheering fans. The lights shining on him blinded his view of more than just the first two rows of people from the stage.

Mary and the multitude cheered as he stood debonair, confident, *and damn good-looking*, she thought. It still boggled her mind when she thought about such a man actually loving her. She inconspicuously dropped her left hand to rest just above her pubic bone. Knowing there was a little piece of her and Alan growing inside her made her smile. The desire to tell him was overwhelming, but the timing wasn't right. Their relationship wasn't all about the public; no, she would tell him once they were alone. In her mind, she'd replayed his anticipated reaction a million times.

She could see the broad, deeply dimpled smile on his face; the overjoyed crinkles on the edges of his eyes; the delighted tears freely streaking his stubbly, chiseled cheeks. He'd wrap his strong arms around her and spin her around in elated joy. Yes, she could see the entire scene. Once they finally left Angela's stupid party, Mary would tell him.

She carefully watched him as he moved across the stage, waving to his fans and smiling at their cheers. The confident way he carried himself made Mary's heart skip beats. She couldn't wait for the party to be over.

"Ok, ok," Angela said with a big smile and motioned for the noise level to decrease.

Alan seemed to eat-up his admirers' adoration.

How can he walk away from this? Mary thought. *He's crazy if he thinks he can. But then again, a baby changes everything.*

"Alan," Angela loudly stated into the microphone.

The cheering subsided.

She turned to face him. "As everyone here knows, we've certainly had our ups and our downs. I guess that's to be expected with any marriage."

There was barely a sound as Angela continued.

Mary's heart thumped in her throat. Surely Angela would produce signed divorce papers, and finally Mary and Alan could move toward being a family. There'd been no word from Arizona from anyone other than Tunda, and everything she'd said was insignificant. Such silence both terrified and comforted her.

"In celebration of your triumphant return from rehab, my gift to you is very small, but very big too." Angela placed her hand over her navel. "Alan, we're going to have a baby!" she nearly shrieked in excitement.

"We're... what?" Alan's chin dropped to his chest.

"We're going to have a baby! You've always dreamed of becoming a daddy, and now you are!"

A choral "Aww" broke out across the multitude.

"Nu-huh."

Angela beamed and said, "Yes."

"You mean, there's a-a b-baby Brooks growing in there?" he asked as he looked down at her. His eyes glistened with the hint of a tear.

Angela tucked her long blonde hair behind her ear as she smiled proudly up at him and nodded enthusiastically.

Alan grabbed her around the waist, picked her up, and spun her around as he hugged her.

The crowd collectively cheered.

For Mary, everything suddenly became warped and slow-moving. It felt as if the entire world was moving in a bizarre frame-by-frame fashion, and she was the only one able to hear the never-ending thumping of her heart.

People's smiling, distorted faces laughed in front of her as she tried to scurry out of the place Alan once promised would be her home.

"When are you due?" a voice shouted out over the crowd.

"Valentine's Day," Angela answered.

She and Angela have the same due date? There's only one way – Mary and Angela got pregnant at the same time. Alan's two-day absence from Mary precipitously made sense. He was with Angela the whole time – making a baby with her, too. Mary's heart completely exploded inside her chest.

Like a wave as it crashed upon the shore, applause filled the room and assaulted her ears.

She couldn't breathe! What had just happened? Her head felt light as her mind flashed memories of their past few months together. She remembered when he'd asked her to marry him. She remembered agreeing. She remembered how his eyes gleamed with what she thought was love for her. Phantasmagoric, cloudy images of him slipping the engagement ring on her finger flickered before her.

She thought of Alan's reaction to Angela's news. In her mind she'd planned for the same reaction to be for her. Now Angela was getting it. He was supposed to spin her around, not Angela. He was supposed to cry tears of joy for their child, not Angela's. And yet, there he was on the stage doing everything she dreamed he'd do, only it was for Angela and not her.

Finding her way outside felt like she was running in Jell-O. Her legs disobeyed every command to leave as quickly as possible.

"Kiss her! Kiss her!" the audience began chanting.

Her soul ached. The knife of bitter betrayal stuck out from between her shoulder blades, which made movement increasingly painful. Her mind tormented her with images of Alan making love to Angela, just like he'd done to her – his face filled with ecstasy; his eyes filled with love. She struggled to push those thoughts aside and get outside as quickly as possible! Her heart pounded, and she gasped for breath – breath that was impossible to inhale.

He played you, the thought ricocheted around inside her mind, shattering every bit of trust she'd developed for him.

Every look, every smile, every assurance indicating he loved her were suddenly thorns of betrayal tearing at her flesh and everything she held dear. Her soul bled. Her heart lay shattered at her feet. Humpty Dumpty had fallen and would never be put back together again. The door closed behind her before she could see what happened next.

Amidst the intoning crowd, Ted stoically stood. His face was stern. His steely hands readied themselves for what he knew would happen next. The pistol's unrelenting request rang inside his head. The impending end to all the suffering was within his grasp. Coldly, he reached into his jacket and pulled out the silencer first, and then the demanding pistol. Inconspicuously, he screwed the silencer on the end of the barrel.

The crowd cheered as Alan knelt down in front of Angela. All eyes were focused on the couple.

"Kiss her, kiss her," the crowd continued to chant.

Ted raised the pistol, while keeping it concealed against his body. Methodically, he lifted the gun to his neck, and then to his head, moving it near his eye level. His arms moved out from his body, aiming the gun at the back of Alan's head.

Alan puckered his lips and kissed Angela's belly. "This doesn't change anything," he quietly said loud enough for her to hear. *Or does it,* he thought. His father's words immediately entered his head: "Your boy's gonna need his daddy, just like you needed me."

Is this what he meant?

"What?" Angela leaned down and asked just as Ted pulled the trigger.

Like watching a movie in painstakingly slow motion, Alan helplessly watched as a thick string of horror spurted from Angela's chest. Seconds felt like minutes. Alan's immediate thought was, *What the hell?!* The dull thud from the bullet hitting her chest rang in the air, even above the crowd's noise.

A woman screamed in a low, distorted voice as a second stream shot from the stage and directly onto her.

Blood, rang in his ears but didn't register what it actually was or why it was there. He looked to the left of him, terror was written on the crowd's faces. He turned back to Angela, who staggered back, grabbed her chest, and with her frightened eyes fixated on Alan, collapsed to her knees. The stage quivered and then nodded in response to the force of her landing.

Her blood shot again, this time spattering on Alan's white button-down shirt. As if he could hardly make his body obey, his head looked down, but his eyes couldn't focus on the dark crimson splattered across his chest. *Blood*, replayed in his mind. His fingers touched it – thick and still warm. Turning his hand over, his jaw dropped to his chest. *Why is this here?*

His mind finally registered what was happening: *Angela's bleeding!*

"Ssoommeebbooddyy hheellpp!!" he tried to shout urgently, but to him, his words sounded slow and lackadaisical.

He reached out to catch her from falling farther, but his arms were heavy, taking inordinate effort to move. It amazed him when she fell into them.

The men near the stage moved as if they were crawling, yet the reality was quite different. They were by his side before he could lay Angela flat on the stage.

Without a thought, they threw their hands over her chest, trying desperately to stop the thick lifeblood shooting out from between their fingers. Multiple sets of hands joined them; they collectively pressed firmly against Angela's chest.

"You're going to be ok," Alan told Angela. The foreign, alkaline smell of blood permeated the air. More and more poured onto the stage floor; Angela's previously light blue dress was stained a deep red.

"Noooooo!" a single male voice cried out above the crowd's growing furor. Ted was able to fire off one more shot before two men tackled him to the floor. "No! No!" Ted continued to sob and fight against them. He had to shoot Alan – not Angela!

"Get off me!" he demanded and struggled against their grip.

"Drop the weapon!" one of the men commanded.

"Drop it!" the other reiterated.

"Call an ambulance!" one of the men on the stage shouted.

The two large men pinned Ted's legs against the floor, refusing to allow him to move. Nevertheless, before they could secure the gun from Ted, he turned the pistol on himself and pulled the trigger inside his opened mouth. His blood sprayed out behind him and then poured out from his head, soaking into the mahogany floors Angela had requested be installed over the original hardwood floors. His body instantly went limp.

A wave of murmured panic washed over the crowd. Many panicked and pushed their way to the door. Some people fainted at the sight of the blood.

"Angela, Baby, hold on. Is there a doctor here? James!?" Alan shrieked.

From the sea of anxious people, Dr. Sabia appeared. "I've called for an ambulance. Keep pressure on the wound," he instructed the others as he put his hands on top of the guests' hands. Thick cerise ribbons occasionally shot through their hands and rained down on those around her and onto the dark-colored stage.

"Angela! Hold on!" Alan's frightened words commanded her.

"I...," she weakly said.

"Shh. Don't talk now. Save your strength. James! Stop the bleeding!" Alan peremptorily requested of his doctor. Blood soaked into the knees of his Levis, splattered onto his face, and dripped down his shirt.

"I can't! I think it's coming from her aorta. Angela. You've got to stay calm. The more upset you get the faster your heart will beat and the faster you'll bleed out," James instructed her.

"Alan," she demanded.

He looked down at her ashen face; her once vibrant blue eyes were pale, glistening with tears.

Angela's entire body shook as she reached for his worried face.

"Just hold on, Honey. The ambulance is on its way."

"Forgive me," she weakly whispered as her blood-soaked fingers brushed his cheek. With those words, her hand limply fell to her side, and she drew her last breath. Her eyes remained fixed upon Alan.

"Angela?"

No response.

"Angela!!??" Alan shouted.

No response.

James immediately began CPR, but with each chest compression, blood shot out of her wound. He hung his head and sat back from her lifeless body. "I'm so sorry," he said and turned to Alan. "There's nothing more we can do."

"Nooo!!!" Alan screamed. "Angela! No!!" He embraced her body, pulling her against him while he sobbed.

CHAPTER 42

"Kiss her! Kiss her!" the audience's chanting muffled behind the closed door. Wind wickedly blew outside, carrying the sounds of their voices away from Mary. She ran across the veranda and down the stairs into the night. The shattered shadows of her life with Alan swirled around her, taunting and tormenting her. The very thought of her heart once again descending interminably into the pit of despair, left her in a repugnant dizziness which hindered cohesive thought.

Where was she? Nothing looked familiar. Utter darkness surrounded her, adding to her disorientation. Of one thing she was certain – she had to get as far away from the main house as she could. She couldn't cry. Her eyes could only watch her feet run away from the source of her pain and into the increasingly thicker night.

The hair on the back of her neck stood up as the air charged with electricity. Thunder crashed and blue lightning flickered in the sky, flashing images of familiarity, but just as quickly the darkness sprang up from the depths of the unknown to obnubilate those once familiar things.

Alan had a choice to make, and it was clear what his choice was – Angela.

Frantically, her nails clawed at her neck to find the pearl necklace. No one would ever wear it again as she broke the delicate strand, allowing a few loose pearls and the remaining strand to fall to the ground.

Thunder crashed, but she couldn't hear it. The wind whipped

around her, yet she couldn't breathe. It was as if there were no more oxygen to be had. She gasped as she ran through the night's thick forest of blackness. Her brain screamed at her not to cry, but her heart, which lay barely clinging to life, was incapable of doing anything but.

She felt panicked. Claustrophobic. Getting away from Alan seemed to feel as if she were swimming upstream in freezing water. As hard as she tried, she couldn't get away fast enough.

Thunder crashed again, followed by a deluge of rain. It felt as if the sky were falling down all over her, soaking through her beautiful white dress, pelting her with its tears. Black mascara ran down her cheeks, branding her with the darkness of the night.

Out of the corner of her eye, she spied the lights of the barn. It was the only source of light, but it seemed so far away. With a concentrated effort, and all the strength she had, she pushed her legs to run faster toward the faint barn lights.

The heels of her high-heeled shoes continually stuck into the ground, causing her ankles to twist. Repeatedly she fell face-first into the wet grass. Her beautiful white gown soon became tarnished with grass stains. Each time, her arms trembled as she forced herself up from the ground. Part of her wanted to stay down; there was no point in getting up again. She was defeated. The night seemed to cling to her and keep her in its ubiquitous embrace.

Roger's shadowy image stood before her. "Come home to me. Everything will be all right, if you'll just come home." He had his arms opened wide toward her; the familiar longing look in his eyes invited her and made her heart long for the expected normalcy only he could provide.

"No!" she shouted and pushed onward. Rain battered her face. Her eyes stung, making it difficult to see the lights of the barn. The comfort she knew she'd find next to Sun pushed her to return to her rapid pace. He would understand. He would soothe her hurts. "Sun!" she cried out just before she tripped again and fell into the red clay mud.

"Leave this chaotic world behind you. Close your eyes and listen to your heart. You know you belong to me," Roger's voice continued its torment.

She tried to turn her face away from the images of him, but even still, his voice continued to coax her.

"Look at you wallowing in the mud. I protected you. I made you feel important. I lifted you upon a pedestal. There's no one in the world for me but you. You nearly killed me when you left. Come home to me. I love you. I'll never leave you. Look where he's put you – in the mud. Turn away from him and his deceitful ways. With me you always knew where you stood. We can be everything we ever dreamed of, and more," Roger's image told her.

For a moment, Mary's head dropped. If only all of those things were true, she could be happy. *Get up*, her mind commanded. *Get up out of the mud!*

"Listen to me! We had a good life, and it can be even better! The life I know you long to have. We can be happy," Roger said. "Things will be different this time. I promise all the bad stuff won't ever happen again."

Her legs trembled as she stood on them; her knees were skinned from the rocks she'd landed on. Mud, rain, and blood oozed down her legs. Her brow furrowed as her heart longed for the security she got from Roger. At least with him, she always knew what to expect. With him, she never felt like this. "No," she weakly said and continued.

By the time she burst through the barn door, the rain had washed off most of the mud from her legs. Scarlett streaks marbled down into her shoes. Her hair hung as a dripping mix of hairspray and spray-on glitter. Her face was marred with dripping makeup. The dress she'd so carefully shopped for clung to her thin body. The right heel of her shoe was broken. Squish-click-squish-clump, squish-click-squish-clump she ran down the cement barn hallway straight to Sun's stall. Inside stood the magnificent sleeping horse.

Limply, Mary clung to the bars. Every part of her was in tattered ruins. She hadn't the strength to slide the stall door open. Her world – her future – was over. The hope she'd held onto so fervently had slipped through her fingers. The one glimmer of light she had was a precipitous lie. It was the train she so feared. Limply, she was falling into the interminable abyss of perfidy all over again.

Fear began attaching his puppet strings once again to her limbs.

Her tears were a noticeable contrast to the cold rain on her face.

"No, please, no," she weakly begged Fear.

"You knew it was too good to be true," Fear hissed.

"No, please, don't," she begged.

"You won't escape me this time!" he said as he tied each restraint.

"Please!!" she shrieked with the last bit of resistance she had.

"If Alan loves you so much, where is he? Why hasn't he come running after you? Why hasn't he come to your rescue?" Fear shouted as frenzied threads of spit clung to the edges of his boney mouth and shot toward her.

Mary didn't answer.

Alan's betrayal hurt so much worse than Roger's had. At least with Roger, she knew what to expect. But with Alan? Alan had played on all of her emotions, trust, and security. Worst of all, he'd validated her hope for a future, and like a fool, she'd let him into her inner circle of trust – a place very few people were ever allowed to enter. Once he was inside, he shattered the circle.

Fear laughed maniacally. "It's because it was all a lie! You don't belong here! Roger was right. You've proven that. You can't live without him! Roger is the only one you belong to!"

The thick fog of bondage crept around her.

Her soul screamed a terrified, insane, reticent scream as she once again yielded control over to Fear and his cronies: Distrust, Panic, and Betrayal.

Roger's voice filled her head: "Come home to me. Your heart is safe here. There's hope here."

Sun nibbled her fingers, letting her know he was there.

"Oh, Sun," Mary said with an all-encompassing sob. For a split moment, she had the strength to open his stall. In a defeated lump, she collapsed into the wood shavings of his stall.

Sun lowered his head to her and gently nuzzled her.

Mary sincerely wanted to die right there at his hooves. There was no point living anyway. Her hands shook as they reached for his halter. Her fingers blindly and mindlessly adjusted his forelock. "You're all I have left to live for," she barely whispered. She clung to him as if he represented the last throes of her existence.

Sun sneezed on her, blowing wood shavings across the stall.

Bits of sawdust clung to her when she lifted her face and leaned it against his; her cheek lying right between his eyes. "What now?" Her knuckles turned white from the death grip she had on each side of his halter. "What do I do now? There's no Alan. No Roger. No one. Just me and you, and we have nothing but each other."

Sun lifted his head, effectively raising her to her wobbly feet.

"He knows everything, you know? He could easily destroy us." Mary buried her face into his flaxen mane. "We've got to leave. There's no other way." The words burned like acid pouring off her tongue. Leaving Alan was the equivalent of leaving Sun.

"Why did I let him in? Why? Why did I trust him?? I should've known this would happen. No affair with a married man ever turns out the way you think it will. Why did I think this would be different?"

Flecks of bedding clung to the entire side of her body. "I'm a fool," she matter-of-factly stated. "Johe warned me, and I didn't listen." She sighed deeply. "She was right." The words were bitter on her tongue.

"Come home to me. I've never stopped loving you. I never stopped searching for you," Roger's voice echoed.

"At least Roger did love me," she whispered to Sun.

Sun nudged her with his head. Instinctively, she started brushing some of the shavings off. Bits of wood stained with the blood from her knees fell to the floor.

"Alan," she said with a shuddering sigh. "I should've known better," she told Sun while leaning against his powerful shoulder.

"Yes, but it's over now. You belong in Arizona," Roger's voice said.

"Arizona," she whispered. "The world is right in Arizona."

Sun sneezed and nodded; his forelock flung up and down with his head.

"Arizona," she gently joined Sun's nodding. "Where it's warm and dry and the world makes sense."

Without another thought, she kissed Sun between his eyes and closed his stall door behind her. *Arizona*, replayed in her mind. Thunder shook the ground where she walked. Mary didn't notice.

There was no more hope left for her in Georgia. Nothing would be strong enough to pull Alan from his child. Angela knew it. Why else would she have gotten pregnant? There was no point confusing things by staying.

Mary took her shoes off as she let the rain wash the rest of the shavings off of her. It made no sense trying to wear them in the rain. With a primal growl, she threw each of them as far as she could.

Deliberately and with the wind and rain stinging her face, she walked straight to her truck to hook up the trailer. Her mind was in complete control. No emotional thoughts of Alan were going to change her course. He wasn't even there to try to change her mind. He was instead there with Angela, worshiping her and the baby growing inside her.

The rain strafed her and dripped from her eyelashes while she hitched the trailer to the truck. Perfunctorily, she moved around the barn collecting her tack, Sun's feed, and finally Sun himself. After loading the trailer, she made her way to her cabin.

The windshield wipers flung the pouring rain to and fro as Mary walked determinedly from the truck and trailer into the cabin. Her first goal was to get out of the ruined dress as soon as possible. The delicate fabric hadn't held up very well through everything. It didn't matter anyway. She didn't deserve to look pretty. Ripping it off seemed preferable. She tried to tear it to shreds with her bare hands, but the fabric wouldn't give. Instead, she let it fall into a wet crumpled pile on the bathroom floor.

She caught a brief glance at herself in the mirror. There, tucked into a fold at the base of her neck was a loan pearl from Alan's pearls. Without feeling, she reached up and flicked the pearl as hard as she could. It bounced off the cold tile floor.

The image in the mirror showed someone she thought she knew, but the only familiar remnant was her green eyes blazing against their smeared black backdrop.

Numbly, Mary pulled her hair into a hair clip, wet a washcloth, and scrubbed her face. She scrubbed away every one of Alan's kisses – every one of his caresses. Her face was red when she'd finished.

A tear began in her right eye. "Don't you do it," she shouted at her image. "Go and get dressed. Pack your shit and get out of here."

Thunder rumbled outside, shaking the walls of her cabin. Despite her previous fears, Mary didn't notice the thunder. She was a robot performing every necessary duty in order to put her life back together and get as far away from Alan and Babbling Brooks as she could get.

Quickly, she piled garbage bags with her clothes and belongings by the back door.

The cell phone Alan had given her sat on the dark brown coffee table, right next to her laptop. She packed the laptop in a trash bag and placed it by the back door.

The cell phone beckoned her. It was her last chance to say anything to Alan, but what would she say?

"You're a lying ass!" she venomously said aloud. She held the cell phone in her hands; what should she say? Instead of sending a text message, she thought she'd type out a note:

Dear Alan,

I don't know if you'll ever get this, but ~~I want you to understand I never want to hear from you again. What you did to me devastated me! I don't ever want to hear your voice again, taste your kisses, feel your touch~~

She backspaced over the words. "Stay strong, Mary. Don't give him anything he can use to hurt you."

I want you to know I understand your situation. You had a choice to make, and you obviously made it. I, too, had a choice, and given my departure, I hope you understand what my choice was. ~~In the future, I would encourage you to forgo the lying to Angela. It's quite destructive, and with the impending birth of your child, perhaps total honesty would be the best. I guess Jobe was right about you, I'm just another notch on your bedpost. I only hope Angela doesn't abort this child too~~.

"Stop it, Mary," she told herself and deleted the text. "Get focused and stay professional."

You deserve happiness. I hope you achieve everything you want to. I wish you and Angela all the best. ~~I'll love you always,~~ Regards, Mary.

She sniffled while reading back over the message. "Good. Nothing too mushy," she said aloud and stiffly placed the phone back on the coffee table.

Taking the black gift bag she'd used to store all of Alan's CDs, she neatly placed it on the table next to the cell phone. For a moment, she stopped to admire the 4-carat diamond ring one more time. It would never grace her finger again. For the first time since Alan had slipped it on her finger, she removed it and placed it on top of the cell phone.

Moving to the couch, she sat down and reached into the bag of Alan's CDs. Randomly, she produced one and opened it. Inside was one of the notes Alan had written:

Dear Mary:

Thanks for helping me again discover the music I used to love. I hope you enjoy listening to the music I now love.

Love,
Alan Brooks

It was all written in his elegant longhand. "So unlike the strong block letters of ELF," she said as her brow furrowed. Her eyes blinked back tears. "Stop it!" she demanded. "You can't think about this kind of stuff right now!"

Emotionlessly, she reached into the coffee table drawer and produced the 9mm pistol Tunda had given her over a year ago to kill Roger. The cool, moist steel barely felt like anything in her hands. For a split second, she contemplated killing herself with it.

"Let me go," her soul begged her. "I'll never be free if you don't let me go. It was foolish for you to think otherwise."

Blankly she stared next to her at the seat on the couch where Alan often sat. New, warm tears welled up in her eyes. Her heart pounded inside her head. She desperately wanted to snuggle into his spot and breathe nothing but the spicy bourbon aroma his breath may have left or the outdoorsy way the pines smelled when it rained which reminded her of Alan. She could then kill herself while feeling the last bit of his presence and being somewhere where she felt certain she was loved, even if the end result was a lie.

Just as her body began moving toward Alan's spot on the couch, she coldly shouted at herself, "Don't you dare!" Her legs pushed her to standing; she shoved the gun into her pocket. "Then Angela would see your dead body and think she'd won. Besides, he's not worth it. He's out of my life, and that's all that matters," she said trying to sound determined, but really was struggling to keep from crying.

Moving from the couch and back toward the door where her belongings were piled up, she stopped briefly and turned back to look at the stuff she'd left on the table for Alan. Her head shook; her eyes closed. "Fine. For the baby," she whispered to herself. Immediately, she walked back into the living room and scooped up the bag of CDs, leaving only the cell phone and engagement ring behind.

In the pouring rain, she loaded the trash bags into the passenger's seat of the truck, climbed into the driver's seat, and pulled away from the cabin.

The lane down the Brooks driveway held no fear for her now. It was her pathway to somewhere away from all the agony – away from Alan. Freedom. Where she was going mattered much less than how quickly she would get there.

"Maybe we'll go to Tunda's for a while," she said to Sun as she wiped the dripping rain from her cheeks. "Tunda will hide us until we can figure out what to do."

"Return to me," Roger's voice echoed.

She turned onto Brooks River Road, toward the interstate. Arizona was where she belonged. It was where she'd always belonged. "Screw Georgia," she angrily shouted.

The night's darkness was split by the light of four police cars heading rapidly toward her. Obediently, she pulled her rig over as the flashing blue lights and sirens raced past her. But before she could pull out again, three ambulances appeared with their lights piercing the darkness. The sirens echoed inside her head as they zoomed past.

The still small voice of her shattered heart pleaded with her to go back to Babbling Brooks.

"No!" she shouted. "It serves you right," she vocalized what her head was thinking. "You knew better, and yet you let yourself get caught up in his frenzy. What did you think would happen?"

Her heart's sad voice whispered, "At least we still have his baby."

Mary sighed and placed her hand upon her belly. "Yeah," she weakly replied. "I guess, Tunda will be thrilled to be a grandma."

ABOUT THE AUTHOR

Nicole Renee Wyatt was born in the tiny town of Franklin, Virginia, but was raised in Georgia. After facing a most difficult divorce, Nicole relocated her family to Athens, Georgia, where she found work at the nearby University of Georgia and soon after became a student. Life as a single parent to two daughters was a struggle in extremes. Nicole worked non-stop to provide for the family and keep up her studies, but something had to give, and she was forced to discontinue her educational pursuits. Since there was little money to seek professional therapy to help her cope with her divorce and her failures, Nicole channeled her emotions into writing stories. Those stories became a form of self-therapy for her, and before long, the stories turned into entire novels. *Butterflies are Free?* (The Butterfly Stories) was the first in a series of novels, and was followed by *Butterflies in the Storm.* These novels are based on a very vivid dream which was nearly a premonition of things to come. When *Butterflies are Free?* was nearly completed, Nicole's writing skills were attacked with a serious case of meningitis that left her completely unable to imagine or write. It took several years for her brain to heal and for her imagination to return. She hopes her writing will help others to remember the importance of perseverance. She firmly believes living is not just about surviving, but also about flying and obtaining those dreams and goals, even through insurmountable odds. Nicole currently lives in the quaint city of Commerce, GA and works as an academic advisor at the University of Georgia.